Four Plays of Minoru Betsuyaku

Translated and introduced by **Masako Yuasa**

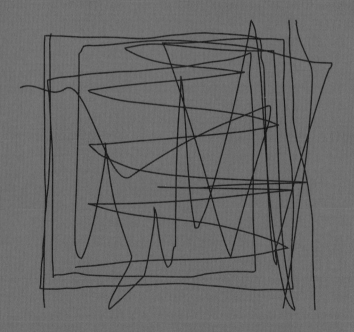

社会評論社

Four Plays of Minoru Betsuyaku
Translated and introduced by Masako Yuasa

Published by Shakai Hyōronsya
Bunkyo-ku, Tokyo, Japan
http://www.shahyo.com/
© Masako Yuasa, 2023

Printed and bounded in Japan by Kurashiki print Co, Ltd. December 2023
ISBN978-4-7845-1167-9

The Kangaroo

SCENE I
(from left) Hat Seller, Old Man,
Man and Hat Seller's Wife

Man

Prostitute

SCENE V
(from left) Man, Pimp and Prostitute

Stage photos by Christopher Jowett
Costume design by Kitty Burrows

3

(from left)
Bakabon and
Constable

(from left)
Rerere,
Woman 1,
Mama,
Constable,
Papa and Bakabon

Seargeant and
Constable

Auntie Rerere

Stage photos by Christopher Jowett
Costume design by Kitty Burrows

4

the Man and the Woman

the Man and the Woman

Stage photos by Christopher Jowett

SCENE II
Knight 2 and Knight 1

SCENE I
(from left) the Nurse and
the Doctor

Stage photos by Christopher Jowett
Costume design by Kitty Burrows

SCENE I
(from left) the Doctor, Knight 2, the Innkeeper, Squire 2,
the Daughter, the Nurse, Squire 1 and Knight 1

the Nurse   Squire 1

Contents

~ FOREWORD ~

Yoshie Inoue

I was introduced to Dr Masako Yuasa by the late Emeritus Professor Bunzo Torigoe of the University of Waseda in Tokyo in 1995 when she was in Japan on sabbatical. As I was teaching at a regional university at that time, we could not meet very often. Later, when I was staying in London as a visiting fellow of SOAS at the University of London, I had an opportunity to visit Leeds and spend time with her. We talked about theatre and other matters, and I learned that she conducted research on Kunio Shimizu for her Master's degree and on Minoru Betsuyaku for her doctorate. That PhD thesis is the basis of this book.

When I asked her why she had focused her research on Japanese playwrights from Shimizu to Betsuyaku, she said, "It is because, once one reads their plays, understands them and stages them, while being very honest to the play texts, their theatrical worlds will appear by themselves," and "Theatrical language in some Japanese plays is written in a roundabout way which becomes a problem to translate into English, while their theatrical language does not and is easier to translate into English." As the works of these two playwrights have a high degree of abstractness, I am not so sure whether it is as easy to stage their plays as she said. However, it is true that their languages are poetic and fluent. Either through play-reading or stage performance, their plays are worth taking up. I see her good sense in theatre here. She also said that when she was a postgraduate student, neither Betsuyaku nor Shimizu were much known as playwrights in the United Kingdom. She hoped that their plays could be better known, so chose them as the subjects of her research. I see her spirit as a researcher in the field of Theatre Studies there. I hope that the readers of this book will see it, too.

Minoru Betsuyaku was an ardent admirer of Kafka and Beckett in his student days. There is a hint of their influence in his plays, and some of them are almost too abstract to understand. He began his career as a writer with the play ***A, B and a Woman (A to B to Hitori no Onna)*** in 1961 and subsequently became one of the leading figures of the Small Theatre Movement in Japan.

When Dr Yuasa was writing her doctoral thesis in the latter half of the nineteen eighties, she chose comparatively easy plays to translate: *The Kangaroo* from the sixties, *I'm the Father of the Genius Idiot Bakabon* from the seventies, and *A Corpse with Feet* and *Two Knights Travelling around the Country* from the eighties.

Betsuyaku died on the 3rd of March 2020 at the age of eighty-two. In 2018, *Ah! And Yet, and Yet (Aa Sorenanoni Sorenanoni)*, first staged by the Natori Office, became his one hundred and forty-fourth and last new play. There have been no other playwrights as prolific as him in Japan.

I would like to offer my hearty congratulations on the publication of this book.

(Emeritus Professor of Toho Gakuen College of Drama and Music)

～ 序 ～

井上理惠

　湯浅雅子さんとは、1995 年に彼女が研究休暇で日本へ帰国したとき、鳥越文藏先生に紹介されて知り合った。その頃私は地方大学に勤務していたからしょっちゅう会うことは出来なかったが、97 年にロンドン大学 SOAS に visiting fellow で滞在した時、リーズを訪ね、さまざまな話をして修士論文が清水邦夫論で、博士論文が別役実論だと、聞いた。その博士論文が今回の本である。

　清水邦夫から別役実へ進んだのは、何故かと聞いたら、「戯曲を理解して素直に舞台化すると自ずと彼らの劇世界が出来てくる。」「日本語は迂遠な表現が多いから英訳は大変なのだが、彼らの日本語は英語にしやすい」からだという。
　二人の戯曲は抽象度が高いから「素直に舞台化」できるかどうかはいささか疑問だが、彼らの戯曲は、詩的でしかも口の端に乗りやすい。読むにせよ演ずるにせよ、やりがいがある対象だ。劇に対する彼女のセンスの良さが伺われるところだろう。
　彼女が院生の頃、別役も清水も、イギリスではあまり知られていなかったという。それで彼らのすばらしさを知ってほしくて取り上げたのだ。そこに演劇研究者の心意気を感じる。今回の本を読めば、それが真実であることが理解されるであろう。

　別役実は、学生時代にカフカやベケットに傾倒した。戯曲にはその影が見受けられ、抽象的で分かりにくい作もある。1961 年に「A と B と一人の女」で劇作家のスタートを切り、日本の小劇場演劇運動の先頭を歩いた一人である。論文執筆時が 80 年代後半であるため別役作品の内、比較的理解しやすい作品、60 年代から「カンガルー」、70 年代から「天才バカボンのパパなのだ」、80 年代から「足のある死体」、「諸国を遍歴する二人の騎士の物語」の 4 作が選ばれている。
　別役は 2020 年 3 月 3 日 82 歳で亡くなったが、2018 年に書き下ろした 144 作目の「ああ、それなのに、それなのに」（名取事務所が初演）が最後の作品になった。日本の劇作家でこれほどの多作な作家はいない。

　本の上梓を心から祝いたい。

（桐朋学園芸術短期大学名誉教授）

～ PREFACE ～

This book is based on my PhD thesis, which I completed in 1990. I had hoped to publish at that time but was unable to do so, and my wish was left unfulfilled.

Minoru Betsuyaku died on the 3rd of March 2020. Many years had passed since the writing of my thesis, and in that interval, Betsuyaku had written more plays and widened his theatrical activity. I believed, therefore, that my work was out of date. However, I then received an email from Ms Kana Nakajima, one of the editors of the *Theatre Yearbook 2021*, published by the Japanese Centre of the International Theatre Institute. She asked for details of my staging of the plays of Betsuyaku for the memorial section they were putting together, which included a list of publication and performances overseas.

When I received my copy of *Theatre Yearbook 2021* and read the memorial, I realised that very few translations of his plays were available in print. I had translated and staged four of his plays into English at the University of Leeds in the United Kingdom. Only one of these, **The Story of the Two Knights Travelling Around the Country**, staged as part of my post-doctoral project, had been printed as a booklet and was listed in *Theatre Yearbook 2021: Theatre Abroad*. Another of the four plays, **A Corpse with Feet**, had been published in the *Asian Theatre Journal* together with an article on the activity of The Snail Theatre Company (*Katatsumujri no kai*), but this was not listed in the Yearbook. I, therefore, felt obliged to publish the remaining translations left untouched on my desk.

This is how and why I have decided to publish now. Taking advantage of this opportunity, I have been through the translations line by line in detail once more and tried to make them, as far as possible, more precise and closer to the original. I humbly hope that the book will be of use to the international theatre community and audiences, and will allow them to more fully enjoy the works of Minoru Betsuyaku.

Dr Masako Yuasa
October 2023

Acknowledgements

I am deeply in debt to the great work of Minoru Betsuyaku, from which I have learned so much. I also owe much to Akihiko Senda for his in-depth knowledge of contemporary Japanese theatre. The monthly magazine *Shingeki* by Hakusuisha was the source of essential information throughout. I am grateful for the fine, definitive editions of Betsuyaku's plays by Sanichi Shobo, which I have used throughout as the basis for my translations.

I wish to thank Emeritus Prof. Martin Banham of the Workshop Theatre in the School of English of the University of Leeds in the United Kingdom for his unwavering understanding and encouragement as my supervisor throughout my research and for many years since.

Among the many staff and students of the Workshop Theatre who made the productions of the plays so successful, I would particularly like to thank Trevor Faulkner, Kitty Burrows and Chris Jowett.

Among my friends, Tanya Lees and Terry Ram supported me enormously on many occasions, both on and off stage: Stephanie Hoare kindly proofread my original manuscripts with unfailing patience.

All those who work in the theatre rely on the goodwill and generosity of the most important contributors to any performance: the audience.

In the creation of this book, I would like to thank Emeritus Prof. Yoshie Inoue of Toho Gakuen College of Drama and Music for her encouragement and support. My publisher, Kenji Matsuda of Shakai Hyōronsya, gave me time to prepare the thesis for the book, and the book designer, Taeko Nakano, has done splendid work preparing it for publication. I am truly grateful to all of them.

My sister Ikuko allowed me to use one of her artworks as the book cover. She knows how grateful I am for all her support and love.

Note on names and translations

Japanese names are presented in the order of given name followed by family name.

The translations of quoted material from Japanese publications are mine unless indicated otherwise.

CHAPTER ONE
Introduction

[I]

Biography of Minoru Betsuyaku until 1990 (1)

There are two main aspects that must be considered in order to see Betsuyaku's plays in their correct context; firstly, it was Betsuyaku's position in and relation to Japanese theatre as a whole and secondly it was the social background against which he has lived. These elements are especially significant in Betsuyaku's case because his war and post-war experiences were extraordinary, and his sensational debut into the theatrical world coincided with the revolutionary days of New Theatre (*Shingeki*), in Japan in the nineteen-sixties.

The first important point to make about Betsuyaku's life and upbringing is that he spent his early days outside Japan, and in a different cultural and linguistic environment from most Japanese people of his generation. These wider influences on him have inevitably affected the way in which he looks at the world. Betsuyaku was born in Manchuria in 1937 and lived there until 1946; his father worked in the general affairs division of the government of Manchuria.(2) At first Betsuyaku's family lived in Harbin,(3) a town originally built by European Russians. He grew up therefore living in a Russian-style house, eating Russian food, visiting Russian families in the neighbourhood, and with an old Russian woman as family maid. Afterwards, Betsuyaku's family moved to Shinkyo,(4) a Japanese town walled in to protect it from the vast wasteland of Manchuria, with the Manchurian town outside the walls. They lived in an official residence in an American condominium-type building, very different from the traditional Japanese-style house of those days. Under his father's influence, Betsuyaku read children's stories such as those of Hans Andersen, the Brothers Grimm, and Peter Pan in translation. His neutral middle-class Japanese language originated in this early experience of growing up in a foreign atmosphere, hearing a mixture of foreign languages and colonial Japanese, not experiencing his traditional and native culture.

His father became ill and died in 1944 and it was the time the situation of the Japanese army in the Pacific War was deteriorating. The Japanese in Manchuria had to move out. In his memoirs Betsuyaku tells how the traumatic events during the Japanese withdrawal from Manchuria provided recurrent images in his plays. Only few trains were running and the people left behind even contemplated committing group suicide by sharing poison. Betsuyaku and his family and their friends barricaded themselves in the studio of the Manchuria Film Company and all calmly prepared for death. But the military officer and head of Manchuko Film Association Amakasu committed suicide just before the Russian army's invasion. This incident eased the despair in the peoples' minds and released them from their single-minded idea of committing suicide, because it told them of the collapse of Imperialist Japan. Betsuyaku's family and others began the return journey to Japan. On this journey the boy Betsuyaku saw bandits steal their belongings, travelled in open railway waggons, walked many days, and heard the Imperial edict of the termination of the war read out, accompanied by people's sobs. In the end, however, the refugees had to go back to Shinkyo as there was no transportation available from the town of Hoten[5] to the coast. Back in Shinkyo, the food situation was very bad and on one occasion all the family's neighbours broke into the warehouse and took food left by the Japanese army. Russian soldiers raided the Betsuyaku's house while Betsuyaku's mother was out, and examined the inside of the urn containing his father's ashes folded in white cloth on the family altar.

In 1946, when all the Japanese finally began returning home, Betsuyaku's family joined the others. Diseases such as typhoid and dysentery broke out because of the unhygienic drinking water and the primitive toilet facilities. Betsuyaku also suffered from diarrhoea but had to hide it because everything was run on military lines and, if the boy's illness had been discovered, everyone in his group would have had to stay longer in this ever-worsening and ever-more-dangerous situation. From these traumatic times, Betsuyaku retained the image of the dirty latrine and was left with a horror of going to the toilet. The extraordinary experiences from his childhood became the source materials for episodes in some of his plays[6] and he has used them repeatedly.

The first sight that Betsuyaku had of his hitherto unseen home country, from the deck of the ship, was of a land covered with green trees and a fantastically blue sea. As Manchuria was a place of dry desolate wasteland, and the sea which he had seen there was always greyish, this first sight of Japan gave him the impression that it was a marvellously beautiful country. Initially Betsuyaku and his family went back to the home of his father's family, Kochi in Shikoku, moved to the home of his mother's family, Shimizu in Shizuoka, and finally settled down in Nagano, a central prefecture of mainland Japan, where a friend of his late father wanted his mother to help with his small business. First his mother took up peddling and soon she began to run a fried dumpling stall. Later, all these foods and drinking stalls were moved by a decision of the local council, to a more prestigious site, a building called 'A town of recreation and relaxation.' Betsuyaku's family was not well-off, having only the income of a single parent, and they received the state benefit for poor families, although their position gradually became better as time went on.

Nagano Prefecture is well known for the high standard of its public education. Betsuyaku had an ambition to become an artist and in his upper school days studied sketching as well as reading much literature, including, for example, the novels of Dostoevsky, and attending a Sunday School Bible class. As the art college entrance examination was hard to pass and he thought that the world of fine art was too abstract and intellectual for him, Betsuyaku applied to two universities, the Tokyo University of Foreign Languages (*Tokyo Gaikokugo Daigaku*), so that he could become an interpreter, and the Department of Politics and Economics of Waseda University (*Waseda Daigaku*) in order to become a journalist. In any case, he wanted a well-paid job to be able to support his sisters.

In 1958 Betsuyaku was accepted by Waseda, which was, and is, one of the centres of student theatre activity. In Tokyo, he was to experience another period of exposure to foreign influences. This was as a result of his lodging in the house of his paternal grandmother, Kazue. After her first husband's death, Kazue had married an Englishman who taught in an upper school; with him she had gone to Beijing, leaving her four children from the first marriage with her mother, who was an elder sister of Torahiko Terada, a famous literary figure in Japan. When her second husband died, Kazue had returned to Japan, with Mary, her daughter from the second marriage, and settled at Meguro in Tokyo. Mary spoke three foreign languages, English, French and German, and was also a stenographer, and in the post-war period was involved in work related to the American army of occupation. Their house was partly furnished in the Western style, containing, for example, crucifixes and a Western-style toilet, although it was otherwise an ordinary post-war wooden Japanese house. Kazue and Mary were devout Roman Catholics and when Betsuyaku and his sisters stayed at the house, they all went to the Sunday services, except for Betsuyaku who was no longer interested in religion and refused to attend. However, this day-to-day contact with Christianity gave him a wider knowledge of it than he would otherwise have had, and his frequent use of the character of a Christian priest in his plays may be seen as originating in the influences of this time. His non-traditional and Western-influenced background was reinforced in this period.

Soon Betsuyaku joined the student drama group at Waseda, the Freedom Stage (*Jiyū Butai*). He was persuaded to become a member by one of the actors of the group who happened to be from the same upper school as Betsuyaku. He told Betsuyaku that he was tall enough to make a good actor. Although he did not intend to become an actor and worked on the administrative side at first, this was the beginning of Betsuyaku's career in the theatre.

These student days coincided with the first outbreak of political unrest against the renewal of the ten-year treaty between Japan and the United States of America, the Pacific Security Treaty (*Nichibei Anzen Hoshō Jyōyaku*),[7] which had established a military alliance between the two countries. Many left-wing students and intellectuals supported this movement (*Ampo Tōsō '60*) for the political independence of Japan. The Freedom Stage, which was strongly left-wing, was deeply involved in the movement. The protests ended in failure however and the government signed the revised Treaty for the next ten years. Betsuyaku, undoubtedly one of the angry young men of his time, lost the interest and motivation to complete his degree in order to pursue a good profession in society, and left Waseda in the middle of his course in 1960, the year of the renewal of the treaty.

In 1961 he took part in the political movement known as the Niijima Conflict (*Niijima Tōsō*), a movement supporting the farmers and residents opposing the establishment of a missile base on Niijima Island in Tokyo prefecture. While he was staying on the island among the local people, he gained a different impression of the political movements which he had joined. Before this time such movements had seemed to him somehow dismal and solemn, but after the failure of Ampo '60, Betsuyaku looked at them in a more relaxed way, and because of this the movement now seemed rather peaceful, pleasant, and light-hearted. As a result of these experiences, Betsuyaku began to have doubts about the role of Marxist class-conflict analysis and social-realism in theatre, and came to abandon them. He moved in the direction of forms of expression free from restrictive ideologies. It was at this time that Betsuyaku was influenced by Beckett's plays; I shall discuss this influence in the next chapter (see [II] [A]). He wrote his first play, *A, B and a Woman (A to B to Hitiri no Onna)*,[8] 1961, which deals with the endless, insoluble social conflicts of the day.

In 1962 the New Freedom Stage (*Shin Jiyū Butai*), was formed for former Waseda students on the initiative of Tadashi Suzuki, the theatre enthusiast who was to become the founder and the artistic director of SCOT.[9] Betsuyaku joined as a founder member while he was working as a trade union secretary in a building company. In the same year, he wrote **The Elephant (Zō)**, which was to become one of the most important plays of the nineteen-sixties. The first production of The Elephant was staged by the director Suzuki and Ono,[10] one of the leading actors of the New Freedom Stage (see [II] [B] (1) for a discussion of this play). The same people had put on **Death of a Salesman** by Arthur Miller just before this production, and Betsuyaku thinks that **The Elephant** was somehow influenced by this. In addition, Betsuyaku had been inspired by **The Hungry Artist** by Franz Kafka around this time and tried to write a play which was objectively a comedy but structurally a tragedy.

The late nineteen-sixties saw the second wave of protest movements and political upheaval in Japan. These focussed on opposition to the further renewal of the Pacific Security Treaty between Japan and the United States of America. in 1970, and its conversion into a permanent pact. The world-wide influence of 'hippy culture' gave impetus to this social phenomenon. Many Japanese, especially of the young generation, began to believe that society needed to change. Japanese universities saw radical protest movements and demonstrations against the authorities. These spread outside the campuses as time went on. The New Theatre of Japan (*Shingeki*) reflected these trends. The younger generation rebelled against their lack of influence over the repertoire and organisation of the theatre and looked for new places to express their ideas. The small theatre movement came out of this need. Many of the small theatre groups were formed by these young people. They used any place, such as streets, campuses, the precincts of a shrine, coffee-shops, warehouses, second-class film theatres, wherever they could find space to stage their plays. The Waseda Small Theatre Company was a successful example of these groups. The most influential included the Kobo Studio of Kobo Abe, the Situation Theatre (*Jokyō Gekijō*) of Juro Kara, the Upper Circle (*Tenjōsajiki*) of Shyūji Terayama, the Centre 68/70 of Makoto Sato, and the Contemporary People's Theatre (*Gendaijin Gekijō*) of Yukio Ninagawa and Kunio Shimizu. The work of these groups and individuals changed the New Theatre in its various phases and became another milestone of the contemporary Japanese theatre. The critic Akihiko Senda called this period "The Dramatic Renaissance."[11]

The New Freedom Stage was reformed in March 1966 with the same group of people and called the Waseda Small Theatre Company (*Waseda Shō Gekijō*). They staged Betsuyaku's newly written play **The Gate (Mon)** as its opening production in May, and in October they opened their own studio above a coffee shop in Waseda. From this time onward Betsuyaku began to concentrate on writing. He wrote not only for the WSTC but for other theatre groups such as the Drama Project 66 (*Engeki Kikaku 66*) and the Atelier Group in the Literature Theatre Company (*Bungaku-za Atorie no Kai*). In 1968 Betsuyaku received the prestigious 13th Kishida Playwright Award (*Kishida Gikyoku Shō*) for **The Match Girl (Matchi Uri no Shōjo)** and **A Scene with a Red Bird (Akai Tori no Iru Fūkei)**. This was the period when he established himself as a playwright.

> ...the days when I was in the Freedom Stage could be described as the time when I had the chance to work with two extraordinarily talented people, Suzuki and Ono. Our relationship in the theatre lasted until we left the university and formed the Waseda Small Theatre Company... The extent of Suzuki's talent is related to the depth of his hatred and that of Ono to his sense of isolation. When their collaboration was at its best, the working atmosphere became very tense because Ono tended to expand his own alienation metaphysically while Suzuki tried to pin his down to a concrete reality.[12]

In 1969, Betsuyaku left the Waseda Small Theatre Company. The immediate reason for this was the suicide of Ono. Betsuyaku felt that this marked the end of the nineteen-sixties for him. He felt that he could no longer write plays just developing something with the words which spontaneously came out of his deepest feelings. The differing views which Betsuyaku and Suzuki held of the theatre also contributed to their separation. Suzuki expressed his thoughts on theatre in his critical piece: 'Acting and Situation (*Engi to Jōkyō*)'[13] in the July 1969 issue of *Shingeki*.[14]

> So far many of the productions have been supported by a spirit of disciplined collaboration. In regard of this, actors are only parts and the sum of these parts make the whole. The whole is the subject matter of

the play which is called its theme. In staging a play this false hierarchy has undeniably existed and required strong cooperation. But actors are whole in themselves and cannot be simply parts of the greater whole. It has been self-evident that an actor expresses the whole and does not help to express some concept of a play or the theme scripted by a playwright. A play, once dead, lives today only in the actor and revives through their consciousness and the emotions. We do not go to the theatre to hear the read-out script, but to share the experience of intense moments existing in a non-everyday world, to witness the moments when an actor needs the audience, and to encounter his potential. If we cannot recognize the situation surrounding us through the creative consciousness of an actor, why should we bother to go to the theatre?[15]

In Suzuki's theatre acting takes pride of place. His method requires actors to use loud or half-shouting voices and stiff stylized movements in which they keep a low centre of gravity. After Betsuyaku left the WSTC, Suzuki collected dramatic scenes from Kabuki plays as well as from Japanese and Western plays, and adapted them into scripts like mosaic work.[16] The plays created in this way were sensational successes with the collaboration of the actress, Kayoko Shiraishi, who embodied Suzuki's acting method.

On the other hand, Betsuyaku's plays are written as literature and it is said that they do not need rewriting during rehearsal. What is demanded of the actors is straight acting, with the actor serving as mediator between the lines and the part in the play. On the whole "what Betsuyaku's theatre aspires to is a well calculated calmness."[17] Betsuyaku characterises his time at Waseda as his amateur rather than his professional career.[18]

In 1970 Betsuyaku received the 5th Kinokuniya Theatre Award (*Kinokuniya Engeki Shō*) for his individual work and in 1972 he was chosen to receive the Art Prize Newcomer Award (*Geijutsusen Shō Shinjin Sho*).

As Japanese society returned to normal in the nineteen-seventies, this new wave in the theatre lost some of its radical qualities. In 1972, Betsuyaku formed the theatre group Hand (*Te no Kai*) with Masakazu Yamazaki, a playwright and academic in theatre studies,[19] Toshifumi Sueki, a director and translator of the contemporary French theatre,[20] and Taketoshi Naito and others. *The Move (Ido)*, 1973, was the first of Betsuyaku's plays staged by the Hand. Betsuyaku had written about twenty plays before this, and he thinks that after *The Move* his method of playwriting changed:

> I took notes whenever I came across any unusual atmosphere, things
> that might lead us to behave in an unlikely way, and which interested
> me greatly. When the situations behind these were revealed, I began to
> write a play using them... Since *The Move* the way I write a play has
> been different; in short I see on the one side the human relationships
> such as the parent-children relationship and the family-relationship,
> and on the other I see the everyday routine of life. When these two in-
> teract mechanically and seem to have independent life, I began to write
> a play...[21]

From this time, 1973, to the end of the nineteen-seventies Betsuyaku's
plays display two approaches: one which looks at human relationships rather
mechanically in an abstract situation, as in **Chairs and the Legend (Isu to
Densetsu)**, 1974, and the other closely related to everyday life in present-day
Japan, which Betsuyaku calls plays with a sense of daily life. The plays in the
latter category were mostly staged by the director Shinpei Fujiwara[22] with the
Atelier Group of the Literature Theatre Company. In 1978, Betsuyaku's new
play, **The Short Months (Nishi Muku Samurai)**, as presented by the Atelier
Group, was given the 5th Teatoro Theatre Award (*Teatoro Engeki Shō*).[23] Two
years before this the Circle Theatre Company (*En*) had chosen his newly written play **A Demolished Scene (Kowareta Fūkei)** as part of its repetoire. The
fourth company to produce Betsuyaku's work regularly was to be the Snail
Company (*Katatsumuri no Kai*). In 1978, a woman director and producer,
Shimako Murai[24] and the actress Yuko Kusunoki,[25] who is Betsuyaku's wife,
formed a two-woman theatre group, inviting Betsuyaku to be a founder member and a writer for the group. Kusunoki recalls the circumstances in an interview in the July 1989 issue of *Shingeki*:

> At first we did not have a name for the group when we were staging
> **Dance, Dance, Snails (Mae Mae Katatsumuri)** as our first produc-
> tion. We just picked up our group name from the title of the show.
> This was the start. It was still very rare ten years ago to form a women's
> theatre group although it was at the time when professional women in
> society attracted attention with the catch-phrase: 'a high-flying woman
> <*tonderu onna*>.' We wished to carry out work which was very much

down to earth...that's how the name of our group came about... We had the desire to make Betsuyaku's theatre better understood. That was the motivation for forming the group. We want to believe that we have been the best group staging his plays and the fact that we have been given the staging rights of any play which Betsuyaku writes for us encourages us a lot.[26]

Since the formation of the Snail, Betsuyaku has been writing for mainly these four theatre groups: the Atelier Group of the Literature Theatre Company, the Hand, the Snail and the Circle Theatre Companies. For about ten years from then, he had written on average four to five new plays yearly. In 1987 his new play, *Giovanni's Journey to His Father (Jobanni no Chichi e no Tabi)*, written for the Literature Theatre Company, was chosen to be a production in its main theatre and to be part of their touring repertoire. He was given a major award, the 31st Yomiuri Literature Award (*Yomiuri Bungaku Shō*) of 1988,[27] for the play, *The Story of the Two Knights Travelling Around the Country-from Don Quixote- (Shokoku wo Henrekisuru Futari no Kishi no Monogatari)*,[28] written in 1987. In a newspaper interview[29] after this award, he describes how this play came to be written and what he has gained through it:

I have changed. The plot of a play and its emotional movement tended to be disrupted. When I gave a lot of thought to the structure of the play, it would become too abstract and as a result, turned out to be a bad example of an Absurd Play. But I think I have succeeded in combining the dramatic structure and the exposure of emotions in a harmonious way in this play...

The Story of the Two Knights Travelling Around the Country was written with two famous actors, Ken Mitsuda[30] and Nobuo Nakamura,[31] in mind for the two leads. As it had long been his wish to have the opportunity to work with them in this way, Betsuyaku became very nervous and sensitive about finding a world which they could share in theatre. However, the search for the play helped him to develop into a new theatrical phase.

In the same interview, Betsuyaku regrets that sincerity and seriousness towards the subject matters discussed or examined in plays have been given less consideration by successive generations in the New Theatre, and that theatre in

Japan has been becoming superficial and mere entertainment:

> Recently the Japanese Theatre has been losing the richness which used to be there. And it makes me feel as if I were watching a theatre which does not have room for a backstage.[32]

Despite this dissatisfaction with contemporary theatre, and despite the crowning of his career by the general acclamation of his work by a wide range of audiences - from the successful national tour of *Giovanni's Journey to His Father* in 1987, to the star performances of *The Story of the Two Knights Travelling Around the Country* at a fashionable Tokyo venue - Betsuyaku seems not to have lost any of his enthusiasm for writing. Once he said that he will write at least one hundred plays before he dies.[33] Words, words, words, Betsuyaku must keep writing, for it is through this extraordinary flood of words, the constant flow of plays, that he examines the ineffable forces: <etain-oshirenai> [34] forces, within us and without which mould our whole lives.

The time that Betsuyaku was writing the postscript to the seventeenth collection of his plays, *Count Dracula's Autumn (Dorakura Hakushaku no Aki)*, 1990, coincided with the death of Samuel Beckett. I will discuss the immense influence of Beckett's theatre on Betsuyaku's in the next chapter (see [II], [A]). In the postscript Betsuyaku writes, with his usual calmness, of the deep emotion aroused in him by Beckett's death:

> Samuel Beckett died. This was not that surprising considering his age and the rarity of his work in recent years. However, I felt that something had passed, solemnly and absolutely. For myself I began playwriting inspired by his plays and theatre, and at the same time was forced to struggle to break their spell. It seems as if his existence has been part of my consciousness all the time. When the news of his death was announced, I re-read some of his latest plays and was very much moved by the speech from the ending of *Ohio Impromptu*; "Nothing is left to tell."…[35]

Perhaps, I think, all Beckett's work could be seen as a progress to 'being silent.' It was not his death which brought 'the silence.' He made his plays quieter, led them into 'the silence' and died saying "Nothing is left to tell".... and, it (Beckett's death) has become a silent existence like a fossil, and I feel a little better. I feel that 'the weight' is taken away. Of course, this does not mean that his death will not give some new direction to my work in the future.... As in the plays in the collection, a 'Beckettian fragrance' remains in my work - this sort of thing will last a long time. I only think that I might be able to use this 'Beckettian fragrance' more consciously now.... I know that the time when I must think about Beckett's work will come, but I want to forget about Beckett for a while and in that sense his death also means a lot to me. 15th January, 1990[36]

I understand these words as Betsuyaku's paradoxical but sincere mourning for Beckett. As he says here, Beckett's death must have released him from the spell of this other great artist; however, since Betsuyaku himself has developed his theatre with Beckett's theatre always in his mind, and has become another great artist of the same theatrical tradition, "to forget about Beckett" will not be very easy.

Notes for [I] ───────────────────────────────

(1) For much of the material in this section I am indebted to Akihiko Senda's book *The Dramatic Renaissance (Gekiteki Runesansu)* (Tokyo: Libroport, 1983).
(2) Manchuria (1932-1945).
     The Japanese military government had colonised three provinces of the northeast of China, and part of inner Mongolia between 1932 and 1945, and set up a puppet government under Pu Yi.
(3) Harbin.
     Today it is the capital of Heilongjiang Sheng Province.
(4) Shinkyô.
     In Chinese called Xinjing.
(5) Hôten.
     Today it is called Shenyang, and is in the province of Liaoning.
(6) For example in ***The Legend of Noon (Shogo no Densetsu)***, 1973, Invalid 2 refuses to go to the toilet, in ***Water-Bloated Corpse(Umi Yukaba Mizuku Kabane)***, 1978, Invalid 1 dies through refusing to go to the toilet, in ***I am the Father of the Genius Idiot Bakabon (Tensai Bakabon no Papa Namoda)***, 1978, the characters share poison and commit group suicide, and in ***The Story of the Two Knights Travelling Around the Country (Shokoku wo Henrekisuru Futari no Kishi no Monogatari)***,

1987, there is a long list of diseases associated with travelling people.

(For further information on this topic see Appendix [II] Table of Betsuyaku's plays)

(7) Japan/U.S. Pacific Security Treaty (Nichi-Bei Anzen Hosho Jyoyaku).

The Original Pacific Security Treaty was made at the San Francisco Peace Conference in 1957, at which the U.S.A. was able to demand the establishment of U.S. military installations on Japanese territory.

(8) For bibliographic information on all Betsuyaku's published plays see Appendix [I].

(9) Tadashi Suzuki (1939-), director.

He graduated from the Dept. of Economics and Politics at the University of Waseda. He founded Toga Theatre in a converted traditional farmhouse in Toga, Toyama Prefecture, in 1976. He changed the name of his group from the Waseda Small Theatre to the SCOT (Suzuki Company of Toga), and set up the Japan Performing Art Centre in 1982. Every summer at Toga he organises the Toga International Theatre Festival, and invites international performance groups. He lectured on his dramaturgy and acting method at the Julliard School in New York, and Wisconsin University.

(10) He played the part of Willy Loman in **Death of a Salesman** by Arthur Miller, and the Invalid in **The Elephant**.

(11) Akihiko Senda, The Dramatic Renaissance (*Gekiteki Runessansu*) (Tokyo, Libroport, 1983).

(12) Ibid. p.120, footnote.

(13) Tadashi Suzuki, "Acting and Situations", collected in *The Sum of Interior Angles (Naikaku no Wa)* (Tokyo: Jiritsu Shobo, 1973).

(14) *Shingeki (New Theatre)*, a monthly theatre magazine from Hakusui Sha Publishers, Tokyo, (1954 - 1992). The prestigious theatre award, the Kishida Playwright Award is announced in this magazine.

(15) *The Sum of Interior Angles*, p.51.

(16) **Dramatic Passions, Part I (Gekitekinaru Mono o Megutte, Pâto I)**, first performed in 1966, Tokyo; **Dramatic Passions, Part II (Gekitekinaru Mono o Megutte, Pâto II)**, first performed in 1970, Tokyo.

(17) Ibid. (13). *The Dramatic Renaissance*, p.134.

(18) *The Collected Interviews of Tadashi Suzuki (Suzuki Tadashi Taidan Shu)*, ed. Michiaki Ogawa, (Tokyo: Libroport, 1984), p.13. Suzuki interviews Betsuyaku about the days in which they worked together.

(19) Masakazu Yamazaki (1934 - 2020), playwright, theatre critic and lectured at the University of Osaka. Received the Kishida Playwright Award for the play **Zeami (Zeami)**, 1963. A member of the Hand Company.

(20) Toshifumi Sueki (1939 - 2017), director, translator.

Read French Literature at the University of Gakushyuin. Translated Ionesco's plays into Japanese. A member of Hand.

(21) *The Dramatic Renaissance*, p.108.

(22) Shimpei Fujiwara (1931 -), director.

A member of the Literature Theatre Company (*Bungaku Za*), he received the 13th

Kinokuniya Theatre Award, 1978, and the 5th Teatoro Theatre Award, 1978, for *The Short Months (Nishimuku Samurai)*.

(23) Teatoro Theatre Award (*Teatoro Engeki Sho*).
Teatoro (*Teatoro*), a monthly magazine from Teatoro Publishers, (1951 -). The Award is selected and given annually by this magazine.

(24) Shimako Murai (1928 - 2018), director, translator, and playwright.
Read Japanese Literature at Tokyo Women's University.

(25) Yuko Kusunoki (1933 -), actress.
Yuko Betsuyaku. She graduated from Haiyu Za Drama School, and was a founder member of the theatre company Snail.

(26) Tsuneo Kawamura, 'The Snail Company is Eleven Years Old' in *Shingeki*, no. 436, (July 1989), p.89.

(27) Yomiuri Literature Award.
The Yomiuri is one of Japan's national newspapers.

(28) This play is one of the four which I chose to translate and stage for this research, (see [III], [D]).

(29) 'The Winner of the Yomiuri Literature Award (*Yomiuri Bungaku Shō no Hito*)' in *The Yomiuri*, (1st February 1988).

(30) Ken Mitsuda (1902 - 1997), actor, member of the LTC.
He also acted in Betsuyaku's play *Giovanni's Journey to His Father*, and received the 6th Kikuta Kazuo Theatre Award, 1981, and the 22nd Kinokuniya Theatre Award, 1987.

(31) Nobuo Nakamura (1908 - 1991), actor, member of the L.T.C.
He acted in Ionesco's *The Lesson*, Betsuyaku's *A Demolished Scene, A Corpse which Creates an Atmosphere* and others. Received Shijuhō Shō from the state in 1967 and Kinokuniya Theatre Award in 1982.

(32) 'The Winner of the Yomiuri Literature Award'.

(33) Postscript to *Collected Plays of Minoru Betsuyaku* (Vol. 10), p.236.
His one-hundredth play was *Wearing Gold-embroidered Satin-damask Obi (Kinran-donsu no Obi Shimete)*, *"Biography of Minoru Betsuyaku 1937-1997," Programme of the 11th Aoyama Engeki Festival*, 18th October - 9th November 1997.

(34) Betsuyaku frequently uses this term.

(35) *Ohio Impromptu* in *Collected Shorter Plays of Samuel Beckett*, (London: Faber and Faber, 1984), p.288, ll.8-11.

(36) Postscript to *Collected Plays of Minoru Betsuyaku* (Vol 17), p.249.

Minoru Betsuyaku
photo by Masako Yuasa

[II]

Betsuyaku's Theatre

Betsuyaku wrote more than seventy plays by the end of nineteen-eighties since he began playwriting in the nineteen-sixties, and almost all of which were staged by various theatre companies. Every year from ten to twenty of his plays were staged by small and large theatre companies during this period, and Betsuyaku became one of the most popular and important figures among the playwrights of the New Theatre (*Shingeki*) in Japan.

For my doctoral research I studied seventy-two of his plays in detail between 1961 and 1988. Most of the plays have been published in the seventeen-volume collection of his work[1] produced by Sanichi Shōbō in Tokyo. And two plays[2] have been published by the Shinchōsha in Tokyo. I have drawn up a table (see Appendix [II]) analysing each of the seventy-two plays under various headings: the year when the play was first staged, the staging group and the director of the first production, the length of the play, the number of acts and scenes, the number of characters, the style and genre, the subject matter, the relationships among the characters, the significant costumes and properties, the design, the location, the time of the day and the season of a year, the sound effects including the songs to be used, the lighting effects and a general note on each play. It has been important and useful to complete this table in order to see Betsuyaku's work both as a whole and in detail. This is especially so since the number of Betsuyaku's plays is large and he is a playwright who repeatedly uses certain theatrical elements which are indispensable in creating his dramatic world.[3]

In order to look at the whole body of Betsuyaku's theatrical work from August 1960 to 1988 and to offer some analysis of it, I divide his work into three periods: (1) from 1960 to August 1973, (2) from September 1973 to 1980, (3) from 1981 to 1988. Each period represents a different phase of his work, although his basic theatrical ideas remain consistent throughout.

An alternative way of viewing Betsuyaku's theatrical work is to approach it through theatrical style. There are three major styles of theatre which Betsuyaku employs in his plays: they are naturalism, surrealism, and absurdism. Betsuyaku's drama is fundamentally a mixture of the three, depending on the play, characteristics of one style or another are evident.

When Betsuyaku is concerned with universal themes, such as life and death, the emphasis is on the absurdist style; on the other hand, when the subject matter is in some way directly related to the social problems of present-day Japan, the emphasis is put on the naturalist style. The surrealist elements are seen in both categories of plays as a consistent refrain. In those plays of the first category with more elements of the absurdist theatre, Betsuyaku often distinguishes the characters by number – for example, Man 1, Man 2, Woman 1, Woman 2. Here the characters' relationships, the procession of events and the orientation of time and place are all non-concrete. In the second category of plays, those more in the naturalistic mode, the characters are named according to family relationships - the father, the mother, the husband, the wife, the son, and the daughter. By using this nomenclature Betsuyaku immediately presents the compressed husband-wife and parents-children's relationships, and those between an individual and society.

There are perhaps ten plays which have a 'fantastic' quality of fantasy in addition to the three elements of absurdism, naturalism, and surrealism. These are the plays which borrow characters from fantasies or children's stories; they are the puppet plays, and the plays of a diorama where miniatures of the people and the setting, such as a station and a house, are used on the same stage with the human actors and the ordinary-sized scenery. The line between real and unreal becomes unclear and these plays show more of the surrealistic elements. However, when we remember that one of the big movements in the theatre since the late nineteenth century has been the stream from Symbolism to Surrealism to the Absurd,[4] it is no surprise that we should see this mixture or the co-existence in Betsuyaku's plays of elements from more than one of these styles of theatre.

I shall analyse Betsuyaku's theatrical work by examining the major phases and characteristics of his plays, using some of them as examples, following a chronological order. However, there is one aspect of Betsuyaku's work which we must consider first, which is the influence of Beckett's theatre, introduced to Japan in the late nineteen-fifties. It was Beckett's theatre which Betsuyaku studied, and it was Beckett's influence from which he initially gained most.

Betsuyaku's life-long commitment to being a playwright was inspired by Beckett's revolutionary experiments in theatre. Betsuyaku's creative writing began with interpretations and copies of Beckett's work. Indeed, if one could give a short account of Betsuyaku's whole career in theatre, it might be as follows; how he encountered Beckett's theatre, escaped from the extremes which Beckett had reached, and how he thereafter established his own theatre as a positive presence on the contemporary Japanese theatre scene. In this chapter, first I shall discuss what Betsuyaku learned in Beckett's work, and then examine Betsuyaku's plays in other contexts.

[A] Beckett's influence and post-Beckett

It was in the nineteen-sixties that Japanese theatre began to be influenced by Beckett. If I may talk about myself, I must admit that it was my first encounter with Beckett's plays which gave me the initial motivation for choosing theatre as my vocation - yes, that is true. I can still remember that sensational excitement when I read *Waiting for Godot* for the first time in Shinya Ando's translation.[5] Everyone sensed that a very new concept of theatre had been introduced, although we could not yet say precisely how this new theatre would differ from the pre-Beckettian. We felt as if we were having raw theatre thrown in front of us. Enthusiasm for Beckett's theatre grew and we competed in studying Beckettian theatre craft in order to learn Beckettian theory. We were eager to study how the characters in his plays behaved and how the contrivances of Beckett's dramatic language worked in the seemingly illogical dialogues. We foresaw that we would be able to have direct contact with our audience once we could change our old dramatic movements and language to those of Beckett. Formerly we had debated whether 'drama' should identify itself with 'theatre' or 'literature.' In contrast, after Beckett's appearance, we began to debate whether 'drama' should identify itself with 'theatre' or 'meaning.'[6]

In the quotation above Betsuyaku looks back at the theatre of the nineteen-sixties, as one of the young playwrights who followed Beckett. The plays which inspired Betsuyaku at that time were *Waiting for Godot, Endgame, Krapp's Last Tape, Happy Days* and *Play*.[7] Beckett still believed in the function of dramatic language and movement, although his work was already showing signs of moving in the direction of non-language and non-movement theatre. Some of Betsuyaku's plays in the nineteen-sixties, such as *Another Story (Aru Betsuna Hanashi)*, 1962, *The Fallen Angel (Da-Tenshi)*, 1966, and *An Old Banger and the Five Gentlemen (Ponkotsusha to Gonin no Shinshi)*, 1969, show a close resemblance to Beckett's *Play* and *Waiting for Godot* in features such as the setting, the movements, and the dramatic language. For example, in *Another Story*, the three characters, the Father, the Mother, and the Daughter, talk in a fixed order all the way through, just as the Man, the Woman 1 and the Woman 2 do in *Play*. Beckett's characters are in urns somewhere in purgatory and "their speech is provoked by a spotlight projected on faces alone."[8] Betsuyaku's characters meanwhile sit at a table and change their seats in a fixed order. Their movements are ritualised and their speech is conventional and reserved. The conversation is constantly turning to mealtimes and health until at the end of the play the Man from an old people's home comes to take the parents away. Only then is it revealed what they have been talking about. Thus, the language cycle of false conversations in a closed situation creates very much a Beckettian world.

In *The Fallen Angel* and *An Old Banger and the Five Gentlemen* Betsuyaku experimented with Beckett's theatre in a straightforward way by borrowing similar dramatic situations, characters, and subject matter to those of *Waiting for Godot*. The characters A and B in *The Fallen Angel* have been living in a wasteland, somewhere near a small hill, for the last three years. During this time, they have witnessed a procession of the Six Blind People pass them every three and a half hours. The characters A and B decide to get away to somewhere else by following the Six Blind People when they next come past. But only the blind people reach anywhere else and the two who have chased after the blind people return to the same place near the hill. In *An Old Banger and the Five Gentlemen* Betsuyaku uses five male characters in tramp-like, Chaplinesque costumes exactly like those which Vladimir and Estragon wear in *Waiting for Godot*. The location is on a road. The five Gentlemen A, B, C, D and E who seemingly live in "these parts,"[9] enter one by one and argue over whose shoes are smelliest and whether or not wearing shoes is indispensable in that situation. Their speech and behaviour suggest that they repeat this nonsensical act every day. They receive a letter saying that someone is coming to visit them. They do not know when he or she is coming because they cannot work out what day or time it is now. A fruitless discussion goes on about how they might find out the correct date, reminiscent of the messenger boy sequence from *Waiting for Godot.*

While Betsuyaku experimented with his thoughts in the theatre using the elements of Beckettian theatre in his playwriting, he also analysed Beckett's use of dramatic space and sought to formulate a theory concerning it. In the post-script of the third collection of his plays, *The Rebellion of the Soyosoyo Tribe (Soyosoyo Zoku no Hanran),*[10] 1971, Betsuyaku explained his thinking on stage space:

> For my plays I need a clear bare stage behind the proscenium arch. In other words I do not need any of the conventional settings which the modern theatre tends to have. I do not think that we should change the dynamics of the stage space which theatres possess by their nature. Instead of the overdone settings, I might put an electricity pole, a pillar box, or a set of table and chairs in the centre stage, objects which function in the same way as "a tree" in Beckett's *Waiting for Godot.*[11]

Betsuyaku's plays of the nineteen-sixties were written assuming the presence of a proscenium arch. Although many of them were produced in small studio-type theatres without the arch, none of the plays used a radically alternative space. In the same postscript Betsuyaku gave his interpretation of Beckett's dramatic space and praised the function of "a tree" as expounded by Beckett:

> What is the dynamic structure of Beckett's stage? The stage in the modern theatre has walls on three sides and they tend to create a centralizing power. The stage in Beckett's plays, on the other hand, has an object in the centre stage which tends to create a centrifugally spreading power. In this situation it does not matter whether the central object is 'a tree in the desert,' as the context of the play would suggest, or 'an object made of paper and wire which looks like a tree' on the stage. However, this object must interact with the infinite space created by the uncharacteristic stage. The important point is that 'an object' is a 'part' relating to the infinite 'whole.' A small tree radiates meaning throughout the bare stage. But of course, the infinite and futile world surrounding the tree begins to fight back, tending to make the existence of 'a tree' or 'a

small object' meaningless. The dynamics of the space of Beckett's the-atre always depend on the ambivalence between the power to expand and the power to eliminate.[12]

Many of Betsuyaku's plays employ outdoor locations. He places an elec-tricity pole, a pillar box, a bus-stop, a bench, a table with some chairs or a straw mat, all described as old and worn, out in the open, for example, in the corner of a town or on a street or in a park. The typical stage directions for the opening of a Betsuyaku play might be: "There is nothing on stage. Simply dazzlingly bright," or "There is an electricity pole standing on stage. Evening. The wind blows." These directions tell us that the stage is bare and there are no walls which cut off or enclose the acting area. Even when Betsuyaku locates a scene indoors, he will only use a little furniture and decor, and again no doors, no windows, and no walls. The styles of decoration which he employs may be either Japanese or Western, depending on the play. This unlimited staging space developed directly from Beckett and has become the fundamental ele-ment in Betsuyaku's theatre.

The counter-art of the visual-gesture, movement and setting - is language, and here again Betsuyaku was deeply inspired by Beckett's theatre. Later in the same postscript quoted above Betsuyaku analysed the mechanisms of the dra-matic language of Beckett's theatre and of the modern theatre:

> Language in modern theatre aims to justify the existence of 'the char-acters.' The language in Beckett's theatre meanwhile aims to affirm the fact of the existence of 'the actors' or 'the characters' in their dramatic space. While in modern theatre the speeches are regarded as the sum of the meaning of the words, in Beckett's theatre they are regarded as the means of communication, in other words speeches are merely acts of delivery. The audience in the modern theatre ought to listen to what the actors say and those of Beckett's theatre ought to listen to why the ac-tors say it. Furthermore, having been delivered, the lines in the modern theatre expect a reply, but those of Beckett's theatre are delivered sim-ply to emphasize the distance between the stage and the audience. The dramatic language of modern theatre aims to perpetuate the existing format while Beckett's dramatic language works to create a new format which has not been seen until that moment.[13]

This analysis of Beckett's dramatic language and that of the conventional theatre reveals Betsuyaku's vision of his own dramatic language. Betsuyaku gives the reasons for his use of short sentences and the repetition of simple everyday words in a critical article, 'Words into Sentences (Kotoba kara Buntai e)' in The Space with an Electricity Pole (Denshinbashira no Aru Uchu),(14) 1980. Here he recalls the summer he spent as a private tutor in Karuizawa, a mountain resort of the Japanese Alps, when he was a university student. He had to be with his pupil most of the day, except on Sundays when the boy went to a Catholic church to be given French lessons by a French nun. It was Betsuyaku's job, however, to take the boy to the church and every time the nun opened the door, she greeted them with, "You are most welcome (Yoku irasshaimashita)." He was fascinated by the slow and elegant way in which she spoke this sentence. He thought she must be hesitating between two languages whenever she said it, and heard an implicit criticism of the Japanese language in the nun's tone of voice. Later he used this sense of unsmoothness, 'a feeling of hesitation,' when he chose the words for his plays. In his early playwriting he repeatedly used simple words and sentences such as the moon (o-tsuki-sama), the fish (o-sakana), Good evening (Konbanwa), and Good-bye (Sayonara), words which can be spoken falteringly while at the same time being transformed into symbols.

In the following quotation Betsuyaku defends his use of simple words and short sentences which have the potential for growing into deeper symbolic expressions:

> People called them children's words. I was not annoyed by this, because I knew that the function of the words which I used in my plays was not the same as that of children's words. Children's words depend on the unclearness of their meanings, and on their images. But the simple words in my plays tend to grow as much as possible in respect of the meanings and images until the ends of the meaning and image are supposed finally to meet at a certain point. This is the big difference. In short, the simple words such as 'the moon (o-tsuki-sama)' or 'the fish (o-sakana)' are not meant to be spoken innocently and sweetly. They should be said as if searching for the purified meanings of the words while projecting the intelligence coming out of the simplified images.(15)

Using such simple words was one way in which Betsuyaku developed his dramatic language. But there is another distinctive cornerstone to his verbalism, especially in the work of his early period. It is periphrasis. He often uses expressions such as "I would say I feel almost sad", "I feel as if I were sad," or "I might feel sad." These round-about expressions give the speeches the unsmoothness and unnaturalness of manner which was hinted at in the French nun's greeting. Again in *Words into Sentences'* Betsuyaku explains that he used periphrastic phrases in order to search for the purified meanings and images of the words. When he used a sentence like, "I would say I feel almost sad," he thought that

> ...the emotion approaches closer to "sad" as a result of the use of the word "almost," at the same time, I put a distance to the emotion of sadness by using, "I would say" as an opposing element.[16]

By extracting the purified image of a word such as "sad" and projecting that purified image over the stage, he distilled the images of the words.

Nevertheless, as time went on, Betsuyaku had to face the problem of maintaining a language which was opposed to the natural manner of human speech. He noticed that words should be chosen by human nature. And if the words were chosen in this way, in his theory, they had to be alienated from the natural human feelings soon after they were said. The difficulty was that the choice of words by human nature and alienation of them by the same human nature could not possibly stand together. As the result of this dilemma, he faced a situation where he could not write any plays. However, after all this confusion, he reached a new stage where he was very conscious of 'the logic of the dialogues,' another dimension of dramatic language:

> Roughly speaking, I tried to be sensitive to the logic of dialogues to find my own language style. 'Dialogues' possess their own logic. Of course, words are chosen by the characters who deliver them but 'dialogues' are not formed only by them, because the logic of the 'dialogues' themselves must be working for the conversations to materialize. Paradoxically, if I know 'the logic of dialogues,' even if the words are borrowed from somebody else, the lines which I write can be formulated...

Every speech in my playwriting became even shorter. This was because I was concerned more about the combination and the flow of the lines than about the content of the speeches. I broke down dialogues into several patterns at the beginning and then reunited them. Later my job became easier when I learned that the patterns of the dialogues associated and collaborated by their own nature.[17]

Betsuyaku broke the rules which he had formerly established for his dramatic language. As he says, this change came out of the necessity of developing his own theatre. This was a departure from the direct influence of Beckett's theatre. It is very interesting to note that Beckett moved more and more towards the non-mobile, non-visual, non-verbal, towards the extreme of anti-theatrical drama, while Betsuyaku returned to verbal, visual theatre, towards the Absurd. Betsuyaku writes of how Japanese playwrights at this time reacted to the extremes of Beckett's theatre:

We thought Beckett had fallen into the bottomless muddy swamp in the consolidation of his theatre, which stood in isolation, far away from the theatre which Pinter described as 'a public activity.' Once we realised this, we quickly rushed away from his theatre. From the late nineteen-sixties to the early nineteen-seventies, we ran away from the Beckettian world at full speed. For us, theatre was still alive. We saw clearly where in theatre we could find the parts which had not been demolished after Beckett showed us its skeleton. I followed the general trend. If I may justify my stance at that time, I felt healthiness rather than insensibility of theatre…

I fought a desperate fight to cure my theatre of the addiction to the Beckettian. Once having known the strong aromatic touch of the Beckettian world, I felt uncomfortable when I looked at the non-Beckettian theatre. I felt as if I were in a weightless state and seeing the ghostly shapes. The emotions caused self-intoxication, the logic ended up by turning into an ordinary pattern and the perspectives flattened into the old-fashioned plain scenes. What saved me at that time was the indescribable nature which theatre traditionally possessed. At that time, I wrote, "Theatre consists twenty percent of what is conscious and has been theorised about, and eighty percent of what has traditionally been left untouched." My theatre was softened unconsciously by relying on the untouched eighty percent. I became less restless and I was beginning to forget Beckett's theatre.[18]

The change referred to was the second turning point in Betsuyaku's career as a dramatist. Coincidentally, this happened at the time when another new wave of the younger generation[19] in New Theatre in Japan was prospering, a radical trend which, in the end, drastically changed the whole view of New Theatre. Nevertheless, whatever is sometimes argued, there had been a Beckettian element in the contemporary Japanese theatre influencing and disturbing it. As with the Western theatre, the 'drama' before Beckett and that after Beckett could not be the same in the Japanese theatre - and neither could Betsuyaku's theatre. He found his own world, but we still see Beckettian dramatic elements breaking through in his plays now and then. I shall examine how Betsuyaku inherited and developed or disinherited these elements in the following section.

[B] Betsuyaku's Plays

In this section I shall review Betsuyaku's theatrical work in the years 1960-1988, by dividing the time into three periods: (1) from 1960 to August 1973, (2) from September 1973 to 1980, and (3) from 1981 to 1988. In each period there are certain characteristics which link the plays as a group, although there is a fundamental unity in all Betsuyaku's theatre. I shall look at some individual plays among them to illustrate the characteristics of his style of theatre and the subject matters of each separate period.

(1) The First Period: 1960 - August 1973

I count the play *The Room to Let (Kashima Ari)*,[20] 1960, as Betsuyaku's first serious theatrical work, although it has never been published, and is not generally credited as such. The play was produced by the Freedom Stage (*Jiyū Budai*) at the University of Waseda in the year it was written. And I treat the first period as ending with the two puppet plays, *A Blue Horse (Aoi Uma)*, 1972, and *The Sea and the Rabbit (Umi to Usagi)*, 1973. This is because the fresh innocence of his early writing, producing images like crystal fade about this time, and is replaced by more mature and complex writing.

We see four major currents in the plays of this period. These are: the plays which deal with the war issues, those which show the direct Beckettian influence, those which contains the elements of 'fantastic' stories and music, including the puppet theatre, and those in which Betsuyaku explores the possibilities of his own dramaturgy through a blending of the other three currents.

The plays with war issues: *The Elephant (Zō)*, 1962, made Betsuyaku's name as a playwright. The Invalid, with keloidal scars on his back suffered in the atomic bomb raid on Hiroshima, tries to prove the meaning of his individual life. For he does not want to be regarded as simply that of another nameless victim of a senseless holocaust. His antithesis is the Man, also a victim of the A-bomb, who sees his own life as purposeless and absurd in contrast with the real world around him. David Goodman analyses the conflict between the characters as follows:

> ...whether to accept or reject the devaluation of experience... [This conflict] comes direct from the 1960 demonstrations and has specific political implications. Should one continue to struggle in the knowledge that to do so would be futile and even absurd? Or would it wiser (or at least less painful) to accept defeat and resign oneself to a life of passive resignation. These were the questions young Japanese like Betsuyaku were left after 1960, and because they were crystallised most clearly in the experience of hibakusha (a victim of the A-bomb), Betsuyaku invested these conflicts in them.[21]

This goes some way to explaining why Betsuyaku chose the issue of the A-bomb in the nineteen-sixties, years after the event. The war issues in Betsuyaku's plays are significant in two ways: because of the painful experiences suffered in the last war by himself and by Japanese society, and because of the anti-war political movements of the period. *The Match Girl (Matchi Uri no Shōjō)*, 1966, and *Dr. Maximilian's Smile (Makushimirian Hakase no Bishō)*, 1967, may also be placed with *The Elephant* within this first group.

The plays *An Old Banger and Five Gentlemen (Ponkotsusha to Gonin no Shinshi)*, 1969, *Another Story (Aru Betsuna Hanoshi)*, 1962, and *The Fallen Angel (Da-Tenshi)*, 1966 are the plays with direct Beckettian influence in the characters, setting and costumes. (See Chapter One [II] [A])

The plays with the elements of 'fantastic' stories and music, and the puppet theatre: *I am Alice (Ai amu Arisu)*, 1970, and *Alice in Wonderland (Fushigi no Kuni no Arisu)*, 1970, in which Betsuyaku borrowed characters from Lewis Carroll's stories. In these, Alice, standing in a similar position to Sophocles' Antigone, that is, in opposition to authority, searches for her own identity. The fantastic element appears most strongly in a court scene in the second Alice play, in which all the characters except Alice wear the masks of animals. Two puppet plays, *A Blue Horse, and The Sea and a Rabbit*, are also with the 'fantastic' elements. Some of the puppet characters are described as having surrealistic appearances, and can display the horror and the anxiety of our lives more visually and dynamically than human actors. These plays show obvious kinship with Betsuyaku's other major field of work, the writing of 'fantastic' stories for both adults and children, although Betsuyaku himself advised me in the interview which he gave me in summer, 1987, not to pay much attention to these 'fantastic' stories. He seemed to draw a distinct line between the two different creative fields. In this third current we can clearly see Betsuyaku's world of 'fantasy' in his theatrical creations. *The Spy Story (Supai Monogatari)*, 1969, is the one musical among Betsuyaku's plays. The actors in minor roles remain on stage as a chorus throughout the play and dress themselves as their given characters as they come out to centre stage. The Spy does not know when and why he has been a spy. This is another play about looking for an identity, and the scene in which the Spy sells his own identity reminds us of Brecht's play *Man is Man*. In *The Spy Story* we also see the electricity pole's first appearance in Betsuyaku's plays.

Lastly the plays with a blending of the other three currents are *The Kangaroo (Kangarū)*, 1967, *The Town and the Zeppelin (Machi to Hikōsen)*, 1970 and *The Rebellion of the Soyosoyo Tribe (Soyosoyo Zoku no Hanran)*, 1971 and so forth. The dramatic quality is rich and unique, because Betsuyaku here synthesises the other three forms and creates his own style, which comprises a sense of dry absurdity in the language, a surrealistic or 'fantastic' atmosphere and the universal questions of our human world as subject matter.

Among the plays of this group *A Scene with a Red Bird (Akai Tori no Iru Fūkai)*, 1967, was exceptional. We see the familiar characters of Betsuyaku's plays, such as the Woman, her Younger Brother, Mother and Father, the

Mayor, the Traveller, and the Postman. There are also stage properties such as coffins, a pram, an umbrella, a parasol, a bicycle and a set of table and chairs, which later Betsuyaku uses repetitively in his plays. The background of the play is a mixture of Japanese and Western cultures. There is a funeral conducted in something like the Japanese Buddhist rites, and on the other hand there is a carnival held in a town square with a clock tower which would seem very Western for a Japanese audience. The plot of the play is as follows. The Blind Woman and her Younger Brother's parents borrowed much money from the money-lender, and then committed suicide because they could not pay it back. The people of their home-town want to help and to support the sister and brother left behind, and to pay back the money to the money-lender. However, the blind sister thinks they ought to pay it back by themselves, and forces the brother to work to earn money for that. The brother steals money, is caught, and is put in jail. He tries to escape but his blind sister shoots him when she finds him on the wall of the prison. She believes that they must atone for their parents' misdeeds. She refuses all sympathy and mercy. The Woman believes that we must face reality and find our own way out of our problems, because otherwise nothing is solved. We cannot simply forget what has happened even if others show their sympathy. Betsuyaku is here discussing the same issues as he raises in **The Elephant**, that is, whether to accept or reject the devaluation of experience. I shall be discussing the play **The Kangaroo**, which falls into this period, in the annotation on the four plays in Chapter Two. (See Chapter Two [I])

(2) The Second Period: September 1973 - 1980

In this period Betsuyaku steadily wrote about three plays a year, and most of them were staged by the four theatre groups: the Hand (*Te no Kai*), the Atelier Group of the Literature Theatre Company (*Bungaku-za*), the Circle (*En*) and the Snail (*Katatsumuri no Kai*). In the postscript to the sixth collection of his plays, **The Short Months (Nishimuku Samurai)**, 1978, Betsuyaku remarks that he does not write plays with particular stage groups in mind.[22] But when we look at the plays and their productions, we find in fact that each group's distinctive qualities give Betsuyaku the confidence, and enable him to expand his theatrical world. For Hand, Betsuyaku experimented with plays which have rather metaphysical features in the foreground and, by contrast, the plays which have a more concrete, realistic sense of our everyday life were written for the Atelier Group of the LTC. The plays written for the Circle and the Snail include both types, the major distinction between them being that those written for the Snail are all two-handers (See (3) The Third Period: 1981-1988, for discussion of two-handers). So in general we can see that Betsuyaku's plays of the second period are written with two contrasting approaches. One approach is to bring out the true meaning of our daily life through the artificial arrangement of the characters and the situations of the play. The characters begin to react to the situation, and, as the play develops, to recognise and face the issues which confront them. Meanwhile the audience witnesses the process, at first contemplating the metaphysical question objectively and then soon thinking about the problems with Betsuyaku's own absurd logic. The other approach is to reach the universal issue through the impact of the repetitive routines of everyday life.

In the postscript to the fifth collection of his plays, **Bubbling Boiling (Abuku Tatta Nitatta)** 1976, Betsuyaku puts down his thoughts on the 'three spaces'[23]; 'the living space,' 'the abstract space' and 'the language space,' and also how he actually uses these three spaces in his playwriting. And this explanation gives the logical base to the two approaches identified above:

> Drama develops in three different spaces: these are 'the life space,' 'the language space' and 'the abstract space.' Similarly, an actor on stage can be a 'dweller' in the drama, 'a presenter' of the drama and also 'a centre of the fictional world' to focus the meaning of the drama. 'The life space' tends to enclose the events within itself, in other words, it is a unit of 'the infinite nothing' of space. On the other hand, 'the abstract space' tends to open up the events, in other words it is a unit of 'the infinite all' of space. And 'the language space' works to chain them together and create a balance between them. This means that 'the life space' and the 'abstract space' cannot stand by themselves without relating to 'the language space.' Or rather it can be understood thus; 'the life space' and the 'abstract space' at present are simply the predictable reflections of 'the language space'... 'the abstract space' would be better called 'the space which gives out the abstract impulse' and likewise 'the life space' would be better called 'the space which gives out the emotional impulse'... [24]

The present is 'the third era' of theatre and in this era, we again begin to think about our theatre as simply comprising 'the living space' and 'the abstract space.' However, as both spaces have been eroded by 'the language space,' we cannot extract the 'living space' and 'the abstract space' by themselves. They are only 'living space' and 'abstract space' in 'the dramatic irony,' as the predictable reflections of 'the language space.' 'The theatre of the third era' consists of these two spaces.[25]

Betsuyaku explains his ideas on the three spaces and the two approaches in his playwriting in the same essay, by using as examples of his experiments in the two approaches, the two plays *A Demolished Scene (Kowareta Fukei)*, 1976, from the first approach, and *Boiling Bubbling* from the second approach. Also, since he believes that 'the life space' and 'the abstract space' can only stand in our own time supported by 'the language space,' he calls 'the life space' 'the life space in the dramatic irony' and 'the abstract space' 'the abstract space in the dramatic irony':

> *Bubbling Boiling* follows a path from 'the living space in the dramatic irony' towards 'the abstract space in the dramatic irony' and, on the other hand, *A Demolished Scene* follows a path from 'the abstract space in the dramatic irony' towards 'the living space in the dramatic irony.' In other words, the first play is an attempt to examine the phenomena of 'the living space' acknowledging them as the central activity in 'the abstract space' without their passing through 'the language space.' And the second one is an attempt to examine the central activity of 'the abstract space' acknowledging it as a phenomenon in 'the living space' without it passing through 'the language space.' I would like to say that the former is an attempt to see the universe by examining in detail a stone on the street and the latter is that of making a substance exactly similar to a human being by drawing some lines, colouring the space, adding some hair.[26]

The other plays written with the first, 'realistic' approach include *The Story Written with Numbers (Sūji de Kakareta Monogatari)*, 1974, and *A House, a Tree, a Son (Ikken no Ie, Ippon no Ki, Hitori no Musuko)*, 1978. Although the play *I am the Father of the Genius Idiot Bakabon*, 1979, is based on a comic book (see Chapter Two [II]), the comic characters were nationally well-known figures in contemporary Japan and so this play could perhaps belong to this group.

The plays of the second, 'metaphysical' approach include **Chairs and the Legend (Isu to Densetsu)**, 1974, **A Place and Memories (Basho to Omoide)**, 1977, and **A Little House and the Five Gentlemen (Chiisana Ie to Gonin no Shinshi)**, 1979. These are the plays which manifest the characteristics of the Theatre of the Absurd more directly.

At the end of this period Betsuyaku developed the first (i.e. 'realistic') approach further, and wrote plays using very raw materials: he writes his thought about these plays in the postscript to the ninth collection of his plays, **The Blooming Tree (Ki ni Hana Saku)**, 1981:

> I used to avoid using materials for a play 'raw' and used to adjust them to fit in with 'the dynamism of the dramatic space' and locate them in 'the place where we can see both the whole and the part' and to add to them the new 'sense of everyday life' in order to make them work better with 'the actor's sense of his body.' I saw this as the first rule in my playwriting. However, recently I began to have doubts about this. I realised that I could not ignore the strengths of materials used as they are. Needless to say, this way of thinking is risky, because 'the raw materials' have too many unrefined facets and so they fail to merge into the dramatic space. What is more they sometimes show very unexpected and profound aspects. If we become too used to this effect, we tend to rely more on the unexpected and our work strays in the wrong direction. I am losing the clear sense of a boundary between 'the pure dramatic elements' and 'the rough elements.'[27]

The Blooming Tree, 1980, **The Red Elegy (Sekishoku Eregi)**, 1980 and **A Corpse Which Creates an Atmosphere (Funiki no Ari Shitai)**, 1980 are the plays written using the 'rawer' materials.

The Move (Idō), written in 1971, and first staged in 1973, is the play which marks the transformation in Betsuyaku's writing from the first 'realistic' to the second 'metaphysical' period. As such it broke much new ground, and it shows characteristics of both the approaches which Betsuyaku was to develop separately in the following years. **The Move** is about a family moving house from one place to another. Their journey does not last a day or a week but seems to be never-ending. The family do not adjust their way of life as they travel with their belongings. They keep the times for tea, meals and washing, although on each occasion they have to find the necessary equipment in the mound of luggage on their bicycle-cart. The effect is to make the audience, who see the enormous efforts needed for each trivial daily ritual, feel tired. In fact, the characters on stage look exhausted from the opening of the play and the elderly father, the mother and the small baby die one by one because of the harsh routine of the move. At one point they come across a couple who are moving in the opposite direction, and the husband and wife realise that the place they are heading for has nothing to justify their efforts to get to it. They seem shocked but continue their move. The basic idea behind their determination is that it will all be in vain if they return. They cannot change their decision. They might not gain anything by going on but returning means losing all. As the play proceeds, we come to realise that the actors are illustrating our daily routine in their actual horizontal movement from stage right to stage left, and are making visual what is usually observed only with the passing of time. This dramatic experiment of using stage space to create a sense of time passing gives us a more concrete vision of what we repeat in everyday life. The wife is determined not to look at the unpleasant reality confronting her. She becomes more and more talkative and frantic in her movements. Her husband tries to soothe her and suggests she should rest - they have no reason to hurry. The wife says she understands this, but she cannot change, she cannot stop.

(3) The Third Period: 1981 - 1988

Fundamentally, Betsuyaku's work does not change direction between the second and third periods, any more than it did between the first and the second periods. Betsuyaku holds to the two approaches and the main feature of his theatre continues to be the interweaving of the naturalistic and the 'fantastic' strands with the 'surrealistic' and the 'absurdist.' Also, the main staging groups continue to produce his work. However, there are two distinctive characteristics of the third period. They are the two-handed plays and the plays which utilise a large number of actors and a grand backdrop.

From 1981 to 1988 Betsuyaku wrote seven two-handers, but, as I mentioned in the previous section, he had already written five others during the second period. The earlier two-handers are: *A Scene with a Corpse (Shitai no Aru Fukei)*, 1974, *A Scene with a Bus-stop (Bustei no Aru Fukei)*, 1976, *Dance, Dance Snails (Mae Mae Katatsumuri)*, 1978, *Days for Insects (Mushitachi no Hi)*, 1979, and *The Information Desk (Uketsuke)*, 1980. Both the 'metaphysical' and the 'realistic' approaches are used in these plays; the groups which produced them were various until the Snail Company began its productions. In the third period the two-handers include: *I am not Her (Sono Hito dewa Arismasen)*, 1981, *A Corpse with Feet (Ashi no Aru Shitai)*, 1982, *Star Time (Hoshi no Jikan)*, 1983, *The Room (Heya)*, 1985, and *An Escaped Convict Who Carries a Hot-water Bottle (Yutampo wo Motta Datsugokushū)*, 1986. All the seven plays were staged by the Snail; their themes are like those of the second period two-handers, the problems of man-woman relationships, and in all twelve plays the two characters are 'the Woman' and 'the Man.' The long heritage of conservatism in Japan is still felt in society. The conventional social customs which often restrict people's thoughts and attitudes especially about marriage, love relationships, and marital status are still very strong. Using the two characters in simple situations, Betsuyaku discusses in a direct way the pressures which society thus exerts on individuals. The approaches followed in the playwriting are again what we have called the 'metaphysical' and the 'realistic,' as in the previous period, but the plays show more of a 'fantastic' quality, and more of Betsuyaku's surrealism and absurdism. I shall be discussing this further in the annotation on *A Corpse with Feet* (see Chapter Two [III]).

Betsuyaku himself comments on the other distinctive quality found in some of his work in this third period, its grandness of scale, in the postscript to the eleventh collection of his plays, *The Snow Lies on Taro's Roof (Taro no Yane ni Yuki Furitsumu)*, published in 1983:

> The three plays published in this collection are all longer than those I had written before. *Ten Little Indians (Soshite Dare mo Inaku Natta)*, 1982 and *The Snow Lies on Taro's Roof*, each consists of about one hundred and forty *genkō yōshi* which is a sheet of Japanese manuscript paper with space for 400 characters. *Who's Right Behind Me (Ushino no Shōmen Dare)*, 1983, has about one hundred and thirty sheets of *genkō yōshi*. The plays which I had written up to now usually had about one hundred *genkō yōshi*, which shows that my plays have become a little longer. And this change in the number of the sheets - about twenty

or thirty extra - makes a big difference in staging. This is because a play of one hundred sheets makes a performance of 'one and a half hours without intermission' possible, but a play of one hundred and thirty to forty sheets becomes a performance of 'two hours without intermission'... This makes quite a big difference when I write a play. I do not intend to write a longer play, but I suppose that something inside me forces me to do so. It is, so to speak, like one's 'breathing rate.' In future my plays will change depending on the motif and on the style of the performance and I would like to experiment more with this 'breathing rate.'[28]

The Snow Lies on Taro's Roof uses the 2.26 Incident in 1932[29] to examine the emperor system (*Tennō Sei*) of Japan, in relation to the power of individuals. In fact, although the play is based on the 2.26 Incident, the subject matter is closely connected with Betsuyaku's 'war-issues' and with the political movements of the nineteen-sixties, discussed in (1) the First Period. In addition, characters called Invalids 1, 2, 3 and 4 appear in the play, and this is another 'invalids play,' like *The Elephant* or *The Water-Bloated Corpse (Umi Yukaba Mizu Tsuku Kabane)*, 1978.

The play *Ten Little Indians* has the very Betsuyakuesque explanation and subtitle: "The detective story by Agatha Christie, which is rather tragic, comic and absurd, developed in a Beckettian theatrical way with a Monty Pythonic[30] twist. - *the ten little Indians who are waiting for Godot* -." The absurdity of this explanation and subtitle prepares us for the main characteristics of the play. Although Betsuyaku borrows the characters from Agatha Christie, the location he uses is different from the original: "Somewhere in the wasteland. A thin tree. Nothing else. In the evening."[31] All the characters have come to this place at the summons of the absent Mr. Godot. The basic plot follows Christie's story, but what the play discusses is whether Mr. Godot exists. And at the end of the play when the murderer is unmasked, Betsuyaku adds a further surprise of his own something like in the style of the Monty Python television series. Here we see that Betsuyaku is still studying Beckett's *Waiting for Godot* for both its subject matter and its theatrical method.

The plays *Giovanni's Journey to His Father (Jobanni no Chichi e no Tabi)*, 1987, *Lieutenant Shirase's Expedition to the South Pole (Shirase-chūi no Nankyoku Tanken)*, 1986, *The Story of the Two Knights Travelling Around the Country (Shokoku wo Henrekisuru Futari no Kishi no Monoga-*

tari), 1987 are also on a grand scale and each play illustrates certain currents in Betsuyaku's work of this period.

Giovanni's Journey to His Father was based on Kenji Miyazawa's[32] 'fantastic' story, *The Night of the Milky Way Train (Ginga Tetsudō no Yoru)*. Betsuyaku borrows the characters from another author's original story, but this time the play begins twenty-three years after the end of *The Night of the Milky Way Train*, when the main character, Giovanni, returns home. Visually the play reminds us of those of the first period - the 'fantastic' elements, such as the big puppet characters hanging from the lighting bar, while there is also a big clock hanging down. It is also interesting to note that the epilogue from **The Spy Story** is repeated in **Giovanni's Journey to His Father** with slight adaptations. Overall the play is fantastic and surrealistic.

Lieutenant Shirase's Expedition to the South Pole displays more of the elements of absurdity. The nine characters, such as Man 1, Man 2, Woman 1 and Woman 2 and so forth are heading for the South Pole but always end up back where they started. Lieutenant Shirase is a historical figure who was the first Japanese to reach the South Pole. In Betsuyaku's play, more than one Lieutenant Shirase appear and claim to be the real Shirase. The journey from one place to another, the characters distinguished only by numbers, and the bare stage, are all the common characteristics of Betsuyaku's absurd plays. **The Story of the Two Knights Travelling Around the Country** is based on Cervantes' novel, **Don Quixote**.

These large-scale plays share the same subject matter, 'returning.' In the previous period Betsuyaku was much concerned with the issue of parent-child relationships; here in the third period he concentrates on the disintegration and reuniting of the family. There is a play, **Father Comes Home (Chichi Kaeru)** by Kan Kikuchi,[33] the story of which, Betsuyaku says,[34] stayed in his mind all the time he was writing these plays. The story is that of a father who left his wife and children and who now comes home after a long absence. Each play that Betsuyaku writes in this third period examines different aspects of 'returning.' I shall be discussing further how Betsuyaku interprets the meaning of 'returning home' in Chapter Two [IV] **The Two Knights Travelling Around the Country**.

Notes for [II] ————————————————————————

(1) See Appendix [I], Bibliography of Betsuyaku's plays.
(2) *The Move* (Tokyo: Shinchōsha, 1971).
     Chairs and the Legend (Tokyo: Shinchōsha, 1974).
(3) See Appendix [II], Table of Betsuyaku's plays (1960-1988).
(4) J.L. Styan, *Modern Drama in Theory and Practice, Vol. 2: Symbolism, Surrealism and the Absurd* (Cambridge: C.U.P, 1981).
(5) **Waiting for Godot (Godo wo Machinagara)** in *Collected Plays of Beckett, Vol. 1 (Bekketo Gikyoku Shū 1)*, trans. Shinya Ando & Yasunari Takahashi (Tokyo: Hakushi Sha, 1967).
(6) Minoru Betsuyaku, *'Analysis of the Beckettian Space'* in *Lines in Scenes (Serifu no Fūkei)* (Tokyo: Hakusui Sha, 1984), pp.201-202.
(7) **Endgame (Shōbu no Owari), Krapp's Last Tape (Kurappu no Saigo no Tegami)**, in *Collected Plays of Beckett, Vol. 1 (Bekketo Gikyoku Shū 1)* trans. Shinya Ando & Yasunari Takahashi (Tokyo: Hakushi Sha, 1967).
     Happy Days (Shiawasena Hibi), Play (Shibai) in *Collected Plays of Beckett, Vol. 2 (Bekketo Gikyoku Shū 2)* trans. Shinya Ando & Yasunari Takahashi (Tokyo: Hakushi Sha, 1967).
(8) **Play** in *Collected Shorter Plays of Samuel Beckett* (London: Faber and Faber, 1984).
(9) Samuel Beckett, **Waiting for Godot** (London: Faber and Faber, 1956).
(10) See Appendix [I], *Collected Plays of Minoru Betsuyaku (Vol. 3)*, p.273.
(11) "A country road. A tree. Evening."
     Opening stage direction to Samuel Beckett's **Waiting for Godot**.
(12) See Appendix [I], *Collected Plays of Minoru Betsuyaku (Vol. 3)*, pp.275-76.
(13) Ibid. pp.276-77.
(14) Minoru Betsuyaku, *'Words into Sentences'* in *The Space with an Electricity Pole (Denshinbashira no Aru Uchū)* (Tokyo: Hakusui Sha, 1980).
(15) Ibid. pp.194-95.
(16) Ibid. p.196.
(17) Ibid. p.198.
(18) Minoru Betsuyaku, *'Analysis of the Beckettian Space'* in *Lines in Scenes*, pp.203-204.
(19) The playwrights who belong to the second generation of the New Theatre (*Shingeki*) are Kōhei Tsuka, Kōday Okabe, Juichirō Takeuchi, Sō Kitamura, etc. Their theatre activities began to prosper in the mid-seventies.
(20) See Appendix [II].
(21) David Goodman *'The absurdity of the real'* in *After Apocalypse* (New York: Columbia University Press, 1986), p.191.
(22) *Collected Plays of Minoru Betsuyaku (Vol. 6)*, p.225.
(23) See Appendix [I], *Collected Plays of Minoru Betsuyaku (Vol. 5)*, pp.217-219.
(24) Ibid. p.217.
(25) Ibid. p.218.

(26) Ibid. p.219.

(27) See Appendix [I], *Collected Plays of Minoru Betsuyaku (Vol. 9)*, pp.241-242.

(28) See Appendix [I], *Collected Plays of Minoru Betsuyaku (Vol. 11)*, pp.311-312.

(29) This incident occurred on the 26th of February 1932 (hence the name 2.26) when it snowed heavily. Young generals opposed to the military government attempted to assassinate the ministers, using one hundred troops. They failed, and were all caught and killed.

(30) Monty Python.
   The UK television comedy series and films produced since the late sixties by the following team of actors and scriptwriters: Graham Chapman, Eric Idle, Terry Jones, Michael Palin, John Cleese, Terry Gilliam.

(31) See Appendix [I], *Collected Plays of Minoru Betsuyaku (Vol. 11)*, p.7.

(32) Kenji Miyazawa (1896-1933), poet and 'fantastic' story writer.
   He graduated from Morioka Agricultural College and remained there as a researcher. *The Night of the Milky Way Train (Ginga Tetsudō no Yoru)* was not completed when he died.

(33) Kan Kikuchi (1880-1948), novelist and playwright.
   Father Comes Home (Chi Chi Kaeru), a one-act play of half an hour, was published by Shincho (Literary Magazine) in 1917.

(34) See Appendix [I], *Collected Plays of Minoru Betsuyaku (Vol. 16)*, p.247.

CHAPTER TWO

Four Plays Of Minoru Betsuyaku

Translations of four plays with annotations

The initial work for this research was the translation and staging of four of Betsuyaku's plays. The purpose of this was to give the plays a new life through a new language and a new theatre and to understand the mechanism of Betsuyaku's theatre with an objective view and at the same time to see how the plays would be received by the British Theatre and its audience.

The plays which I chose for the experiment are: *The Kangaroo (Kangarū)*, *I am the Father of the Genius Idiot Bakabon (Tensai Bakabon no Papa nanoda)*, *A Corpse with Feet (Ashi no Aru Shitai)*, and *The Story of the Two Knights Travelling Around the Country (Shokoku wo Henrekisuru Futari no Kshi no Monogatari)*. The choice of the four plays was governed partly by the time when they were written - *The Kangaroo* dates from the late nineteen-sixties, *I am the Father of the Genius Idiot Bakabon* from the mid nineteen-seventies, *A Corpse with Feet* from the early nineteen-eighties, and *The Story of the Two Knights Travelling Around the Country* from the late nineteen-eighties. I hoped to see how the characteristics of Betsuyaku's work developed through the three decades.

I staged *The Kangaroo* in December 1987, *I am the Father of the Genius Idiot Bakabon* in November 1988, *A Corpse with Feet* in June 1989, *The Story of the Two Knights Travelling Around the Country* in November 1990.

In furtherance of the aims of this research, the producing and staging of the plays were carried out by myself. Most of the decisions made during the rehearsing period, for example some movements, the properties, the costumes and so on, were based on my personal knowledge on both Japanese theatre, and culture and society. The experiment was taken place in the Workshop Theatre, the School of English of the University of Leeds of the United Kingdom. For each production I was helped by my colleagues of the WT, and many MA and BA students as cast and staff.

In this chapter I present my translations of four plays with annotations.

The Kangaroo
Stage photo by Christopher Jowett
SCENE VI (from left) Hat Seller's Wife, Hat Seller, Old Man,
Pimp, Prostitute, Mistress, Man in the Black Hat, Follwer 1 and 2

The Kangaroo
Stage photo by Christopher Jowett
SCENE IV (from left) Man in the Black Hat, Prostitute and Man

[I]

The Kangaroo

About the play

The Kangaroo was written in 1967 and staged in July by Shimpei Fujiwara and the grop of actors from the Literature Theatre Company (*Bungakuza*) known as the Atelier Group. It was at the beginning of Betsuyaku's career as a professional playwright, and soon after the staging of the award-winning plays, **The Match Girl (Matchi Uri no Shōjo)** in 1966 and **Scenery with a Red Bird (Akai Tori no Iru Fūkei)** in 1967.

Among Betsuyaku's plays of this time *The Kangaroo* is remarkable for its abundance of the theatrical elements which Betsuyaku was later to go on to experiment with, develop and bring to maturity. Betsuyaku seems to use most of his theatrical elements in this one play. So we find fairly sophisticated absurdity, surrealism mixed with the quality of 'fantasy' and symbolism, the use of short simple words and sentences in repetition, the Beckettian bare stage, the early evening to midnight setting which Betsuyaku liked in his early plays and also very familiar properties such as a coffin at a funeral and a rag doll: all of them in a two-hour play with six scenes. It is true though that some of these elements are still in a crude state or not aptly employed and also that the play could be said to lack definite direction. This is perhaps why it did not have such a strong impact as other plays such as **The Match Girl**. Nonetheless, **The Kangaroo** is rich in theatre and it is interesting to see that Betsuyaku's work was already presenting so many features of his later theatre.

The social background of this play is the two political protest movements over the *Ampo Tōsō* in the nineteen-sixties and seventies. As I have described in Chapter One [I], many intellectuals were involved in these movements and experienced the bitterness of the failure of the struggle against the authorities. Betsuyaku had himself experienced the movement of the sixties and at the time of writing **The Kangaroo** was anticipating the *Ampo Toso* re-emergence in the coming seventies. The world-wide spread of the 'Hippy Culture' should also not be ignored as another general influence on the author at this time.

The Man, the leading character of the play, wishes to go abroad, anywhere out of the country, but preferably to India. His hopes however are condemned to disappointment firstly by his being given the wrong sailing ticket, and secondly by the people at the quay, some of the other passengers, deciding that he is a kangaroo and so could not get on the ship even with the correct ticket. Although Betsuyaku used 'a kangaroo' to label the Man, it does not matter whether he is called 'a kangaroo' or 'a chameleon.' What matters here is that he is different from the other people. The Man is a heroic symbol of angry young men of that time in Betsuyaku's world. Betsuyaku's hero is angry but does not become aggressive. The anger turns inward and grows into despair. Now the only desire left in the Man is to run away from his own country and to die of hunger in India, hoping that his bones would be licked by Buddha. The Man's attitude represents the desolate spirit of young people disillusioned by the failure to change the conservative Japanese society.

The mid nineteen-sixties was also the time when Japan, having survived the severe damage of the last war, was looking forward to the economic prosperity which blossomed since and which lasted to the early nineteen-nineties. Behind this economic success, however, other important matters were being neglected and devalued: the destruction of the environment speeded up, business success was glorified above everything else and so forth. Young people like the Man in the play, and Betsuyaku himself, regretted the emphasis upon material prosperity, lamenting the loss of richness in Japanese society and culture and the spiritual impoverishment which accompanied the economic triumphs.

The Man is judged to be a kangaroo simply because the other people believe that he is. This tendency to abide by the decision of the group is one of the more noticeable characteristics of society in Japan. I would like to call it 'the group logic.' In general, I think, there are two contrasting attitudes which a group of people may adopt when relating to an individual amongst them. The one is to go towards the individual to offer him or her help. If the kindness is excessive, even if it arises from the best of motives, it invades the privacy of the individual. The other reaction is to stay away from an individual and give him or her a chance to sort things out by themselves. But if it is taken too far, it turns into ignoring even the existence of the individual. Japanese society has former tendency – it is like a child who smothers small animals.

To return to the point: when the Man is called a kangaroo, why does he accept what the others say without making any effort to defend himself? There are two possible reasons for this: he is too demoralised to protest by being prevented from leaving the country, and that he has perhaps had to deny that he is a kangaroo many times in the past. He has explained his behaviour and his attitude towards life and declared his own thought and opinions and yet it has either never listened to, or people have always thought that he was wrong, simply because his ideas were different from the majority view. The play ends with the funeral of the Man, but what is going to happen at the quay next day? Perhaps they will find another kangaroo, a misfit of society, and play the same trick on him or her.

Style and Structure

The theatrical style of the play is very much a mixture of absurdism, surrealism, and symbolism. Although the play consists of six scenes, in terms of style it can be divided into three parts, Scenes I and II, Scenes III and IV, and Scenes V and VI.

In Scenes I and II we see Betsuyaku building up the world of absurdity by using one of his theatrical devices, 'the leap of logic,' again and again. This 'leap of logic' mainly appears in the Old Man's speeches. For example, the Old Man tells the passengers what is indispensable on the ship (KANGAROO p.76, l.28-34). His manner of explanation sounds very logical although we soon notice that he is talking nonsense. The Old Man presents his passengers with a riddle, which is "WHAT IS THE ROUND THING IN THE SKY?" (KANGAROO p.79, l.22 & 24, p.80, l.18). This straightforward, rather childish absurdity appeals to the audience, and their sympathy further validates the rules of Betsuyaku's dramatic world. It could be because most of us have been through the world similar to Betsuyaku's in our childhood. Therefore, when the Old Man gives the justification for believing that the Man is undoubtedly a kangaroo, his words oddly convey some truth and convince us of the soundness of his logic. He says, "To their shame, none of them has ever thought that they might be the kind of THICK OAF who'd be called a kangaroo. No one believes other people's description..." (KANGAROO p.81, l.17-19).

The Man's story about India (KANGAROO p.88, l.34-p.89, l.2), the Pimp's brother being able to suck up two strings of noodle with his nose at the same time (KANGAROO p.89, l.17-19), and 'the French style friendship' between the Pimp and a stranger (KANGAROO p.91, l.4-p.92, l.2), in Scene II are also episodes which are somehow strangely comprehensible and credible when we judge things by the laws of Betsuyaku's absurdism.

Betsuyaku uses the Old Man to establish the world of 'the leap of logic' and in the same way he chooses the Hat Seller and his Wife to establish the pace of the play by giving them short, simple, and rather poetic sentences to say in a quick exchange of lines right from the start of Scene I (KANGAROO p.75, l.7-27). This use of the short sentence will be seen again in Scene V when the Man and the Prostitute have a meal as a married couple.

In Scene III and Scene IV, we see the elements of action, drama and slapstick comedy in addition to the use of 'the leap of logic' and of short sentences which have so well created the dry and absurd atmosphere of the previous two scenes. Betsuyaku cleverly borrows the traditional characters represented by the Man in the Black Hat, his Mistress and his Followers 1 and 2 to install the two new elements of action and humour into the play. Torturing, killing, fighting a duel, being rescued by a hero, and several exciting moments involving all the cast are incorporated into these scenes.

The Black Hat Gang are desperate to find out the secret which the Old Man, the Hat Seller and his Wife are keeping, and argue about what torture they should use to extract it. Followers 1 and 2 suggest several elaborate tortures but what they actually do on stage is to slap the Hat Seller and pull his ears; they have decided that the Old Man and the Wife would take longer to coerce. The cruel tortures are only heard about and not shown simply because the would-be torturers do not have any of the right equipment with them. The Followers play the role of clowns and get the laughs. The Man in the Black Hat understand things very slowly and as he is controlled by his Mistress who has a strong character, he also looks silly. In fact these gangsters play the traditional characters of the 'silly baddies' in Betsuyaku's absurd world, his world of nonsensical logic, and make the stage active and vivid, and this lightens the play which otherwise might tend to get too serious and monotonous as some absurd plays do.

We should notice here two very interesting movements which are borrowed from Japanese traditional theatre and which we do not find in any of Betsuyaku's other plays. When the Man in the Black Hat and his Mistress enter, they look at the moon and admire its beauty (KANGAROO p.96, l.18-20). The stage directions do not indicate the particular movement, but the lines require that they should make some stylized posture. Again, when the Pimp comes to rescue the Prostitute and the Man, he enters saying, "Wait! Wait for a moment!" (KANGAROO p.114, l.13-15). This is one of the typical entrances in *kabuki* for a hero who is supposed to take up a pose. They are common comic devices used in the traditional style of slapstick comedy. But we do not expect to see them in a play like **The Kangaroo** with its different theatrical style. Its unexpected silliness makes the play funnier, more visual, and richer as a comedy.

In Scene V and scene VI, the style of theatre moves towards surrealism and symbolism. Scene V is an imaginary scene which in staging the play we called 'a dream sequence.' The Man, killed at the end of Scene IV, returns and is playing house with the Prostitute on a straw mat in a field. Because the play begins in the evening and ends at midnight, the choice of daytime for this scene changes the whole atmosphere on the stage. The language used here is simple, poetic, and beautiful, and forms short dialogues. Some of the earlier characters appear unexpectedly on the stage, disguised as unwanted visitors to the home, such as a constable, a house-to-house saleswoman and telephone salesman, implying that they have always been intruders into the private life of the individuals. What is more, every one of them oppresses the couple by warning them of the danger of the existence of a cow, which is peacefully grazing far away in the distance. Here is Betsuyaku's ironic observation of society. He is pointing out from another angle the problem of 'the group logic.' The cow is not seen on stage and is used to symbolise everything people in society are forced by custom, by fear of others' disapproval, to pay attention to.

Scene VI is the funeral scene of the Man. The time is already midnight and all the characters except the Man, who has been killed twice, at the end of both Scenes IV and V, gather at the quay to attend the funeral. Even the Hat Seller who we thought was killed in Scene III returns alive saying that he failed to die. There is the coffin in which the Man lies dead placed in Centre Stage. The characters are led into a line surrounding and circling the coffin. The stage direction of this scene says:

Everyone except the MASKED SINGER and the PROSTITUTE moves slowly in this scene. They sometimes stop walking and meditate or have a look at the corpse in the coffin. They converse with one another but they are not tied down by their talking. Each of them lives in his or her own world.
(KANGAROO p.128, l.8-11)

Because of this stage direction the scene begins at an extremely slow speed with restricted movements. We see Betsuyaku's interpretation of the funeral rite in

Japan. The Prostitute, who is playing the role of a chief mourner stands beside the coffin holding a red rose as if she were the Man's wife in the real life of the play. This red rose is handed from character to character when each one comes to console the spirit of the dead man, while at a real funeral in Japan people come close to the altar of the coffin to burn incense instead. A red rose is used as a symbol of the incense and mourners' consolation. The people attending the funeral sing a song, 'Kangaroos Are Sad,' and altogether dance around the coffin. The song is also a symbolised feature of the chant of the sutra of Buddhism, and the dancing is the ritual movements and gestures of the funeral-goers. Both the song and the dancing sound and look ridiculous. The characters eat peanuts at the end of the rite and by this time the stage looks almost bizarre. The undeniable absurdity spreads and covers the stage.

The scene of the midnight funeral on stage represents the world lying between the real and the unreal. As I have already pointed out, there is a sense of implausibility in this scene created by the return of the Hat Seller, the rose, touching the corpse, singing and dancing and eating peanuts and so on. Here is a world of symbolism and absurdism.

Songs

There are a few plays of Betsuyaku's which contain songs. In *The Kangaroo* the Masked Singer sings a kind of theme song in each scene, at the beginning of the scene or at the end. In Scene VI the singing almost leads the action. All the songs: 'In the Old Days,' 'Sayonara Brazil,' 'The Moon, My Friend,' 'When Somebody Dies' and 'Kangaroos are Sad,' were newly composed by Peter Still in Guildford (at the time of the performance) for this production.

Language

Betsuyaku's Japanese has little of the native and local taste of Japanese culture. We may call it the neutral middle-class Japanese. It is easy to understand this when we recall his biographical background. Betsuyaku says that he refused to pick up the local accents.* It was difficult for Betsuyaku as a boy to accept the very different environment in the countryside of Japan after the years in Manchuria. For example, he remembers that the wet muddy earth was so different from the dried earth in Manchuria that he walked on tip-toe for years when he was barefoot.

The tendency toward cultural and linguistic neutrality makes Betsuyaku's language simple. This is one of the main reasons I have chosen Betsuyaku's theatre as the central subject of my doctoral research. The concepts which Betsuyaku uses in his theatre are generally internationally comprehensible, and the language he uses should produce less difficulty and confusion when translated into English. Given the simplicity of Betsuyaku's dramatic language, we can say that it ought to be easy to translate his plays, although there are still the usual problems of finding the right equivalents without losing the original meaning, length, rhythm and stress, especially as the words are all meant to be spoken on stage.

However, there were two additional fences I had to go over because of his being a Japanese playwright whose work belongs to the Theatre of the Absurd: one is the problem of the different culture and the other is that of its absurdity. And these two qualities tend to be easily mixed up and this produces more confusion than that in the original script. The audience, especially when it is not familiar with Japanese culture, could be driven into the uncomfortable position of not being sure whether lines are serious, jokes or nonsense.

One of the most immediately obvious problems, present in all Betsuyaku's plays, is his unconventional use of the Japanese writing system. There are three kinds of letters used for writing in Japanese. Normally most of the writing is done with the mixture of *hiragana*, *katakana* and *kanji* (Chinese characters). *Katakana* is used for imported words and some mimetic words. However, Betsuyaku sometimes uses *katakana* for words which are normally written in *hiragana* or *kanji*. There is a reason for his usage of *katakana* on each occasion. In my translation I used capital letters for some of the words in *katakana*.

Things absent in British Culture

(a) Objects

∗ noodles (*udon*): different table manners.

When Japanese people eat noodles in soup with chopsticks, they sometimes suck up the soup and noodles holding the bowl to the mouth. The Prostitute talks about the Pimp's younger brother, who can suck up two noodles together into his nostrils at the same time. The image conjured up is very visual and funny and I therefore remained loyal to the literal translation; to the Western audience the image is so unexpected and unfamiliar that the joke becomes even more absurd than in the original.

* a Japanese abacus (*soroban*): a method of torture.

The beads of a Japanese abacus have a very sharp edge, so it can be used to torture people by forcing them to sit on it and putting heavy stones on their laps. A large washboard-like jagged board and stones were familiar torturing tools in old Japan. Betsuyaku must have used a Japanese abacus in place of it to express a traditional and cruel torture tool.

* salted Japanese radish (*takuan*) and miso soup (*miso shiru*).

The yellowish salted Japanese radish <*takuan*> which has a strong unpleasant smell like some kinds of cheese. Miso soup also has a distinctive smell. These two traditional Japanese foods symbolise the cultural elements of the play.

(b) Animals

* kangaroos, dogs, camels (Scene I); lizards, horses, cows, larks, busy warblers, snakes, roaches (Scene V):

Animals have slightly different roles, meanings and of course even sizes and shapes in every culture. Therefore, we must pay special attention when animals are used in plays. Kangaroos, the Australian animals, look awkward because of their large back legs and the pouches in which they carry their babies, and generally the image of them which the Japanese have is as peaceful animals who do not fight back, perhaps because of their gentle expressions. I think that this impression of kangaroos is the reason the Man, who is a misfit in society but not aggressive, is called a kangaroo. The very interesting point which I found during the rehearsals is that in the West kangaroos are not regarded like that and at first my actors did not understand why Betsuyaku had chosen 'a kangaroo' as the name for the Man.

* dogs:

In the West dogs are allowed to come into the house and to share the same space with people. However, in the old days Japan, usually they are kept in a kennel outside in the garden or in the backyard. This is because of the different architectural style of houses.

"It's a hard world. However, everything has a front and back and dogs live in backyards." (KANGAROO p.79, l.3-4). In the original Japanese text, there is a pun on the word <*ura*> "the reverse side" and <*ura niwa*> "a backyard." Finding a translation for puns is hard work in general, and what might make the audience in the West more confused in this line is the different assumption of where dogs usually live.

(c) Customs
* greetings for meals:

We are grateful for this meal (*Itadaki-masu*) and Thank you for the delicious meal (*Gochisō-sama*).

As people in the West often thank God for the meal before they eat, so the Japanese have the same custom. However, Japanese thank gods and goddesses, or people who grow or cook the food for them. To avoid having an image of the Christian God this is what I did in my translation. The greeting before the meal became, 'We are grateful for this meal' and the greeting after meal, 'Thank you for the delicious meal.'

(d) The Culture of Sentimentality
* to feel lonely, to cry:

Japanese culture could be called a sentimental culture and a good example of this is 'to feel lonely' and 'to cry.' It is natural that people feel lonely or cry at unhappy moments. But what makes the Japanese people's attitude look different is that while they are crying or feeling lonely, on one hand they feel sorry about the unhappy matters and on the other hand they are taking pleasure in the extremity of their emotion. The examples which I listed from **The Kangaroo** come out in the odd and abrupt manner; it is making the play more absurd.

> OLD MAN: I feel lonely. Hey, don't you feel lonely?
> MAN: Yes.
> OLD MAN: Lonely, very lonely. Very, very, lonely. (*He puts his arm around the Young Man's shoulder.*)　　(KANGAROO p.83, l.19-22)

> OLD MAN: Oh, it's so nice to be good to others. Well, everybody, let's go to my place and cry about our goodness.
> 　　　　(KANGAROO p.85, l.31-32)

> PROSTITUTE: ...I want to have a good cry sitting on a straw-mat there. I want to cry for you...　　(KANGAROO p.94, l.15-16)

Chapter Two

Notes: ─────────────────────────────

* Akihiko Senda, *The Dramatic Renaissance* (Tokyo: Libroport, 1983), footnote to p.112.

THE KANGAROO

By
Minoru Betsuyaku

Translated by Masako Yuasa

The original text for the translation is from *Collected Plays of Minoru Betsuyaku: The Match Girl/The Elephant, pp.87-146 (Matchi Uri no Shōjo/Zō: Betsuyaku Minoru Gikyoku Shū, pp.87-146)*, Tokyo: Sanichi Shobo, 1969.
©1969 Minoru Betsuyaku

CHARACTERS

MAN
PROSTITUTE
HER PIMP
HAT SELLER
HIS WIFE
MAN IN THE BLACK HAT
HIS MISTRESS
FOLLOWER 1
FOLLOWER 2
OLD MAN
MASKED SINGER

A play in six scenes

Performance Poster (Leeds in December 1987)

The English translation of **The Kangaroo** was staged at the Workshop Theatre from the 1st to the 4th of December 1987.

The cast and the technical staff for the first English production of **The Kangaroo** in the Workshop Theatre in 1987:

CAST

The Young Man	John Britton
The Prostitute	Emm Gilding
Her Pimp	Ian Connaughton
The Hat-Seller	Mark Hanson
His Wife	Terry Ram
The Man in the Black Hat	Ted Motohashi
His Mistress	Melanie Jones
His Follower 1	Panayotis Domvros
His Follower 2	Rebecca Kempster
The Old Man	Peter Ettridge
The Masked-Singer	Mandy Lewis

TECHNICAL STAFF

Director	Masako Yuasa
Stage-Manager	Melanie Jones
Design	Haibo Yu and Masako Yuasa
Set Construction	Haibo Yu and Chris Jowett
Costumes	Kitty Burrows
Lighting	Trevor Faulkner
	Kwong Wai Lap, Jamal Soliman & Jose da Sliva Beja
Original music	Peter Still
Sound effects	Melanie Jones
Lighting board Operator	Kwong Wai Lap
Follow spot Chris Banfield	
Properties	Melanie Jones & Masako Yuasa
Technical advisor	Chris Jowett

This is a play for a humble variety hall. The hall must be decorated to suit it and a prologue of the play like the following one should be given in front of the hall.

Prologue

PROSTITUTE: Good evening, everyone.

>Please be pleased. A long-waited play, ***The Kangaroo***, is going to open.

>It's true, everyone.

>We've been looking forward to this moment like you have. Tonight, miraculously, the play is going to open, (*after the previous line, as if muttering*) really, hardly believe this.

MAN: Hi, everyone in Shinjuku.

>The people who are just about to pass by the Shinjuku Pit Inn.

>You, not someone else, just you, have you heard that?

>A play is going to open.

>A humble two-act farce, ***The Kangaroo***, is about to open here, now, in this hall.

MAN IN THE BLACK HAT: Everyone! This is confidential, but to tell you the truth, the play is a lot of fun, and a lot cheap.

>You only give five of one-hundred coins, or one five-hundred note, or if it's a one-thousand note, don't get surprised, you'll receive change.

WIFE: Now everyone, who are passing by in front of the Pit Inn, and who have passed by the Pit Inn, let's stop and return.

>If you miss ***The Kangaroo*** tonight, you'll have a bad dream.

>If you miss ***The Kangaroo***, (*after the previous line, as if muttering*) don't know if you'll have a nice wake-up tomorrow morning, really…

CAPTAIN (OLD MAN): Gather around, ladies and gentlemen,

>It's no good to keep standing there idly.

>It's no good to keep giggling there foolishly.

>Watermelons need to be tapped; ladies need to be touched… (*sounding of wooden clappers of kabuki*); and plays need to be seen to be appraised.

PIMP: Well, ladies and gentlemen,

>It's an avant-garde play, very much on trend now, presented by the Project 66.

>It has a theme and thought, fight and love, and an enough view of world.

>We believe (*making a posture accompanies by sounding of wooden clappers of*

kabuki), we won't be damned even if we call it a work of art.

THE FOLLOWERS: Now ladies and gentlemen,
> *The Kangaroo* is starting!
> *The Kangaroo* is beginning!
> Oh, how fretful this is!
> We're telling you that the play is going to start!

This prologue was used when the Project 66 staged the play at the Shinjuku Pit Inn in August 1968.

SCENE I

At the quay. Evening. An old-fashioned bench under a shabby streetlight. Melancholy and gasping ships' whistles are heard now and then.

The MASKED SINGER comes onto the stage playing the guitar in a stylish way and sings the following song.

MASKED SINGER: In the old days,
> I might have been a one-eyed pirate,
> Sailing under the moonlight and drumming,
> My ship might have run after a catch,
> Three days and three nights like a wolf.

> Perhaps as I was strong,
> I might never have been beaten when I fought.
> The white sails of my ship
> Might always have looked red
> With the spray of blood.

> Perhaps I might have aged and,
> My ship might have sunk
> Deep in the sea.

During the song a shabby looking OLD MAN in a flashy striped jacket and a sailor hat comes in from Stage Left with a megaphone in his hand. The MASKED SINGER goes off while singing.

OLD MAN [*holding a megaphone and gazing sadly into the distance*]: The ship's going. The ship's leaving. It's off...It's off...

The HAT SELLER and his WIFE in travelling clothes with suitcases come in from Stage Right.

HAT SELLER: Good afternoon, Captain.

OLD MAN: Good afternoon. What do you want?

WIFE: We're getting on the ship.

OLD MAN: Getting on the ship?

HAT SELLER: Yes, we're going abroad.

OLD MAN: Huh! Have you had the jabs?

WIFE: Yes, we've had seven of them. Big ones like this.

OLD MAN: Did you say good-bye to everyone...? That always causes trouble afterwards.

HAT SELLER: Of course, we went to see everyone and said to them, "Please don't feel sad. We will meet again..."

WIFE: We missed three people, so we left letters to them.

HAT SELLER: We used a light blue note pad with flower patterns on it, and wrote,

WIFE: 'Good-bye. We're getting on the ship...

HAT SELLER: Crossing the sea...

WIFE: Going south.

HAT SELLER: To a warm place.

WIFE: When the wind blows,

HAT SELLER: Please remember us.'

WIFE: We sealed them and left them on the table.

OLD MAN: Did you close the window? If not, they'll be blown away by the first gust of wind.

HAT SELLER: We put the paper-weight on them.

OLD MAN: You put the paper-weight on them. O.K., then I must ask you to wait about there for a while. We still have time before the departure of the ship.

HAT SELLER: Did you say near here? [*He wanders around looking for the place to wait.*]

OLD MAN [*using the megaphone again*]: The ship's leaving. The ship's about to be off...

A young MAN comes in carrying a small bag.

MAN [*waiting for the end of announcement of the OLD MAN*]: Good afternoon.

OLD MAN: Are you getting on the ship?

MAN: Yes.

OLD MAN: Going south?

MAN: Yes.

OLD MAN: The south's good. Flowers are in bloom.

HAT SELLER: Birds are singing, too, Captain.

WIFE: Streams are flowing, too, Captain.

OLD MAN: You've got to make a queue behind them.

MAN: Thank you. [*He stands behind the HAT SELLER and his WIFE.*]

OLD MAN [*breathing in deeply*]: The ship's about to leave... [*giving the announcement and listening to it as if he were trying to see how far it went.*]

HAT SELLER [*listening to the announcement in the same way as the OLD MAN*]: No one's coming any more, Captain.

OLD MAN [*a little displeased*]: No, they aren't, it seems. [*Slowly going to the three and walking around them*] From now on, things become more difficult. Before you get on the ship, we've got to sort a few things out. Don't think all you have to do to get on the ship is to come to the pier. It's wrong.

WIFE: Indeed.

OLD MAN: It's wrong.

HAT SELLER: Absolutely.

OLD MAN: There are three indispensable things before you get on a ship. Do you know what they are? They're a tie, a handkerchief and courage. If you don't wear a tie, you are not allowed to go in the ship's restaurant. If you don't have a handkerchief, you are not allowed to go in the ship's restaurant. If you don't have courage, you are not allowed to go in the ship's restaurant. If you are not allowed to go in the ship's restaurant to eat, you'll starve and die.

HAT SELLER: Absolutely.

OLD MAN [*unpleasantly*]: Have you got a TICKET?

HAT SELLER: Yes, we have. [*He indicates his breast pocket.*]

OLD MAN: Show it to me.

HAT SELLER: Here?

OLD MAN: Yes, here.

HAT SELLER: To you?

OLD MAN: Yes, to me.

HAT SELLER: But...? [*He looks around.*]

OLD MAN: Do you know how this port is organized and who does what?

HAT SELLER: No, we don't.

OLD MAN: Well, this is the point where you show your tickets - here - to - me. [*He holds out his hand.*]

The HAT SELLER takes two big sheets of paper out of his breast pocket. The OLD MAN takes them, looks at them and gives them back to the HAT SELLER.

HAT SELLER: Why?

The OLD MAN hands them back silently.

HAT SELLER: Look, this time the tickets are properly stamped.

WIFE: Why?

OLD MAN [*to the MAN*]: TICKET, please...

The MAN takes a similar sheet of paper out of his breast pocket. The OLD MAN takes it, looks at it and gives it back to the MAN.

MAN [*receiving it*]: Is it all right?

OLD MAN: I'm sorry...

MAN: Why?

OLD MAN: It isn't a TICKET.

HAT SELLER: What about these? Why aren't they valid?

WIFE: Stamped! They've been stamped.

OLD MAN: [*to the HAT SELLER and his WIFE*] The destination isn't written on it. Listen carefully. Tickets must have the destinations on them and to be stamped.

MAN: My ticket has the destination.

OLD MAN: It isn't stamped. All it says for the destination is "a foreign country."

MAN: To a foreign country. I want to go to a foreign country. I don't mind which country it is.

OLD MAN: Nor me. Any country's all right as long as it is a foreign one. Because it isn't here. We all think the same. But it won't get you on the ship.

HAT SELLER: Our destination is clear.

WIFE: We're going to Egypt. People say the fish are very tasty over there.

HAT SELLER: I'd rather go to Argentina. They have delicious cabbages.

OLD MAN [*to the young MAN*]: You've been cheated. There're many crooks in this town.

MAN: But...

OLD MAN: You've got to be careful. We human beings must live our lives always wondering whether we are being cheated, or not.

HAT SELLER: We... cannot get on the ship?

OLD MAN: It seems not.

MAN: A man in the black hat came and sold me the ticket.

HAT SELLER: He's the one.

WIFE: He's the one.

OLD MAN: It's him. At least three people who've bought his tickets come here every day. It's because of them I have been employed. That's to say my job is to soothe their wounded souls. You've been cheated, too. I'm sorry. How unfortunate! I hardly know how to comfort you. And the thing is it's not your fault at all. Yes, it's true. If it happened through your own mistakes, it would be easier to accept ... I do feel sorry for you. I really don't know how to comfort you... Dear me! It's a hard world.

WIFE: Shall we go?

HAT SELLER: Where?

WIFE: Home. It's already time for tea.

HAT SELLER: What can we say to them? We've said good-bye to everyone.

WIFE: Just say our ship didn't go.

HAT SELLER: Again?

OLD MAN: I'm very sorry. First, it's a pity... And... [*putting his arm around the young MAN's shoulders*] ... I don't know what to say to comfort you...

MAN [*breaking away from the OLD MAN*]: Where's the ship?

OLD MAN: The ship?

MAN: Yes.

OLD MAN [*seeing the MAN's determination*]: All right, I give in. I'll give you three special chances. Mind you, this is all that I'm allowed to do for the three poor people who come here every day. It's a hard world. However, everything has a front and back and dogs live in backyards ...so... the first is ROCK-PAPER-SCISSORS.
MAN: Rock-paper-scissors?
OLD MAN: If you win, you are allowed to get on the ship.
MAN: If I win...?
OLD MAN: Here we go, ROCK-PAPER-SCISSORS... [*putting himself in position for rock-paper-scissors*] hang on. You were going to make PAPER, weren't you?
MAN: Yes, I was.
OLD MAN: I was going to make SCISSORS. Sorry, you lost. Right, next, we DRAW LOT'S. [*He takes several paper strips out of his breast pocket.*] Choose one.

The MAN draws a paper strip.

OLD MAN: Unfold it.

The MAN unfolds the paper strip.

OLD MAN: What do you see?
MAN: A triangle in a circle.
OLD MAN: I'm sorry. You nearly won though. The last chance is the RIDDLE. Ready? Tell me, 'WHAT'S THE ROUND THING IN THE SKY?'
MAN: ...?
OLD MAN: 'WHAT'S THE ROUND THING IN THE SKY?'
MAN: The sun...
OLD MAN: It's the moon.
WIFE: It's the moon. I thought so too.
OLD MAN [*comforting the MAN*]: It's just luck. You just had bad luck.
WIFE [*to the HAT SELLER*]: I thought it would be the moon, honest.
OLD MAN: How about you two? Would you like to try, too?
HAT SELLER: Well, but I don't think we'll pass...
OLD MAN: You can't tell. You can't tell yet. This is a hard world. However, ...
WIFE: Yes, we should try it. Everything has a front and back. And dogs live in

backyards.

OLD MAN: Will you try?

HAT SELLER: Well, then, I will put my trust in your encouraging words...

OLD MAN: Shall we start with ROCK-PAPER-SCISSORS?

HAT SELLER: Yes, please...

OLD MAN: Then, let's play ROCK-PAPER-SCISSORS... [*putting himself in the position for rock-paper-scissors*] yours is SCISSORS, isn't it?

WIFE: Isn't yours STONE, my dear?

HAT SELLER: Yeah.

OLD MAN: Look. Mine is PAPER.

HAT SELLER: I was afraid it might be so.

OLD MAN: Do you want to try the next one?

WIFE: Yes, please.

OLD MAN [*taking out the paper strips*]: Choose one.

WIFE: That thick one.

The HAT SELLER draws a thick paper strip.

WIFE [*taking it from the HAT SELLER and unfolding it*]: A triangle in a circle.

OLD MAN: 'WHAT'S THE ROUND THING IN THE SKY?'

WIFE: The moon.

OLD MAN: It's the sun.

The MAN suddenly tries to dash away...

OLD MAN [*stopping him*]: Where are you going?

MAN: Let me go.

OLD MAN: What are you going to do?

MAN: I'll ask the other people.

OLD MAN: It'll be a waste of time

MAN: Let me go.

OLD MAN [*forcing down the MAN*]: It'll be a waste of time, a waste of time, a waste of time...

MAN: Leave me alone. [*He shakes himself free from the OLD MAN's grasp.*]

OLD MAN: You don't know why it'll be a waste of time, do you?

MAN: ...?

OLD MAN [*pointing to him*]: Because you are a kangaroo.

MAN: Kangaroo?

OLD MAN: Kangaroos are not allowed on the ships ever since the old days. Even you've had lots of jabs or a big farewell party, if you are a kangaroo, you are not allowed on the ship. Everybody ought to know that. It's the rule. [*To the HAT SELLER*] You know it, too.

HAT SELLER: Of course, I do.

OLD MAN [*to the WIFE*]: Kangaroos can't get on the ship.

WIFE: Kangaroos can't. If you are a camel, it's another story.

OLD MAN [*to the MAN*]: You are not allowed on.

MAN: I'm...I'm not a kangaroo.

OLD MAN [*to the HAT SELLER and his WIFE*]: Did you hear that?

WIFE: What impudence!

HAT SELLER: Yes, impudent, very...

MAN: I'm not a kangaroo.

OLD MAN [*going up to the MAN and gently*]: Have you ever been to the zoo and seen kangaroos? You must have seen them. Just think which of all kangaroos knows that it's a kangaroo. Do you see? To their shame, none of them has ever thought that they might be the kind of THICK OAF who'd be called a kangaroo. No one believes other people's descriptions of them. You are a kangaroo, that's why...

WIFE: Because you're a kangaroo. That's why.

HAT SELLER: That's why.

MAN: But I don't look like a kangaroo at all.

OLD MAN: No, you don't. You don't look a bit like a kangaroo. I could hardly believe my eyes. I never have thought you were a kangaroo.

WIFE: But I did, I thought he could be a kangaroo... Because he doesn't look like a camel.

HAT SELLER: He can't be a camel. To be a camel he'd have to have a tail.

MAN: No one has ever said such a thing to me before.

OLD MAN [*More gently*]: It's their consideration. It's their delicacy. Listen, the more warm-hearted they are, the harder it is for them to tell you the truth.

HAT SELLER: But I think the true kindness would be...

WIFE: Yes, that's the point.

OLD MAN: There! You, see? Real kindness is not hiding the truth but revealing it as it is and encouraging the person to stand up again. [*He looks Up Stage Left, takes out a whistle and blows it.*] Everybody, take out your handkerchief and wave it. [*Pointing to the ship*] It's leaving. Your ship's leaving now... [*He whistles and waves his handkerchief.*]

The ship blows a low whistle. It whistles again.

OLD MAN [*madly*]: Leaving. It's leaving. Look! That's your ship. The ship you were trying to get on. Look, it's going... Everybody, take out your handkerchiefs and wave to her. Say good-bye to her. Heey, sayonara... Heeey.

The ship blows a low whistle. The MAN sinks onto the bench disappointingly. The HAT SELLER and his WIFE wave their handkerchiefs.

OLD MAN: She's going. She's sailing ... I love it when ships leave. Look, they are waving to us. They are thinking of us. It would be nice to go away somewhere feeling nostalgia for friends.

The ship blows a low whistle. The MAN becomes downhearted and sits down on the bench. The HAT SELLER and his WIFE wave their handkerchiefs.

OLD MAN: Going! The ship's going! How great a ship's departure is! Look, they are waving at us. They are thinking of us with fondness. It must be good to go away while thinking of the others with fondness.

The ship blows a low whistle. The three see off their ship absent-mindedly.

OLD MAN: [*Dazedly*] It's going ...going like fate... [*He dries his tears with his handkerchief.*]
WIFE: I don't know why, but tears just come to my eyes.
HAT SELLER: To mine too. Perhaps it's the weather.
WIFE: The Captain is crying, too.
HAT SELLER: A friend of his might be on board. Maybe that's why. These things often happen.
OLD MAN: No, I don't know any of them. They're all complete strangers to me. But even though they're just strangers, they are thinking of us... [*He dries his tears.*] In the old days I had friends on board. When all of my cousin's family sailed away, I cried for three days. That time was terrible. The quay was packed with people who came to see them off. They were

clinging to each other, to anybody and cried as though they were howling.

HAT SELLER: I remember that day. Our sons were on the ship, too.

WIFE: Our daughters were with them, too.

HAT SELLER: They've gone away.

WIFE: We cried.

HAT SELLER: It was awful. I couldn't stop crying for a week.

WIFE: But you smiled on Tuesday.

HAT SELLER: The milkman made me so. But soon after that I began to cry again.

OLD MAN: Going... Why do ships set off so painfully and slowly as if the sun were setting.

The low ship's whistles are heard a few times.

WIFE: I'm hungry.

HAT SELLER: We have some peanuts.

WIFE: Only a few...

HAT SELLER: Better than nothing. [*They squat down and eat the peanuts.*]

OLD MAN [*To the MAN*]: Did you see it?

MAN: Yes...

OLD MAN: I feel lonely. Hey, don't you feel lonely?

MAN: Yes.

OLD MAN: Lonely, very lonely. Very, very lonely. [*He puts his arm around the MAN's shoulders.*]

HAT SELLER: No peanuts left?

WIFE: No.

HAT SELLER: How many did you eat?

WIFE: Seven.

HAT SELLER: I had three. It's always the same... I get less than half of what you get... Do you feel lonely?

WIFE: No, I don't.

OLD MAN: Lonely. What's more it's cold. When we feel lonely, most of the time we feel cold. How about staying at my place tonight, mister?

HAT SELLER: Captain, could we come with you too?

WIFE: We don't snore and hardly talk in our sleep, either.

OLD MAN: There's only one bed at my place.

HAT SELLER: We don't mind sleeping under the bed.

OLD MAN: I keep two big trunks under it.

WIFE: How about in the corner of the storeroom?

OLD MAN: I'm living in the corner of the storeroom.

HAT SELLER: How about in a nook in the corner of the storeroom?

OLD MAN: Gorō lives there.

WIFE: Gorō?

OLD MAN [*to the MAN*]: My dog. She's an old bitch with a bad skin disease. Every morning I dissolve sulphur and spread it on her. When I do that, it must give her a tingling pain, she rages about madly. But it can't be helped. I haven't got anything else to do to her. Because, if I stopped, she'd die tomorrow.

WIFE: Let's go.

HAT SELLER: Go where?

WIFE: I'd rather stay with a dog at least hasn't got a skin disease.

OLD MAN: Come along. She won't bite you. Gorō is a very well-behaved dog.

MAN: Why am I a kangaroo?

OLD MAN: Kangaroo? You are a kangaroo… after all.

MAN: But you said…

WIFE: This man is a kangaroo.

HAT SELLER: I never thought he was, though…

OLD MAN: Oh, God! You are.

MAN: But you said…

OLD MAN: Sshhh! It's not good to speak loudly. This sort of thing is better not made public. You two, will you please check that nobody has heard our talk.

WIFE: O.K.

HAT SELLER: Certainly.

The HAT SELLER and his WIFE examine Stage Left and Right.

WIFE: No one is here.

HAT SELLER: Not a soul…

OLD MAN: Good. How lucky you are! You came within an inch of being killed.

MAN: Why?

OLD MAN: Sshh! Now everyone, listen to me carefully. The point is only the three of us know that this man is a kangaroo. Agreed?

WIFE: Yes.

HAT SELLER: Yes.

MAN: Will you please listen to me?

OLD MAN: You'd better be quiet for a second.

WIFE: I think so, too.

HAT SELLER: You can trust us.

OLD MAN: Now then, if I may say what I think, I myself will hold my tongue for his sake.

WIFE: I've made up my mind, too. I won't tell anybody for his sake.

HAT SELLER: I won't tell, either. Just for his sake.

OLD MAN: Good. We've made a resolution. [*To the MAN*] Did you hear? We are on your side. We are determined to be so. Now then, although this isn't easy to say, but... to put it simply... well let me explain from the start. Think, [*thinking at the same time*] first, you were driven into a tight corner. Some people are holding your secret. Then what you are going to do next is to appeal to their sympathy and say, "Please don't tell anybody, please hold your tongues." Then the people, means us, realise we need courage to keep your secret because we become your accomplices. If we cared about ourselves, it wouldn't be surprising if we said "no." Yet, our goodness won't allow us to do so. For justice, for truth, for history we must keep silent at the risk of our lives. We were resolutely fighting back our fear. We'll keep quiet, won't tell, won't talk... Do you understand? So, one word is quite enough. Please give us one word... in appreciation of our goodness...

WIFE: Just one word will do, if you understand us...

HAT SELLER: Well, just show us your feelings.

MAN: Thanks... thank you very much.

OLD MAN: Lovely! That's wonderful. But don't worry about us too much. We have done what we ought to do.

WIFE: We did what we must do.

HAT SELLER: We did the right thing.

OLD MAN: Oh, it's so nice to be good to others. Well, everyone, let's go to my place and cry about our goodness.

HAT SELLER: You mean, us, too?

OLD MAN: Why not?

WIFE: Isn't Gorō there...?

OLD MAN: She died last year...

WIFE: Died last year?

OLD MAN: Could be the year before last. Well, let's go comrades!

Led by the OLD MAN, all go off the stage singing. The MAN comes back and sits on the bench. The HAT SELLER comes after him.

HAT SELLER: What's the matter, mister?
MAN: Please go ahead.
HAT SELLER: Don't take this so seriously. To tell you the truth [*looking around*] we're kangaroos, too.
MAN [*lowering his voice*]: To tell you the truth, I'm not a kangaroo.
HAT SELLER [*lowering his voice more*]: To be very completely honest, we aren't kangaroos, either. Hih! [*He laughs and goes off.*]

SCENE II

*The same place as **SCENE I**. Night. The MAN sits lonely on the bench. The moon rises straight. Tears run down the MAN's cheeks as he hears the sorrowful music and the low ships' whistles.*

The MASKED SINGER slowly comes in and sings.

MASKED SINGER: Sayonara Brazil
　　　Sayonara Argentina
　　　Sayonara Egypt
　　　Sayonara India
　　　My ship has gone

　　　Sayonara onions in Brazil
　　　Sayonara cabbages in Argentina
　　　I feel sad like a camel

　　　Sayonara pumpkins in Egypt
　　　Sayonara cucumbers in India
　　　My ship has gone

Sayonara Brazil
Sayonara cabbages
Sayonara Egypt
Sayonara cucumbers
My ship has gone.

The MASKED SINGER goes off slowly but still singing. A PROSTITUTE, who is big and grotesque or small and cute, comes in from Stage Right. She has a straw and a small bottle in her hands, in other words she is making bubbles with them. She slowly passes in front of the MAN and turns back towards him.

PROSTITUTE: What's the matter?
MAN: Eh?
PROSTITUTE: What are you thinking about?
MAN: Yeah.
PROSTITUTE [*sitting next to him*]: Do you want me to guess...? Right. You're thinking about your mother at home... Aren't I right?
MAN: Yeah.
PROSTITUTE: I understand. Everybody is like that. When we're lonely, we tend to think about our mother at home. Aren't you hungry?
MAN: No, I'm not.
PROSTITUTE: Good. But I'm sorry for you. Because even if you aren't hungry, if you are unhappy, then you are unhappy. I think in that way. You look very sad. [*Making soap bubbles to show the MAN*] How about these?
MAN: Well...
PROSTITUTE: Aren't they pretty?
MAN: Pretty, very.
PROSTITUTE: Won't you try it? It's easy.
MAN: Yes...but...
PROSTITUTE: It's all right. Don't be shy. This is cheap. [*She gives the straw and the small bottle to the MAN.*]

The MAN makes soap bubbles.

PROSTITUTE: You're doing very well... Do it again.
MAN: Thanks. [*He makes soap bubbles.*]
PROSTITUTE: You're marvellous. Hey, do you want to have them?

MAN: No. [*He tries to give the straw and the bottle back to the PROSTITUTE.*]

PROSTITUTE: If you want, I don't mind giving them to you. As I said before, they're very cheap.

MAN: But...

PROSTITUTE: That's all right. Keep them.

MAN: Then, I'll have them. Thank you.

PROSTITUTE: That's it. Keep them. If you had something, I wouldn't mind taking it. I mean something cheap.

MAN: Yes, let me find you something. [*He feels inside his pockets.*]

PROSTITUTE: If you don't have anything, it's all right. I didn't mean to embarrass you.

MAN [*taking something out*]: Here you are...

PROSTITUTE [*receiving it*]: What's this?

MAN: It's a stamp of a foreign country.

PROSTITUTE: A foreign stamp? It's very pretty. But it must be expensive. I can't take it.

MAN: It's all right. I'll give it to you. To show my gratitude.

PROSTITUTE: Gratitude! I, I didn't mean it. Honest. I feel bad. But can I still use it?

MAN: Yes.

PROSTITUTE: So, we can send a letter to a foreign country?

MAN: Yes, you can

PROSTITUTE: Even to India?

MAN: India? Yes, you can send a letter even to India.

PROSTITUTE: I wouldn't mind writing a letter to India. Is it all right just write 'India' for the address?

MAN: Yes, just write 'India'.

PROSTITUTE: But I wonder what they would think about it in India.

MAN: I suppose they'd be surprised.

PROSTITUTE: I agree, they'd be surprised. But I'm afraid they wouldn't think well of me. A woman in my line of work to send a letter to India...

MAN: I don't think so. People in India are all admirable.

PROSTITUTE: Are they? Why?

MAN: India is a wonderful country. There are cows, and a big river flows. The red water flows slowly. People in India sit by that river and worship Buddha. All of them put on deep, calm expressions. Because they believe in Buddha. When they have a famine, millions of people die of hunger...

PROSTITUTE: Die of hunger...? I don't want to die of hunger.

MAN: Starving...but still alive...just a bag of bones...that must be awesome...

PROSTITUTE: Well, I don't know. It wouldn't suit my job. They don't like bony women. They say they feel very lonely when they see women like that.

MAN: Hmm.

PROSTITUTE: Do you want to die of hunger?

MAN: Yes, if I was in India...if I was to die in India, I wouldn't mind dying of hunger. When we die in India, Buddha licks our bones.

PROSTITUTE: Isn't it obscene to lick bones?

MAN: No, it isn't. Licking bones is a very generous way of giving comfort. But maybe bones being licked feel very lonely.

PROSTITUTE: You're very odd. But I like a strange person. Because they aren't boring to be with. The man I'm keeping company with now, he can breathe his cigarette smoke out of his nose and then breathe it into his mouth again. Can you do that?

MAN: No.

PROSTITUTE: I'm not surprised. He says it is very difficult to do. But his brother is even more extraordinary. He can suck noodles with his nose. Two noodles together at the same time... I'd like to see that.

MAN: Are you a kangaroo?

PROSTITUTE: Ah! Do I stink?

MAN: No.

PROSTITUTE: You are right. Everybody says I'm a kangaroo.

MAN: I'm a kangaroo, too.

PROSTITUTE: Are you, too?

MAN: Yes.

PROSTITUTE: Then we're in the same category.

MAN: Category?

PROSTITUTE: The same sort.

MAN: I see.

An ugly big man, who is the PROSTITUTE's Pimp comes in from Stage Right. He is trying to pull out the hairs of the nostrils. He pulls one out at last.

PROSTITUTE: Won't you stop that?

PIMP: Umm.

PROSTITUTE: Come and join us. I was talking to him... about India. He can talk about India very well. And he says he wants to go to India... He wants to go to India and die of hunger. I also talked about you. You don't mind, do you? I told him that you could breathe cigarette smoke out of your nose and get it into your mouth again ... Why don't you show it to him here now? He was very impressed and said, "Is it possible?"

The PIMP pulls out the hairs of his nostrils.

PROSTITUTE: Will you stop it?

PIMP: Umm.

PROSTITUTE [*to the MAN*]: See, this is the person, I was talking about a moment ago. I've just asked him to demonstrate it to you. You want to see it, don't you?

MAN: Well...yes.

PIMP: I won't do it...

PROSTITUTE: Why not? It won't cost you anything, and once you told me about your little brother... It is true... sucks up noodles with his nose...? It's true, isn't it?

PIMP: Yeah.

PROSTITUTE: Did you hear? It's true. He sucks up two strings of noodles at the same time. You did see it, didn't you?

PIMP: I saw it. Two went in together. [*He pulls out the hairs of his nostrils.*]

PROSTITUTE: You'd better stop it. Otherwise, you'll lose them all.

PIMP: They'll grow again.

PROSTITUTE: You're not a lizard. [*To the MAN*] Did you hear? He saw it. It's true. His younger brother's going to show me next time. We've already asked him to. [*To the PIMP*] Do you remember? You said he would demonstrate it for me sometime, didn't you?

PIMP: Yea, sometime.

PROSTITUTE [*to the MAN*]: Sometime. It'll be soon. When he has time, he'll let us know.

PIMP [*yawning*]: Now, it's time to go.

PROSTITUTE: Don't worry. We don't have to rush. Yes, darling, why don't you tell him that story?

PIMP: Which story?

PROSTITUTE: Which? The story you know, there's only one. The story about French style friendship.

PIMP: No, I won't.

PROSTITUTE [*to the MAN*]: He's timid, very shy. He is. But, it's a lovely story. [*To the PIMP*] Go on. This guy has already told his story.

PIMP: I was walking, while smoking a cigarette…

PROSTITUTE: Yes, you were. [*To the MAN*] Can you hear?

MAN: Yes.

PIMP: When I came to the slope where that chimney is, I threw the cigarette-end aside.

PROSTITUTE: Threw it aside…

PIMP: When I was about to stamp on it, it was rolling over…

PROSTITUTE: Rolling over…

PIMP: A man, who came behind me, stamped on it…

PROSTITUTE: Wow!

PIMP: I was very pleased about that.

PROSTITUTE: And after that?

PIMP: And after that we happened to walk along together for a while.

PROSTITUTE: Did you part ways after the walk?

PIMP: I was going to do so…

PROSTITUTE: But it became difficult to do…

PIMP: Yeah…

PROSTITUTE [*to the MAN*]: Don't you think that's the way to be?

MAN: Yeah…yes.

PIMP: So, we had a drink at my usual place. We talked of many things. He was a very nice bloke.

PROSTITUTE: What did you talk about?

PIMP: Umm, we talked about, for example, life. He was deeply concerned about it. After all life was an inexplicable thing for him.

PROSTITUTE: It's a wonderful story… [*To the MAN*] It makes me feel all warm.

MAN: Yes, it is very…

PROSTITUTE: And after that?

PIMP: And after that…we said SAYONARA…

PROSTITUTE: What's his name?

PIMP: I didn't ask.

PROSTITUTE [*to the MAN*]: Did you hear that? He didn't ask his name. I like this part very much. They parted without asking each other's name… just left it to chance that they would meet again…

PIMP: That's it. We said we'd like to meet again when we parted ways.

PROSTITUTE: Don't you think it's the so-called French style.

MAN: Yes.

PROSTITUTE: I love this story...

PIMP [*yawning*]: Well, it's time to go.

PROSTITUTE: No need to hurry. Darling, do you know how to show friendship in the Indian style?

PIMP: Indian style?

PROSTITUTE: By licking. They show their friendship, by licking.

PIMP: Kidding. We'll be late.

PROSTITUTE: We won't. I've got more to talk to him.

PIMP: Oi, come on.

PROSTITUTE [*to the MAN*]: He's jealous. You see, I've become your friend, so he's jealous... Silly, isn't it? [*To the PIMP*] I've got a stamp. Look, it's a foreign stamp. I'll send a letter to India with it.

PIMP: To India?

PROSTITUTE: Yes, to India. Please don't spoil it. It's expensive. He says he wants to give it to me, free. It was very precious for him, next to his life. But he wants to give it to me. [*To the MAN*] Isn't that so?

MAN: Amm, yeah.

PIMP: Give it back to him.

PROSTITUTE: No, I won't. He's given this to me.

PIMP: You'd better give it back to him.

MAN: No, I don't mind giving it to her.

PROSTITUTE: Did you hear? He's given this to me.

PIMP: Stand up.

PROSTITUTE: No, I won't.

PIMP: Move.

PROSTITUTE: You said you'd swallow the smoke from your nostrils into your mouth. I'll go, after you do that.

PIMP: I won't do that tonight. I don't feel like doing it.

PROSTITUTE: For his sake.

PIMP: No, I won't.

PROSTITUTE: You're embarrassed, aren't you?

PIMP: Piss off.

PROSTITUTE: He's embarrassed. Although he's a big man, he's very naive. In the evening, when it's getting dark, he misses his mum like you did. He says, "I feel lonely," with tears in his eyes.

PIMP: Come on. [*He grabs the PROSTITUTE by the hand.*]

PROSTITUTE [*shaking herself free from him*]: No.

PIMP: Won't you come?

PROSTITUTE: No, I won't.

PIMP: Come on. [*He tries to catch her again.*]

PROSTITUTE [*fleeing from him*]: Please hit him. He's a beast. He hits and kicks me. He takes all my money from me. I have nothing ever. Please, will you please hit him? He's a bastard. Beat him up and punish him. He always bullies me. He's very cruel. He pulls my hair and ... I often cry. Often, often cry. I cry all the time. Please, please hit him. Hit him hard and punish him...

PIMP [*amazed*]: Oi... Don't be silly...what's the matter with you...

PROSTITUTE [*appealing to the MAN and circling around him, fleeing from the PIMP*]: Hurry up, quick! Hit him. Finish him off. Otherwise...I bet...he's going to strangle me. Please, help me.

MAN: But, you...you'd better... [*He tries to calm down the PROSTITUTE.*]

PROSTITUTE [*pointing to the PIMP*]: Kill him! Beat him! Knock him down. He forces me to do this job and he himself is sitting pretty. I won't take it anymore. [*Clinging to the MAN's sleeve*] Look, can you guess how much I've suffered from it...... what's more he hits and kicks me saying that I don't earn enough.

PIMP: Won't you stop it. That's enough.

PROSTITUTE: Knock him down. Please. Finish him off. I can't stand any more. His face makes me sick. Kill him. Kill him. Please kill this bastard. [*She falls on the floor and cries heavily.*]

The PROSTITUTE cries for a while in front of the two who stand astonished.

PIMP [*going close to the PROSTITUTE and speaking gently*]: Hey, let's go. I won't hurt you. Stop crying. Now, let's go. [*Lifting her in his arm*] This man's not... he can't...

The PROSTITUTE stands up feebly. The PIMP gives her his handkerchief. She dries her tears with it.

PIMP [*gently*]: Let's go. Well, just trust me. I'll think about it, too. No, in fact,

I've thought about it. I've thought we'll go to the countryside, say once a month, renting a car.

PROSTITUTE [*drying her tears*]: I wish I could have a good cry somewhere by myself once in a lifetime.

PIMP: All right. Whenever you want.

PROSTITUTE: Will you look the other way?

PIMP: Yeah, whenever you like.

PROSTITUTE: Somewhere, in a quiet place?

PIMP: You mean, somewhere near a lake?

PROSTITUTE: Yes, there. We'll spread a straw-mat there. I want to cry on it from morning till night.

PIMP: I'll take you there. I'll rent a car, borrow a straw-mat and buy a packet of peanuts.

PROSTITUTE [*standing up and still looking down*]: Sayonara. I'll go with him. I think you've heard. We'll go to a lake. I want to have a good cry sitting on a straw-mat. I want to cry for you. He'll turn away while I do it. Please don't forget me. [*Turning back*] I could have gone away with you, if you wanted. I've said so. It's your fault. But I'll send a letter to India writing about you... Sayonara.

The two go off. The ship blows a sad whistle. The MAN sits on the bench absent-mindedly.

The HAT SELLER comes in on tiptoe turning backwards.

HAT SELLER: Things aren't looking good. You'd better hide yourself quick.

MAN: Why?

HAT SELLER: It's dangerous. The Black Hat Gang become eager to know your SECRET.

MAN: My secret?

HAT SELLER: The SECRET we talked about.

MAN: What is that?

HAT SELLER whispers to the MAN.

MAN: Eh?

HAT SELLER whispers to the MAN.

MAN: Eh?

HAT SELLER: Can't you hear?

MAN: No.

HAT SELLER: The SECRET that you are a kangaroo.

MAN: But that is...

HAT SELLER: Sshh! Don't you know what sort of danger you're facing now?

MAN: Is it dangerous?

HAT SELLER: Your ears might be cut off.

MAN: It can't be.

HAT SELLER: You must hide yourself as soon as possible. [*Pointing to Stage Left*] When you go further on, you'll see a small coal ship moored. Our people are waiting for you there. The password is CAT, right?

MAN: Cat?

HAT SELLER: Yes. They'll say CHIMNEY. CAT and CHIMNEY, please don't forget. Go right now. And don't worry about us. Do you understand me? Don't worry. We'll be all right.

MAN: No... Thank you.

HAT SELLER: You'd better go straight away. Further down there. Hide yourself until there is a signal. [*He goes off to Stage Right on tiptoe.*]

MAN: All right. [*He keeps sitting on the bench.*]

The ships' whistles at a distance. The MAN makes soap bubbles by blowing through the straw.

SCENE III

*The same quay as **SCENE II**. The MAN is still making soap bubbles by blowing through the straw. The MASKED SINGER comes in and sings.*

MASKED SINGER: The moon, my friend,
   The one hanging from the electricity pole,
   That is the earthworm suffering from the flu.
   The moon, my friend,
   The one walking on the roof,

That is the herring suffering from Basedow's disease.

The moon, my friend, cry for me.
For a long time
My soul was a salted herring.
The moon, my friend, cry for me.
For a long time
My soul was a dried earthworm.

The moon, my friend,
Cry for the herring.
The moon, my friend,
Cry for the earthworm.

During the song the MAN stands up frightened by something in the air and goes off. The MASKED SINGER also goes off, singing.

After a while the HAT SELLER and his WIFE and the OLD MAN, who are bound with the rope, come in from Stage Right. FOLLOWER 1 and 2 of the MAN IN THE BLACK HAT hold the other end of the rope. The MAN IN THE BLACK HAT and his MISTRESS come in after them.

MISTRESS [*stopping*]: Look at the lovely moon. [*... she could say something like that...*]
BLACK HAT: Yes, the lovely moon. [*...he could answer something like that...*]
FOLLOWER 1: Boss!
FOLLOWER 2: It's ready.

The HAT SELLER and his WIFE and the OLD MAN are tied to the street lamp. The MAN IN THE BLACK HAT and his MISTRESS sit on chairs prepared by FOLLOWER 1 and 2.

BLACK HAT: By the way, who are they?
FOLLOWER 1: They've got a secret.
BLACK HAT: What is their secret?
FOLLOWER 2: They won't tell us.

BLACK HAT: That means their secret must be an important one.

FOLLOWER 1: We were walking in the town this evening. When we passed them, they giggled to one another in a funny way.

BLACK HAT: I see.

MISTRESS: That's funny.

FOLLOWER 2: It rang a bell. So, we followed them. Then they giggled again looking back towards us.

MISTRESS: Giggled again?

FOLLOWER 1: That's right, Boss. They giggled twice.

BLACK HAT: I see. That's strange.

FOLLOWER 2: Boss, please get them to talk about everything they know. They must be keeping a big secret.

The OLD MAN whispers to the HAT SELLER. The HAT SELLER whispers to his WIFE. The three of them giggle.

FOLLOWER 1: Look, Boss. They giggled again. It's the third time.

FOLLOWER 2: Boss, we must get them to tell us their secret. Otherwise, we don't know what might happen to us.

FOLLOWER 1: Boss, that's true. People in the town kind of knew. I'm sure these three must have been doing the same thing everywhere before they met us.

FOLLOWER 2: The grandad at the watchmaker's told us that they must've grabbed a big secret...

MISTRESS: Darling, we must get them to talk.

BLACK HAT: I know.

FOLLOWER 1: But how to make them talk is the question, isn't it, Boss?

BLACK HAT: That's the problem.

FOLLOWER 2: I think the easiest way to make them speak is to hurt them a bit.

The three look at one another and giggle.

FOLLOWER 1: They're giggling again. How irritating! Damn!

BLACK HAT: Don't be rash. We'll get them to talk little by little. Who's likely to open their mouth easily?

MISTRESS: It's no good picking on the old one.

FOLLOWER 2: If you want to get women to talk, the best way is to starve them.

BLACK HAT: That takes time.

FOLLOWER 1: How about hurting the husband?

FOLLOWER 2: He looks the easiest, Boss. That sort would scream with pain if we pulled his ear just a bit.

BLACK HAT: How about the old chap?

FOLLOWER 1: I don't think he's any good. He'd take time. He's the sort whose sentiment you've got to appeal to, slowly by taking time, otherwise he'll never open his mouth.

BLACK HAT: Well, then, lets hurt that sweet husband a little. No, no, we don't have to do it that severely. Just like licking him gently.

FOLLOWER 2: It's an easy job.

BLACK HAT: You, do it.

FOLLOWER 2: Me?

BLACK HAT: Yeah, do it a bit.

FOLLOWER 2: But how?

BLACK HAT: Well...pull his ear.

FOLLOWER 2: Alright. [*He goes close to the three.*]

OLD MAN: Oi!

FOLLOWER 2: What?

OLD MAN: Whatever you do to us, we'll never tell.

FOLLOWER 2: Why?

OLD MAN: Because it's a SECRET.

The three giggle.

FOLLOWER 2: When you get hurt, you'll want to talk. I'm sure everyone would rather not be hurt than be hurt.

OLD MAN: Will you tell when he pulls your ear?

HAT SELLER: No, never, Captain.

WIFE: Will you be all right?

HAT SELLER: Of course, I will. Only ears.

OLD MAN: Right. Hey, won't you pull his ear?

FOLLOWER 2: What shall we do, Boss?

BLACK HAT: Just pull.

FOLLOWER 2 gets hold of the HAT SELLER's ear as if he were touching something dirty and pulls it.

HAT SELLER [*assuring himself that his ear is pulled*]: Ouch!
FOLLOWER 2: Will you talk?
HAT SELLER [*thinking*]: No, I won't.

FOLLOWER 2 pulls the HAT SELLER's ear.

HAT SELLER: Ouch!
FOLLOWER 2: Won't you talk?
HAT SELLER: No, I won't.
FOLLOWER 2: This isn't working, Boss.
BLACK HAT: Do it hard.
FOLLOWER 2: All right. [*He pulls the HAT SELLER's ear hard.*]
HAT SELLER: Ouch, ouch, ouch, ouch...
FOLLOWER 2: Won't you talk?
HAT SELLER: No, I won't.
FOLLOWER 2: Boss, it still isn't working.
BLACK HAT: He's a tough customer.
OLD MAN: Well done.
WIFE: You were wonderful.
HAT SELLER: Thanks, but it hurt a lot.
BLACK HAT [*to the FOLLOWER 1*]: You do it next.
FOLLOWER 1: Me?
BLACK HAT: Give him a few slaps on his cheeks. Who cares!
FOLLOWER 1: Yes, Boss. [*He goes close to the three.*]
OLD MAN: Well, mister, have you ever been beaten?
HAT SELLER: No, Captain.
OLD MAN: I see. Don't worry. It won't hurt as much as being pulled by your ear.
WIFE: Do your best.
HAT SELLER: Yes, I'll try.
FOLLOWER 1: Boss, shall we use a stick?
BLACK HAT: Have you got one?
FOLLOWER 1: No.
BLACK HAT: Then use your hands. They'll do if we hit him a lot.

FOLLOWER 1 [*taking up a posture*]: Take that! [*He hits the HAT SELLER.*]

HAT SELLER: Ouch!

FOLLOWER 1: Won't you talk?

HAT SELLER: No, I won't.

FOLLOWER 1: Take this!

HAT SELLER: Ouch!

FOLLOWER 1: Won't you talk?

HAT SELLER: No, I won't.

FOLLOWER 1: Damn! Take this, this, this... [*He keeps hitting the HAT SELL-ER.*]

HAT SELLER: Ouch, ouch, ouch, ouch...

FOLLOWER 1: Won't you talk?

HAT SELLER: No, I won't.

FOLLOWER 1 [*disappointed*]: He said "No," Boss.

BLACK HAT: I see.

OLD MAN: Well done. You were wonderful.

WIFE: I'm proud of you.

HAT SELLER: Well, thank you.

BLACK HAT: Haven't you any better ideas?

FOLLOWER 2: How about pinching him, Boss, pinch him on some soft parts of the body?

FOLLOWER 1: It doesn't sound very exciting.

MISTRESS: And it wouldn't look elegant, either.

BLACK HAT: See, we need an exciting and elegant way on this occasion.

FOLLOWER 1: We need tools for it, Boss. If only we had enough tools, we could show you some smashing torture.

FOLLOWER 2: Boss, let's say there are two carriages. Tie his right leg to this carriage and tie his left leg to that carriage and move the two carriages in that direction and in this direction at the same time.

BLACK HAT: What did you say?

FOLLOWER 1: You see, Boss, there are two carriages.

BLACK HAT: I see.

FOLLOWER 1: Tie his right leg to this carriage and tie his left leg to that carriage and move the two carriages in that direction and in this direction at the same time.

BLACK HAT: But... don't you think his crotch would be torn?...

FOLLOWER 2: That's why we call it torture.

BLACK HAT: I see.

MISTRESS: Are we going to do that?

FOLLOWER 1: We don't have any carriages, ma'am.

MISTRESS: Then, it isn't any good.

FOLLOWER 2: Still, there's another way. Think there is a large Japanese abacus and big stones.

MISTRESS: A large Japanese abacus and stones?

FOLLOWER 2: Yes. Get him to sit on the Japanese abacus and put the stones on his lap one by one. The sharp edges of the Japanese abacus beads eat into his legs and the blood comes out of the cuts on his legs.

MISTRESS: And?

FOLLOWER 2: That's all, ma'am. But when they're tortured as much as this, they'll tell us everything.

MISTRESS: That's true.

BLACK HAT: Is that your idea?

FOLLOWER 2: Yes, more or less.

FOLLOWER 1: Mine is much simpler, Boss. We don't need many tools, only a thin bamboo-stick. Stick it in between the nail and the finger and set fire to the tip of the bamboo-stick. When it's burning, the bamboo-oil comes out into the nail.

BLACK HAT: I see.

FOLLOWER 1: That's my idea.

MISTRESS: Have you got a bamboo stick?

FOLLOWER 1: No, I haven't...

FOLLOWER 2: All he thought about was the nursing after the torturing. He brought the first-aid kit with him.

FOLLOWER 1: But, Boss, I just cared...

MISTRESS: Well, all right. I'll do it.

BLACK HAT: Will you?

MISTRESS: Yes, I will.

BLACK HAT: Better not.

MISTRESS: Why?

BLACK HAT: You'll be injured.

MISTRESS: I don't think I will. I won't do anything violent. [*She opens the first-aid box and takes out a syringe.*]

BLACK HAT: What are you going to do?

MISTRESS: Injection.

FOLLOWER 1: Are you going to give him an injection?

MISTRESS: Yes.

OLD MAN: Oi!

BLACK HAT: What?

OLD MAN: What injection is she going to give him?

BLACK HAT: Shut your gob! [*But after he says this, he becomes anxious about the injection and asks his MISTRESS.*] What injection is it?

MISTRESS: I suppose it's a vaccination jab for some disease.

WIFE: You mustn't. He's had them all already.

MISTRESS: Don't worry. It'll just work as extra prevention.

OLD MAN: Hey, be careful. I don't think we should get the same jab twice or three times.

BLACK HAT: Stop making a fuss! But, are you sure it'll be all right?

MISTRESS: Don't worry. We'll see when it's done.

HAT SELLER: No! Don't! Don't give me the same jab twice. It might kill me.

FOLLOWER 1: I hope he won't be killed.

FOLLOWER 2: He won't be killed.

WIFE: I won't allow you to do that to my husband.

OLD MAN: I won't either. I'll tell everybody about your villainy if you do that to him.

BLACK HAT: How about a different way, something rather weak?

MISTRESS: I agree, but we can't think of anything like that. It doesn't matter what sort it is. It's just an injection. It's much more elegant than using carriages and also it's easier.

HAT SELLER: No. Don't do that! If you come any nearer, I'll bite you.

WIFE: And I'll kick you.

MISTRESS: Hey, guys, go and roll up his sleeve.

FOLLOWER 1: O.K. [*He goes to the HAT SELLER but cannot roll up his sleeve.*]

MISTRESS: Then, go and cut the sleeve, enough for the injection. [*She gives the scissors to one of the Followers.*]

WIFE: You're joking! He's just got the order-made suit. I won't let you do that.

HAT SELLER: I won't let you do that, either.

MISTRESS: Go on!

FOLLOWER 1 and FOLLOWER 2 go close to the three.

BLACK HAT: Friends, how about telling us your secret?

HAT SELLER: What should we do, Captain?

OLD MAN: No, still we mustn't tell. Because we promised to one another we'd never tell our SECRET even if we were going to be killed, didn't we?

HAT SELLER: Yes, we did, but...

WIFE: It'll be all right. It's only a suit.

HAT SELLER: But, how about the jab? I might be killed.

MISTRESS: Now, are you ready?

FOLLOWER 1 and FOLLOWER 2 make a hole in the sleeve of the HAT SELLER's suit.

WIFE: Do you think it'll be all right, Captain?

OLD MAN: Yes, it's only a vaccination, not poison.

WIFE: Shall we tell, Captain?

OLD MAN: No. Stop kidding. They'd just say we were traitors.

BLACK HAT: Spill the beans. We'll keep secret what you tell us. We won't tell anybody.

OLD MAN: I'll kill you. If you betray us, I'll kill you later.

WIFE: Stop worrying, my dear. It's just a vaccination. There must be the people who've had the same jab twice by mistake.

FOLLOWER 1 and FOLLOWER 2 have finished their job.

MISTRESS: Well, you'd better face the other way.

BLACK HAT: Have you ever given an injection?

MISTRESS: No, never.

BLACK HAT: Then, I suppose you don't know how to do it.

MISTRESS: I've seen it done.

OLD MAN: Oi, stop it. Stop letting her do it. You've mistaken if you think giving an injection is easy. I know people who've been killed by being injected in the wrong way.

WIFE: Are we going to be killed?

OLD MAN: Of course, we are. There are various ways of injecting. The one sticking in the needle deep or shallow or the one sticking it into the vein and so on.

BLACK HAT: Do you know about that?

MISTRESS: When you give an injection, the deeper it is the better.

OLD MAN: It's wrong. Fool! Oi, stop her. She doesn't know anything about injections.

BLACK HAT: But it's all because you haven't told the secret. Or will you tell?

OLD MAN: No, no I won't.

MISTRESS [*to the Followers*]: Disinfect his arm with this.

FOLLOWER 2: Yes, ma'am. [*He wipes the HAT SELLER's arm with the cotton wool and alcohol.*]

HAT SELLER: Spare me, Captain!

OLD MAN: Do you want to be a traitor?

MISTRESS: Make up your mind. [*She holds the syringe to the light and looks at it.*]

HAT SELLER: No. I wouldn't let you do that. [*He struggles.*]

WIFE: Open your mouth. It's all right. What's wrong about being a traitor. If we ask, that Boss could do anything to this old man.

BLACK HAT: Yes, open your mouth. I'll protect you from this sort of old crock.

OLD MAN: Will you talk?

HAT SELLER: Yes, I will, Captain.

WIFE: Yes, he will, Captain.

BLACK HAT: O.K. That's it!

MISTRESS [*looking at the syringe and mumbling*]: Stop the chatter. You are too late. Whether you tell or not, I've already decided to give him an injection. I want to try it and see what's going to happen to him.

BLACK HAT: But, honey...

MISTRESS [*quietly to the HAT SELLER*]: You ought to make up your mind. I reckon you'd like to try it, too, wouldn't you? Nobody has ever been given the same jab twice... You're going to do something very new. This might be an adventure. And it's not me but you who's going to have it. I expect you had dreamed of having adventures when you were young. But you thought you needed savings before you took action. Although true adventures can only be had by killing somebody or setting fire to houses or stealing something. Don't you think so? You've made a mistake. But listen. Now, if you want, you can have a wonderful adventure. You're going to be killed through keeping your friend's secret, if you like. In other words, if you intend to do it, I could tell you that this liquid, the liquid in the syringe is not a vaccine but poison which can kill you.

HAT SELLER [*blankly*]: Adventure...

MISTRESS: You wanted to be a pirate.

HAT SELLER: I wanted to be a pirate's man...

MISTRESS: You wanted to set sail, to light a signal fire...

HAT SELLER: To sound the departure gong...

MISTRESS: Well, will you keep the secret or will you betray your friends and have your life spared?

HAT SELLER: I'll keep the SECRET. I will.

MISTRESS [*to all*]: Did you hear that? This man's made up his mind. [*She injects the HAT SELLER.*]

The HAT SELLER stands for a second and falls slowly and gradually. All the people cast down their eyes. Only the MISTRESS walks back briskly to the first-aid box and tidies up the box.

BLACK HAT: Is he dead?

MISTRESS: Yes, for his honour.

The MAN comes in vacantly from Stage Left. FOLLOWER 1 and FOLLOWER 2 notice him and stop him. The MAN IN THE BLACK HAT and his MISTRESS also surround the MAN unintentionally.

MAN: Good evening.

FOLLOWER 1: Who are you?

MAN: I came to this town today, but couldn't get on the ship.

BLACK HAT: I see. Was it you who bought a TICKET from me?

MAN: Yes, it was you who sold it to me. The problem was, that TICKET had no stamps on it...

BLACK HAT: Stamps? Who told you TICKETS should be stamped?

OLD MAN: Run away! Hey, mister, you must run away.

MAN: Oh, Captain!

OLD MAN: Run straight away. We haven't told them anything. In the end we didn't. Look at him. He didn't open his mouth even though he was killed for it. He was killed by them because he kept his mouth shut...

FOLLOWER 1: I've got it. Boss, it's this man whose SECRET they're keeping.

OLD MAN: Go, get away!

The MAN hesitates to go away.

BLACK HAT: Why don't you run away.

MAN: But...why?

WIFE: My husband died for you. For you.

MAN: For me?

BLACK HAT: He kept your SECRET.

MAN: Is he dead? [*He approaches the HAT SELLER.*]

WIFE: Yes, he died for you.

MAN: Why?

MISTRESS: Because he didn't tell us your SECRET.

MAN: My SECRET?

MISTRESS: Yes, he died for it. Look at him. Isn't he dead?

MAN: Yes, he is...

MISTRESS: He died. If you want to avoid more killing, tell us.

MAN: What am I supposed to tell?

OLD MAN: Don't tell. Remember he died for it.

WIFE: He died for it.

MISTRESS: This wife and the old man intend to die for you, too. What do you think of this?

OLD MAN: I'm intending to die. I'm positive, mister.

WIFE: So am I. I don't mind.

MAN: But...

MISTRESS: Won't you talk?

MAN: What? What am I supposed to say?

OLD MAN: Listen, mister. If you talk, you'd be betraying me and her.

MISTRESS: What is your SECRET?

MAN: Ah, my SECRET... It's that I'm a kangaroo.

MISTRESS: Kangaroo...

All become silent for a second.

OLD MAN [*speaking low*]: Now I see, you really are a kangaroo.

WIFE: After all... he's a kangaroo.

MAN: But you started...

MISTRESS: That's enough. Whatever you say, you betrayed these two. Guys, you tie him up and release the old chap and the missus. We don't need them anymore.

BLACK HAT: That's right. We'll leave the rest to you.

The MAN IN THE BLACK HAT and his MISTRESS go off. FOLLOWER 1 and FOLLOWER 2 do the job as ordered and go off.

OLD MAN: Someday, you'll see... what you've done...
MAN: I don't understand at all.
OLD MAN: You killed this man. You changed his honourable death into just a daft sacrifice of life.
WIFE: You killed, killed my husband. You'll see...

The OLD MAN and The HAT SELLER's Wife leave the MAN who is tied up, and go off the stage carrying the HAT SELLER.

To put the intermission here and to let the audience go to the loo is one idea. If we have an audience...

SCENE IV

*The same place as **SCENE III**. The MAN is tied to the street-light. Midnight. The MASKED SINGER comes in slowly and plays the guitar looking at the moon. He goes off after a while.*

The PROSTITUTE comes in from stage right holding a big doll. She goes to the bench as if she were dancing, and puts the doll to sleep on the bench.

PROSTITUTE: You must sleep now because it's night. Everyone sleeps at night.
MAN: Good evening.
PROSTITUTE [*turning round*]: Oh, dear!
MAN: Good evening.
PROSTITUTE: What happened?
MAN: I've been tied up.
PROSTITUTE: Really, you're tied up. You're a funny man. Every time I meet you, you surprise me.
MAN: Haven't you gone to bed yet?
PROSTITUTE: No, I've been very busy tonight. What do you think of my doll?

Pretty?

MAN: Yes, pretty, very...

PROSTITUTE: One of my clients gave her to me. When she drinks milk, she pees.

MAN: Pees?

PROSTITUTE: Yes, she does. Do you want to hold her in your arm?

MAN: Yes, I do. But my hands...

PROSTITUTE: Oh, of course. Shall I untie the rope?

MAN: No, don't, or you'll get into trouble.

PROSTITUTE: I don't care.

MAN: You don't need to untie the rope. I'm all right. But if you don't mind, will you please give me a pinch?

PROSTITUTE: Do you feel as if you were dreaming?

MAN: No, I don't feel like that, it's just that I really want to be pinched. Or you can hit me or kick me.

PROSTITUTE: No, I won't.

MAN: Why?

PROSTITUTE: Because it's weird.

MAN: Is it weird?

PROSTITUTE: Yes, it's weird, no matter what.

MAN: I don't know why but I want to feel a sharp pain.

PROSTITUTE: Forget it for now. How about kissing this doll?

MAN: All right.

PROSTITUTE: Here you are. [*She holds her doll close to the MAN.*]

The MAN kisses the doll.

PROSTITUTE: How was it?

MAN: It was nice.

PROSTITUTE: You're very good at it.

MAN: I might be killed.

PROSTITUTE: Do you want to die?

MAN: I don't mind dying. But not here, if possible.

PROSTITUTE: In India?

MAN: Yes.

PROSTITUTE: I thought so. You'll die of hunger in India, won't you?

MAN: Yes, I want to go to India. I haven't known where I wanted to go until now. But now I feel like going to India. I'm sure I want to go to India to die of hunger. Or maybe India is calling me.

PROSTITUTE: Is it..?

MAN: India is calling me, saying, "come to India..." If I were in India, I'd dig a small hole in the desert and get in it with only my head sticking out. The moon in India must be big and I would shed tears looking at it.

PROSTITUTE: Would you remember me?

MAN: I'm sure I would. And the sun rises in the morning. As the sun in India is big and strong, my nose would bleed when I was fiercely burnt by it. All the waste inside me would come out with the nosebleed. And after that my heart would go pit-a-pat even if I only just sat quietly and wasn't tied up like this. And a lot of thin Indian people might gather around me, and cry for me silently day after day...

PROSTITUTE: I'd cry for you, too.

MAN: Thank you. Cows would also be gathering meantime and they'd be licking me gently.

PROSTITUTE: Bones?

MAN: Yes, various parts of my body. The wind blows, the rain falls, time slides away and I'd been dead unnoticed. The people in India and the cows would cover my head with sand and walk away...

PROSTITUTE: Don't you want to be spared?

MAN: Yes, if it's possible?

PROSTITUTE: I'll help you.

MAN: But even if I was spared, I wouldn't be able to go to India.

PROSTITUTE: A person I know, he wears a black hat, he deals in TICKETS for foreign countries.

MAN: I was cheated by that man.

PROSTITUTE: Were you? But sometimes he doesn't. One of my acquaintances bought a TICKET from him and has gone somewhere...

MAN: I bet even if I tried a dozen times, I'd be cheated every time.

PROSTITUTE: That might be true. Still, you don't need to die now.

MAN: You're right. No need to die now.

PROSTITUTE: How about living on for a while?

MAN: I don't mind living some more. But I have neither an umbrella nor a toothbrush.

PROSTITUTE: I'll lend you mine.

MAN: They must be for women's

PROSTITUTE: You could borrow the ones for men's if you want...

MAN: A pillow, too?

PROSTITUTE: Sure, a pillow in a new cover.

MAN: Who's that man?

PROSTITUTE: Which one?

MAN: The big man I met a moment ago...

PROSTITUTE: Ah, he's just a friend.

MAN: You're going to lend me his?

PROSTITUTE: No, I'm not. Don't be silly. I have things my clients have given me.

MAN: I see.

PROSTITUTE: Well, do you want to live?

MAN: Yes, I don't mind trying it.

PROSTITUTE: Then, I'll untie you. [*She tries to untie the rope.*]

The PIMP comes in from Stage Right.

PIMP: Oi, what are you doing?

PROSTITUTE: Ah, darling, will you please untie this rope? It's ever so tight.

PIMP: You, fool! Get away quick. If you keep hanging around here, nothing good will come of it.

PROSTITUTE: What's going on?

PIMP: Twenty or thirty people are coming with knives. They're coming to kill him.

MAN: Me?

PIMP: Yes, it seems like that.

MAN: It could be. They said so before. They said they would make me see...

PIMP: Yeah, they were talking like that.

PROSTITUTE: I've decided to rescue him. Will you help me?

PIMP: Help you? Me?

PROSTITUTE: Yes. This man must go to India.

PIMP: No, I can't. It doesn't suit my character, I mean, helping people doesn't suit me.

PROSTITUTE: No. You must help him. Don't you care if he's killed in front of you?

PIMP: I won't be around.

PROSTITUTE: But you'll hear his shriek. It'll be stuck in your head and stop you sleeping at night.

PIMP: Fuck off. Stop the bloody joke. If you want to help him, you go on, but not me. [*He is about to go off.*]

PROSTITUTE: Darling!

PIMP: What?

PROSTITUTE: Don't you want a friend? How long are you going to be alone? Men are supposed to have some good friends. But you haven't got any. Why? Tell me why? Don't you feel lonely? If you help him, he'll become a sincere friend of you. Next time when you are in trouble, I'm sure he'd help you. Don't you want a friend like that?

PIMP: It won't be bad to have a good friend. But it's a different thing whether he'll become my friend.

PROSTITUTE: Why?

PIMP: Because he'll go to India when he's rescued, won't he?

PROSTITUTE: He'll write you a letter.

PIMP: A letter...

PROSTITUTE: You've never received any letters. You don't know how nice it is to have letters from friends far away occasionally and unexpectedly.

PIMP: Will he write me a letter in India?

PROSTITUTE: He will. Because you'll be his life saver.

PIMP: Still, I won't do it. I'll be done before I save him because they are in great numbers.

PROSTITUTE: But you're strong, aren't you?

PIMP: Yes, I am. Still, I can't face them with my bare hands. They have sharp weapons.

PROSTITUTE: You won't lose if you fight with a will. Somebody says when you do your best, you can do anything.

PIMP: Still, I won't. I don't feel like doing my best.

PROSTITUTE: Darling! Please!

PIMP: No, I can't. Really, I can't do it. You'd better stop too, or you'll get into trouble. [*He goes off.*]

PROSTITUTE [*to the back of the PIMP*]: RABBIT! COWARD! BASTARD! TRAITOR! I don't need your help. I'll do it myself.

MAN: He's gone.

PROSTITUTE [*discouraged*]: He used to be not like that. He was very gentle and strong. [*Noticing the doll in her hands*] I don't need this. [*She throws it away.*]

MAN: You got it from him.

PROSTITUTE: Yes. He treats me like a child all the time. Don't worry. I'll save you by myself.

MAN: No, it's all right. Honest! Just one thing, will you do me a favour?

PROSTITUTE: What is it?

MAN: I'm sorry about this, but while I'm killed, will you watch me from a distance?

PROSTITUTE: Watch you being killed?

MAN: Yes.

PROSTITUTE: No, I won't. I can't do such a thing.

MAN: Just looking at me is enough. If I know you are watching me, I won't be afraid of death anymore.

PROSTITUTE: No, don't say such things. I'll rescue you. Really, if I try hard, I can do it. [*She goes behind the MAN and tries to untie the rope.*]

The MAN IN THE BLACK HAT appears unexpectedly from Stage Right and picks up the abandoned doll.

BLACK HAT [*politely*]: Good evening, miss. Is this yours?

PROSTITUTE [*standing up scared*]: Yes, I'll give it to you. So, please don't kill him.

BLACK HAT: Well, that's quite an offer. But, miss, this is not playschool. I'll give this back to you. In exchange, will you stay away from that man. You might be stained by the blood.

From Stage Right the MISTRESS is the first to come in, the OLD MAN, the HAT SELLER'S WIFE, FOLLOWER 1 and 2 and other people come in one after another carrying knives, cutters, or axes in their hands. The PROSTITUTE clings to the MAN.

MISTRESS: What's that woman doing?

BLACK HAT: She's the owner of this doll.

MISTRESS: How about asking her to get out of the way?

BLACK HAT [*to FOLLOWER 1 and 2*]: Ask her to get out of the way.

FOLLOWER 1 and 2: Yes, Boss. [*They go to the PROSTITUTE and grab her by the neck and tear her away from the MAN.*]

PROSTITUTE: Stop it! [*She turns around and at the same time she kicks the*

FOLLOWERS.]
FOLLOWER 1: Ouch!
FOLLOWER 2: You, bitch! [*He tries to get at her.*]
MAN: Hang on! Didn't you come here to kill me?
FOLLOWER 1: Yes, we did. But this tart is in the way so...
MAN: She won't bother you. Say you won't.
PROSTITUTE: I will. I'm not joking. I won't let you touch him, not even one
finger.
MISTRESS: Pull her ear. Pull it and drop her in the sea.
FOLLOWER 2: All right. [*He pulls the PROSTITUTE's ear.*]
PROSTITUTE: Ouch! You brute! [*She kicks in FOLLOWER 2's belly.*]
FOLLOWER 2: Uh! [*Holding his belly*] Damn you! You slut!
FOLLOWER 1: Take that! [*He tries to grab her.*]
PROSTITUTE: Piss off! [*She kicks in FOLLOWER 1's belly, too.*]
FOLLOWER 1: Uh! [*He holds his belly and hunches up.*]
PROSTITUTE: See, I knocked them down. Look, they're still groaning. Did
you see that?
MAN: Thank you, but you'd better move away. It's dangerous. They have sharp
weapons with them.
MISTRESS: Hey, miss?
PROSTITUTE: What?
MISTRESS: Are you serious?
PROSTITUTE: Yes, I am.
MISTRESS: Right. Someone, give her a knife.
BLACK HAT: Honey!
MISTRESS: Don't worry. [*She takes a big knife from one of the FOLLOWERS
and gives it to the PROSTITUTE.*] How about this?
PROSTITUTE [*shaking the knife*]: Fine.
MISTRESS: You might be killed.
PROSTITUTE: I might, but so might you.
MAN: Stop being silly. Or you'll be killed.
PROSTITUTE: Don't worry. I won't be killed easily.
MISTRESS [*to all*]: Who's going to fight?
OLD MAN: Me. [*He goes to the PROSTITUTE unhesitatingly, slaps her cheeks
mercilessly while she winces terribly, and knocks the knife from her hand.*]
Mind your own business. You're only a woman. [*Going to the MAN*] Did
you intend to involve her in your affairs?

MAN: Of course not. I thank you for what you've done.

OLD MAN: But she was nearly killed for your sake.

MAN: I told her to stop it.

OLD MAN: But she didn't stop. [*He takes a knife out of his breast pocket and touches the MAN's nose with it.*] She didn't...

MAN: I wished her to stop...

OLD MAN: So, what? [*Standing up*] At least, she would have been killed, for your sake.

The PROSTITUTE, who has been squatting, suddenly stands up and dashes herself against the OLD MAN.

OLD MAN [*staggering*]: You slut, what've you done to me? [*He holds the knife.*]

Everybody is startled at it.
"Wait!" Saying this, the PIMP comes in slowly from stage right. It is a very impressive moment. He may fascinate the gallery and get cries such as "Excellent!" "Wonderful!" from the audience.

PIMP: Wait a moment!

PROSTITUTE: At last, you've come back to me, my darling.

PIMP: I'm not a RABBIT.

PROSTITUTE: No, you are not a RABBIT.

PIMP: I'm not a COWARD.

PROSTITUTE: No, you are not a COWARD.

PIMP: I'm neither a BASTARD nor a TRAITOR.

PROSTITUTE: Of course, you are. I know that you've been gentle and strong.

PIMP [*taking out the dagger out of his breast pocket*]: I went back to get this. All of them have sharp weapons. If I didn't have one, it wouldn't be fair. Right?

PROSTITUTE: Yes, you should have one, otherwise it's not fair.

PIMP: Look at it. Flashing brilliantly. I've just sharpened it; because I haven't used it for a long time. It'll cut superbly. I should hurt them a bit with this. Now, where shall I slash?

PROSTITUTE: Well, they pulled my ear. So why don't you cut off their ears first?

PIMP: Ears. That's a good idea. Let me try. [*He assumes a posture holding the dagger.*] But which ear? The right one or the left one?

PROSTITUTE: Both. Please cut off both.

PIMP: O.K., I'll cut off both [*He assumes a posture.*] But if I cut off both their ears, they may not answer when I call them.

PROSTITUTE: It doesn't matter. Whenever we need them, we can beat them up to let them know.

PIMP: I see. That's another way. Then it doesn't matter if I cut off both their ears. Well, who wants to be the first?

BLACK HAT: Wait a moment!

PIMP: You're to be slashed first?

BLACK HAT: I didn't mean that. Listen, I have no intention of fighting you. But it isn't because I'm weaker than you. I have a dagger, too and many followers as you see. However, please listen to this carefully. The person we want to hurt is not this woman but that man.

MISTRESS: We don't need that slut, nor you.

PIMP: I see. You only want this man. I didn't know that.

BLACK HAT: Now you've understood this, go away, and take that bitch with you.

PROSTITUTE: Darling!

PIMP: I know. [*He cuts off the rope tying up the MAN. When all the people close in on him, he threatens them with the dagger.*] Oi, what on earth do you want? Do you want to have your ears cut off? To tell you the truth, he used to be my follower. Anyone who's wanting to lay a hand on him, come to the front. Mind you, losing your ears isn't all you'll get... [*He assumes a posture.*]

BLACK HAT: Mister, are you serious?

PIMP: Very. He must go to India.

BLACK HAT: India?

PIMP: Yes, India. He wants to have his bones licked by Buddha in India. Until he leaves here, he's my follower. Do you understand? Now you'd better put your swords back in their sheaths and draw off quietly. I won't be as foolish as to run after you to cut your ears off.

BLACK HAT: O.K. As he says that, shall we withdraw? It doesn't mean we lost. We have more weapons and more people. How can we lose the fight? We'd win without a question. However, if we were injured in the silly fight, it'd be silly after all.

All the people begin to withdraw in a stream.

PROSTITUTE [*going behind the MAN IN THE BLACK HAT and kicking his backside*]: You worm!
BLACK HAT: You bitch! [*He is about to grab the PROSTITUTE.*]
PIMP [*holding the dagger*]: Hang on! She's just a woman.

The OLD MAN takes the opportunity, runs to the MAN swiftly and stabs him in the breast. The MAN utters a long shriek, which is almost incredibly long, and he falls gradually. The PROSTITUTE covers her ears with her hands and falls prostrate.

While lights are getting dim, the MASKED SINGER appears singing.

MASKED SINGER: When somebody dies, the wind blows.
　　When nobody dies, the wind still blows.
　　So when the wind blows,
　　It doesn't say somebody dies.

　　When somebody dies, the night falls.
　　When nobody dies, the night still falls.
　　So when the night falls,
　　It doesn't say that somebody dies.

　　But somebody died.
　　The wind blew and the night fell,
　　And somebody died.
　　Somebody might have died.
　　The wind blew and the night fell,
　　And somebody died.

SCENE V

Daytime. Anywhere. If possible, it is a field. The sun shines. The weather is balmy. The straw-mat is spread and the PROSTITUTE and the young MAN sit on it.

They are playing house. The big doll is sleeping by them. The PROSTITUTE is cutting the leaves of Japanese daikon radish on a chopping board. The MAN is reading a newspaper.

PROSTITUTE [*while cooking*]: Darling.
MAN: Yes?
PROSTITUTE: It's a lovely day.
MAN: Yes, it's a lovely day.
PROSTITUTE: The wind's blowing gently.
MAN: Yes, the wind's blowing gently.
PROSTITUTE: Ah, darling, can you hear?
MAN: What?
PROSTITUTE: I just heard a bird singing.
MAN: It was a lark.
PROSTITUTE: But it sounded like a bush warbler.
MAN: It may be a cow.
PROSTITUTE: A cow isn't a bird.
MAN: Is a horse a bird?
PROSTITUTE: Birds can fly.
MAN: Horses can run.
PROSTITUTE: Snakes can creep.
MAN: That, standing in the distance, is a cow.
PROSTITUTE: Those, looking yellow, are dandelions.
MAN: Those, swimming in the river, are roaches.
PROSTITUTE: We'll hear the noon-siren soon. Then we'll have the meal. Aren't you hungry, darling?
MAN: No.
PROSTITUTE: That's no good. A man who has no appetite is as bad as a woman who's constipated. It might be lack of exercise. How about taking a walk around here until lunch?
MAN: Yes, but I can't be bothered.
PROSTITUTE: Men are always like that, always say 'I can't be bothered.' But you must look after yourself, my dear. You're young and you've got all your life ahead of you.
MAN: Ah, I heard a cow mooing.
PROSTITUTE: It can't be. It horses that can whinny. How do you like your miso-soup, weak or strong?

MAN: Well, I'd like to have it medium.

PROSTITUTE: All right, then I'll make it medium. How about pickled-daikon radish? Do you like slices thick or thin?

MAN: I prefer thin ones, if it's possible.

PROSTITUTE: You prefer thin ones. I'll cut them thin.

MAN: Something smells nice.

PROSTITUTE: It's miso-soup.

MAN: Wasn't it the fragrance of the plum-blossoms?

PROSTITUTE: Miso-soup being boiled or pickled-daikon. How's our baby, darling?

MAN: She's sleeping.

PROSTITUTE: Are you sure?

MAN: Yes.

PROSTITUTE: Oh, liar! She's awake. Now you see why I can't trust men. [*She takes the doll in her arms.*]

MAN: Is she awake?

PROSTITUTE: Yes, she is, but I'll let her lie down during the meal. Will you please put her to sleep over there?

MAN: All right.

PROSTITUTE: Lunch is ready. [*She prepares the table.*]

MAN: But we haven't heard the noon-siren.

PROSTITUTE: Doesn't matter. Soon we'll hear it. [*Serving rice in the rice-bowl*] Here you are.

MAN [*receiving the rice-bowl*]: Thank you.

PROSTITUTE: I put tofu in the miso-soup.

MAN: What else did you put in?

PROSTITUTE: Spring onions.

MAN: We are grateful for this meal.

PROSTITUTE: We are grateful for this meal.

The two eat lunch in a modest way.

PROSTITUTE: Is it good?

MAN: Yes, it's tasty.

PROSTITUTE: What is tasty?

MAN: The pickled-daikon radish tastes delicious.

PROSTITUTE: How about the miso-soup?

MAN: That's delicious, too.

PROSTITUTE: How?

MAN: Umm, for example...it's very, terribly, irresistibly, a lot...

The PIMP in a policeman's uniform comes in from Stage Right.

PIMP: You're having lunch.

PROSTITUTE: Oh, how annoying you are!

PIMP [*sitting down*]: Looks delicious.

PROSTITUTE: Stop it. Aren't you rude?

PIMP [*standing up*]: Then, I'll walk around here until you finish lunch.

PROSTITUTE: Don't! If you stroll around here, you'll make it dusty.

PIMP: But ...

PROSTITUTE: What do you want?

PIMP: As a matter of fact, I have something to ask you.

PROSTITUTE: Why don't you sit down. You're obstructing the nice view.

PIMP: Then, excuse me.

PROSTITUTE: Then, I'll give you a cup of tea.

PIMP: Cheers. It tastes nice, madam.

PROSTITUTE: What's your question about? Has a thief got away?

PIMP: No, madam. It's not a thief but a murderer who's got away.

PROSTITUTE: Goodness! A murderer?

PIMP: Yes, madam.

PROSTITUTE: Why have you let him get away? Wasn't that careless?

PIMP: You're right. It was very careless.

PROSTITUTE: You should arrest him quick.

PIMP: Yes, we should. That's why I came here to make some inquiries. Have you seen anyone who looks like a criminal?

PROSTITUTE [*to the MAN*]: Have you seen anyone?

MAN: Is he big?

PIMP: No, he isn't. He is rather a hairy bloke.

MAN: Only a cow lives here apart from us.

PIMP: Is there a cow here?

PROSTITUTE: It's over there. It's yawned right now.

PIMP: I see, it's yawned. Absolutely that is a cow because it's got horns. If it hadn't got horns, it'd be a horse.

PROSTITUTE: But why does the cow live there? Do you know?

MAN: No, I don't.

PROSTITUTE: How about you?

PIMP: Is this a RIDDLE?

PROSTITUTE: No.

PIMP: Then, I don't know.

PROSTITUTE: I don't know, either.

PIMP: By the way don't you ever think that cow might run straight in this direction?

MAN: Why in this direction?

PIMP: Of course, it might be that direction. But don't you ever think it could happen that it run this direction?

PROSTITUTE: It might happen. Yes, it might.

PIMP: Yes, it might run in this direction. In fact, we never know what cows are thinking. Well, I'm afraid I've bothered you rather a lot. But I think it'd be worthwhile your being careful. [*He goes off to Stage Right.*]

PROSTITUTE: I wonder if it'll run towards us?

MAN: It's facing the other way.

PROSTITUTE: How about a second helping?

MAN: I've had enough.

PROSTITUTE: Then I'll serve you tea.

MAN: Thank you for a delicious meal.

PROSTITUTE: Not at all. What are you going to do this afternoon?

MAN: Hmm, this afternoon.

PROSTITUTE: In the afternoon, usually people have a nap, mow the lawn, dig a pond in the garden or make a kennel.

MAN: Shall we make a kennel?

PROSTITUTE: But we don't have a dog.

MAN: A cat house?

PROSTITUTE: They don't need it.

MAN: Why not?

PROSTITUTE: They move too quickly.

MAN: Then, shall we sing a song at the tops of our voices?

PROSTITUTE: But I don't think it'd last long. The longest song I know has only got four verses.

MAN: Then let's laugh.

PROSTITUTE: Laugh?

MAN: Yes, laughter has no limits.

PROSTITUTE: I doubt if it goes on that long.

MAN: If it doesn't, we can stop.

PROSTITUTE: You may be right.

MAN: Shall we do that?

PROSTITUTE: Yes.

MAN [*trying to laugh but failing*]: Will you start us off?

PROSTITUTE: But I don't want to laugh at all. You've started this, so you go first.

MAN: Sure. [*He tries to laugh.*]

The WIFE of the HAT SELLER comes in from Stage Left as an insurance saleswoman.

WIFE: Good afternoon.

PROSTITUTE: Oh, good afternoon.

WIFE: What a lovely day!

PROSTITUTE: Yes, indeed. It is a lovely day.

WIFE: I think the good weather is better in every way.

PROSTITUTE: I agree. The good weather is better in every way.

WIFE: The washing dries fast.

PROSTITUTE: We don't need an umbrella.

WIFE: We feel better.

PROSTITUTE: And best of all, it's warmer.

WIFE: But, madam, it is on these fine, peaceful, and balmy days that most accidents happen.

PROSTITUTE: Accidents?

WIFE: Yes. Madam, can you see a horse standing over there?

PROSTITUTE: That's a cow.

WIFE: Goodness! Is it a cow?

PROSTITUTE: It's a cow because it's got horns.

WIFE: That's right. It's got horns. As it's got four legs, I simply thought it was a horse... Never mind. Suppose that cow runs straight in this direction. Well, if that is a cow like you say, it would come charging over here it's horns first.

PROSTITUTE: Yes, it would.

WIFE: And the cow would run at your husband here...

PROSTITUTE: Oh, dear!

WIFE: The horns would stick into your husband's body ever so deeply... The

121

blood would flow non-stop and your husband would be killed. For cows horns usually stick in very deeply.

PROSTITUTE: Really?

WIFE: Yes, it's true. Then, what would happen to you and your small baby left alone?

MAN: Am I going to be killed?

WIFE: Yes, you are. Then, what would happen to you and your small baby left alone?

MAN: Is that a RIDDLE?

WIFE: No.

MAN: Then, I don't know.

PROSTITUTE: Tell me what'd happen to us?

WIFE: I would say... perhaps you'd be badly off.

PROSTITUTE: Yes, we'd be badly off.

WIFE: You agree? That's why I came here to have a word with you madam... [*She takes documents out of a bag.*] As a matter of fact, I'm a house-to-house insurance saleswoman.

MAN: House-to-house insurance saleswoman?

PROSTITUTE: Have you ever heard of it?

MAN: No.

WIFE: Insurance is very useful. When you get it, for example, as I said just now, even if your husband died unexpectedly, madam, you'd receive a lot of money.

PROSTITUTE: Oh!

WIFE: Really a huge amount. Most of our customers are surprised at it and say, "Is it all right for you? We've received so much."

PROSTITUTE: Then, I'll feel guilty.

WIFE: No, you shouldn't. You don't have to worry about it. Because we collect a little money as a membership fee from each customer.

MAN: I see. Under your system if we die, you pay us, but if we don't, all the membership fees go to you.

WIFE: No, no you're wrong, sir. Even if you don't die, when the terms of the contract expire, you'll be given back all your membership fee.

PROSTITUTE: Under that system only you suffer a loss.

WIFE: Yes, we do.

PROSTITUTE: Can you manage to carry on like that?

WIFE: Yes, we manage one way or another. We do everything for the sake of

the wives and babies who are left.
PROSTITUTE: I can't believe it.
WIFE: But everybody trusts me and gets insurance. Anyway, won't you join us?
PROSTITUTE: Darling, what do you think?
MAN: I can't believe it.
WIFE: But madam, don't you believe in that horse, standing over there, or that cow if you like, don't you ever think it might dash this way?
PROSTITUTE: It might.
WIFE: It will. It was eating grass some time ago and now it's nearly time for its exercise. Cows always do exercise after meals. They run.
PROSTITUTE: Does that one run?
MAN: I'm afraid it might.
WIFE: Please get your insurance. It'll work.
PROSTITUTE: Shall we?
MAN: I don't mind.
PROSTITUTE: We'll get insurance.
WIFE: Thank you so much. [*Hastily puts the documents in her bag*] Then I'll send the person in charge immediately... Needless to say, in case you die before our clerk comes and completes the contract, we won't be able to guarantee payment.
PROSTITUTE: Will your clerk come before the cow starts running?
WIFE: We'll send him down here right away. Well, I'm so sorry to have bothered you. [*She goes off.*]
PROSTITUTE: We're lucky, aren't we?
MAN: Why?
PROSTITUTE: Because we'll get insurance.
MAN: Hum.
PROSTITUTE: Do you think that cow runs?
MAN: I have no idea. [*He tries to laugh.*]
PROSTITUTE: What's wrong?
MAN: I still can't do.
PROSTITUTE: What can't you do?
MAN: I can't laugh.
PROSTITUTE: You'll feel like laughing soon.

The MAN IN THE BLACK HAT comes in swiftly, disguised as 'a pushy telephone salesman.' He brings a telephone wrapped in a wrapping cloth.

123

BLACK HAT: Mister, it's hush-hush but I've got a good telephone here for sale. Won't you buy it?

MAN: A telephone?

BLACK HAT: Yes. It's a good machine. To tell you the truth, JT, Japanese Telecom's gone bankrupt and they gave us these telephones as redundancy payment. If I can't sell them, my wife and kids will be out on the cold streets. Hey, mister, will you please buy one? It's a bargain.

MAN: He's selling a telephone.

PROSTITUTE: A telephone? Wonderful! Do you have it there?

BLACK HAT: Yes, I do. Would you like to see it? It sounds like I keep saying the same thing, but this is a very good one, made by reliable manufacturers. [*He shows the telephone to the PROSTITUTE.*]

PROSTITUTE: I see, it's a good one.

BLACK HAT: Look at the gloss on it.

PROSTITUTE: Can we hear well through it?

BLACK HAT: Of course, you can. Try it. [*He gives the receiver to the PROSTITUTE.*]

PROSTITUTE [*putting the receiver to her ear*]: I can hear.

BLACK HAT: Can you tell what you're hearing?

PROSTITUTE: No.

BLACK HAT: It's the grunt of a hippopotamus.

PROSTITUTE: A hippopotamus?

BLACK HAT: Yes.

PROSTITUTE: You've phoned up the zoo, haven't you?

BLACK HAT: Yes. Why won't you try it, too, mister?

The MAN listens to the receiver.

PROSTITUTE: Can you hear?

MAN: Hmm.

PROSTITUTE: What's wrong?

MAN: Somebody's laughing...

PROSTITUTE: Laughing?

MAN: Yes. They sound like they're enjoying themselves a lot. Who are these people?

BLACK HAT: They're Indians.

MAN: Indians?

BLACK HAT: Yes, I've phoned up India. So, they're Indians. You can call foreign countries with this telephone.

PROSTITUTE: Good gracious!

MAN: But do Indians laugh?

BLACK HAT: Of course, they do, mister. When I was at work, I often talked to an Indian and he certainly laughed. Mister, Indians usually laugh before meals and before going to bed.

PROSTITUTE: Darling, let's get one.

MAN: Get what?

PROSTITUTE: This telephone. It's brilliant.

BLACK HAT: Mister, please buy one. You can have it at a special discount.

MAN: But I can't believe that Indians would laugh.

BLACK HAT: Please, mister. Madam is saying yes. Please buy one to save me and my family.

PROSTITUTE: Won't we buy it, darling?

MAN: Eh? Yes, we'll buy it.

PROSTITUTE: He said we'd buy it. [*She pays.*]

BLACK HAT: I thank you for this, mister. Now my wife and kids won't have to be out in the streets in misery. Well, it's time to leave now. So, if you'll excuse me. [*He goes off.*]

PROSTITUTE [*listening to the receiver*]: Darling, I can hear a train coming. I wonder where it's going. Don't you want to get on the train...?

MAN [*trying to laugh*]: Aa, haa...

PROSTITUTE: What's the matter?

MAN: Well, I may be able to laugh.

PROSTITUTE: Really?

MAN: Yes, Aa, aa, aa, ha...

PROSTITUTE [*putting the receiver to her ear again*]: Somebody is on the other end. He must be just near the receiver. He's keeping quiet. I'm sure he's listening to me. Who is it? Is it an Indian? No, it can't be. If he was an Indian, he'd speak something in Indian...

MAN [*trying to laugh desperately*]: Aa, hahaa, hahaa, aa, aa, ha, hahaa, ha, ha, hahaa. [*He gradually begins to laugh. We wonder if we can call it laughter, though.*] Hahaa, hahaha, aa, hahaha, aa, hahaha, hahaha...

PROSTITUTE [*noticing*]: You laughed. You're laughing, aren't you?

MAN: Hahaa, hahaha, aa, hahaha...

PROSTITUTE: How wonderful. You're laughing. [*She laughs.*]

At first the two laugh low and then little by little they get to bursting their sides with laughing. They keep laughing. They do it for a while. Then they stop. Both become worn-out and dejected. They calm down their breathing for a while facing each other. Soon the MAN lies down holding his stomach with his hands.

PROSTITUTE: What's wrong?
MAN: It's aching.
PROSTITUTE: Where? Where is it aching?
MAN [*holding his stomach with his hands*]: Here.
PROSTITUTE: Is it hurting badly?
MAN: Yes, it's killing me. It's hurting terribly.
PROSTITUTE: Why did it come on? Because of the laughing? Well, we must send for a doctor.
MAN: No. You don't have to send for a doctor. Please don't.
PROSTITUTE: Yes. We must. It might be appendicitis. If you've got appendicitis and are left any longer, you'll die of it. [*Takes up the receiver*] Hello, hello, is that a doctor? Hello, you're a doctor, aren't you? Will you please come down here as fast as you can? My husband's got a serious stomach ache. Eh? A stomach ache! His stomach is aching. I'm not lying. It's hurting badly. He might have appendicitis. Could you come and see him. Eh? No, he can't go there. Because it's aching so terribly... He's lying down. He can't get up. Because he is seriously ill. No, he can't. You must come to see him. I'm telling you this is true. Are you really a doctor? Can't you hear that my husband is groaning? That groaning voice is my husband's. He's in danger of dying. If you don't come soon...

The OLD MAN disguised as a doctor comes in while the PROSTITUTE is talking on the phone. The PROSTITUTE keeps talking to the receiver.

OLD MAN [*patting the PROSTITUTE on the shoulder*]: Hello.
PROSTITUTE [*hanging up the receiver*]: Oh, dear! You're very late; my husband is tortured by the pain.
OLD MAN: I ran down here, though. Where's the patient?
PROSTITUTE: He's here. He's got a stomach ache.
OLD MAN: I see. Stomach ache. What has he done?

PROSTITUTE: He laughed.

OLD MAN: I see. He laughed.

PROSTITUTE: He was convulsed with laughter. It might have caused the pain.

OLD MAN: Yes, that was the reason. When we laugh, we must be very careful, otherwise... [*He takes a stethoscope out of his bag and holds it against the MAN.*]

PROSTITUTE: How is he?

OLD MAN: Very poorly.

PROSTITUTE: Will he recover?

OLD MAN: Of course, he will. I have lots of good medicine and injections.

PROSTITUTE: Are they expensive?

OLD MAN: I don't take money from the poor patients.

PROSTITUTE: Oh, how kind of you.

OLD MAN: Is there a cow?

PROSTITUTE: A cow? It's not ours but yes, over there...

OLD MAN [*looking at the cow and then turning his eyes from it*]: I see, over there. I felt that I was being watched by a cow.

PROSTITUTE: Is it watching us?

OLD MAN: Yes, it is. But it's better to leave it. Because cows often get excited once they know they are being watched.

PROSTITUTE: My husband hasn't completed the insurance contract yet.

OLD MAN: That's bad. He must get it: insurance isn't a bad thing to have.

PROSTITUTE: He's already got it but the person in charge of the contract hasn't brought the document.

OLD MAN: That's very bad. It's just the same as he doesn't have the insurance at all.

PROSTITUTE: What's happened to them? We've been waiting a long time.

OLD MAN: Madam, which shall I use, medicine or an injection?

PROSTITUTE: They say injections work quicker...

OLD MAN: You're right, madam. [*He takes a big knife out of his bag and sticks it into the MAN's breast slowly.*]

The MAN's long, long cry echoes. The PROSTITUTE covers her ears with her hands and falls prostrate. The scene moves to the quay at night quietly...
The MASKED SINGER appears quietly and sings. His song is the same as the ending of SCENE IV, "Somebody Died."

SCENE VI

The quay at night. A white coffin is put at centre stage. The MASKED SINGER sits on the end of it and is playing the guitar into the distance.
The PROSTITUTE, who is holding a red rose, stands by the coffin and stares down at it. There is no lid on the coffin and instead a white cloth covers the corpse.
From Stage Left the HAT SELLER and his WIFE, the OLD MAN, from Stage Right the PIMP, the MAN IN THE BLACK HAT, his MISTRESS, FOLLOWER 1 and 2 come in and all walk slowly.
Everyone except the MASKED SINGER and the PROSTITUTE moves slowly in this scene. They sometimes stop walking and meditate or have a look at the corpse in the coffin. They converse with one another but they are not tied down by their talking. Each of them lives in his or her own world.

MISTRESS [*noticing the HAT SELLER and blankly*]: Oh, you missed it again?
HAT SELLER: Yes, I'm sorry.
WIFE: When we got home, he was alive. He's hopeless...
HAT SELLER: I'm hopeless. I've got no talent.
OLD MAN: It's not a question of whether you're talented or not. You have no passion, no passion at all...
HAT SELLER: That's right. I have no passion.
OLD MAN: Look at him. He did it well.
HAT SELLER [*looking at the coffin*]: How nice it is, to be still!
PIMP: It was a good cry...
WIFE: It wrung my heart.
HAT SELLER: You mean, it was like the whistle of the ship?
FOLLOWER 1: It was quite different. Listen, the whistle of the ship sounds like this. [*He mimics the sound.*] But his cry sounded like this. [*He tries to mimic the MAN's cry but fails. To FOLLOWER 2*] You do it for them.
FOLLOWER 2: Look. First the knife was stuck in him like this. And then... [*He tries to cry but fails.*]
BLACK HAT: Stop it. You silly fools! You've got to do it like this. [*He gives a cry.*]
MISTRESS: That's totally different.
BLACK HAT: It was not quite the same, yet, similar somehow.

MISTRESS: No, it bore no resemblance at all. I've ever heard that voice some-where, some day when the wind blew...

PROSTITUTE: In the town where we see tall chimneys...

MISTRESS: Yes, there...

PROSTITUTE: I heard it, too and I cried then.

HAT SELLER [*hesitatingly*]: I feel I can do that cry if I try...

OLD MAN: You never can. You were sound asleep and snoring loudly, then.

WIFE: He wasn't snoring but sleeping well. I'm ashamed of him...

HAT SELLER: Still, I think like this; the injection wasn't poison but something like calcium or that sort... I've gained weight. See!

MISTRESS: You'd gain weight whatever injection you were given.

WIFE: You gain weight even if you eat parsley.

HAT SELLER: But if it wasn't poison but something like nutrition, I would feel as if I had been betrayed.

BLACK HAT: Listen and don't be too much concerned about that. The crucial point is the determination. In fact, there was a man who was killed by an injection of calcium...

PIMP: Some people were killed even without any injections.

OLD MAN: How?

PIMP: To tell you the truth, I twisted them a bit.

HAT SELLER: Still, is he truly dead? [*He is about to touch the corpse in the coffin.*]

PROSTITUTE [*suddenly furious*]: Don't touch him.

HAT SELLER: No, Ma'am. [*He steps aside reflectively.*]

At this point everyone wakes up slowly from the half-dreaming condition.

OLD MAN: How dare you put on airs like that? This slut thinks the corpse belongs to her.

PROSTITUTE: I found him first.

OLD MAN: Before you, I had seen him with these people.

WIFE: Yes, we were before you. You had also seen him, my dear.

HAT SELLER: That's right. Off course, I had seen him. What's more I had talked to him.

MISTRESS: Sweetheart.

BLACK HAT: Yeah, I was the first, I mean, to see him. And, the first to talk to him, needless to say... However, it doesn't mean I want to have it. [*He casts a strong glance at the PROSTITUTE, goes away from the coffin and moves to the corner of the stage.*]

FOLLOWER 1 and 2 go after the MAN IN THE BLACK HAT.

OLD MAN: I don't want it, either. I only wanted to tell her it wasn't hers. [*He casts a stern glance at the PROSTITUTE, goes away from the coffin and moves to the corner of the stage which is the opposite side where the MAN IN THE BLACK HAT and his FOLLOWERS are.*]

The WIFE goes after the OLD MAN.

MISTRESS: Did you understand? It's not yours! [*She goes to the place where the MAN IN THE BLACK HAT and his FOLLOWERS are.*]
PROSTITUTE [*to the PIMP*]: Darling!
PIMP [*standing apart from the others*]: Let them touch it. It's everybody's.
PROSTITUTE: But...
PIMP: Let them touch it.
HAT SELLER [*also standing apart from the others*]: It's all right. I don't need to touch it as long as I know he's dead.
WIFE: Why don't you feel it, my dear?
HAT SELLER: No, I'm fine.
MISTRESS [*coldly*]: Mister, you must feel it.
HAT SELLER: If you say so, then... [*He looks at the PROSTITUTE, bows his head slightly, squats and feels the corpse.*] Thanks... [*He bows his head to the PROSTITUTE slightly.*]
PROSTITUTE: That's all right. If anyone wants to touch it, I don't mind you doing that.
MISTRESS: Guys! Go and feel it.
FOLLOWER 1: No, ma'am, we really don't need to...
MISTRESS: Go and touch it!
FOLLOWER 1: Yes, ma'am. [*He reluctantly walks to the coffin, bows his head to the PROSTITUTE, feels the corpse nervously, bows his head to the PROSTITUTE again and comes back.*]
MISTRESS: And you!
FOLLOWER 2: Yes, ma'am.

About this point the scene becomes like the rite of incense burning for the repose of a departed soul at a funeral. People feel the corpse with fingers instead of burning the incense. Needless to say, the PROSTITUTE, holding a red rose and standing by the coffin, is like the chief mourner and the HAT SELLER is like the chief of the funeral committee. Only the MASKED SINGER is strumming the guitar as if he did not notice what the others are doing at all.

MISTRESS: Sweetheart.

BLACK HAT: I know. [*He feels the corpse extremely formally.*] Honey, you do it, too.

MISTRESS: Yes, I will. [*She feels.*]

OLD MAN: You go and do it, too.

WIFE [*standing up*]: But, how about you, Captain?

OLD MAN: Me? Let me think. O.K., I will.

The WIFE feels the corpse.

OLD MAN [*feeling the corpse*]: It was a wonderful cry...

PROSTITUTE [*bowing back to the OLD MAN who is the last mourner and noticing that everybody except the PIMP have finished touching the corpse*]: Why don't you go and do it, too?

PIMP: I'm all right.

PROSTITUTE: Why?

PIMP: I'm all right. I don't feel like doing it. You go ahead.

PROSTITUTE: All right, then. [*She goes to the coffin, bows her head to the group with the MAN IN THE BLACK HAT and then to the group of the OLD MAN, and feels the corpse with her fingers.*] He was nice. His cry was fantastic, and he told the story about India nicely, too. [*She puts the rose on the corpse.*]

HAT SELLER: Won't you do it too, once?

PIMP: I'm fine.

HAT SELLER: But...

PIMP: I don't feel like doing it.

MISTRESS: Why?

PIMP: No reason! I just don't want to do it.

OLD MAN: You're a funny bloke.

PROSTITUTE: Go and feel it. It's very nice.

PIMP: I'm all right.

FOLLOWER 1: He's too shy to do that, Boss.

BLACK HAT: Shut your gob...

WIFE: You should do it, if you wanted.

MISTRESS: I agree. You aren't honest with yourself.

PIMP: What!

PROSTITUTE: Please, please do it for my sake.

PIMP: Umm, I don't mind doing it. Only these people are...

PROSTITUTE: Leave them. Come... [*Taking him to the coffin*] Look, there, the forehead, that's the good part.

PIMP: Here? [*He points to the forehead of the corpse and notices the people around him.*] You look the other way.

MISTRESS: What!

PROSTITUTE: Don't! Leave them. You see, there...

PIMP feels the corpse nervously.

PROSTITUTE: Isn't it nice?

PIMP: Hmm.

HAT SELLER: Now then, as everybody's finished, let's move on to the memorial service.

PIMP: The memorial service?

HAT SELLER: Yes.

BLACK HAT: What's that?

HAT SELLER: It is... well, we often do it when somebody's died...

WIFE: Mourning for the dead.

OLD MAN: That's it. And after that, we cry for the dead.

PROSTITUTE: I don't mind crying.

MISTRESS: Who's going to give the mourning speech?

BLACK HAT [*to FOLLOWER 1*]: You, try it.

FOLLOWER 1: I can't, Boss.

BLACK HAT: Why?

FOLLOWER 1: I've never done it.

BLACK HAT [*to FOLLOWER 2*]: How about you?

FOLLOWER 2: I can't, either. I'm not in the mood.

HAT SELLER [*to the OLD MAN*]: How about you?

OLD MAN: No, not me. I'm bored with it.

PROSTITUTE: Then, why don't you go somewhere else! We don't care!

OLD MAN: I don't feel like going somewhere else, either.

PIMP: Then, keep quiet!

OLD MAN: I don't feel like keeping quiet, either.

HAT SELLER: Well, we've got to move on to the next thing. Otherwise, we'll just get stuck.

WIFE: Stop worrying and sit down, darling.

PROSTITUTE: I wonder what his mother's like?

OLD MAN: The things you think of are always out of tune.

PROSTITUTE: What's wrong?

HAT SELLER: It's reasonable. That's to say, there must have been a mother, so he could be born...

BLACK HAT: You'd better not say any more.

HAT SELLER: But we must sort this out.

About this point the people begin to go back to their own world and meditate absent-mindedly. Strumming of the guitar is heard as if nothing had been happening.

MISTRESS [*blankly*]: All right. Everyone, stand up and surround him. Come on...

All the people slowly stand up and surround the coffin in a half circle. They put hands together in front of the body and are looking down. The following conversation should be said in a special way: it is that only the speaker looks up and delivers his or her lines into midair.

BLACK HAT: And..?

MISTRESS: And we'll do various things.

PIMP: What are they...?

HAT SELLER: How about eating something? Something we have with us?

MISTRESS: All right. Do you have anything to eat?

WIFE: We have some peanuts.

MISTRESS: Good. Pass them round.

The peanuts are passed to everyone hand to hand. When everyone has received one each...

MISTRESS: For this man...

ALL: We're grateful for this meal.

All the people eat peanuts while they are having a taste of them in their own world. When they have finished eating, they fold their arms in front of them again and look down.

BLACK HAT: And...?
MISTRESS: We'll talk about him. Anything... You, go ahead...
FOLLOWER 1: This man went to India...
FOLLOWER 2: This man died of hunger in India...
BLACK HAT: Buddha licked his bones.
HAT SELLER: Dug a hole in the desert in the moonlight...
WIFE: Got into it and cried there...
PROSTITUTE: The wind blew and I cried, too...
PIMP: It was cows that licked him, not Buddha...
OLD MAN: This man is a kangaroo...
PIMP: Did he move?
OLD MAN: No.
PROSTITUTE: He was a real kangaroo.

The sound of the guitar stops for a second.

BLACK HAT: Let's go.
MISTRESS: Why?
BLACK HAT: It's over.
WIFE: Let's go.
HAT SELLER: Where to?
WIFE: We'll go to bed.
FOLLOWER 1: Let's go.
FOLLOWER 2: You go.
FOLLOWER 1: And you?
FOLLOWER 2: I'll go, too.
OLD MAN: It's over.
PIMP: It's over.
BLACK HAT: Let's go.
WIFE: Let's go.
FOLLOWER 1: Let's go.

FOLLOWER 2: Let's go.

Nobody moves. The MASKED SINGER stands up and moves away slowly from the coffin. At the same time, the PROSTITUTE begins to sing a song which sounds like muttering or cursing. They all join her and their movements slowly become dancing.

PROSTITUTE: Kangaroos are sad.
ALL: SAARD, SAARD.
PROSTITUTE: Because.
ALL: BEA-CAUSE.
PROSTITUTE: They are kangaroos.
ALL: ARE-ROOS.

Surrounding the corpse, they all sing and dance sorrowfully but gracefully.

PROSTITUTE: I'm a kangaroo.
ALL: QUANGWEARU, QUANGWEARU.
PROSTITUTE: I eat peanuts.
ALL: WEEEAT.
PROSTITUTE: I shed tears.
ALL: SHWED, SHWED.
PROSTITUTE: Kangaroos are kangaroos.
ALL: QUANGWEARU, QUANGWEARU.
PROSTITUTE: Kangaroos are sad.
ALL: SAARD, SAARD.
PROSTITUTE: Kangaroos are smelly.
ALL: SUMERRIE, SUMERRIE.
PROSTITUTE: Kill the kangaroos.
ALL: KWIILL, KWIILL.
PROSTITUTE: I am smelly.
ALL: SUMERRIE, SUMERRIE.
PROSTITUTE: I do stink.
ALL: SWEATINK, SWEATINK.
PROSTITUTE: Please kill me.
ALL: KWIILL, KWIILL.
PROSTITUTE: Kill the kangaroos.
ALL: QUANGWEARU, QUANGWEARU.

PROSTITUTE: Kill the kangaroos.

All stand rigidly all of a sudden.

OLD MAN [*crying out sorrowfully*]: QUANGWEARU!
ALL [*unhappily*]: KWIILL. [*All heads down.*]

A second of silence.

BLACK HAT: And...?

A second of silence and blackout.

Curtain calls.

When the lights come up, they all stand in the half-circle surrounding the coffin. We still hear the notes of the guitar. The corpse gets up from the coffin and bows holding the red rose. The rose is handed to the PROSTITUTE. She bows and hands the rose to the PIMP. The following is done in the same way. The red rose is handed to the HAT SELLER, the MAN IN THE BLACK HAT, his MISTRESS, FOLLOWER 1 and FOLLOWER 2, the WIFE of THE HAT SELLER and the OLD MAN. When the person is handed the rose, he or she bows holding it, hands it to the next person and goes off stage. During this, the applause of the audience shouldn't be stopped. The OLD MAN, who is the last to be handed the rose, bows holding it and calls the MASKED SINGER. The MASKED SINGER goes to Centre stage, bows, gets into the coffi, and lies in it. The OLD MAN covers it with the white cloth and goes off. The lights stay on for a while. The audience give up after a while and go home.

END

[II]

I AM THE FATHER OF
THE GENIUS IDIOT BAKABON

About the play

Betsuyaku borrowed the characters and the situation for this play from the popular comic, **Genius Idiot (Tensai Bakabon)** by the cartoonist, Fujio Akatsuka,[1] and wrote *I am the Father of the Genius Idiot Bakabon (Tensai Bakabon no Papa Nanoda)* in 1978. The first staging took place in October 1978 by the Atelier Group of the LTC *(Bungaku-za Atorie no Kai)*. **The Kangaroo** had been this group's first production, and after several years' absence Betsuyaku wrote four more plays for the group, and this play being their sixth.

Betsuyaku often takes ideas for his plays from real life incidents or crimes, or from fantasies or other authors' stories. On this occasion he used a funny and innocently silly popular comic written for children. The title of the comic had been translated to be **Genius Idiot**. It must have been because *tensai* means 'genius,' and *baka* means 'idiot.' But *bon* meaning 'a small boy' has been missed in this. The whole word *Bakabon* sounds like 'vagabond,' and making a pun. What's more, Bakabon is one of the main characters' names. So I decided the English title of Betsuyaku's play as *I am the Father of the Genius Idiot Bakabon* in order to capture it.

Akatsuka first drew for girls' comic magazines and became well-known as the "King of the gag" in the nineteen-sixties when he began drawing for boys' comics. Schodt writes:

> In the 1960s, under the influence of old American slapstick movies, Akatsuka began creating serialized gagstrips for newly formed boys' comic magazines. Previous children's humor strips had been short, restrained and naive, often depending on quaint puns and scenes of characters bumping into each other. Akatsuka's strips were around sixteen pages per episode, fast-paced and wacky. In his topsy-turvy world, idiot fathers fished for birds in rivers, policemen wore dresses, and everybody lied, cheated, and stole from his neighbor. Akatsuka's comics were

simply drawn and not particularly erotic or violent, but the new style of irreverent parody of the real world delighted readers of all ages and cleared the way for later, more radical artists.[2]

When the comic strip **Genius Idiot** was made into a thirty-minute television animation for broadcasting in the early evening,[3] Akatsuka's nonsensical 'topsy-turvy' world was no longer only for school children. In the same book, under the title '*The Gag Guerilla*,' Schodt describes how Akatsuka's humour is received by the Japanese public:

> Children read Akatsuka's comics for their simple, funny pictures; teenagers read them for their gags and the clever puns to which the Japanese language is so well suited; adults read them for their social satire. Akatsuka, through his Fujio Productions, has subsequently fostered the work of other gag artists who share his style, and he continues to promote his zany vision through comics, books, movies, and TV appearances. In doing so he is helping transform the humor of Japanese comics and, indirectly, of Japanese society.[4]

Some of the main characters in **Genius Idiot** speak in an odd way in Akatsuka's original comic strip, and this characteristic, as a common phenomenon in cartoon worlds, was developed and emphasised by the vocal actors in the television adaptations. Betsuyaku praises and analyses Akatsuka's work in the postscript of the collection of his plays, *I am the Father of the Genius Idiot Bakabon*:[5]

> Needless to say I wrote *I am the Father of the Genius Idiot Bakabon* by borrowing the elements from Akatsuka's **Genius Idiot**. I had admired the unique dramaturgy in **Genius Idiot** and if I may explain his dramaturgy simply, the main plot of the story develops into many irrelevant sub-plots. Normally these sub-plots are used principally to support the main plot, the central story line, and so they are supposed to go back to the main plot so as to unite. But in Akatsuka's dramaturgy, things do not happen in that way. On the contrary we even tend to consider the sub-plot as the main plot because the sub-plot continues to receive the main emphasis. And what is more, once we begin thinking in this way, another sub-plot starts taking over the previous sub-plot...

In this way the plots are divided and added up endlessly and in the end they do not unite with the main story line but get lost. This is Akatsuka's dramaturgy and it is this which I borrowed in this play.[6]

Betsuyaku's decision to write a play based on a popular comic strip was courageous as well as clever. If his play version of **Genius Idiot** did not amuse or impress its audience, it would have meant that his humour was not as strong as Akatsuka's; and then even if he succeeded, much of the credit for the success would go back to the original. This attempt to adapt an art to a new form must have presented a real challenge. However, from a different point of view, the play could be seen as a kind of copy, a study and interpretation of a successful creative work, allowing one artist to learn and build on another artist's labours. This reminds us of when Betsuyaku studied Beckettian stage craft and from it developed his own theatre. Of course, Betsuyaku already had the theme for his play version of **Bakabon** and only borrowed the format from the comic, and so perhaps it would be better to understand this piece as a kind of collaboration between these two artists of the same generation.

Style and Structure

The play lasts about one hour and, since there are no scene changes, there is no chance, once the curtain has risen, for either the actors or the audience to relax from the intensity of the play. The entrance of the two policemen begins the play, and the other characters join them one by one: first Bakabon, then his mother: Mama, his father: Papa, the woman in the neighbourhood: Rerere, Woman 1 and finally Man and Woman 2. Each character adds more confusion. The nature of their communication is always the same. One person asks a question and the other answers it from an unexpected point of view, thus making the thread of the discussion more tangled.

Although **I am the Father of the Genius Idiot** is written as one continuous act, because of the characteristics of the play, when I staged it, I divided the play into six scenes based on the appearances of the characters. This in the first instance was for entirely practical reason: so that we did not have to call the actors for rehearsals in which they had no parts to act. But soon it became apparent that every character adds a new dimension when he or she joins the others, and the division was extremely useful. Here is a table of scenes I made for the rehearsals.

Scene 1 (Sergeant, Constable)
Scene 2 (Sergeant, Constable, Bakabon, Mama)
Scene 3 (Sergeant, Constable, Bakabon, Mama, Papa)
Scene 4 (Sergeant, Constable, Bakabon, Mama, Papa, Rerere)
Scene 5 (Sergeant, Constable, Bakabon, Mama, Papa, Rerere, Woman 1)
Scene 6-1 (Sergeant, Constable, Bakabon, Mama, Papa, Rerere, Woman 1,
    Man, Woman 2).
Scene 6-2 (Sergeant).

As can be seen, when the number of actors on stage swells, the intensity of the play grows alongside this. At the end of the play when the other characters commit group suicide and Man and Woman 2 go off stage, leaving the Sergeant alone, the level of energy on stage suddenly falls off.

Scene 1 (BAKABON p.153 - p.158, l.16)
When the curtain rises, the audience sees two objects on stage. One is a public toilet with an unusual device for holding the toilet-paper on its outside wall and the other is an electricity pole. Betsuyaku uses a street in which the events take place. The electricity pole stands as the central focus and the balance of energy expands endlessly outwards from it. So here the design of the play is already setting up one of Betsuyaku's characteristic elements, the Beckettian dramatic space (see Chapter One [II] [A]). The ridiculous device on the public toilet represents an element from Akatsuka's humour.

The two policemen walk onto the street, their hands full of equipment for setting up their new police station. They are a Sergeant and a Constable. It will be the Constable who will use this new station regularly; the Sergeant's responsibility covers this station, but he has others under his charge as well. So, the conditions of the new police station are more important to the Constable. A dialogue takes place between the two about the electricity pole because the Sergeant chooses a spot next to the pole for the site of the station, giving as his reason, "...it'd be nicer if we had something to centre on... say to create an atmosphere..." (BAKABON p.153, l.13). He sounds reasonable and we may be taken in. However, although on the surface we can agree with his idea, there is no chance of course that the logic will go unchallenged because the place being considered for the police station is just part of a public street. The conclusion of the logic sounds correct, but its basis is absurd. The Sergeant at first thinks that the pole is an electricity pole, but the attitude of the Constable, who is confused and perhaps embarrassed to find that the office he is going to work in is in the street, makes the Sergeant sceptical as to whether it really is an electricity pole. The conversation tails off into details and loses its overview of the whole matter. The world of absurdity is firmly established as the framework of the play. This conversation without meaningful communication has drawn us into the absurd world of the characters, and the first ten minutes of, literally, physical scene-setting has completed the visual frame of the play too.

There now follows a scene involving a call to test if the telephone is working. The Constable's insensitive way of talking to Mr. Yoshida, who is on the other end of the line, worries the Sergeant, who is a little over-sensitive about public relations. It is obvious that, under the circumstances, the line cannot be connected,[7] and the combination of the conversation over a useless instrument, with the Constable's embarrassingly bad attitude towards Mr. Yoshida and the Sergeant's anxiety as a background, doubles the nonsense. Another thread which runs behind and through the plot is the hierarchical nature of the world of the policemen. Most of the Constable's answers to the Sergeant are not clearly expressed. One of the reasons for this, apart from his bewilderment about his new office, is the effect on him of this hierarchical structure.

Scene 2 (BAKABON p.158, l.17 - p.164, l.13)
Bakabon, followed by Mama, enters, putting up an umbrella, although it is a fine day. The young Constable, who has not learned well how a policeman is supposed to talk to the public, as has been seen in Scene 1, stops Bakabon in an autocratic way which makes the Sergeant nervous. The entrance of Bakabon and Mama expands the world from that of the policemen alone to one which includes contact with the public. However, the reactions of these supposedly ordinary decent citizens towards the policemen are unusual. Bakabon and Mama bring the nonsensical world of Akatsuka's comic strips to Betsuyaku's absurd world which has been created by the two inharmonious policemen, and the play quickly changes the nature of its humour with the collision of these two styles.

As we see through the Sergeant's speeches, Bakabon's character in the play appears mischievous, and overturns the common viewpoint of everyday life. The main victim of this new logic is the Sergeant, because he tends to see the world as a place always at peace, where nothing wrong can be happening. He wants to avoid conflict with the public; here is an echo of the democratic attitude taken up by the Japanese police after World War II to make amends for the militaristic style of former times. But the Sergeant's pretentious and unrealistic standpoint leads him to be antagonized by the other characters right through the play to the very end.

Scene 3 (BAKABON p.164, l.14 - p.171, l.27)
When the Sergeant is leaving, or rather, running away to another police station, abandoning the Constable to the confusion created by the peculiar woman and her son, Bakabon's father, Papa, enters abruptly on all fours, wearing a pair of Japanese wooden clogs. He is howling because he believes he is an Iriomote cat. This entrance of Papa brings into the play a 'game-like' quality. There are now three dimensions to the play: Betsuyaku's absurdity, Akatsuka's nonsense, and the game-playing. The introduction of the Iriomote cat adds a topical element since they were becoming recognised largely in the nineteen-seventies as an endangered species in Japan. The play has now taken a serious problem on with the absurdism and the cartoon fantasy and has created from all this a bizarre world.

The family, Bakabon, Mama, and Papa, at first happily enjoy their game, but Papa suddenly becomes dubious as to whether Bakabon really believes that he is a cat, and ends up forcing his son to hit the Sergeant to prove that he does. The who's-going-to-hit-whom-with-what game begins here, choosing the Sergeant as its first victim. This is the beginning of the sequence of crazy, irrational logic which will be developed at high speed to involve all the other characters on stage. The audience is also swallowed up by the distorted logic and quickly becomes engaged in it.

Scene 4 (BAKABON p.171, l.28 - p.178, l.23)
Rerere, the woman in the neighbourhood, passes by in the middle of an argument as to whether or not the Sergeant has agreed to pull down his trousers when Bakabon hits him. Despite our expectations of her as a middle-aged decent woman from the ordinary world, she in fact takes the conversation and the victimisation of the Sergeant in a new direction, and to even greater extremes. The discussion is changed by Rerere's contribution from an argument to agreement, and the Sergeant is further baffled. The dialogues bring more and more irrelevant subjects into the main stream as subplots, and it becomes impossible to halt the expanded, scattered and swollen conversations, as the

people become more and more excited. The tension of the craziness, absurdity, silliness and cruelty rises mercilessly. The play shows the quality of Akatsuka's dramaturgy which Betsuyaku praises in his postscript quoted earlier, exceptionally enhanced by Betsuyaku's own dramatic language.

The sequence in which Mama and Rerere try to guess why the Sergeant does not pull down his trousers is hilarious. The Sergeant becomes embarrassed and feels insulted. He declares that he wears men's underwear not women's, and that it is clean and decent and does not have any holes. He has been pressured into this declaration by the implications of the others' words. Here the play exhibits a typical instance of Betsuyaku's superb skill with language. One of the characters is chosen and persecuted until finally he loses his temper and reacts to the others in an unexpected way which can be ridiculous or violent, exploding the tension of the situation that has developed. And often, of course, the scene looks absurd because of the ridiculous subject-matter that is being discussed.

During these who-will-hit-whom and what-sort-of-underwear-is-the-Sergeant-wearing arguments, Bakabon, who cannot wait any longer to start the hitting, hits the Constable and leads the action into physical conflict - between the representatives of authority and the general public.

Scene 5 (BAKABON p.178, l.24 - p.187, l.29)
Woman 1's entrance breaks up the fighting scene and brings the play forward to the next phase. She has a problem: she is being watched through the window every night by a fat woman. The policemen are questioning her but the other characters interrupt them and take over. This develops into a petty quarrel over the right to take off clothes, and the dispute between the Constable and the ordinary citizens becomes serious. Despite his usual caution the Sergeant draws a pistol to halt it. Now the role of the Sergeant becomes that of the only person who retains his common sense, and an ordinary attitude towards events, although sadly the Sergeant's reaction shows itself in odd ways - but the unexpected is an essential quality of the play. The Sergeant becomes more and more confused and loses confidence in his own judgement, influenced by the bizarre people's unpredictable behaviour.

The episodes of smoking together, and then taking cyanide to commit group suicide as a solution to Woman 1's problem appear in a way to be fair, because everybody is given an equal portion. But when we look at them clear-headedly, what the people are accepting in the play has nothing to do with equality. This false democracy, echoing the dispute about the right to take off one's clothes, is another vital element of the play. Betsuyaku's sarcasm is sharply directed against all such false democracy.

Scene 6-1 & 6-2 (BAKABON p.187, l.30 - p.193)

The spotlight falls on the public toilet when Man calls someone to help him to reach the toilet-paper hung on its outside wall. Woman 2, who is passing by, helps him. This odd entrance of the last two characters again abruptly breaks up the extreme tension. Of course, the unusual system for reaching the toilet-paper causes laughter and is one more factor in the play's topsy-turvy world.

All the characters are given some of Woman 1's cyanide, and actually take it and die, except for the Sergeant who in his bewilderment has omitted to take his. They do this to surprise other people, but when Man and Woman 2 pass by again, they are not surprised at it at all. This is the final ironic reversal. The dead then rise up, dance and sing and leave the stage. The totally confused Sergeant is left alone.

The episode of the group suicide reminds us of Betsuyaku's experience in war-time Manchuria (see Chapter One [I]). The madness of the play, of our own busy and materialistic lives, and of the War, are somehow crossing over and merging.

Things absent in British Culture

Betsuyaku's frequent use of repetition and suspension creates the confusion which takes the play into the nonsensical world of his absurdity and forms the general basis of the play. It also creates the major difficulties in translating the play. But there were other features which needed attention in order to transfer them into the British theatre. I listed the things that are very much from Japanese culture, and additional information would be helpful to understand the meaning of the original play clearly and correctly.

* Papa and Mama

After World War II, it was fashionable, under the influence of the new wave of postwar Westernisation, to call parents 'papa' and 'mama' instead of using the Japanese words *otōsan* (father) and *okāsan* (mother). Dressing Bakabon's father in the old-fashioned Japanese outfit and then addressing him in this modern way creates another absurd imbalance.

✳ Rerere, the woman in the neighbourhood
Are? is an interjection which would be translated as 'Listen!,' 'Look!,' 'What!,' 'Oh, dear!' etc. in English. *Arere* and *arerere* are just longer versions of *are* and *Rerere* seems to have been formed by dropping *a* from *arerere*. In Akatsuka's comic Rerere is a man who calls and stops the people in his neighbourhood for everyday greetings and chats while sweeping the street.

✳ Mr. Yoshida
One of the common Japanese surnames, like Tanaka, Nakamura etc.. Calling the man on the other end of the telephone Mr. Yoshida indicates that the policemen are talking to one of the ordinary citizens whom they are supposed to be protecting.

✳ Iriomote cat *(Iriomote yamaneko)*
One of the species of animals designated for special protection, inhabit only on the Iriomote Island of Okinawa prefecture, the southern-west Islands in Japan. The near-extinction of the Iriomote cat was a topical problem at the time the play was written. The Okinawa islands were once called Ryukyu and had their own language before they were colonised and became part of Japan. *Kanji* (the Chinese character) *nishi/sei* is therefore read as *iri* in this place-name, which is very unusual and sounds foreign. The unfamiliar sound of the word probably influenced Betsuyaku's choice.

✳ Maruei
A common name for a shop; this is why the characters argue about 'Maruei Removal Service' and 'Maruei Bakery'. The name works to confuse the conversation further, while giving the atmosphere of the town where the people live.

✳ Woman 1's room (BAKABON p.181, l.15-22):
The followings are the phrases to describe the location of her room.
- around the corner from the tobacconist's: *tabakoya no kado*
- on this side of the post box: *posto no kocchi no*
- at the end of the passage: *tsukiatari no*
- a house with a lattice door: *koshido no (ie)*
- the two storeyed-house: *nikaiya*
- the room upstairs: *nikai*
- the four and half tatami-mattress sized room next to the balcony for drying:

monohoshi no yoko no yojohan

The description of Woman 1's room is that of what used to be a typical rented room. This sort of accommodation and district has become hard to find in recent years and, in a very brief exchange of the speeches, Betsuyaku conjures up an atmosphere which seems very old-fashioned now.

Design

I staged the play in the Workshop Theatre (now Banham Theatre) where **The Kangaroo** had been staged. I changed the shape of the acting area once again. The story develops on the street alone, and it is in the nature of the play that the audience do not have to think what has already happened before the first scene. Because of this I wanted to create an intimate atmosphere where the audience could experience and live the events close to the actors. To do this I designed the acting area to run diagonally from Upstage Left to the other end of the theatre. I raised the area of the original audience seats and made the theatre completely flat to create a long-acting space to look like an ordinary street. The seats were placed on both sides of the staging area; this meant of course that the audience on each side faced one another. The aim was that the audience should see the actors' movements and listen to them chatting and arguing as if they themselves were walking along the street and witnessing it all by chance.

There are two objects on the street in the stage directions: a public toilet and an electricity pole. In Japan an electricity pole in the conventional sense is a wooden pole.[8] Nowadays, new poles are not wooden, being made rather of concrete. For this production we used an old telegraph pole given by British Telecom, which gave the right effect of an old Japanese electricity pole.

I had an image of the public toilet as the sort of small hut we might see in a place like a park. However, when I thought how it would look on stage, I realised that both the design and its location were problematic. The structure could not be big in case it obstructed the movements of the actors and the audience's view. But then, the stage being very close to the audience, we could not use anything which would look obviously like a stage device: there was not enough distance to fool the audience. Our final decision was that we should get a real Porta-loo. This meant that there would be a real electricity (real telegraph) pole, and a real Porta-loo on stage. Fortunately, we were able to borrow a Porta-loo from a construction company. We then added a further realistic touch by putting several traffic cones on the stage.

Notes: ───

(1) Fujio Akatsuka (1935-2008), cartoonist, media presenter and actor. Born in Manchuria, and began drawing cartoons in 1956. *Genius Idiot* was first published in a boy's comic magazine: *Weekly Boy's Magazine (Shūkan Shōnen magagine)* in 1967. The comic appeared serially in a few comic magazines and ended it in 1978.

(2) Frederik L. Schodt, *Manga! Manga! The World of Japanese Comics* (Tokyo: Kodansha International Ltd, 1983).

(3) The TV series was broadcast from 25th September 1971 to 24th June 1972.

(4) Ibid. of (2), '*The Column - The Gag Guerilla*', p.121.

(5) See Appendix [I], *Collected Plays of Minoru Betsuyaku Vol.7*, (1), p.4

(6) Ibid. pp.252-53.

(7) Telephones in the nineteen sixties were landline telephones. Betsuyaku used a black phone as one of his recurrent stage properties. A black phone was given by the Nippon Telegraph and Telephone Public Corporation when people subscribed telephone in 1952-1985.

(8) Undergrounding in Japan is only 15% on average in 2021 and not advanced. It is a kind of urban landscape of Japan seeing running power lines along with standing electricity/telephone poles. An electricity pole standing on stage is one of the typical sceneries in Betsuyaku's plays.

I'm the Father of the Genius Idiot Bakabon
Stage photo by Christopher Jowett
(from left) Constable and Sergeant

I'm the Father of the Genius Idiot Bakabon
Stage photo by Christopher Jowett
the Sergeant

I AM THE FATHER OF THE GENIUS IDIOT, BAKABON

By

Minoru Betsuyaku

Translated by Masako Yuasa

The original text for the translation is from *Collected Plays of Minoru Betsuyaku: I am the Father of the Genius Idiot Bakabon, pp.5-83 (Tensai Bakabon no Papa Nanoda Betsuyaku Minoru Gikyoku Shū, pp.5-83)*, Tokyo: Sanichi Shobo, 1979.
©1979 Minoru Betsuyaku

CHARACTERS

THE SERGEANT
THE CONSTABLE
BAKABON (the boy GENIUS IDIOT)
MAMA
PAPA
AUNTIE RERERE (the woman in the neighbourhood)
WOMAN 1
WOMAN 2
MAN

Performance poster (Leeds in November 1988)
Illustrarion by The Workshop Theatre of the School of
English at the University of Leeds in the United Kingdom
"The Genius Bakabon" ©Fujio Akatsuka

I am the Father of the Genius Idiot Bakabon was the second Betsuyaku play in English which I staged in the Workshop Theatre. The performances took place between the 8th and the 12th of November, 1988.

The cast and the technical staff for the first English production of *I am the Father of the Genius Idiot Bakabon* in the Workshop Theatre in 1988:

CAST

The Sergeant	Hohn Sharp
The Constable	Greg Preston
Bakabon	Eli Wood
Mama	Rachel Efemay
Papa	D. Sidney Montz
Aunti Lelele	Terry Ram
Woman 1	Jeanette Tterney
Woman 2	Tanya Lees
The Man	Nick Issac

TECHNICAL STAFF

Director	Masako Yuasa
Stage-Manager	Park Chu-Wan
Assistant Stage Manager	Alyson Campbell
Prompter for rehearsal	Tanya Lees
Set Design	Masako Yuasa with Trevor Faulkner and Chris Jowett
Set Construction	Chris Jowett, students from the Workshop theatre
Costumes	Kitty Burrows
Costumes Assistant	Emma Davies, D. Sidney Montz, Jane Coppola
Lighting Design	Trevor Faulkner, MA students from the Workshop Theatre
Musical Arrangement	Chiaki Yamase and Graeme Pounder
Lighting board & Sound Operator	Chiaki Yamase
Properties	Masako Yuasa, Alyson Campbell
Technical supervisor	Trevor Faulkner
Production supervisor	Chris Jowett

The corner of the town where the public toilet and an electricity pole stand. There is a device on the wall of the public toilet. It is a small hole in the wall covered with a lid and when people open it from inside, they can reach their hand out through it. The loopaper is hanging on a roller on the wall, in other words people who have relieved themselves reach out their hand and get the loopaper.
THE CONSTABLE and SERGEANT enter with their hands full carrying two chairs, an office desk, a telephone, some documents and so on.

SERGEANT: Oh, yes, well, about here would be all right.

CONSTABLE: About here? Whereabouts?

SERGEANT: Oh, well, this...how about under this electricity pole...that's what I meant. This is an electricity pole, isn't it?

CONSTABLE: Yes, it is. It's an electricity pole...I suppose...

SERGEANT: I mean, it'd be nicer if we had something to centre...say to create an atmosphere... What do you think?

CONSTABLE: Yes, I think so...

SERGEANT: Shall we put the desk down here?

CONSTABLE: Here?

SERGEANT: You don't like it here?

CONSTABLE: No, I didn't say so, but...

SERGEANT: Just have a go. Around here would be good. It's also sunny here...

CONSTABLE [*putting down the desk*]: So, am I to understand that this will be my working place?

SERGEANT: Am I to understand? Please. If you don't like it here, just say so. I've been consulting with you about it...saying, how about here...

CONSTABLE: Yes, I know that.

SERGEANT: You don't like it here?

CONSTABLE: I don't say so.

SERGEANT: Then, no problem. It'd be nice here. An electricity pole is standing. This is only an electricity pole, but it'd be better than having nothing around. Don't you think so?

CONSTABLE: Yes, I think so, too.

SERGEANT: But do you think this is really an electricity pole?

CONSTABLE: Isn't it an electricity pole?

SERGEANT: Are you thinking this might not be an electricity pole at all?

CONSTABLE: No, I'm not. I just said so. I think it's an electricity pole.

SERGEANT: No, I didn't mean that, I said it wrong. Of course, although I did say it wrong, it wasn't that bad. Just a small mistake... What I meant was...are you listening? If this isn't an electricity pole, don't you like it?

CONSTABLE: What?

SERGEANT: Oh, no, listen, this isn't that serious question. I'm just asking you. For instance, supposing this wasn't an electricity pole...you see, just now we chose here simply because we assumed that this was an electricity pole. So, if it wasn't an electricity pole at all, you wouldn't like it? In other words, if it wasn't, although we've already made our choice, here wouldn't do...so... Do you see the point?

CONSTABLE: Yes, I think so.

SERGEANT: You wouldn't like it?

CONSTABLE: You mean, this electricity pole?

SERGEANT: No, I said if this wasn't an electricity pole at all...

CONSTABLE: Oh, I see. You're saying that this isn't an electricity pole.

SERGEANT: What are you saying? I've not said something like that at all. I'm saying if it wasn't. If this wasn't an electricity pole...in that case, this would.

CONSTABLE: Yes, that's it. I said so just now. In short, assuming that this is not an electricity pole at all for now, in that case...

SERGEANT: Who assumed that?

CONSTABLE: Pardon?

SERGEANT: Who assumed that this wasn't an electricity pole?

CONSTABLE: But, Sergeant, you said so just now... So, I thought that we would take it that way...

SERGEANT: No, that's not it. It's not like that. This is a very simple thing. Assuming? Don't take it like that. You'd better take it simply, straightforwardly. Listen carefully, suppose this electricity pole was... Shall we stop? Yes, let's stop. Well, it doesn't matter. It's not so important. Will you please organize the desk properly? Put the telephone there.

CONSTABLE: Here?

SERGEANT: Yes. Put it where it goes. Yes. What does it matter if you understood my question and answered it right? Where is the diary?

CONSTABLE: The diary? [*Pulling out the drawer*] It's here, Sergeant.

SERGEANT: If it's there, that's fine.

CONSTABLE: In other words what the Sergeant said to me was if this wasn't an electricity pole, would I be unhappy...?

SERGEANT: Stop it, well...let's stop talking about it. I told you just now that

I had finished with it. If we went on, we'd only make things worse... Also...well, I'm just explaining...what I mean by the phrase, "Don't you like it?" wasn't whether you liked the electricity pole or not, but if this wasn't an electricity pole...this... Here... This place would...

CONSTABLE: In other words what Sergeant's saying is if this wasn't an electricity pole at all...

SERGEANT: Stop it. We've already finished with that. Don't you see we've finished with it? Forget it. About the chairs. Which will you use? You can use the better one and our clients can use the other one.

CONSTABLE: I see, then, I'll use this one.

SERGEANT: All right, I give in. You can say it if you like.

CONSTABLE: Say what?

SERGEANT: I thought...you were about to say something just now. You were saying if this wasn't an electricity pole at all... But please remember that I'm only listening. I have no intention of discussing it. Right?

CONSTABLE: Yes, Sergeant. I was about to say that in other words...

SERGEANT: Can't you avoid that phrase in other words? As soon as you use in other words, things get more confused...

CONSTABLE: I see, Sergeant. Err...umm...yes, if this wasn't an electricity pole at all, in other words in that case...oh, excuse me. Er...in that case, it would mean that this wasn't an electricity pole at all, so it wouldn't mean whether I was unhappy about an electricity pole or not but, it would mean whether or not I was unhappy about the thing which isn't an electricity pole at all...

SERGEANT: What are you saying, you fool! It was a good decision to drop the subject. Shall we make a phone-call?

CONSTABLE: Was I wrong, Sergeant?

SERGEANT: Yes, you were. I've told you again and again that I'm not asking you whether you are unhappy about the electricity pole.

CONSTABLE: So, I said whether or not I was unhappy about the thing which isn't an electricity pole at all...

SERGEANT: You're wrong. Well, that's O.K. Let's stop. There's no end to this. Let's check if the telephone is connected by making a phone-call. I simply said if this wasn't an electricity pole at all...I'd drop this, but...if it wasn't one, would you like it here?

CONSTABLE: You mean being here?

SERGEANT: Yes, that's what I've been saying all the time.

CONSTABLE: If this wasn't an electricity pole at all?

SERGEANT: Yes.

CONSTABLE: But please just a minute. I don't understand what you mean by that.

SERGEANT: So, I've been telling you to forget it. Just make a phone-call, go on...

CONSTABLE: Yes, Sergeant. Where shall I ring?

SERGEANT: Any number you like.

THE CONSTABLE dials a number.

SERGEANT: It's ever so simple. If this wasn't an electricity pole at all, would he like it here or not? That's all...

CONSTABLE [*to the receiver*]: Ah...hello... Yes? Well, excuse me, just a minute please. [*Covering the receiver with his hand*] Sergeant, I'm through.

SERGEANT: That's fine then. You must tidy up the things on your desk and give the impression that you are very efficient. That sort of thing works for mutual trust.

CONSTABLE [*to the receiver*]: Sorry? Yes, that's why I'm telling you to hold the line. [*To THE SERGEANT*] Sergeant, what am I supposed to do?

SERGEANT: What?

CONSTABLE: The telephone. He's saying something to us.

SERGEANT: Who's on the phone? [*He takes the receiver.*]

CONSTABLE: It's a man called Mr. Yoshida.

SERGEANT [*to the receiver*]: Hello, this is a different person speaking. Eh? What? Well, excuse me. Will you wait a moment? Eh? No, no, won't be long. [*To THE CONSTABLE*] Who's this man?

CONSTABLE: He said that he's Mr. Yoshida.

SERGEANT: Who is Mr. Yoshida?

CONSTABLE: I've no idea. I just dialled to give it a try.

SERGEANT [*to the receiver*]: Eh? No, no, it won't take long. Only a second. We are talking about it now. Anyway, please wait. [*To THE CONSTABLE*] Did you say that you just dialled to give it a try?

CONSTABLE: Yes, I did. You told me so...to dial any number.

SERGEANT: Yes, I said so. But in that case you have to explain it to him. [*To the receiver*] Hello, we've sorted it out. We're sorry about this. I'll let the first person explain all about this. Eh? That's why I'm saying that...I'll let him explain. Eh? Oh, please. Please don't talk like that. Yes, so... Eh? What are you saying? Oh, no, please don't be so...he's going to explain... In a minute. Soon... [*Covering the receiver with his hand*] What a bugger... [*To THE CONSTABLE*] Explain to him.

CONSTABLE: But how do I explain?

SERGEANT: How do you explain? Tell him the facts as they are... Don't forget to tell him first that it's the first caller speaking.

CONSTABLE: Yes, Sergeant. [*To the receiver*] Err... hello, I'm going to explain about this...umm...to explain the facts in other words...

SERGEANT: Can't you hear me? Tell him it's the first caller speaking now.

CONSTABLE [*covering the receiver*]: Pardon?

SERGEANT: You must tell him that the first caller is speaking.

CONSTABLE [*to the receiver*]: Eh? Yes, I know. Please wait a moment.

SERGEANT: Listen. That bugger's still thinking that it's me who's talking to him. So I'm saying that you must let him know that what he's thinking is wrong and it's you who's talking to him now.

CONSTABLE: Am I supposed to tell that to him?

SERGEANT: Doesn't matter. Anyway...just tell him this one thing. A different person is speaking.

CONSTABLE [*to the receiver*]: Hello, err, now a different person's speaking.

SERGEANT: It's not now. If you tell him "Now," it sounds as if you took over again just now. I'm not saying that...well, it'll be all right. If he thought it was me on the phone and now you've taken over...well, it's OK. Go on.

CONSTABLE: Is it all right?

SERGEANT: Yes, it's fine. No, hang on… Well, after all, it's fine.

CONSTABLE: Hello, hello...

SERGEANT: Explain to him in a polite manner and no shouting.

CONSTABLE: Hello, hello...

SERGEANT: What's the matter?

CONSTABLE: It sounds like he's hung up.

SERGEANT: Hung up? [*Taking the receiver and listening*] Yes, he's hung up... That's why I told you so much you must explain in a polite manner.

CONSTABLE: But he'd hung up before I explain.

SERGEANT: Well, it's OK now... But should we call him again and explain it all? What do you think?

CONSTABLE: I would think it'd be the better thing, but I'm not sure I can find his number.

SERGEANT: Why can't you find his number?

CONSTABLE: Well, because...

SERGEANT: Did you dial at random?

CONSTABLE: Yes, but, Sergeant, you told me to. You said just to try any number I liked.

SERGEANT: OK. OK. Enough. This is enough. Let's not use but or in other words. It sounds a bit persistent. Don't you think so? We are talking to each other freely. Did you dial at random? Yes, I did. See? That's it. That's fine. Still...well, it's OK. It's all right now. What's wrong? We know that the telephone is working... Then I'm off now. I'll leave everything to you. You know what to do?

CONSTABLE: What should that be?

SERGEANT: Look, will you listen to me. I've been telling you that your attitude is wrong, that attitude. Didn't I tell you? Just speak freely, naturally. You know what to do? Yes, Sergeant. See? That's all. The world is much more common, uneventful and run-of-the-mill than you think...

BAKABON enters putting up an umbrella. THE CONSTABLE stops him by blowing a police-whistle.

CONSTABLE [*blowing a police-whistle*]: Oi! You!

SERGEANT: What? What's the matter?

CONSTABLE: Well, nothing. Only that boy is coming in...

SERGEANT: It's all right. Fine. This is that sort of...see...an ordinary place.

CONSTABLE: But he's putting up an umbrella.

SERGEANT: It doesn't matter. Does it? I wouldn't be surprised if he was even singing a song.

BAKABON: Do you want me to sing a song?

SERGEANT: No, we don't want it, fool. You shut up! [*To THE CONSTABLE*] You see? What's wrong with you is that you show too much interest in every little thing. Isn't that so? This is nothing extraordinary, this sort of thing is... [*To BAKABON*] But why are you putting up an umbrella?

BAKABON: Because it's not raining.

A short silence.

SERGEANT [*to THE CONSTABLE, as if asking for his agreement*]: See. [*He is about to say it's a simple matter, but he notices that it is not simple.*] No, maybe not. What did this kid say just now?

CONSTABLE: I think he said he was putting up an umbrella because it wasn't raining.

SERGEANT: Is it so?

BAKABON: Is what so?

SERGEANT: No, that's fine. Fine. [*To THE CONSTABLE*] See. This is OK... Of course if we thought about it seriously, it might seem a bit awkward but it's not worth bothering about. Is it?

CONSTABLE: Maybe not.

SERGEANT: Aren't you happy about this?

CONSTABLE: No, I'm not saying that, only...

SERGEANT: Then, it's fine. Let's give an end to this for now. [*Muttering*] It's not raining, so he's putting up an umbrella... Well, fine. Yes. Fine. I'll leave everything to you. I'm off now. About that kid...just leave him. Right?

CONSTABLE: Yes, Sergeant. I should be fine.

SERGEANT [*about to go off, feeling uneasy and turning round to BAKABON*]: You...are you still stopping there?

BAKABON: Yes, I am.

CONSTABLE: What do you want with us?

SERGEANT [*to THE CONSTABLE*]: Don't! [*To BAKABON*] Do you mean that...you're just stopping here? Is that it?

BAKABON: Yes, it is.

SERGEANT [*to THE CONSTABLE*]: Did you hear that? He's just stopping here. Well...he can...because this place is... Do you understand?

CONSTABLE: Yes, I do, Sergeant.

SERGEANT: Gooood. That's it. [*He looks at BAKABON who is standing still and feels uneasy.*] You won't do anything wrong, will you?

BAKABON: No, I won't.

SERGEANT: Good. He won't do anything wrong. [*To THE CONSTABLE*] Don't pay too much attention to him. This is just the same as if he weren't here. He isn't here. Good. [*He is about to go off.*]

BAKABON's MAMA comes in carrying a shopping basket in her arm.

MAMA: Oh dear, Bakabon, what's wrong?

BAKABON: Nothing's wrong.

MAMA: Oh dear, why is nothing wrong?

SERGEANT [*returning*]: Err...well...madam...

MAMA: Oh dear, good afternoon, officer.

SERGEANT: Good afternoon, madam...

MAMA: It's a lovely day...

SERGEANT: It certainly is a lovely day but... [*Seeing that THE CONSTABLE is looking up*] What's the matter?

CONSTABLE: No, nothing in particular... I was just checking because this lady said the weather was fine.

SERGEANT: Right, I wouldn't say any... [*To MAMA*] Don't take any notice of him. He's new. I must tell you one thing...err...I've forgotten what I was going to say. Oh, yes, that's it. Madam, just then you asked him what was wrong. But as a matter of fact...nothing was wrong.

MAMA: Pardon?

SERGEANT: Oh, well, you didn't mean that. Then that's fine. I just thought that you meant that.

MAMA [*to BAKABON*]: Did anything happen?

BAKABON: Nothing happened.

SERGEANT: Yes...it's true, madam. Nothing happened. I wanted to tell you that. In other words, madam, you asked him what was wrong when you came in, so I mistakenly thought that you had thought that something had happened to him. That's why I told you that there was nothing wrong. Right? So, that's all. Do you understand?

MAMA: Yes...

SERGEANT [*to THE CONSTABLE*]: She understood. Right? Is it clear? This is just an ordinary case. A neighbour passed by and we simply had a little chat.

CONSTABLE: I understand, Sergeant.

SERGEANT: Good. [*To MAMA*] Excuse me, madam, I'm in a hurry to get to another job... But, umm...maybe alright... Yes... Err that's that, so excuse me. [*He is about to leave.*]

CONSTABLE: Err... in other words, madam, you say that the weather is fine today, don't you?

SERGEANT [*stopping and turning around*]: What the hell are you saying to her?

CONSTABLE: Oh, I'm just talking about the weather.

SERGEANT: Talking about the weather? [*To MAMA*] I'm very sorry. You must

おなまえ　　　　　　　　　　　　　　　　　　　様

（　　才）

ご住所

メールアドレス

購入をご希望の本がございましたらお知らせ下さい。
（送料小社負担。請求書同封）

書名

メールでも承ります。　book@shahyo.com

書名

be shocked. He often talks like this although I've kept telling him to behave properly.

CONSTABLE: What's the matter?

SERGEANT: Just keep quiet, you idiot. [*To MAMA*] Well, are you going somewhere from now?

MAMA: No, nowhere in particular.

SERGEANT: But you seem to be going shopping or something like that...

MAMA: Yes, I came out for that but I remembered the market isn't open today...

SERGEANT: I see. [*To THE CONSTABLE*] Closed. The market isn't open
today. Can't do anything about that. [*To MAMA*] Then, you are going to
stay here for some more time?

MAMA: No, I didn't intend to...but if something's happening here, I don't
mind...

SERGEANT: No, no, nothing's happening here. [*To THE CONSTABLE*] Isn't
that right? Nothing's happening here.

CONSTABLE: Err...yes... Umm...nothing's going to happen...I suppose...

MAMA: Then, can we leave now?

SERGEANT: Yes, yes madam, you can. That's just what I was going to say.

MAMA: But I feel sort of guilty.

SERGEANT: You feel guilty? Not at all, madam. It's me who should feel guilty.
[*To THE CONSTABLE*] Isn't that so?

CONSTABLE: Yes, it is, Sergeant. In other words, madam, why you shouldn't
feel guilty is...

SERGEANT: Didn't you hear me to tell you to stop talking like that...

BAKABON slowly closes his umbrella.

CONSTABLE: Hey, you! Why are you closing the umbrella?

BAKABON: Eh?

SERGEANT [*to THE CONSTABLE*]: What?

CONSTABLE: Well, this kid was closing the umbrella.

SERGEANT: Doesn't matter.

CONSTABLE: No, it doesn't but I just wondered why he had closed the umbrella.

MAMA: Is anything wrong?

SERGEANT: No no nothing's wrong. Only this child has closed his umbrella

161

right now.

MAMA: Oh dear, Bakabon, why have you done that?

SERGEANT: No no, it's all right. He's only closed his umbrella.

MAMA: Are you sure?

SERGEANT: Yes, I am. It's the sort of thing everybody always does, as a rule. We didn't mean he shouldn't do it. What bothered my man was why he was doing that? In other words...he simply asked the boy a question. [*To THE CONSTABLE*] Isn't that so?

CONSTABLE: Err...yes, it is. To tell you the truth...

SERGEANT: It's not important whether you tell the truth or not. Just say "Yes," "Yes, it is."

CONSTABLE: Yes, it is.

MAMA: Bakabon, tell us.

BAKABON: Tell you what?

MAMA: Don't say "what!" Just now you were asked a question.

SERGEANT: Madam, it's better to leave it now.

MAMA: But, aren't I right? Just now this person asked him why he had closed his umbrella, didn't he?

SERGEANT: Yes, he did. But he simply asked. It's OK now. [*To THE CON-STABLE*] Hey, are you alright with it? Or are you still wondering why he closed the umbrella?

CONSTABLE: Yes, I am still wondering about it, but it's all right.

MAMA: Bakabon, tell us.

SERGEANT: "Yes, I am still wondering about it!" Why the hell you talk like that?.

MAMA: Bakabon.

SERGEANT: There, there, madam...

MAMA: No. You can easily answer that simple thing. Can't you, Bakabon, tell us. Why did you close the umbrella?

BAKABON: It was because I wanted to.

MAMA: It was because you wanted to? That's not an answer at all.

SERGEANT: Oh, yes, madam. It sounded a good answer to me. [*To BAKA-BON*] Yes? [*To MAMA*] Because he wanted to close his umbrella, he did it. This is a good answer. [*To THE CONSTABLE*] Don't you think so?

MAMA: No, it can't be an answer. What's more where are your manners, Bakabon? Have you got something in your mouth?

BAKABON: No, I haven't.

MAMA: Really?

BAKABON: Yes, really.

CONSTABLE: You liar! I'm sure something's in your mouth. Open your mouth.

SERGEANT: Don't! You fool! What are you saying?

CONSTABLE: But, Sergeant, please leave this to me this time. There's something in his mouth. I'm positive. This kid's just lying. [*He is about to approach BAKABON.*]

SERGEANT [*stopping THE CONSTABLE*]: Don't!

CONSTABLE: Why not, Sergeant? He's been doing that for some time. If we examine inside of his mouth, we'll find out.

SERGEANT: Can't you hear I've been telling you "Don't!"? How many times do you want me to say it? Does it matter if he's got something in his mouth?

CONSTABLE: Doesn't it matter?

SERGEANT: No.

CONSTABLE: Won't he get bad teeth?

SERGEANT: That doesn't matter. [*To MAMA*] No, no, madam, I didn't mean to say that, not at all. If you tell him to open his mouth, madam, it's OK because you're his parent. Err... are you his parent?

MAMA: Yes, I am.

SERGEANT [*to THE CONSTABLE*]: See? It's OK because she's his parent. But what are you to him?

CONSTABLE: What am I?

SERGEANT: You're nothing to do with him. You see? A person who is nothing to do with him shouldn't say that sort of thing. What's more, we are not sure that there's something in his mouth.

BAKABON: There has been something in my mouth actually. [*He takes the chewing-gum out of his mouth.*]

MAMA: Bakabon...

CONSTABLE: ... [*He looks to THE SERGEANT.*]

SERGEANT: It's fine... Don't you see? I didn't say that there was nothing in his mouth. I said it wouldn't matter if there was something in his mouth.

MAMA: Throw it away.

SERGEANT [*to THE CONSTABLE*]: Right? Don't you ever think I told you a lie.

CONSTABLE: I know.

BAKABON sticks the chewing-gum from his mouth on to THE CONSTABLE's uniform.

MAMA: Bakabon...
CONSTABLE: What shall we do?
SERGEANT: Well...so...
MAMA: Err...I don't think he meant any harm.
SERGEANT: That's right. I agree with you, madam. [*To THE CONSTABLE*]
See? That's it. As he didn't mean any harm... there's no point doing any-
thing about it, isn't it?
MAMA: Shall I take it off?
CONSTABLE: Well, it's all right.
SERGEANT: Look, I've told already. Right? Don't pay too much attention to
this kind of thing and just behave naturally as usual... Then things go
smoothly...I'll leave this to you. I really must go now. [*To MAMA*] I'm
in a hurry. There's another case to attend to.

BAKABON's PAPA comes in on all fours wearing geta(1) *on his hands. He sometimes howls somewhat like "Wooow!" unenthusiastically.*

CONSTABLE: Sergeant ...
SERGEANT: Yes, well...of course some funny things could happen because
that's the way the world is. But haven't I been telling you not to show too
much interest in them. When you see something very peculiar, then you
can do a bit about it. But as for this...is it very peculiar?
BAKABON: It's a cat.
CONSTABLE: A cat?
MAMA: He is my husband.
SERGEANT: "My husband"? Your husband?
MAMA: Yes. But he thinks he's a cat now...
SERGEANT: I see, he thinks he's a cat.
CONSTABLE: But he howled wooow just now.
SERGEANT: I told you, don't talk too much. It doesn't matter since he himself
thinks he's a cat.
BAKABON: Because it's a wildcat.
CONSTABLE: A wildcat?
BAKABON: He howls wooow because he's a wildcat.
CONSTABLE [*to THE SERGEANT*]: Is that true?

SERGEANT: I don't know... [*To MAMA*] Is he always like this?

MAMA: No, not always... Yesterday he thought he was a dog.

SERGEANT: Then only today he becomes a wildcat?

MAMA: Yes. That's right.

SERGEANT: In that case... [*To THE CONSTABLE*] Did you hear? It doesn't matter because it's only for today. Does it?

CONSTABLE: Maybe doesn't... But please let me think about it for a moment.

SERGEANT: I'd say that it's no use thinking about this sort of thing...

MAMA: But... everyone around also must think he's a cat.

SERGEANT: Must we?

MAMA: Yes... Otherwise he comes to realise that he mightn't be a cat, either.

SERGEANT: I see.

CONSTABLE: What shall we do?

SERGEANT: "What shall we do?" We have no choice. [*To MAMA*] In other words, only in our hearts, we must believe that he's a cat.

MAMA: Yes, that's right. But we really must believe it.

SERGEANT: "Really must believe it"? Err...what do you mean by that?

MAMA: Well, I mean, if you think, "Oh, he really is a cat!" then it'll be fine.

SERGEANT: Ah...I see... [*To THE CONSTABLE*] That's it. So, we only need to think he is really a cat. Only to think would solve the matter, in this case...

CONSTABLE: Am I to think that's a cat?

SERGEANT: "Am I to think that's a cat?"... [*To BAKABON*] So, you're saying that's not an ordinary cat but...um...what kind of a cat did you say?

BAKABON: A wildcat.

SERGEANT: Ah...a wildcat... [*To THE CONSTABLE*] Right? It's a wildcat.

BAKABON: It's an Iriomote cat.[2]

SERGEANT: What did you say?

BAKABON: An Iriomote cat.

SERGEANT: Did you say this is an Iriomote cat?

MAMA: He's doing...a female of it.

SERGEANT: Female? But how can you tell that it's female?

MAMA: He said so himself...

SERGEANT: I see... he said so himself... [*To THE CONSTABLE*] Nevertheless, we don't have to take this so seriously... We only have to believe it in our hearts. [*Looking at his watch*] Oh dear, I'm late. [*To MAMA*] Well, excuse me. [*He is about to leave.*]

CONSTABLE: But, Sergeant...

SERGEANT: Don't worry. It's not the case that needs serious consideration...

PAPA gets tired and rises slowly.

PAPA: Oh dear, I'm exhausted. I didn't think being a cat would be so tiring.

SERGEANT: Hello! Hahahahaha, good afternoon.

PAPA: What?

SERGEANT [*wet-blanketed*]: Err... [*to MAMA*] Is he back to being a person?

MAMA: No, he's still a cat.

SERGEANT: Ah...still a cat. [*To THE CONSTABLE*] Remember that he's still a cat. So...see...it's all right...

CONSTABLE: But Sergeant, please give me a little time. I'm still not clear about something.

PAPA: Oi, you don't believe it, do you?

SERGEANT: Eh? No, that's not true. [*To THE CONSTABLE*] Did you hear that? Just think, "Ah, it's a cat." That'll do...

PAPA: Not that chap.

SERGEANT: Not this chap? Eh? Me? I...no, no, I did think so from the beginning. Well, madam, wasn't that so?

PAPA: Mama, I've grazed here. Have you got any medicine with you?

MAMA: No, I haven't. Why don't you lick it?

PAPA: Lick it?

SERGEANT: Yes. That's a good idea. Spit's got sterilizing power. [*Being given a sharp look by PAPA*] I'm sorry... But honestly, I've been thinking that you might be a cat... [*To BAKABON*] Hey, what cat was it?

BAKABON: An Iriomote Wildcat.

SERGEANT: Yes, an Iriomote Wildcat. And a female. It's true, this isn't flattery or anything like that. [*To THE CONSTABLE*] Really. I'm honest. I was...

PAPA: Bakabon, it's you.

BAKABON: What's me?

PAPA: You aren't thinking I'm a cat, are you?

BAKABON: Yes, I am.

PAPA [*without getting angry*]: No, you aren't.

BAKABON [*in the same way*]: Yes, I am.

PAPA: No, you aren't.

BAKABON: Yes, I am.

PAPA: No, you aren't.

BAKABON: Yes, I am.

PAPA: No, you aren't.

BAKABON: Yes, I am.

SERGEANT: Err...how about..? This is...err...a sort of parents and children's thing, so perhaps it isn't right for me to make any comment on it, but... [*To MAMA*] No, it's not. I mean... [*To PAPA*] I think that...he does think you're a cat... [*To THE CONSTABLE*] Don't you think so? Because he was the first to say so...wasn't he?

CONSTABLE: That's right. He was the first to say so. So, I...I think that he thinks so...

PAPA: No, he doesn't.

BAKABON: Yes, I do.

PAPA: No, you don't.

BAKABON: Yes, I do.

SERGEANT: Wait...wait...don't you see? He thinks so because he says so.

PAPA: OK. Then, how about this? [*Pointing at THE SERGEANT*] You hit this chap with your umbrella.

BAKABON: OK...

PAPA: With all your might, right?

BAKABON: All right.

SERGEANT: Hang on, hang on, hang on, hang on!... Hang on a minute. Will you explain how that follows?

PAPA: Yes, because if he does that, he's thinking...that I'm a cat.

SERGEANT: Oh, no, you...don't... [*To MAMA*] Well, madam, it's not that sort of...don't you think so?

MAMA: No, no, listen. He's saying this. Bakabon's going to hit your backside with his umbrella.

CONSTABLE: With all his might, isn't he?

MAMA: Yes, with all his might.

SERGEANT: But...

MAMA: No, no, just listen, if he does that, Bakabon's thinking my husband is a cat... Don't you understand?

SERGEANT: Yes, I do, but...

CONSTABLE: In other words, Sergeant, they're saying...

SERGEANT: You'd better stop...

CONSTABLE: Please, just let me say one word. Just one word...

SERGEANT: What is it?

CONSTABLE: In other words, they're saying... [*To the three*] You've got to be quiet, right?

SERGEANT: Constable...that sort of manner...

CONSTABLE: Yes, I know. [*To the three*] I'm sorry but please keep quiet for a second, I'm going to explain. In other words, that kid is going to hit the Sergeant's backside with that umbrella...

SERGEANT: I've known all that for some time...

CONSTABLE: No, no, please listen.

BAKABON: With all my might.

CONSTABLE: Yes, with all your might. I've told you to shut your mouth, right? I know exactly what I'm going to say.

MAMA: But, Papa, I wonder if his umbrella won't get broken.

PAPA: Well...

CONSTABLE: Didn't you hear me telling you to shut up? You idiots!

SERGEANT: Constable...

CONSTABLE: Yes, I know. I'm all right. Just let me start... Did you say that the umbrella might get broken?

SERGEANT: Please. What exactly do you want to say? I haven't got much time.

CONSTABLE: Yes, I know. So, what I was saying was...err...what was it?

SERGEANT: Dear me! It's all right now. You see, this isn't that important sort of... Anyway, I must really go now...

CONSTABLE: Ah, Sergeant, I've remembered now. Yes, that's it. In other words, if that kid hits your backside...he's thinking it. Please listen to me, as I think this is the most important point, but if he does not hit your backside...he isn't thinking it.

SERGEANT [*considering for a while*]: What on earth do you mean by that?

CONSTABLE: No, no, in other words, if he is not thinking, he might not hit...

SERGEANT: So?

CONSTABLE: So, what I'm trying to say is...how about asking him?

SERGEANT: Asking him what?

CONSTABLE: Well...whether or not he's going to hit you?

SERGEANT: But...I don't think asking him will make any difference.

CONSTABLE: But I do think it's worth a try.

SERGEANT: Asking that brat?

CONSTABLE: Yes, that brat.

A short silence.

SERGEANT: Are you going to hit me?

BAKABON: Yes...

SERGEANT: He's saying that he'll hit me.

CONSTABLE: Yes, he is. In that case, there's nothing to be done.

SERGEANT: What are you saying? All right. Fine. I understand. So, let's leave this problem for later. If I wasted more of my time on this, I'd really...so...

PAPA: I've got it. Yes, this is it. Listen, Mama, this is the way to do it.

MAMA: What are we going to do?

PAPA: I know what. [*To THE SERGEANT*] Is this right? What's annoying you is that BAKABON's going to hit you.

SERGEANT: Well, yes that is one thing but...

PAPA: I know, I know... So it'd be all right if I hit you in place of Bakabon.

MAMA: Papa's going to hit him?

BAKABON: Why?

CONSTABLE: Don't ask why! Shut up you brat! [*To PAPA*] Well, sorry about it, please continue. [*To THE SERGEANT*] It sounds like some sort of new idea.

SERGEANT: It's not new. You idiot!

PAPA: Well, well, please calm down and listen. Why would it be better for me to hit you? It's because I'm stronger than Bakabon. Do you understand?

SERGEANT: Do I understand? But I don't think...it's not that sort of...but this is...

MAMA: Look...what he's saying is...

SERGEANT: I know. I understood it perfectly well. But please spare me one second...only a second...

CONSTABLE: But, Sergeant...

SERGEANT: Shut up! Keep quiet! Excuse me... Yes, it's that but please spare me a second. Right? Let's...let's think about this calmly. Is this right? Did this gentleman just said that he's stronger?

MAMA: Yes, what he said is true.

SERGEANT: No, no...err...that is so but...why is the stronger person hitting me? Isn't that a bit funny?

CONSTABLE: It's simple because he can hurt you more, Sergeant....

SERGEANT: Hurt me more? Of course, I'd be hurt a lot. But, hurting me more won't...you see, it won't make any...it's not that sort of...what are you thinking? You idiot!

MAMA: Would you rather be hurt more?

SERGEANT: No, I'm not saying that...

PAPA: All right then. See, it's that. In that case Bakabon can do it because this man says so. But for that he must promise to do it with all his might.

MAMA: I agree with you.

CONSTABLE [*to BAKABON*]: Can you do that?

BAKABON: Of course, I can.

CONSTABLE: With all your might?

BAKABON: Don't tell me.

CONSTABLE: Oookey. [*To THE SERGEANT*] Now he's saying that and what shall we do?

SERGEANT [*going weak and collapsing onto the chair*]: Please! Just be quiet...

PAPA: What's the matter with you?

MAMA: Don't worry, Sergeant. Although he's still a small child, he's got the strength...

SERGEANT: I know, madam. Please, hold on a minute. And all of you as well...err... wrong...there's something wrong in this... Just let me think about it...

MAMA: But may I suggest...

CONSTABLE: Can't you hear he said shut up! He is thinking.

SERGEANT: Constable...

CONSTABLE: I know. Don't worry. Please take time. Really, it's all right.

PAPA: Ah, I've got it. Let's do this then. Right? This'll be good.

SERGEANT: Just... Be quiet...won't take long...

A short silence.

MAMA [*to PAPA*]: Isn't that so, dear?

PAPA: What?

MAMA: You thought just now. I wouldn't like that...

PAPA: What?

MAMA: Don't pretend to be innocent. Aren't I right? You thought you'd ask the Sergeant to pull his trousers down when Bakabon hits his backside, didn't you?

PAPA: I never thought of that.

MAMA: Yes, you did. Please don't ask for that... It's not decent.

PAPA: But I never thought that at all.

MAMA: Yes, you did. I know. But I wouldn't agree to it. Asking the Sergeant to pull down his trousers when he's hit his backside... Aren't I right? What do you say?

SERGEANT: But, madam. He said he wasn't thinking of that...

MAMA: But as a matter of fact, he was. He's always like this.

PAPA: I'm not. What are you saying? Honestly, I was not thinking at all. To ask him to pull his trousers down...never...

MAMA: Yes, you were. Why are you lying about it?

PAPA: I'm not lying. [*Seriously to THE SERGEANT*] It's true. I wasn't thinking of it at all.

SERGEANT: Yes, I understand. I do understand.

MAMA: It's a lie.

SERGEANT: But madam. He himself is saying that it's not a lie. Didn't you hear? Just let's stop going on about that sort of. In any case he himself says that he wasn't...so, madam, you mustn't force him to do so...

MAMA: He's always telling lies... I say that I wouldn't like it. I wouldn't know where to look.

SERGEANT: Listen to me, madam. Why don't we drop this? He says himself so...that he wan't thinking of that.

MAMA [*to THE CONSTABLE*]: How about you? Were you thinking of it?

CONSTABLE: Me? No, no, I wasn't. [*To THE SERGEANT*] It's true. Well, I never thought of it at all...never...

SERGEANT [*to MAMA*]: Let's put this matter to one side. See? Nobody was thinking of that sort of thing... And I thought about the problem just now... [*to MAMA*] No, not about that... in other words...why this case has got confused like this?

AUNTIE RERERE comes in sweeping the ground with a broom.

RERERE: Well, what's wrong?

CONSTABLE: Nothing's wrong, madam.

RERERE: But you all look as if something's wrong. Tell me, what's wrong?

PAPA: This Sergeant's just about to let Bakabon hit his backside.

RERERE: That sounds wonderful, Bakabon. And who's next?

PAPA: Next?

RERERE: I mean after Bakabon?

CONSTABLE: No no, madam, there won't be a next person.

RERERE: Why not?

CONSTABLE: Why not? [*Noticing THE SERGEANT who has been collapsed helplessly on the chair.*] Is anything wrong, Sergeant?

SERGEANT: No, I'm fine... Just leave me alone.

MAMA: What's the matter with him?

PAPA: Perhaps he's got stomachache. [*To THE CONSTABLE*] Did he go to the loo this morning?

CONSTABLE: Well, I don't know.

PAPA: Then he must have a fever. [*To THE CONSTABLE*] Did he eat a lot for lunch?

CONSTABLE: I've no idea.

PAPA: He might have a sciatica. [*To THE CONSTABLE*] Does he sometimes burst into singing a song?

CONSTABLE: Not really...

PAPA: Then it's not an ear infection.

SERGEANT: Shut up! Don't you hear me saying shut up?

CONSTABLE [*to all*]: Please be quiet. Please. Won't be long. He's thinking now.

RERERE: Oh! What is he thinking about?

MAMA: We are discussing whether the Sergeant should pull down his trousers or not when Bakabon hits his backside.

SERGEANT: We are not, madam! I told you, how many times do I have to repeat it? That's not the point at all.

CONSTABLE [*stopping THE SERGEANT*]: It's all right, Sergeant. I'll sort this out. Please leave this to me. [*Letting THE SERGEANT sit down*] Yes. [*To all*] It...it won't happen. Do you understand? In other words [*punctuating each word*] The Sergeant will not pull his trousers down. This is the correct answer. Do you know why?

A short silence.

[*Sensing the mood around him*] No... it's not... not that reason, I didn't mean that...

RERERE: I've got it.

PAPA: What?

RERERE: Why the Sergeant won't pull down his trousers.

PAPA: Tell me why.

RERERE: No, I can't say such a thing.

BAKABON: Why not?

RERERE: Keep quiet, you child.

PAPA: You can't say?

RERERE: No, I can't. [*To MAMA*] How can I...

MAMA: Then, you mean...that?

RERERE: Yes, it must be.

MAMA: But.

CONSTABLE: Ummm... I think the reason is that... Err, yours is wrong...that what I think.

SERGEANT: What?

MAMA [*to RERERE*]: You're saying that of that?

RERERE: Yes, Just the same as you're thinking.

MAMA: Oh, dear!

RERERE: See.

PAPA: Eh?

BAKABON: What?

PAPA: I don't know yet.

RERERE [*to MAMA*]: Hmm. [*making a sign with the eye: "Isn't it disgusting?"*]

MAMA: Yes, indeed. [*In the same manner: "It's disgusting."*]

SERGEANT [*involuntarily*]: No. That's not true.

CONSTABLE: No, Sergeant, let me explain about this...

SERGEANT: What? What's going on?

CONSTABLE: They, they say... they know the reason why you won't pull down your trousers.

SERGEANT: So, they're wrong...it's not.

CONSTABLE: Yes, they are, but...

SERGEANT: What are they saying the reason is?

CONSTABLE: Well, I don't really know because they won't say. I could make a guess...but, no, I don't know really.

SERGEANT [*to all*]: You are wrong. Look, it's not that. That means, in other words... [*To RERERE*] You thought that, didn't you?

RERERE: No, not that... [*To MAMA*] I didn't.

MAMA: Of course not. Because it's not the thing like that.

SERGEANT: Then, the other one. [*To RERERE*] You mean that?

PAPA: What?

SERGEANT: You, shut up, please.

RERERE [*to MAMA*]: Did you?

PAPA: Which one?

RERERE: That?

MAMA: Yes…

RERERE: Didn't you?

MAMA: I thought so.

RERERE: I thought so too.

SERGEANT: You are wrong, madam.

CONSTABLE: Hold on, please. I'm lost now.

SERGEANT: Just shut up. Listen to me, madam. You are wrong. What do you think I am? I must say that I'm the sort of person who washes his underwear every day…well, even if you don't mean that, in any case, you are wrong. How could you take me like… I'm not. [*Suddenly noticing something*] Eh? You mean that? You! Never!

A short silence.

SERGEANT: It's a bad joke. Just stop being silly. It can't be. Please stop fooling around. I…I'm wearing proper men's thing. Where the hell you've got that idea?

MAMA: But we only… [*To RERERE*] Yes?

RERERE: Indeed.

SERGEANT: Then what are you trying to say? You'd better stop it… It's like… setting a trap for somebody. What? Then are you saying they've got holes?

CONSTABLE: Please calm down, Sergeant. Don't worry about the holes.

SERGEANT: There aren't any holes. You idiot! What are you talking about? At this right moment I am saying that they haven't got any holes.

CONSTABLE: Yes, you're right. There aren't any holes. I know that.

SERGEANT: Why do you know that?

CONSTABLE: No, no…no, I don't mean that…

PAPA: Oookey. That's fine. That's all just fine. Let's drop this. [*To MAMA and RERERE*] Don't you agree? We'll soon see once he takes his trousers off.

SERGEANT: I won't.

PAPA: Sorry?

SERGEANT: I won't take off my trousers. Bugger! Who said I would. It's not decided yet.

CONSTABLE: It's not.

PAPA: Oh, no, but just now …

SERGEANT: Shut up! You, you'd better stop.

PAPA: Stop? Stop what?

SERGEANT: Stop what? You said, "Oookey. That's fine. That's all just fine." What did you mean by that? Stop mucking about?

PAPA: But, Sergeant.

SERGEANT: Don't... Please move a bit away... All of you, too. See? We must leave some space around here. Don't come any nearer. [*To THE CONSTABLE*] Now, will you be all right?

CONSTABLE: Pardon?

SERGEANT: There's another case to attend as I told you before.

CONSTABLE: Are you off?

SERGEANT: Yes, it's time.

PAPA: Are you off?

SERGEANT: I'm in a hurry.

CONSTABLE: Please wait a minute, Sergeant.

SERGEANT: So …

BAKABON goes to THE CONSTABLE and hits his backside with the handle of the umbrella with all his might.

CONSTABLE: Ugh! [*Out of breath and to BAKABON*] What've you done to me, you little bugger!

SERGEANT: What's the matter?

CONSTABLE: What's the matter? Just now this brat hit me on the backside with that umbrella.

SERGEANT: Why did you do that to him?

BAKABON: I've made a mistake.

CONSTABLE: Made a mistake? [*He is about to grab BAKABON.*]

SERGEANT: Stop it. Just forget it.

CONSTABLE: No, Sergeant, I can't. This is clearly an act of violence.

SERGEANT: Yes, it is. But he's saying he made a mistake.

MAMA: You intended to hit the Sergeant's backside, didn't you, Bakabon?

BAKABON: Yes, I did.

PAPA: Then why did you hit the backside of that chap?

CONSTABLE: That chap?

SERGEANT: Don't! [*To BAKABON*] You say that you hit the wrong person?

In that case there is nothing we can do because he made a mistake. Nothing we could do. [*To THE CONSTABLE*] Did it hurt?

CONSTABLE: Did it hurt? Sergeant, he hit me with the handle of his umbrella crooked like this.

SERGEANT: All right. All right. I understand...just sit down... Gooood. Right? This is the end of it.

RERERE: But I'm next.

SERGEANT: What do you mean by next?

PAPA: She's after Bakabon. She's booked her turn.

SERGEANT: Her turn? What are you talking about?

RERERE [*hotly*]: But I certainly did. When I asked who'd be next, nobody replied, did they?

MAMA: No, we didn't. It's true. But it's not true that we weren't booking our turns. [*To PAPA*] Isn't that right, dear? Weren't we saying how it might be a better idea of you went before Bakabon? Weren't we? The reason is my husband is stronger than Bakabon. And the reason why being stronger is better is that he can hurt more.

SERGEANT: Well, well, madam, please hold on.

MAMA: But we don't mind. We are saying she's the first. And my husband is after her.

SERGEANT: Well, madam, I don't think you've quite understood. I suppose it wasn't like that at all.

PAPA: Won't you let us do it?

RERERE: Stop having me on, Sergeant. Please listen. I definitely did book my turn. And now you say this... really, I feel like I've been made a fool of.

SERGEANT: Made a fool of? No no, madam, don't get so upset. See? It's just a matter of...

PAPA: But, Sergeant...

SERGEANT: All right. All right. Please hold on a minute. Let me...let me have a try...to negotiate with him.

CONSTABLE: Sergeant, what's that to negotiate with him?

SERGEANT: No no, umm...it's nothing to get so upset about.

CONSTABLE: I don't like it. Because, you mean...am I going to be hit?

SERGEANT: Just calm down. There's no other way out. They say that they've booked their turns.

CONSTABLE: Their turns! What are you saying?

SERGEANT: Yes, I know. I've noticed that there's something wrong about it, but...

PAPA: All right. I'll explain it to him.

SERGEANT: No thanks. You've been...really...what are you?

PAPA: What am I? Sorry?

SERGEANT: Fine, it's fine. [*To THE CONSTABLE*] See? We can't get out of this. They've all been looking forward to doing it.

CONSTABLE: But why do I have to be hurt in order to let them enjoy themselves?

SERGEANT: You mustn't say anything likely to upset the public's feelings.

CONSTABLE: But, Sergeant, please think about this carefully. This is somewhat funny.

SERGEANT: Yes, it is. That's true. I've thought all along it's a bit funny, too.

RERERE: Aren't you ready yet?

CONSTABLE: Shut your mouth. What do you mean "ready yet?"

SERGEANT: Calm down! Look, there's no other way in this case...

This time BAKABON hits THE SERGEANT's backside with the handle of his umbrella.

SERGEANT: Ouch! What's the little devil done to me?

CONSTABLE: Calm down, Sergeant.

SERGEANT: No, I won't. Arrest that devil! [*Remembering*] Ouch! It hurts!

PAPA: Bakabon, stop doing that.

BAKABON: I did it again because I made a mistake in the first place.

MAMA: Stop being naughty. Don't you understand it's this auntie's turn now?

RERERE: That's right. It's my turn.

CONSTABLE [*to THE SERGEANT*]: Are you alright?

SERGEANT: No, I'm not. What are you doing? I told you to arrest him, arrest the little devil.

CONSTABLE: Please, Sergeant. It seems rather childish.

MAMA [*to BAKABON*]: Apologise to her.

BAKABON [*to RERERE*]: I'm sorry.

RERERE: It's all right. Your apology doesn't make me happy at all. I feel terribly betrayed.

PAPA: Don't worry. I'll ask the Sergeant for you... Well, Sergeant...did you hear?

SERGEANT: Shut up!

PAPA: Eh?

SERGEANT: I said shut up!

PAPA [*turning back*]: Shut up! Bakabon!

SERGEANT: I mean, you! Idiot!

PAPA: But, I wasn't saying anything. I was only...its because she was...

BAKABON: I wasn't saying anything, either.

PAPA [*to BAKABON*]: Shut up, you fool!

MAMA: It's you who should shut up, Papa.

CONSTABLE [*to RERERE*]: Shut your mouth!

RERERE: I'm not saying anything.

CONSTABLE: I warned you because you were about to say something.

RERERE: Look, I wasn't...nothing...

PAPA: Noisy!

SERGEANT: It's you, you're the noisy bugger.

PAPA: Me? Why me?

SERGEANT: Noisy! Noisy, noisy, noisy, noisy! Shut up! Don't come any closer! Did you hear? Do not come any closer! Are you listening? If you come any nearer than that, I'll scratch you! That means all of you. Don't move. [*To THE CONSTABLE*] Hey, watch that side. Don't let them come any nearer. If they do, scratch them. It's OK.

CONSTABLE: Yes, sir... But how can we scratch them?

SERGEANT: How? Just do it like this and that, that's all. What did they teach you at training school?

WOMAN 1 comes in absent-mindedly.

WOMAN 1: Good afternoon.

SERGEANT: Ah, good afternoon.

WOMAN 1: Is this a police station?

SERGEANT: Yes, it's a police station, but is it urgent?

WOMAN 1: No, not really, but...

SERGEANT: If not, we're terribly sorry, but we're very busy now, so...

CONSTABLE: Shall I take her over, Sergeant?

SERGEANT: It's all right. There's other police station farther on. Would you mind going there?

WOMAN 1: Farther this way?

SERGEANT: Yes, farther this way... Er...rr...

MAMA: Over there. Can you see the post box?

WOMAN 1: Yes.

MAMA: Turn right there and go farther on, you'll see a Tofu shop on the right there... Do you know the Tofu shop?

WOMAN 1: No, I don't.

PAPA: You don't know the Tofu shop?

CONSTABLE: Just wait. The Sergeant's showing her the way now.

RERERE: But this lady doesn't know the Tofu shop.

CONSTABLE: Doesn't matter... Sergeant, please carry on.

SERGEANT: Err...well...umm... All right, then, we'll hear your problem here.

CONSTABLE: Will that be all right?

SERGEANT: It's fine. It's not so busy as all that...

WOMAN 1: I'm sorry.

SERGEANT: No, no, it's OK. Please sit down on this chair. You, get out of her way.

CONSTABLE: I'll do it.

SERGEANT: It's OK. Please sit down.

PAPA: Shall I do that?

SERGEANT: It's OK. What on earth are you saying? Idiot! Who the hell are you?

PAPA: Who am I?

SERGEANT: You're nothing. You've got nothing to do with this... How dare you...that sort of...really, be quiet. Don't bother us... [*To WOMAN 1*] I'm sorry. Err... what can I do for you?

WOMAN 1: As a matter of fact, I have a problem.

SERGEANT: Oh, you have a problem? I see... hum. [*To THE CONSTABLE*] She's got a problem.

CONSTABLE: I see...then it must be, err... you must have a problem.

PAPA: What are you saying? Idiot!

SERGEANT: What?

PAPA [*getting hot*]: This lady's having a hard time. She just said she had a problem...

SERGEANT: Yes, she did. And I said so too that she sounded to have a problem. [*To THE CONSTABLE*] Wasn't that so?

CONSTABLE: Yes, exactly. So ... yes, it was that.

PAPA: Look, can't you see? This lady's in trouble right here, at this moment. Aren't I right?

WOMAN 1: Yes, you are.

PAPA: Did you hear? She says I'm right. See? She's really in big trouble. And what the hell was your reaction?

MAMA: Really...

RERERE: Indeed...

SERGEANT: No, no, please listen. I didn't say that she wasn't in trouble. Just now I said that she'd got a problem...

MAMA: Umm...wouldn't this be the thing to do? She's in trouble at this very moment, isn't she? So how about asking her the reason for it?

RERERE: That's the thing.

PAPA: For, she's in trouble really.

CONSTABLE: That's why we are about to ask her the reason. Just keep your mouth shut, you fool.

MAMA [*to THE SERGEANT*]: Why don't you ask her?

SERGEANT: Why? Look, I'm just thinking about it. What do you mean? Just keep quiet. [*To WOMAN 1*] Err...um...why are you distressed?

WOMAN 1: Yes, the thing is... Do you mind if I smoke?

SERGEANT: No no, not at all. [*To THE CONSTABLE*] Oi, cigarettes.

CONSTABLE: She seems to have her own.

SERGEANT: It's for me.

CONSTABLE: Oh, it's for you... [*taking out a packet of cigarettes and offering*] Here you are.

MAMA: Can I have one as well?

CONSTABLE: Help yourself. [*He offers cigarettes to MAMA.*]

PAPA: Me, too. [*He takes one cigarette.*]

CONSTABLE [*being taken aback*]: ....

RERERE: I'd like to have one as well. [*She takes one cigarette.*]

CONSTABLE [*being taken aback*]: ...

BAKABON: Me, too. [*He takes one cigarette.*]

CONSTABLE [*being taken a back*]: ...

SERGEANT: Oi, light.

CONSTABLE: Yes, sir.

THE CONSTABLE lights THE SERGEANT's cigarette first; then MAMA, PAPA, RERERE and BAKABON come to get light for their cigarettes.

WOMAN 1 [*lighting her cigarette and breathing out the smoke*]: Aaaaa...

SERGEANT [*breathing out the smoke*]: Aaaaa...

MAMA [*breathing out the smoke*]: Aaaaa...

PAPA [*breathing out the smoke*]: Aaaaa...

RERERE [*breathing out the smoke*]: Aaaaa...

BAKABON [*breathing out the smoke*]: Aaaaa...

CONSTABLE [*finally lighting his cigarette and breathing out the smoke*]: Aaaaa...

SERGEANT: Now then... What were we talking about?

WOMAN 1: Pardon?

SERGEANT: Err...

CONSTABLE: Weren't you in trouble?

WOMAN 1: Yes, I was.

MAMA: Why were you in trouble?

SERGEANT: Please, madam... I'll ask her. Err...miss...why were you in trouble?

WOMAN 1: I'm... further down here, around the corner of the tobacconist's...

RERERE: On this side of the post box?

WOMAN 1: Yes, and at the end of the passage, there's a house with a lattice door...

MAMA: The two storyed-house?

WOMAN 1: That's right. The room upstairs...

PAPA: Isn't that the four and half tatami-mattress sized room next to the balcony for drying clothes?

WOMAN 1: Yes, there.

BAKABON: You moved in?

WOMAN 1: Yes.

MAMA: Wasn't that three months ago?

PAPA: The removers were Maruei Removals in the third block.

SERGEANT: Shut up! Hold your tongue! She's the one who's talking now. Excuse me, miss, but will you just tell me the essential points briefly. I'm in a hurry.

WOMAN 1: Yes. And that Maruei is.

SERGEANT: The Maruei Removals in the third block?

WOMAN 1: Yes, them.

SERGEANT [*to THE CONSTABLE*]: Write this down.

CONSTABLE: Yes, sir.

WOMAN 1: No, that Maruei has nothing to do with this.

SERGEANT: It's irrelevant. Cross it out.

CONSTABLE: Yes….

PAPA: Which Maruei is relevant, miss?

BAKABON: I suppose it must be the Maruei in the fourth block.

MAMA: But that's a bakery.

RERERE: The Maruei Bakery?

WOMAN 1: No...

SERGEANT: Didn't you hear me say hold on your bloody tongues?

CONSTABLE: Sergeant, shall I take over?

SERGEANT: It's alright. In other words, you say that no Marueis have anything to do with your problem, don't you?

WOMAN 1: They're irrelevant.

SERGEANT: Not the Maruei Bakery, either?

WOMAN 1: No.

SERGEANT: I see. [*To all*] They're all irrelevant. Right? [*To WOMAN 1*] Now you can start. I mean, just the relevant details...

WOMAN 1: Well, it was that Marusei...

SERGEANT [*to THE CONSTABLE*]: Would you please take over?

CONSTABLE: Yes, Sergeant. The Maruei you mentioned is the Maruei Removals Service in the third block, isn't it?

WOMAN 1: Yes, it is.

SERGEANT: But, Miss, you said it was...

CONSTABLE: Please leave it to me, Sergeant. [*To WOMAN 1*] I'll take over. Ummm... shall I take off my shoes? Yes, I think I will. Let's do that. [*He takes off his shoes.*]

SERGEANT: What on earth are you doing?

CONSTABLE: Please take it easy. I've only taken off my shoes. And, what did Maruei do to you?

WOMAN 1: Yes, the thing is, I asked them to carry my bed when I moved in...

RERERE: It's a big bed.

BAKABON: They couldn't bring it through the front door.

CONSTABLE: Is that so?

WOMAN 1: Yes...

PAPA: I've got it. They pulled it up to the balcony.

MAMA: So, your bed is still on the balcony, isn't it?

WOMAN 1: No, it isn't.

SERGEANT: Just listen to me. Right? All of you, keep quiet!

CONSTABLE: And? So, where's your bed?

WOMAN 1: I asked them to put it by the window in the four and a half tatami mattress-sized room.

CONSTABLE: I see. Things are becoming clear, Sergeant. [*Feeling his belt*] Shall I take this off? Yes, let's do that. [*He unfastens his belt with the attached pistol.*]

SERGEANT: Hey...

CONSTABLE: It's quite all right, Sergeant. I'm just psyching myself up. Right, let's move to the next stage. What happened after that?

WOMAN 1: After that I've been sleeping by the window.

CONSTABLE: Still now?

WOMAN 1: Yes.

A short silence.

MAMA: She might catch a cold.

PAPA: It'll be all right...umm...if she shuts the window.

A short silence.

SERGEANT: And... what happened to that... that Removals Service... err... Maruei?

WOMAN 1: I told you that it was irrelevant.

SERGEANT: Ah...it's irrelevant. I thought so. It's irrelevant...?

A short silence.

CONSTABLE: And?

WOMAN 1: Yes... One night I happened to look outside.

CONSTABLE: You happened to look outside. Well, I expected that that was what had happened.

WOMAN 1: I was horrified.

RERERE: Horrified?

WOMAN 1: Yes, someone was watching me.

CONSTABLE: I see. Things are becoming much clearer, Sergeant. Will you please hold on a moment. I'll take off my jacket.

SERGEANT: Stop it. What are you doing, Constable?

CONSTABLE: No, no, please leave this to me. I'm only taking off my jacket.

SERGEANT: Yes, but I think you don't have to take your jacket off, particularly...

CONSTABLE: Never mind. Please take it easy. So? Somebody was looking at you? Who was that man?

WOMAN 1: No, it wasn't a man but a woman.

CONSTABLE: A woman? Did you hear that, Sergeant? It was a woman. Hang on. I'll take my shirt off now...

SERGEANT: I told you to stop it. What the hell are you doing?

CONSTABLE: What the hell am I doing? I'm only taking off my shirt.

SERGEANT: Don't take your bloody shirt off. Idiot!

CONSTABLE: Why not?

SERGEANT: Don't say why not.

CONSTABLE: Why does it matter? It's only a shirt.

PAPA: In that case, I'll take off my shirt, too.

MAMA: You'd better not.

PAPA: Why not?

MAMA: Because if you take your shirt off, you'll have nothing on.

PAPA: Yes, I'll have nothing on. But this bobby won't have anything on either, will he?

CONSTABLE: You'd better not.

PAPA: Why not?

CONSTABLE: You don't need to take off your shirt at all.

PAPA: But you took off your shirt.

RERERE: Yes, you did.

CONSTABLE: In my case I'm... What are you saying? I, I simply took off my shirt. That's all.

PAPA: I'll simply take off my shirt, too. That's all.

SERGEANT: Listen to me, Constable...

CONSTABLE: Please wait a minute, Sergeant. This is a very important point... You bugger, you've got to listen. There's no need for you to take off your shirt. Do you understand? So, don't take off your shirt when there is no need.

MAMA: Although you talk about need, he's simply taking off his shirt.

CONSTABLE: Simply taking off? What are you saying, madam? It's not simply taking off a shirt, but this is...

SERGEANT: All right. It's all right. All of you, too. This isn't what we are doing now.

RERERE: But, Sergeant, I think it's not fair that this person is allowed to take off his shirt and that person isn't.

WOMAN 1: Then, how about...?

CONSTABLE: Keep quiet! Sorry. Please hold on a second. [*To RERERE*] It's not fair. What's not fair? Look, I'm a... whatever you might say, a policeman and whilst... [*to PAPA*] what are you?

SERGEANT: You mustn't!

PAPA: What am I?

CONSTABLE: Just one of the common people.

MAMA: But my husband simply wants to take off his shirt. Isn't it so?

PAPA: Yes, it is. I mean... I, I only want to try taking off my shirt.

RERERE: That's it. Since he wants to take his shirt off, I think he should be allowed to do so.

CONSTABLE: What should we do, Sergeant?

SERGEANT: What should we do?... It doesn't matter... it's... What on earth are all of you doing?

CONSTABLE: Are you sure?

SERGEANT: Just leave it on one side. [*To WOMAN 1*] I'm sorry to keep you waiting.

MAMA: It's all right, you can take it off...

PAPA: Can I? [*He is about to take his shirt off.*]

BAKABON: Then, I'll take off my shirt, too.

MAMA: You'd better not.

BAKABON: Why not?

PAPA: Don't say why not, idiot!

RERERE: You're only a child.

BAKABON: But why not me as everybody else is going to take off their shirts?

CONSTABLE: No, you can't. See? Such a fuss! Let's stop. [*To PAPA*] You, stop it, too.

MAMA: But the Sergeant said that it's OK.

CONSTABLE [*grabbing PAPA who is taking off his shirt*]: I told you to stop it.

SERGEANT: Don't! You idiot!

CONSTABLE: But, Sergeant.

SERGEANT: Be quiet!

WOMAN 1: Umm...then how about doing this?

SERGEANT: Now, now, doesn't matter. Let's continue with your story. A woman was staring at you, was she?

WOMAN 1: Yes, she was. But... there's something I've just realised about it...

MAMA: What is it?

SERGEANT: No, it's all right. Let's leave it. And is it every day that the woman stares at you?

WOMAN 1: Yes, every day. That's why I began to get nervous.

SERGEANT: You would do if it happens every day.

WOMAN 1: And what's more...if she were an ordinary woman, it'd be better but...

CONSTABLE: Isn't she ordinary?

WOMAN 1: No. She's fat, very fat.

SERGEANT: Fat?

WOMAN 1: Yes, she is. It's already disgusting enough, being fat... It is very unexpected thing for me.

SERGEANT [*looking around anxiously*]: Yes, indeed...

PAPA: Even so, I'll take off my shirt.

CONSTABLE: I told you to stop it, you bugger!

PAPA: Leave me alone. This once I really must do it...

CONSTABLE: Shut up! Stop it! You idiot! [*He immobilises PAPA.*]

BAKABON: Stop this violence! [*He hits THE CONSTABLE with his umbrella.*]

CONSTABLE: You cheeky devil! [*He gets up.*]

RERERE: You, stop it! [*She hits THE CONSTABLE with her broom.*]

SERGEANT: I warned you not to carry on with this. [*He immobilises THE CONSTABLE.*]

MAMA: Stop it!

WOMAN 1: Now look, so, how about this? This is my idea...

SERGEANT: Just...you better keep out of this.

WOMAN 1: Please, I've been thinking about it. Since you took off your jacket, I think it's natural that this gentleman should take off his jacket as well.

MAMA: Yes, that's right.

CONSTABLE: But miss, then, how about me? What's going to happen to me?

WOMAN 1: Yes, so, you can take your trousers off as well.

CONSTABLE: Take my trousers off as well... Yes, that sounds good.

MAMA: My husband can only take off his jacket?

WOMAN 1: Yes, you've got to accept it.

PAPA: Why?

CONSTABLE: Why? That's the way it is. Now then, let's do it...

PAPA: Hang on! If this bobby's taking off his trousers, I want to, too.

RERERE: It's a matter of course.

CONSTABLE: It's not a matter of course at all. What are you saying? [*To PAPA*] You're allowed to take off your jacket. Isn't that enough?

RERERE: But you're going to take off your trousers, aren't you?

CONSTABLE: Yes, I am. Look, there's nothing you can do about it. We've reached this conclusion. Didn't you hear her? She's just explained it.

MAMA: In that case, dear, how about being allowed to drop your trousers half-way?

PAPA: Half-way?

MAMA: Are you happy about that?

CONSTABLE: No, no, it's not allowed. No trousers, it's the same whether you drop them all or half-way. At any rate, do you follow me? As this lady said just now, it's only me who's allowed to drop his trousers.

SERGEANT: Enough is that, idiot!

CONSTABLE: No, no, Sergeant, I can't compromise on this matter. He's going to take off his shirt, so please allow me to drop my trousers, otherwise I'll lose face.

SERGEANT: Shut up! Shut up! Shut your mouth, you fool! [*He grabs the pistol on the desk.*] Keep your hands off your trousers. Don't drop them. If you do, I'll shoot you. [*To PAPA*] You, too. Don't move.

CONSTABLE [*astonished*]: What's the matter, Sergeant?

SERGEANT: Nothing the matter... I warned you, don't move!

PAPA: But we're only talking about dropping our trousers.

SERGEANT: You mustn't drop them, you blooming fool!

WOMAN 1: Then, how about this? Seargent, how about you too can drop only your trousers?

SERGEANT: Shut up! Fool! What the hell is all this about? Do you hear? You are all damn fools. Really...you're hopelessly stupid... You must really... [*He squats down holding his head.*]

There's a MAN's voice saying, "Excuse me. Excuse me," somewhere around. We see a hand sticking out of the hole in the wall of the public toilet. The hand is searching for a toilet-roll hung outside. All the people watch it absentmindedly.

MAN [*Voice off*]: Excuse me...excuse me. Is anybody there? Will you please... excuse me... I can't reach the loo-paper... Is anybody there?

WOMAN 2 enters absentmindedly, looks around the people wonderingly, and then hears MAN's voice and approaches the toilet wall.

WOMAN 2: Yes?

MAN: Er, sorry about this. Will you...please let me have the loo-paper?

WOMAN 2: Ah, you mean this. [*She helps MAN's hand get hold of the end of the loo-paper.*]

MAN: Thanks a lot. That was a big help.

WOMAN 2: How is it over there?

MAN: Eh? Umm...it's boring.

WOMAN 2: I see...

MAN: Will you please cut the paper?

WOMAN 2 [*cutting the paper*]: Is it OK here?

MAN: Yes, fine.

WOMAN 2: Was it enough?

MAN: Yes, that's enough.

WOMAN 2: Well, then, sayonana.

MAN: Sayonara. Arigato, thank you...

WOMAN 2 stares at the people once again and goes off absentmindedly. The sound of flushing water.

SERGEANT [*blankly*]: What's that?

CONSTABLE: What?

SERGEANT: The thing on the wall.

CONSTABLE: Maybe the loo-paper.

SERGEANT: Why is it hung there?

CONSTABLE: I have no idea, Sergeant.

The MAN slowly comes out of the public toilet.

MAN [*stretching his muscles*]: Aaaaaa... Damn it! I'm exhausted.

The MAN slowly goes off.

CONSTABLE [*noticing*]: Sergeant, are you all right?

SERGEANT: Yes, I'm fine. [*Standing up*] All right. Listen, everybody. Let's be normal. Just be normal... [*To THE CONSTABLE*] Don't you agree? There's nothing out of the ordinary here, if you think about it. [*Sitting down on the chair and to WOMAN 1*] So, what did you do?

WOMAN 1: Yes, so I think I'm going to put cyanide in her breakfast.

SERGEANT: Err...just hold on. Whose breakfast is that? Umm...her...who's she?

WOMAN 1: So, it's the woman...

CONSTABLE: Staring at you through the window?

WOMAN 1: Yes.

SERGEANT: Of course... Eh? But...it'd kill her if you did that, wouldn't it?

WOMAN 1: Yes, I suppose it would.

SERGEANT: Well, but I think... [*He anxiously looks around the people*] If she were killed, it wouldn't be a good idea, at any rate...

CONSTABLE [*unconfidently*]: Yes, I suppose so...although it could be said there's an unavoidable circumstance...

SERGEANT [*reacting absentmindedly*]: No, no, even so... [*To WOMAN 1*] If she were...if the woman were killed… Then, what would happen?

WOMAN 1: If it did happen, I think she wouldn't be able to watch me...

SERGEANT: She wouldn't be able to watch... Yes, of course, she wouldn't. Because she'd be dead... [*To THE CONSTABLE*] Even so...that's not the point... Let's, let's think about it calmly.

MAMA: Where can you get cyanide... I mean that's the point, isn't it?

WOMAN 1: No, it isn't. I've already got it.

SERGEANT: She's already got it... So, all of you, just be quiet…

RERERE: She might notice cyanide and throw it out when she ate her breakfast. That'd be the thing, wouldn't it?

PAPA: I think putting it in her breakfast could be a mistake. I would put it in her dinner, it'd be much...

SERGEANT: Keep quiet! What are you saying? It's obvious that in her breakfast is better. Because it works better... No, I didn't mean that... [*To WOMAN 1*] There's a kind of problem... err...in your plan... Ummm...

BAKABON: Strangling her might be better. If we go up to her quietly from behind and choke her with a stocking, she'll be killed easily.

CONSTABLE: I see, it might be better?

MAMA: But she's already got cyanide...

SERGEANT: Shut up! Keep quiet! [*To WOMAN 1*] Listen carefully, if, if she were killed...

WOMAN 1: Yes...

CONSTABLE: You've said that already.

SERGEANT: Have I? Yes, I have.

BAKABON: How about setting fire to her house? Secretly...when she's asleep...

MAMA: Stop that, Bakabon. I told you just now that she'd waste her poison if she did it that way.

PAPA: I've got it. How about this? The left-over cyanide... [*To WOMAN 1*] Do you have it with you now?

WOMAN 1: Yes, I do... [*She takes a small packet out of her hand bag.*]

PAPA [*receiving it*]: So ... how about sharing it with all of us and taking it?

RERERE: But if we do that, I'm afraid that all of us would be killed.

PAPA: What's wrong with that? Don't you like it? I think everybody would be surprised if we died here.

MAMA: Would they?

PAPA: They should be. Think, everybody here would be dead.

CONSTABLE: Hang on! That's her personal property.

WOMAN 1: I don't mind giving it away, as it's left-over.

PAPA: See? As it's left-over...

CONSTABLE: Well, since she says so, it's fine. But you must divide it evenly.

PAPA: Yes, I know that... Has anyone got paper or anything like that?

WOMAN 1: I've got some wafers... [*She takes wafers out of her hand bag and gives them to PAPA.*]

CONSTABLE: Ah, they'll do. Let's use them. Sergeant, Sergeant... are you all right? Don't worry... I'll keep yours, too.

RERERE [*to BAKABON*]: Bakabon, don't breathe so heavily. Or the wafers will be blown away.

MAMA: Shall I do it?

PAPA: It's all right... [*He divides up cyanide to the wafers of the number of the people on the desk.*]

WOMAN 1: I wonder what it tastes like?

PAPA: It tastes sour.

RERERE: Does it?

MAMA: If you put that much on those ones, there might not be enough for these ones?

PAPA: I see...

CONSTABLE [*to BAKABON*]: You brat, what are you doing?

BAKABON [*bringing his nose closer to cyanide*]: I'm smelling it.

MAMA: I don't think it's nice to smell it, Bakabon.

RERERE: What did it smell like?

BAKABON: Umm...it smelt like...

CONSTABLE: Well, please... Right? We must calm down a bit.

PAPA: How is this? I think it's even.

WOMAN 1: Don't you think this one has less?

CONSTABLE: It looks fine to me. But this one seems to have less.

PAPA: Which one?

WOMAN 1: But I think my one's still got less.

PAPA: No, it's because yours is lumpy.

WOMAN 1: I'm not happy about it. Remember that all of it is originally mine.

CONSTABLE: Well, well, please calm down. I'm sure this can kill you. It's quite
    enough.

SERGEANT: Please listen to me, in case she were killed...

CONSTABLE: It's alright, Sergeant. We've already been through that...

SERGEANT: Ah, we've been through it already...

MAMA: Darling, mine's less too.

PAPA: No, it's not.

MAMA: Yes, it is, see? I don't want to die unfairly no matter how I'm going to
    die in the end.

PAPA: All right. Then I'll swap mine for yours.

WOMAN 1: Oh, in that case, I want someone to change theirs to mine, too.

RERERE: Don't worry. Yours isn't so different.

MAMA: But do you know that yours is the biggest?

RERERE: It's not. It's because you are looking from that side. If you look from
    this side... [*To THE CONSTABLE*] Is it?

CONSTABLE [*to WOMAN 1*]: I'll swap mine for yours...

WOMAN 1: Oh, how kind! Thank you so much.

MAMA: But I think yours has got more than his if you compare the two.

WOMAN 1: You're right. Then I'm OK.

CONSTABLE: Eh? But...are you OK?... [*To RERERE*] Shall I change mine for
    yours?

RERERE: No thank you.

CONSTABLE [*to PAPA*]: How about you?

PAPA: I'm fine. It doesn't matter.

MAMA [*to THE CONSTABLE*]: I think yours is the smallest.

CONSTABLE: Is that so? But in that case... I suppose it won't be any good...

WOMAN 1: I think that you'll be all right...that must be enough...

BAKABON: Can I die now?

CONSTABLE: Not yet, you fool. We're going to die at the same time when we hear one, two, three, go. Look, this is still no good. It's obvious that mine is the smallest.

PAPA [*to RERERE*]: Why don't you give him a bit of yours?

RERERE: No, I won't. I don't think mine is as big as everybody else thinks.

MAMA: Bakabon, stop sucking your fingers. Don't you see it's dangerous?

CONSTABLE: Please understand. I'm the biggest person here...

PAPA: So what?

CONSTABLE: So I should eat the biggest portion shouldn't I?

WOMAN 1: I wonder if less might work quicker...

CONSTABLE: What are you saying?

BAKABON: Let's die soon.

CONSTABLE: Shut up! Look! How about drawing lots? I think that it'd be fairer.

PAPA: No, we don't need that.

RERERE: It'd be a lot of trouble...now.

MAMA [*blowing nose*]: Dear, some's got up my nose.

PAPA: Don't worry! You'll die when you take it.

CONSTABLE: What will you do if I don't?

PAPA: What?

CONSTABLE: If I don't, remember, it'll be all your fault.

PAPA: That'll be fine.

CONSTABLE: Gooood! Remember that! Damn it! [*To BAKABON*] Not yet, I told you, you cheeky monkey! Are you ready? I'm going to give you the cue. One, two, three.

All of them put their packet in their mouths. For a second they look at one another and die suddenly. Only THE SERGEANT sits at the desk and keeps still.

WOMAN 2 and MAN come in.

MAN: What happened?

SERGEANT: Well, I don't know what happened to them at all.

WOMAN 2: Are they all dead?

SERGEANT: Yes, they've gone. Are you surprised?

WOMAN 2: No, not really.

SERGEANT: Aren't you? But they expected people to be very surprised.

MAN: Sayonana...
WOMAN 2: Sayonana...
SERGEANT: Aaa... Sayonana...

MAN and WOMAN 2 go off. THE SERGEANT keeps still. Soon the song of BAGABON's PAPA, "This is the way" (3) *is going to be heard from a distance. All the dead people slowly stand up and dance gracefully around THE SERGEANT who is sitting still.*

END

I am grateful to the comic-book writer Mr. Fujio Akatsuka for letting me use the title and the characters from his comics. (4)

Notes: ———————————————————————

(1)   Japanese wooden sandals
(2)   Iriomote cat (*Iriomote yamaneko*): One of the species of animals designated for special protection, inhabit only on the Iriomote Island of Okinawa prefecture, the south-ern-west Islands in Japan.
(3)   *Korede iinoda*: the song from the TV animation.
(4)   An acknowledgement by Minoru Betsuyaku

[III]

A Corpse with Feet

About the Play

A Corpse with Feet was first staged by Snail, in June 1981. It was not included in the original plan to be translated and staged for this research. I had thought that the other three plays, ***The Kangaroo, I am the Father of the Genius Idiot Bakabon*** and ***The Story of the Two Knights Travelling Around the Country***, would together adequately show the various features and aspects of the different phases of Betsuyaku's work. However, I found that the more I studied Betsuyaku's work, the more significant I felt his two-handers (see Chapter Two [II] (3)) were, and the more fascinated I became by them. I then decided that it was important to include one in my project.

Betsuyaku rarely introduces any element of romantic love into his plays, except in the two-handers. But in these plays he looks at society through the eyes of a man-woman relationship; the characters are always 'THE MAN' and 'THE WOMAN,' Betsuyaku employs these two people as the smallest grouping in society which reflects the whole society.

Style and Structure

The play consists of one scene only, lasting about half an hour. All the events take place in front of a railway crossing which is built Down Stage Centre and is supposed to be on a road somewhere on the outskirts of a city. The characters are a respectable looking Woman and Man in their late twenties, thirties, forties or more - in other words, ordinary people who could be found anywhere in Japan.

The time of day laid down for the play is "at night," which makes an interesting contrast with Bakabon in which Betsuyaku used bright daylight. Betsuyaku at one time liked to use "the evening when disguises are stripped off and things show their real forms." [1] In this play THE WOMAN says that the neighbours of her dead lover will have gone to bed when she and THE MAN get to the lover's house, so the play must be set sometime between the evening meal and bedtime, a time when people are released from their daily work and are resting at home surrounded by their families. These are the hours when people need company, and THE WOMAN is delivering the corpse of her lover to his legitimate wife and son just at this time of day.

THE WOMAN has lived with her lover for the last five years, and until three days ago believed what he had been telling her, that he did not want their relationship made official because "...he didn't believe in that sort of conventional custom" (CORPSE p.221, l.8-7). But her lover was already married, had bought a small house and lived happily with his wife and three-year-old son. This was his other life, the sort which brings to ordinary people their ordinary happiness in a very "conventional" way, if we may borrow his expression:

> THE WOMAN: You'll see hundreds of matchbox houses just after the factory. The thirteenth house from this end, the smallest one, is his. They haven't paid off the mortgage for the house, but they have a small flower bed just next to the front door and...(CORPSE p.222, l.5-8).

So, her lover had led a double life, the free relationship with THE WOMAN and the orthodox marriage with his legitimate wife - and in a way so had THE WOMAN, although it was not so much a double life as one with double principles. THE WOMAN was not liberated enough and independent enough to live in a free relationship. On the contrary, she strongly wished to have a registered marriage. However, she had to accept the conditions imposed by her lover because there seemed nothing unreasonable if she could just throw off her conservativeness and persuade herself that she was living a life of true love and happiness, free from the old conventional society. And she had pushed herself on into this liberated world even though there had always been some shadow haunting her life, until all the facts were revealed.

Now THE WOMAN's resentment is deep. She had been intrigued by the idea of a new sort of man-woman relationship without ever being convinced by it. The information she was receiving from television, magazines or newspapers gave approval to this new concept of relationships and ill prepared her to argue with her lover about getting their marriage registered. And it was this that Mr. Kimura, her dead lover, used as a weapon to get his own way and to keep his secret hidden. It is very ironic that the thoughts which are supposed to be freeing them from an empty marriage are used by Mr. Kimura to keep his own unfaithful marriage going. Of course, situations like this can often be misunderstood or unethically manipulated on the practical level. But since in Japan, even more than in some Western countries, people tend to pay more respect to the traditional style of marriage, THE WOMAN's feelings of betrayal appear more valid, while Mr. Kimura's attitude seems like selfishness masquerading under the name of freedom.

Despite the tragic climate surrounding her, THE WOMAN does not appear to bear a mood of mourning or depression as she comes on stage at the beginning. It looks as if she were acting normally in a very ordinary situation. In the play it is not made clear whether Mr. Kimura has been killed by THE WOMAN, has died in an accident, or has committed suicide because of feelings of guilt. So we do not know how THE WOMAN is feeling beneath her determination to deliver the corpse to its widow. However, we may legitimately suppose that, subconsciously, she feels that somehow this action will bring her closer to her dead lover. The only way left for her to see him again is to meet the people who know him. She does not admit to her desolation and confusion, but she desperately needs someone to be with or to talk to about her nightmarish experience. Actually, she does express her feelings in a strange impassive way by living out the peculiar logic through which she looks at the recent events in a way convenient and comfortable for her. Her plan of delivering the corpse to its widow will be extremely embarrassing and cruel to the wife if it is carried out as she intends. But however malicious she maybe, we still tend to follow her logic and begin to believe in its soundness as she explains it all in the terms of her own special reasoning.

In *A Corpse with Feet*, it is THE WOMAN who embodies in her actions the logic of Betsuyaku's absurdity. She examines the problems, analyses them, and finds ways to solve them. The logic of her reasoning generally sounds plausible, although at times we cannot help having some doubts about it. The episode in which she makes a phone call to the Ministry of Transport is a good example of this (CORPSE p.220, l.23-35). She is correct that the Ministry of Transport is supposed to sort out the problems of public transportation and that if nobody keeps an eye on one's belonging in the street, somebody might steal them - we can follow her happily this far. However, the problem of the level crossing is not big enough to receive attention from the Ministry of Transport, and nobody is going to want to steal a corpse. This discontinuity in logic, the short distance between seriousness and nonsense or, perhaps, madness, is a fascinating part of Betsuyaku's absurdism. It is developed so cunningly that we sometimes go along with his logic for a while and only later realise its invalidity. The to-and-fro journeys between the absurd world and the real world confuse us and may eventually liberate us into another world where things show their true forms free from whatever we have been taught to believe by our own education and society. This is one of the fundamental techniques of Betsuyaku's playwrighting.

THE MAN's role as the secondary character is to keep living by the logic of the ordinary world, which will unfortunately end up by failing him. He is a representative of the ordinary people who believe that things will happen in a certain predictable way. He is a good-natured man who has the generosity and kindness to deliver a gift from a friend's wedding to another friend who did not attend the ceremony. However, this is the first step that will lead ultimately towards his death. It is bad luck that he should have come across his friend's mistress with Mr. Kimura's corpse, about whom he himself has been gossiping, on her way to Mr. Kimura's house. This funny, sad or cruel coincidence forms the basis of connection between THE WOMAN and THE MAN, and it creates the element of black humour in the play. As if he has been trapped in a dune like an ant, he gradually loses his power of reasoning and is overwhelmed more and more by THE WOMAN's mentality, until he cannot leave her alone with the corpse and he is finally killed by the train.

There was no obligation for him to help THE WOMAN with carrying the corpse at all. He ought to have pitied THE WOMAN in her distress, but he could have been sympathetic and helpful without sacrificing his life. What is it then which made him feel tied by the obligation? Could the reason simply be that THE MAN is good-natured unlike Mr. Kimura, and easily responds to a request for help? There is a point at which THE WOMAN blackmails THE MAN by quoting Mr. Kimura's unfortunate widow. (CORPSE p.218, l.18-26) THE MAN does not want to be thought of as unkind and cold-hearted by THE WOMAN or by Mr. Kimura's widow and other of their mutual friends and acquaintances, and so he cannot refuse to help. This is a glimpse of the attitude often seen among the Japanese, which wants to avoid expressing one's opinion straightforwardly. This is another reason why THE MAN could not ignore THE WOMAN's plea: out of consideration for the other person, he will not give a clear sense of agreeing or disagreeing. Usually this vagueness, this very polite way of saying 'yes' or 'no', is understood correctly using common sense. The Japanese language works efficiently in the same way that other languages do once its nature is understood. But THE WOMAN, exceptionally, does not respect the usual rules, and THE MAN, who retains his polite behaviour most of the time, is at first embarrassed, then puzzled, and soon very confused by her perverse misunderstanding of his replies.

It is in THE WOMAN's role that Betsuyaku expresses his criticism of the ambiguities of Japanese language. He views the problems from an unusual angle, as THE WOMAN does, and uncovers their bare bones. It is of the essence of Betsuyaku's humour that his audience is kept in fits of laughter by the characters' unexpected responses while at the same time being led round to a critical viewpoint. We tend to look at the play as a story of a crazy woman trying to get a passer-by's help and killing him, and we mock the poor man and laugh at him. Nevertheless, the subject matter of the play is profound and nothing like that of the slap-stick type of black comedy. The play depicts well the position which Japanese women hold in society. When THE WOMAN claims to be acting out of "true kindness" (CORPSE p.218, l.32), it is vindictiveness which motivates her, and it is a feeling of isolation and of revenge towards the opposite sex which makes her draw THE MAN's attention to her private life. If THE WOMAN could feel herself independent and perfected as a whole person as many feminists do, she would not get jealous about the registered marriage, and would, on the contrary, feel genuinely sorry for the betrayed wife and her shameless husband. But Betsuyaku sees that Japanese women in the early nineteen-eighties could not feel about themselves in this way. And, sad to say, despite noticeable progress in improving their status in society, women's emotional situation and their wishes and dreams do not seem to have changed much since that time.

Things absent in British Culture

There are references to things which are found in Japan and not in the UK, but their role is important since they are the direct means by which the Japanese cultural background is conveyed to an audience. In this section I shall pick out these things and explain their significance.

(a) Objects
∗ Futon bag (*futon bukuro*)
   A big sack in which a futon is kept.
∗ A gift from the wedding in a bundle (*kekkonshiki no hikidemono*)

A sea bream or a crane and a tortoise - all three creatures are symbols of good luck in Japan - made of sugar, a piece of the wedding cake and any small present such as a pretty vase, cups etc. usually make up the bundle. Giving gifts to the wedding guests is a traditional custom in Japan.

(b) Situation

* A traffic barrier at a train level crossing (*fumikiri no yokobo*)

The private train companies, as well as Japanese National Railways, (which was privatised in 1987), run their commuter services into the major cities through the suburbs. The train network is very efficient and convenient, but on the other hand it causes traffic jams where cars must cross the tracks at a traffic barrier. The sight of a queue of cars at a level crossing is familiar in and near the big cities in Japan. Japanese audience can sympathise with the characters.

(c) Houses

* Hundreds of matchbox houses (*tateurijutaku ga gisshiri narabu*)

The literal translation is 'the ready-built houses stand closely together.' Such houses are usually rather small and collected in large estates, so I chose the phrase, 'a matchbox house' to give a clear visual image. THE WOMAN's description of the dead lover's house and its location also tells us the shape of the town and whereabouts in it she herself lives. Perhaps she lives in a flat in the old district which is located on the other side of the town. In the newly expanded outskirt of the town there are hundreds of ready-built houses and this is where the young families tend to live.

(d) Delivery service

* Kuroneko Yamato's Home Delivery Service (*Kuroneko Yamato no Takkyubin*)

Yamato Transport Corporation: *Kuroneko Yamato* is one of the delivery service companies in Japan. It was the first company to start this sort of service by which the parcels are delivered within a day or two to the most of the places in the country. Their service continues even on Sundays and the national holidays, so the companies offer a better and faster service than the post office on this account. The local rice shops, the off licences and convenient shops take in parcels from customers and the company vans deliver them all over Japan. This is another very common element of Japanese everyday life. The company started playing a commercial song on the radio in 1979. The phrase THE WOM-

AN is singing in the play is a jingle in television and radio advertisements.

(e) Proper nouns
∗ Mr. Kinoshita, Mr. Kimura (*Kinoshita, Kimura*)

The former is the false name which the corpse used and the latter is his true name. Both are common Japanese surnames.

(f)
∗ A sense of humour like this can oil the wheels of our dry everyday life...
(*Koshita yumoa to iumono ga susanda seikatsuni uruoi o motarashi...*) (CORPSE p.222, l.24-25).

The literal translation is that 'humour can moisten our dry everyday life.' As this proverb does not work in English, and so instead I used 'to oil the wheels of.'

(g) Gesture - Body language
THE MAN: ...*(raising the little finger of his left hand hesitantly)*... he seemed to have got a girlfriend lately. (CORPSE p.216, l.10)

This is a common gesture to imply a girlfriend, and the thumb is used for a boyfriend. These gestures are used when people are talking about girlfriends and boyfriends in front of other people. It implies the secretiveness of the talk. The Japanese word for girlfriend used here is '*kore.*' THE WOMAN did not know what a little finger meant, but it is very rare for anyone not to understand the meaning of this gesture.

Notes: ————————————————————————————

(1) Minoru Betsuyaku, 'Why the evening?' in *The Space with an Electricity Pole (Denshin-bashira no Aru Uchū)*, pp.67-69, Tokyo: Hakusuisha, 1980.

A Corpse with Feet
Stage photo by Christopher Jowett
the Woman and the Man

A Corpse with Feet
Stage photo by Christopher Jowett
the Woman

A CORPSE WITH FEET

By

Minoru Betsuyaku

Translated by Masako Yuasa

The original text for the translation is from *Collected Plays of Minoru Betsuyaku (Vol.10): A Corpse with Feet/ The Meeting (Ashi no Aru Shitai/Kaigi Betsuyaku Minoru Gikyoku Shū, pp.5-42)*, Tokyo, Sanichi Shobo, 1982.
©1982 Minoru Betsuyaku

CHARACTERS

THE MAN
THE WOMAN

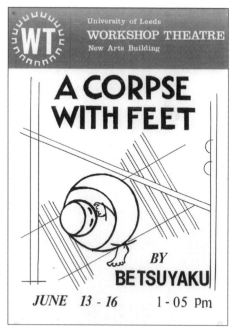

Performance Poster (Leeds in June 1989)
Illustration by Kitty Burrows

*The staging of A **Corpse with Feet**,* took place in the Workshop Theatre at lunchtime on the 12th to the 16th of June, 1989. By chance the members of the crew were all women, although a few male colleagues gave us advice.

The cast and the technical staff for the first English production of *A **Corpse with Feet*** in the Workshop Theatre in 1989:

    CAST
The Woman   Masako Yuasa
The Man   Mine Kaylan

    TECHNICAL STAFF
Director   Masako Yuasa
Stage Manager   Tanya Lees
Design   Masako Yuasa
Lighting   Chiaki Yamase
Sound   Chiaki Yamase, Tany Lees
Costume   Kitty Burrows

At night. In front of a unmanned level-crossing at the edge of a town. There is a shabby bench.
THE WOMAN enters dragging a big object in a futon bag. Two bare feet stick out of the bottom of the bag. When THE WOMAN reaches the level-crossing, the warning-bell suddenly starts ringing and the red light of the crossing-signal flashes on and off, and the barrier of the level-crossing comes down and stops her.

WOMAN [*To nobody in particular*]: Oh, dear, darling, it's again. I hate this...

A train approaches and roars past. After the train has passed, the warning-bell and the red light stop, but the barrier does not go up. Possibly the barrier is waiting for a train from the opposite direction. THE WOMAN gets a little impatient and re-ties the cord of the futon bag.

WOMAN: I wonder if it's always like this here... [*To the inside of the futon bag*] Darling, darling...

THE MAN enters and stands a little away from THE WOMAN. He seems to have been to a wedding and carries a gift in a bundle from the wedding.

MAN: Is he alive?
WOMAN: Eh? [*She notices THE MAN.*] No, he isn't... [*She rises.*]
MAN: But you were talking to him a moment ago... [*He approaches her.*]
WOMAN: I heard a noise, so I wondered if he'd revived...
MAN: A noise?
WOMAN: It was a train. A train has just passed.
MAN: Oh, I see, the noise of a train... [*Looking down at the bag*] Are they feet?
WOMAN: Yes, they are. [*Suddenly noticing*] Haven't you ever seen any before?
MAN: Eh? You mean feet? Yes, yes, I have. I see them every day, whenever I take my socks off. Well, I'm talking about mine, of course.
WOMAN: First I thought I'd have them wearing socks. Because he wore socks all the time, except when he had a bath... He wore them even in bed. But...since things turned out like this...I thought again, maybe it would suit him better not to wear socks...Well, don't you think so? Well, I mean, it would suit the corpse better, not him.
MAN: Well, yes...I agree, it'd suit it...
WOMAN: Do you too?

MAN: What do I...?

THE WOMAN: Do you wear socks when you are in bed?

MAN: [*A little aghast*] No, no, I don't. I take them off. Soon after I come home, I take them off.

WOMAN: Then, as I thought, he was a bit of a funny sort...

MAN: But there must be other people like him... I've heard of a person who wears socks all the time.

WOMAN: Does he wear socks when he sleeps?

MAN: Yes, I think he does.

WOMAN: Who is he?

MAN: Who? It's a friend of mine. Although I say he's a friend of mine, we aren't that close.

WOMAN: Isn't it uncomfortable? Well, I mean, that friend of yours...didn't he say that it was uncomfortable for him?

MAN: I've... never asked him about it...but I suppose it doesn't really bother him...

WOMAN: He goes out in the same socks next day, doesn't he?

MAN: I suppose so...?

WOMAN: Don't they get smelly?

MAN: Yes, they would...

WOMAN [*Pointing at the socks which THE MAN is wearing*]: Are those too?

MAN: Oh, no, ... [*moving away from her*] you've got it wrong. It's not me but a friend of mine I was talking about...

WOMAN [*Slowly noticing something*]: Yes, it is...so, what I said just now is about a friend of yours. [*She glances at THE MAN's bundle.*] Did he get married today?

MAN: Eh? No, no, [*He shifts the bundle from one hand to the other as if to hide it from THE WOMAN.*] you've got it wrong again. The one who got married today is different one, another friend of mine...

WOMAN: But did he come too? I mean, ... the friend who wears socks when he is in bed, did he come to the wedding today, too?

MAN: No, he didn't. Actually he was supposed to come... What's the matter with this level-crossing?

WOMAN: It's waiting for an up train. A down train has just passed.

MAN: Even so... [*He looks at his watch.*]

WOMAN: So, I suppose you have two friends.

MAN: Two friends?

WOMAN: I mean, the one who wears socks when he sleeps and the one who got married today.

MAN: Well, that's right. Of course, I have other friends, too...

WOMAN: I haven't got any, I mean... friends... He was the only one I could talk to...

MAN: Are you going this way too?

WOMAN: Yes, I am. You mustn't worry. It soon goes up if a down train doesn't come soon after an up train goes. Would you like to see the hands too? [*She puts her hand in the futon bag and feels around inside it.*]

MAN: I beg your pardon?

WOMAN [*While searching*]: Well, I thought you might want to see the hands as well.

MAN: The hands? His hands?

WOMAN: Yes. [*She cannot find them easily.*] It's funny...

MAN: It's all right. I don't mind. Really, I don't mind about the hands...

WOMAN: You don't mind about the hands? What do you mean? [*She looks into the sack.*]

MAN: So, I don't mind not seeing... as I have seen them, I mean, hands... mainly mine, when I wash my face in the morning and some other occasions...

WOMAN: Just hang on. I can find them in a minute. I'm sure a moment ago I saw them about here somewhere... [*She looks for them.*] What's happened? They might have moved while I was dragging it. Would you mind my asking you to unfasten the cord?

MAN: Oh, no, please... It's a bit awkward doing that in a place like this.

WOMAN: But I'm sure they are in here.

MAN: Of course, they must be there... But it's all right. Why don't we drop this, really? Since I say I don't mind not looking at them. This is not I'm shy or anything like that.

WOMAN [*Giving up searching for the hands and standing up*]: You doubt that there were ever any hands here, don't you?

MAN: No, I don't. Why should I? Yes, there are hands in there, since we've seen feet. [*Muttering*] When we see feet, most of the time we see hands as well.

WOMAN: That's right... Certainly he's got hands too... [*Indicating the parts of the corpse in the bag by her chin, which seem to be shoulders.*] They were from about here to here, like this...

MAN: That's right...

WOMAN [*Annoyed*]: You haven't seen them, have you?

MAN: No, certainly not, but usually they are there...in other cases, so...

WOMAN [*Deeply*]: They were a lovely pair. The end of the little finger was a bit crooked, but he said it was more convenient when he cleaned his ears...he often said so... [*She dries her tears with a handkerchief.*]

MAN: I see...

WOMAN: He was proud of his hands. Every time he met someone, he showed them to all of them. He said, "Look, this is my little finger." Everybody was very much impressed. You are the first person who doesn't want to see them.

MAN: No, no, honestly... I didn't mean that...

WOMAN: But when I asked you if you'd like to see them, you said, it's all right.

MAN: Yes, I did say so, but...it wasn't because I didn't want to see them, but because I thought, doing that at a place like this was a little...Yes, you see, it's not the thing to do at a place like this...

WOMAN: Do you live near here?

The warning-bell of the level-crossing starts ringing and the red light of the crossing-signal starts flashing on and off.

MAN: What? Will you please wait a minute. It seems the train's coming...at last...

WOMAN: Do you live near here?

MAN: No, I don't.

A train roars through. The warning bell and the light stop but the crossing barrier does not go up.

MAN: It was the up train, wasn't it?

WOMAN: It seemed so.

MAN: Dear, dear... [*He looks at his watch.*]

WOMAN: Is your house farther down this way? [*She points in the direction of the level-crossing.*]

MAN: No, not there. [*Indicates the opposite direction*] It's down that way.

WOMAN: Then why are you going this way?

MAN: Well, I'm [*gesturing with the gift from the wedding in the bundle*], I'm going to deliver this. There was a friend of ours who couldn't come today. I've been asked to deliver this, so... But what's the matter with this level-crossing?

WOMAN: But you must live near here. That's why you've been asked to do it, isn't it?

MAN: Yes, well, you could say, it's sort of near... But why doesn't this go up?

WOMAN: May I just explain why I asked where you live? It's because, I thought, if you live near here [*pointing at the corpse in the futon bag*] I don't mind showing you this at your place, rather than here...

MAN: I beg your pardon?

WOMAN: Well, I said, if you don't like seeing this here, why don't we carry this to your place and...

MAN: No, stop joking! I don't know what you're talking about.

WOMAN [*Sternly*]: I'm not joking.

MAN [*Wincing*]: No, no, ...I didn't mean that, but I don't like it, I don't.

WOMAN: I only said it because you said you didn't want to open this here, so how about at your place... If we go to your place, you can see not only the hands but also all the other parts of the body, too.

MAN [*Breaking away from her*]: It's all right. Why don't we drop this? I'd rather...don't you think this level-crossing is a bit funny?

WOMAN: A down train's coming.

MAN: What did you say?

WOMAN: We are waiting for a down train.

MAN: But we saw an up train a moment ago.

WOMAN: So, when an up train passes and a down train follows soon after that, the levle-crossing waits for a down train and then goes up.

MAN: How stupid! Really! Then we won't be able to cross for ages.

WOMAN: Don't complain to me. It's not me who's doing this.

MAN: Of course, you aren't, but...

WOMAN: If you don't want to do it at your place, I don't mind going somewhere else. Is there any suitable place in your neighbourhood?

MAN: I don't think I can think of any place suitable for that! Let's stop. Because I don't want to look at such things.

WOMAN: Such things! I beg your pardon?

MAN: Oh, no, please. I said such things...I meant, you know, that...

WOMAN: What's more, a moment ago, you said, you wanted to see it, but not here, it'd be a bit awkward here...

MAN: Yes, I'd like to look at it...well. I don't mind, but honestly this place isn't any good for that...neither in my place... Also, I suppose you are going home in that direction, aren't you?

WOMAN: Yea, I'm going this way...but it doesn't mean I'm going home... My house is [*pointing at the opposite direction*] that way... I'm delivering this to its wife and child.

MAN: To its wife and child?

WOMAN: You must remember, once I deliver this to them, there will be no chance to see it.

MAN: I thought he was your husband...

WOMAN: No, he wasn't. Well, I thought he was until three days ago. I believed that he was my husband, but it wasn't true...He had his wife and a child registered farther down this way. I suppose you can guess most of what happened when all this came out.

MAN: Well, more or less...

WOMAN: But it wasn't me who did it. He fell over before I pushed him and he hit this part of his head on the sharp corner of the table in the kitchen. It's true. I pushed him after he fell over. I didn't need to push him that time because he'd fallen over himself...or do you think that he fell over because I pushed him?

MAN: No, really, I don't know.

WOMAN: You're wrong. It was very clear that he had fallen over by the time I pushed him. Of course, I'm not saying that I wasn't pushing him at all, yes, I was going to. Well. it's natural, isn't it? Because he hadn't admitted that he had a wife and a child by up to that very moment. So I lost my temper and I was about to push him, but before I could, he fell over, so I actually pushed him after he fell over. Don't you see?

MAN: I, I don't know. How could I possibly know? I wasn't there.

WOMAN: Perhaps I was holding out my hands to stop him falling over... Now I've calmed down and think about what happened... Because I didn't need to push him if he had already fallen over... This could be right, couldn't it?

MAN: Of course, it could, possibly...

WOMAN: I'm sure it was... I can vaguely remember that I was holding out my hands to catch him...of course, after he began falling over...One thing hadn't been clear, that is, whether I was doing it to push him or to save him. But now you've given me an answer to that. Isn't that right? You think so too...you think that I was trying to save him, don't you?

MAN: Yes, but as I keep saying, I don't know anything about it.

WOMAN: It doesn't matter, as long as that point is clear...

MAN: Clear? I simply said that the case you described could have happened.

WOMAN: So I'm saying it doesn't matter. Taking into the circumstances at the time, it'd be natural for me to push him away, but I wouldn't be happy if people thought that I pushed him when I didn't push him. Because the truth was that I didn't do it. Now, I know...he fell over by himself and I tried to save him.

MAN: Then, well...did he kill himself hitting his head on the corner of the kitchen table when he fell over?

WOMAN: Yes, he did. So, what should we call this? Errr...suicide?

MAN: Suicide... I don't think it was ...

WOMAN: But he fell over by himself... even though I didn't push him.

MAN: Yes, I understand that, but... [*Confused*] Umm...? So, should we still call it suicide after all? No, no, that's not right because he didn't intend to.

WOMAN: I can believe that he might have done it to kill himself. Because he was trapped by a strong feeling of guilt. Can't you see? He had betrayed me for five years up to that time.

MAN: Well, I could see your point, but I think it's unusual to commit suicide by hitting a head on the corner of the kitchen table?

WOMAN: Then what do you call it?

MAN: Well... so how about calling it...an accidental death?

WOMAN: I see, an accidental death. Yes, it could be called that. In other words, you mean it's like a case of tripping over a stone and falling over.

MAN: Well, it would seem...

WOMAN: I've understood. He had an accidental death...

MAN: Just remember that I'm only suggesting there's the possibility of it being considered in that way... In any case, I know nothing about it.

WOMAN: Never mind about that. We can't think of any other possibility, can we?

MAN: No, we can't. But please remember it all depends on whether what you told me did really happen.

WOMAN: Yes, it did happen. What I said is true. It was an accidental death.

MAN: Well...does his wife know about this?

WOMAN: Who do you mean by his wife?

MAN: Well, I mean the registered one.

WOMAN: No, she doesn't. I thought it'd be a good idea to deliver this and at the same time I could tell her all about it. Of course, I'm not obliged to do so. I'm the victim in this case as I told you before. But when I calmed myself down and thought about it, I realised that she must be worried about him too, because he hasn't been home for three days. So I decided to show her true kindness...My late uncle often taught me that...Also there's a child between them, so I concluded that delivering this to his registered wife would be the right thing to do...

MAN: I see...

WOMAN: I've never met her, but I'm sure that she'd appreciate what I'm going to do... Don't you think so?

MAN: Well, I should think so, but...

WOMAN: So, ... will you tell her that as you agree with me?

MAN: What do you mean, tell her that?

WOMAN: We've already talked about it, that he killed himself by accident.

MAN: What are you talking about? No, no way. It's not for me to do that.

WOMAN: But I thought you were going that way?

MAN: Yes, I am, but as I told you a moment ago, I'm going this way only to deliver this wedding gift to a friend of mine who didn't attend the ceremony today.

WOMAN: Then, no problem, his house is just there.

MAN: No, I won't do it. Stop being silly. I have nothing to do with this.

WOMAN: You know why I'm asking you to do this? If you explain all about his death, she will believe it was an accident...If she took his death as suicide, I'd be very sorry...

MAN: In any case, whatever you say, no way...

The warning bell of the level-crossing rings and the red light of the crossing-signal starts going on and off.

WOMAN: Where is it, that you're going?

MAN: Where? It's just over there...

WOMAN: Is that the place of your friend who didn't come to the wedding?

MAN: Yes...

WOMAN: A little while ago you were talking about a friend of yours who wears socks when he sleeps at night, and said that he hadn't come to the wedding.

MAN: ... [*He keeps facing the other way.*]

A train roars through. Needless to say, the level-crossing barrier does not rise.

MAN: ... [*He looks at THE WOMAN.*]
WOMAN: ... [*She looks at THE MAN.*]
MAN [*Looking at the futon bag and pointing at it*]: Errr...is he called Kimura?
WOMAN: Yes, that's his real name...but he told me his name was Kinoshita.
MAN: Couldn't be...
WOMAN: Those feet... [*Pointing at them*] Do you think they're his?
MAN: Well. I'm not sure...because I didn't pay much attention to his feet... As
    I've already told you, we weren't that close...
WOMAN: Then, would you like to see his face?
MAN: No, no, let's not do that...
WOMAN: Why not? If you looked at his face, you could tell…
MAN: Yes, I could... Now, will you please give me some time. It's too sudden
    being asked that sort of thing at a place like this... [*He crouches down.*]
WOMAN: He lived in a two-storeyed house farther down this way. He had a
    wife and a boy of three... Did your friend too?
MAN: More or less…
WOMAN: In that case, I'm positive. It's him. We should have noticed sooner.
    There aren't so many people who wear socks in bed.
MAN: In that case, was that you?
WOMAN: What about me?
MAN: Err, only, I've heard a bit about it.
WOMAN: Well, then have you heard about me?
MAN: Oh, no, it's not like that...I just heard something about you and him...
WOMAN: What did he say about me?
MAN: I'm afraid I don't know. We didn't hear it in that way, I mean, didn't hear
    the details. But... [*He looks at the futon bag thoroughly.*] Goodness! This is
    him...
WOMAN [*Heartily*]: Yes, it's him...But the way he talked, I mean, when he
    talked about me...well, didn't you pick up something about me through
    the way he talked? For example, he sounded annoyed or pleased…
MAN: But as I said, I didn't hear about it from him directly. I happened to hear
    somebody talking about you...
WOMAN: Who was that?
MAN: Who?
WOMAN: Was it a friend of yours?

MAN: Well, I suppose it must've been one of our friends.

WOMAN: Was it the one married today?

MAN: No, I've been telling you I can't tell you exactly who it was. When we were chatting in a group, I heard somebody talking about it...

WOMAN: How did it sound?

MAN: Well, don't you think that we've talked enough?

WOMAN: No, I don't. Because it was about me, wasn't it? I must know how people talked about me.

MAN: We weren't gossiping about you particularly. We were only saying... [*raising the little finger of his left hand hesitantly*] he seemed to have got a girlfriend lately. That's all. [*He hides his left hand.*]

WOMAN [*Criticizing his gesture*]: What do you mean by that?

MAN: Oh, nothing just that it seemed he'd got a girlfriend, you know?

WOMAN: No, I mean, just now you moved that hand in a funny way, didn't you?

MAN: Yes, I did, but it's because you wanted to know how we had been talking about you...

WOMAN: It's all right. Can I see it again?

MAN: Again? [*A little hesitantly*] It's only the gesture you usually make to mean a girlfriend by holding a little finger like this... [*He makes a gesture with the finger.*]

WOMAN: And?

MAN: And what?

WOMAN: Show me how you do it.

MAN: So... [*raising the little finger of his left hand*] he seemed to have a girlfriend recently... [*He is about to withdraw his hand.*]

WOMAN: Don't!

MAN: What?

WOMAN: Please hold that position with your little finger up.

MAN: But, still, I think... [*Unavoidably he keeps his little finger in the same position...*]

WOMAN [*Pointing at it*]: That's me, isn't it?

MAN: Well, yes...

A short silence.

WOMAN: Thank you very much. You can put it down now. I don't want to see it any more... [*She turns back and starts walking upstage.*]

MAN [*To her back*]: But, hey... When we were doing that, we weren't thinking of you particularly... because you know, we didn't know you at all. We were only gossiping, saying that he seemed to have got a girlfriend... And it's, it's very common, especially when we men are together...

WOMAN: It's all right. I'm not upset about it. [*Turning back*] But you must promise me that you'll introduce me to his wife in that way when we meet her...saying she is his this... [*She holds up her little finger while saying the last phrase.*]

MAN: What are you saying? Don't be ridiculous! How can I do that?

WOMAN: But didn't you say that you were delivering it to her?

MAN: Yes, I was, but at that time I didn't know what was going on...

WOMAN: Oh, I think it's a wonderful coincidence. To be very honest with you, although I dragged him this far, I didn't know how I was going to get over the rails. But if you come with me, this might sound a little too much, but how about you helping me to carry this...

MAN: You must be joking!

WOMAN: What's wrong with that? Just to get over the rails? I'll hold your bundle...which, I think you said, was a wedding gift...

MAN [*Moving away from her*]: Wait a bit, please. We can't do that...

WOMAN: Why not?

MAN: Why not? Well, because...the level-crossing isn't up yet... Don't you think that there's something wrong with this level-crossing?

WOMAN: No, it's fine. We're waiting for an up train. I think I'm right. The train just passed was a down one, wasn't it?

MAN: Yes, it was a down train.

WOMAN: So, when an up train comes soon after a down train, the level-crossing waits for it and then goes up.

MAN: But it seems to have been repeating this same thing for some time.

WOMAN: No, that's not true. Before it was a down train coming soon after an up train. But this time it's an up train coming soon after a down train.

MAN: In any case if they keep repeating that, we can never go across the rails.

WOMAN: Don't blame me! I'm not the signalman.

MAN: Well, no, you aren't, but...

WOMAN: I think the same as you do. I want to deliver this to his wife as soon as possible. As I said a while ago, he hasn't been back to her place for three days... I'm sure his wife's worried about him. Don't you see? When we deliver this, surely his wife will feel at peace. What's more, it wasn't suicide but an accidental death. And there you'll hold out that wedding gift and say that the wedding today was splendid... Both the groom and the bride looked so happy and they felt the absence of your husband at the ceremony very much. Because...I think it must be true... Isn't it?

MAN: Yes, it is, but...

WOMAN: I think the three-year-old boy will be delighted when he sees the bundle with the gift... Because I guess, it's something to eat, isn't it? There must be a piece of the wedding cake in too. Aren't I right?

MAN: Well, I don't know what's in it...

WOMAN: I'm sure it is. And also a sea bream this big made of red and white sugar. I like that very much, especially the tail fin which is stretched up like this. It's all made of sugar, but that is the most delicious part. I can imagine the boy's face when he opens the box and sees the big sea bream made of sugar coming out... So, I'll hold that for you while you are dragging it over...

MAN [*Fleeing from her*]: No, don't! I've told you already, you can't, this is...

WOMAN: Why not? Don't you see that his wife is waiting for him right at this moment?

MAN: I understand that very well, but...

WOMAN: And yet, you still want to leave this here like this?

MAN: No, I didn't mean that. I'm not saying that at all.

WOMAN: He's a friend of yours, isn't he?

MAN: Yes, he is.

WOMAN: Then you must agree that we should take him to his wife and son as soon as possible.

MAN: I understand what you are saying very well...But I do not think that I'm necessarily responsible for what has happened to him.

WOMAN: I'm not talking about responsibility. If we think about in that way, it's neither your responsibility nor mine at all... I'm simply talking about what is true kindness...

MAN: Fine! That's all right! I understand that quite well. But please wait.

WOMAN: Wait for what?

MAN: Wait for what? The barrier isn't up yet and...

WOMAN: Soon. Soon it'll go up when an up train comes... Will you please promise me? When the barrier is up, you will do that, drag this?

MAN: Well, so...

The warning-bell rings and the crossing-signal starts going on and off.

WOMAN: Look, here comes an up train. When it's gone, the barrier will soon open.

MAN: Just...please, you must listen to me. No, no, we must deal with this sort of matter only after we've given it serious consideration.

WOMAN: What on earth do we need to consider?

MAN: We must consider this fully... At least, a man died. You see? Died, a man did die. Do you understand? He's dead, he's gone, he's gone ...

A train roars past in the middle of THE MAN's speech. So, the latter half of THE MAN's speech can hardly be heard. After the train has passed, the warning bell and the signal stop but the barrier of the level-crossing stays down.

WOMAN: It's gone... Well, shall we go?

MAN: Please wait. Can't you see the barrier is still there?

WOMAN: It'll go up soon.

MAN: But, please... will you please calm down a little. Let's, let's think about this calmly. Yes, we must consider this sort of matter calmly...

WOMAN: I've been imperturbable.

MAN: That's right. You have been, so I must be imperturbable too. Yes, this is what I have been trying to say.

WOMAN: But it's really funny, this level-crossing. I wonder if it's out of order. [*She shakes the barrier and makes a rattling noise.*]

MAN: You'd better stop!

WOMAN: Why? It isn't working. It's obvious.

MAN: Let's leave it! It's not out of order. It's waiting for a down train.

WOMAN: An up train has just passed...how could it be?

MAN: So ... so, after an up train, if there's a down train coming soon, the barrier waits for it and then opens.

WOMAN: If it keeps doing this, we can never cross here.

MAN: Don't blame me! I'm not a signalman...

WOMAN: No, you aren't, but...

MAN: So, please listen, what I'm trying to say is, when we drag this and get there...

WOMAN: It's not we, it's you who's going to drag this. I told you a moment ago that I would hold the bundle instead.

MAN: What are you saying? Before you said that I would drag it only while we crossed here.

WOMAN: Yes, I did. Then are you saying that you'll just be watching me, standing idle while I'm killing myself dragging it?

MAN: No, I'm not…

WOMAN: If we come across a police car, what do you think you're going to do? Isn't it more natural that you drag it than I do?

MAN: No, it's not. What are you saying? Why do you think that it'd be more natural if I dragged it?

WOMAN: Because you're stronger than me. That's what I meant. Don't worry. I don't think that a police car would pass by because I chose this way to avoid that.

MAN: Whatever it is, what I want to say is that his wife doesn't know about this yet, does she?

WOMAN: Of course not. That's why I'm in a hurry to…

MAN: Oh, yes, yes, I understand that… But if we bring this in when she doesn't know about it at all, can't you see? Surely, it'd be a real shock for her.

WOMAN: Why? It wouldn't be. This is her husband.

MAN: Yes, it is her husband, but, in any case he's dead.

WOMAN: He was killed by accident. He didn't commit suicide.

MAN: But even so, I would think that she'd be extremely shocked…

WOMAN: Would she? Never mind, we can discuss that later. Anyway, we must sort out the problem here right now. Don't you know if there's a public telephone near here?

MAN: A telephone? Well, no. But what are you going to do with it?

WOMAN: Make a phone call and ask.

MAN: Ask his wife?

WOMAN: No, the Ministry of Transport.

MAN: The Ministry of Transport?

WOMAN: After all I think that they are the people who are supposed to deal with problems with the level-crossing.

MAN: You could say that but… I doubt if they'll do anything about this…

WOMAN: It's all right. I'll phone and sort it out. So, will you please keep your eye on this?

MAN: Just a minute. I, I won't.

WOMAN: Why not?

MAN: Why not? Please stop being silly.

WOMAN: Just keep your eye on it, otherwise somebody might carry it away.

MAN: Yes, that might happen, but it's not for me to do that. In any case this isn't mine, don't you see?

WOMAN: But it's not mine either, you could say... As I mentioned earlier, we weren't legally married. Once when I suggested getting our marriage registered, he refused and said he didn't believe in that sort of conventional custom.

MAN: Well...

WOMAN: How could he bloody say "that sort of conventional custom"? He himself was already married behind my back.

MAN: Now now, don't get upset...It'll be all right. You needn't phone them. It'll soon open. An up train has just passed, so once a down one comes, the barrier should open soon after that.

WOMAN: What will you do if it doesn't go up?

MAN: If it doesn't go up? Never! It can't be like that. The barrier of a level-crossing is meant to open. Well, even so, if it doesn't go up, in that case, we could just go under the barrier. It's possible to cross under it. Don't worry, I'll give you a hand pulling that.

WOMAN: Go under it... [*She examines the level-crossing.*]

MAN: Yes, that's right. Now, as I said before, I suppose that it'd be a good idea to think about that a little, well, I mean, she will be pretty much shocked when she receives this, so...

WOMAN [*Looking around*]: Yes, that's right, we could manage to go under this if a train doesn't come... [*Specifically replying to THE MAN's words*] Well, please don't worry about it. You're worrying about his wife, aren't you? It'll be all right.

MAN: All right?

WOMAN: I thought about it over and over. Last night I sat up all night and thought about it in a practical way...

MAN: But, you must really...

WOMAN: Please keep quiet and listen. I'm talking now... After we cross the rails, there's a small printing factory on your right. You're going to drag this in the dark to the wall of the factory...

MAN: Me?

WOMAN: What do you mean?

MAN: Well, it's fine.

WOMAN [*Glancing at her watch*]: I should think the people have left the printing factory by this time of day, but you'd better not sing a song or anything like that when you pass by.

MAN: I never thought of singing a bloody song!

WOMAN: You'll see hundreds of matchbox houses being lined up closely just after the factory. The thirteenth house from this end, the smallest one is his. They haven't paid off the mortgage for the house but they have a small flower bed just next to the front door and...

MAN: What I'm trying to say is, it's not that but...

WOMAN: I've told you I know what you want to say. When we get there, their neighbours probably would have gone to bed already, but only his house would be lit dimly in the living room. Because his wife should be waiting for him to return at any moment. There must be a door-bell with an intercom somewhere around here by the front door... I will ring the bell. And you'll watch the corpse. Rin-don! There's the sound of the bell. We hear a noise from inside and soon through the intercom her anxious voice saying "who is it?" Can't you see it? I'll go closer to the intercom and say gently... [*Moving to the rhythm slightly and as if singing*] It's "Kuroneko Yamato's Home Delivery Service."

THE MAN suddenly tries to run away.

WOMAN [*Catching him by his collar*]: Where are you going?

MAN: No, I'm not going anywhere...

WOMAN: Don't you understand? This is the thing! A sense of humour! It's most important. A sense of humour like this can oil the wheels of our dry everyday life and smooth the sharpest feelings. Isn't it so?

MAN: Well, it can be, but...

WOMAN: Do you think there's any other problem?

MAN: No, no, I'm not worrying about the problem but...

WOMAN: Then, no problem. Let's go. I'm sure that his wife would appreciate that sort of our caring attitude.

MAN: Well, she would, but...

WOMAN [*Gesturing towards THE MAN's wedding gift*]: Shall I carry that?

MAN: Will you please stop? [*He does not give the gift to her.*]

WOMAN: What's wrong? Do you think I'll make off with it?

MAN: Oh, no, I don't.

WOMAN: Didn't you hear me saying I will entrust this to you in place of that?
MAN: Well, I told you I understood that very well.
WOMAN: Don't you see? This is much bigger.
MAN: Well, I'm not talking about that sort of thing... I'm only talking about...
WOMAN: Then, what on earth are you talking about? It's only a sea bream made of sugar in a box, isn't it? Is that a thing that a grown-up man must take great care of?
MAN: All right, then, whatever...I'll hand this over to you for the time being... [*He gives the wedding gift to THE WOMAN.*]
WOMAN [*Receiving it*]: Honestly... [*shaking the gift*] What's in it?
MAN: Please! Don't do that! If it's broken, I don't know what they'll say to me later.
WOMAN: But aren't I right? There's a sea bream made of sugar inside.
MAN: How do I know? I haven't opened it yet.
WOMAN: Oh, then, you don't know what's in the box either?
MAN: No...
WOMAN: In that case I might ask his wife to let me look at it in the box.
MAN: No, you shouldn't.
WOMAN: Well, just look at it. I'm not going to ask her to let me taste it.
MAN: Of course, you aren't, at a time like this...
WOMAN: But first I'll explain to her clearly that I'm not asking her to let me have a look at it because I want to taste it.
MAN: Whatever it is, let's not do it. It's not right.
WOMAN: Don't you want to see it?
MAN: No, I don't. Will you please drop this? I think I've had enough of it.
WOMAN: All right. In that case [*pointing at the head part of the bag*] will you please hold that part?
MAN: Eh? No, no... still, I think we should give more consideration to this matter and...
WOMAN: Please! Hold it! Since I've been already carrying yours.
MAN: Well, I know that, still... [*He reluctantly holds the cord around the head part.*]
WOMAN: You must lift that part a little and drag, as it's his head. Please don't ever bump it against anything... Pull it up...
MAN: Is this all right?
WOMAN: That's right. And just pull...
MAN: Pull? But barrier isn't open yet.

WOMAN: Didn't you say that we were going under the barrier?

MAN: Yes, I did. But only if the barrier doesn't go up after the down train.

WOMAN: It won't come. An up train has passed just now.

MAN: Just now? I don't think it was just now...

WOMAN: Hurry up! If we keep hesitating and don't do things quickly, then, really, a down train will come...

MAN: Well, I know, but...Are you sure? [*He starts crossing over the level-crossing under the barrier.*] If you spot anything, you must let me know quickly... I mean...if the warning-bell rings or anything...

WOMAN: Of course, I will. Don't worry!

MAN: Even if the warning- bell doesn't ring, if you hear a train...do you understand?

WOMAN: I said, I will. Please be careful. The head!

MAN: Eh?

WOMAN: The head!

MAN: What?

WOMAN: The head, I said you must lift the head up and pull it. Lift it up! Up! Don't you see the corpse is bumping against the rail?

MAN: ...

WOMAN: Do you think it's all right?

MAN [*Offstage*]: Pardon?

WOMAN: The train! Do you think it's still not coming?

MAN: Well, I shouldn't think so.

WOMAN: Then, I'll come too... [*She goes under the barrier to cross the level-crossing.*]

Suddenly the warning-bell and the signal go off.

WOMAN [*Coming out of the level-crossing hurriedly*]: Hey, it's coming! Hey, what are you doing? No, no! Don't leave the corpse there. Bring it back. Grab it and... why don't you pull it? Pull it back! Look...the feet. The feet! There! The feet are caught. Move them! There! There! No! Not there! No, how stupid! What are you doing? This side! This! Can't you hear me saying this side? Move the feet! You must move the feet. Quickly! Hurry! Oh, no! Pull it to this side! Lift it up more! To this side! This! What's the matter with you? To this side. To this... [*She screams out and squats down.*]

A train roars along. A foot in a sock and a shoe rolls out from the level-crossing at the feet of THE WOMAN. The train passes by. THE WOMAN stays squatting covering her ears with her hands. The warning-bell and the signal stop.

WOMAN [*Standing up absent-mindedly and looking at the foot at her feet*]: Goodness! This got a sock on! This foot! I think he must've hated being bare foot after all.

Blackout.

END

The Story of the Two Knights Travelling Around the Country
Stage photo by Christopher Jowett
SCENE I (from left) the Nurse, the Priest and the Doctor

The Story of the Two Knights Travelling Around the Country
Stage photo by Christopher Jowett
SCENE II Squire 1 (being on all fours) and Squire 2 (standing)

[IV]

The Story of the Two Knights Travelling Around the Country

About the play

The Story of the Two Knights Travelling Around the Country was first presented in the November, 1987 issue of *The New Theatre (Shingeki)*.[1] Betsuyaku had written it, expecting two experienced actors to be taking the leading parts. (See Chapter One [I]) with actors and crew brought in from a wider range of backgrounds. The people involved in the first staging were in fact not from the groups which usually produce Betsuyaku's newly written plays. Instead, it was presented by the Parco Space Part 3[2] with actors and crew brought in from a wider range of backgrounds.

The play is about two hours long and consists of two scenes. It represents the latest phase of Betsuyaku's work,[3] and the scale on which it is conceived is grand and impressive.

Betsuyaku gained the inspiration for this play from Cervantes' novel *Don Quixote* - he subtitles it - *from Don Quixote* -. The elements used in the play - a desolate wasteland as the setting where the action takes place, the knight and his squire, and the big windmill - are borrowed from Cervantes' novel. Here again Betsuyaku's craftsmanship combines them with his own original dramatic elements - THE DOCTOR, THE NURSE and the itinerant PRIEST, the stage scenery, the mobile inn and the peculiar costumes and properties - and succeeds in creating a world very much the author's own.

Style and Structure

The play takes place somewhere in a wasteland. It begins in the late afternoon in the late summer. The location could be Spain in the Middle Ages. A strange set of objects on stage represents a mobile inn run by THE INNKEEPER and his DAUGHTER. The mobile inn is to the wasteland what an oasis is to the desert, and all sorts of people come together there seeking food, beds, and other comforts. The other stage properties, apart from the desk, table and chairs belonging to the inn, are "a dead tree" (KNIGHTS p.239, l.1), which reminds us of "a tree" in Beckett's **Waiting for Godot**, and "The silhouette of an enormous windmill upstage behind these objects" (KNIGHTS p.239, l.7-8), which links the play visually to the novel, *Don Quixote*.

The atmosphere of the stage is deserted and bare, and rather cold and unfriendly. The space used is unrestricted and open as in most of Betsuyaku's other plays. So the audience could be sitting on a patch of grass or a group of rocks in the arid wasteland, depending on how the design is conceived and how the fantasy shared by the people on stage and in the auditorium develop. This set would possess a strong power which would expand and bring the audience into its world because of its oddity as well as that of the characters. It tends to let us forget the boundary between the stage and auditorium.

SCENE I (KNIGHTS pp.239-259) begins with the entrances of THE DOCTOR and THE NURSE, who are passing by and decide to stop at the inn because THE DOCTOR thinks that there might be a patient for him in this sort of place. He even suggests putting some weak poison into the water jug prepared for the guests so that they get diarrhoea. THE NURSE stops him as he couldn't cure the patients when he tried it before. The travelling PRIEST comes along and annoys THE DOCTOR. THE DOCTOR suspects that the appearance of both their professions in the same place will give a bad impression, implying an inevitable connection between being ill and needing a funeral. THE PRIEST wonders whether some poison might have been put into the jug by THE DOCTOR and THE NURSE, and half believes that it has. All the conversations here focus on 'the poisoned water jug' and add a touch of the comic detective story, although at the same time Betsuyaku is cleverly introducing the feeling that there is 'murder in the air.' The way the play seems to be developing is straightforward, and so we tend to see the conversation among the three characters simply as silly and absurd, and it is only gradually that we come to realise that there is something ominous surrounding them. The mood is deepened by the list of diseases mentioned by THE DOCTOR: appendicitis, peritonitis, diarrhoea, dysentery, cholera. Some of them are the diseases which Betsuyaku came across in the ship from Manchuria when he and his family returned to Japan. (See Chapter One [I]) Betsuyaku is shading in an image of the dark side of human life and revealing the shadow of death.

THE INNKEEPER comes back carrying a basket of food, and shows his contempt for the three parasites, declaring, "Whenever I open the inn, before the customers' arrival, the people who do business with them all turn up…"

(KNIGHTS p.244, l.23-24). He thinks that there will be no customers tonight because the wind is in the wrong direction. At this moment the three men on stage are simply concerned about their own little affairs. All that matters to them is how to make more profit. THE INNKEEPER's DAUGHTER comes back singing the song, *There's No Place Like Home*, (4) and announces that a knight and his squire are on their way to the inn. In defiance of the traditions of plot development, even THE DAUGHTER's entrance does not lighten the mood of the play very much. All the people here are travellers who never settle down in one place and so the song she is singing sounds very ironic.

KNIGHT 1 and SQUIRE 1, and KNIGHT 2 and SQUIRE 2 enter separately. They are the people in rags as in the following stage directions. The play becomes to look very much an old-fashioned slap-stick comedy with these costumes.

> *KNIGHT 1, who wears a helmet made of a squashed washbasin and holds a long cane with some dirty cloth tied on the top end, sits on a chair in a hand-cart.*
> (KNIGHTS p.247, l.33-34)

> *SQUIRE 1, who also wears a helmet made of a squashed saucepan,*
> (KNIGHTS p.248, l.1)

> *KNIGHT 2, who wears a ragged frock coat and a helmet of a squashed wash-basin, slowly walks in with a cane which has a dirty cloth tied on the top.*
> (KNIGHTS p.249, l.14-16)

> *SQUIRE 2, who wears a helmet made of a squashed saucepan, carries a big dirty sack and holds a short cane, comes in almost crawling.*
> (KNIGHTS p.251, l.13-14)

Both Knights treat their Squires rudely but the Squires ignore it and it seems this is their usual manner. Here we see the conventional pattern of a master-servant relationship which will give a firm base to the play. But Betsuyaku's characters go beyond their stereotypes. The two Knights are very old and physically weak. With their age, and perhaps with their experiences, they are losing their self-respect, and becoming extraordinarily greedy and selfish. SQUIRE 2 does not have a pulse and has to talk in order to prove that he is alive. SQUIRE 1 drinks a lot of water and KNIGHT 1 believes that he should not be given too much water in case he gets rusty and too stiff to move. These descriptions of the two squires are not of their characters but of their physical states. However, they indicate that it is not only the Knights who are strange and eccentric. These new elements of the characters of the Knights and the Squires added to the play have a deeply disturbing effect on the atmosphere - from the entrances onwards we more or less lose any ordinary sense of human dignity.

During the quickfire exchange between SQUIRE 1 and KNIGHT 1 over how much SQUIRE 1 should drink, KNIGHT 1 invites THE NURSE to drink from the jug - she does so, and is poisoned to death. (KNIGHTS p.258, l.6-11). It is only when everyone but the Knights go offstage to carry the dead woman away, that the murderer is revealed to be KNIGHT 1 and the conversation continues:

A church-bell rings in the distance.

KNIGHT 1: A church-bell is ringing… Oh, isn't it nice?

KNIGHT 2: What?

KNIGHT 1: I mean… a person died, a church bell rings and the night has fallen…

KNIGHT 2: Yes… and what makes me feel indescribably good is that it isn't me who died.

KNIGHT 1: That's the thing. Yes, that's the thing my friend.

Blackout.   (KNIGHTS p.259, l.23-30)

This last conversation of **SCENE I** between the Knights also indirectly suggests the way that they have lived their lives in the past. They must have seen many people die while they have survived. Now a day is about to be over and they can enjoy their dinner listening to the ringing of a church-bell. The stage direction says, "…they begin to look more like mere old men than knights." (KNIGHTS p.258, l.28-29) Here Betsuyaku is displaying by the subtle transformation in the Knights' appearance when the other characters retreat, this other side of their characters, that these murders are mere frightened old men.

SCENE II (KNIGHTS pp.260-284) begins with KNIGHT 1 and 2 exhibiting their insatiable appetites by eating up all the food in the inn. They are greedy and selfish to forget the others who are waiting for their dinner. This prefigures what is to come. The others become aware of the situation and are deeply shocked that two feeble old men could eat so much and that they themselves will not be able to eat perhaps until tomorrow evening. Now in some way they feel that their lives are at risk - they may die of hunger. Fighting over food is the most fundamental and the ugliest of human acts. In the play the Knights are immoral enough to have eaten up the others' share, but the others' reaction to the shortage of food is not admirable either. They express their anxiety shamelessly and show no compassion towards one another.

THE INNKEEPER and THE DAUGHTER stand apart from the other characters. THE INNKEEPER, already a bitter man, gets very angry when he realises the big mistake which he has made in serving too much to the Knights, who he had at first thought would be his good customers and, on the contrary, have turned out the bad ones. He could have stopped serving before the food ran out, but his own greed let him to serve more in order to earn more, or he was intimidated by the Knights' superior social status, and now he regrets it. THE DAUGHTER has been meekly obedient to her father and to the Knights, waiting on the latter at table. THE DAUGHTER's part is that of the 'good maiden,' who as a rule most of the men admire and love. In Cervantes' novel there are two such characters: "the daughter of the inn" and "Dulcinea." THE INNKEEPER's DAUGHTER in the play is a mixture of both.

The reactions of THE INNKEEPER and THE DAUGHTER are acceptable under the circumstances, as also that of the Squires who are the clown figures in the play. However, THE DOCTOR whose job it is to devote himself to curing patients, and THE PRIEST who should guide confused souls to the divine world, both simply show pettiness of human beings worrying about themselves. Here we see Betsuyaku's cool observation on the realities of human nature coming out. In *The Story of the Two Knights* the greed, selfishness, and the pettiness, all the ugliness of the human heart is shared out among the characters. There is a scene in which the Knights explain and justify their killing of others; KNIGHT 2 says, "It's because if we don't, we get killed," and KNIGHT 1 says, "...it's too late after we've been attacked." (KNIGHTS p.276, l.32-35)

After the Knights come back from a duel for the love of THE DAUGHTER, the other characters are murdered, one by one. Each is killed in a chilling or brutal way, from the poison to a razor. The audience hear the anguished cries of the victims. The continuous murdering scenes, one after another, give us a bloodthirsty image of the play. Betsuyaku often writes a play in which an innocent leading character is killed in the end, sometimes for a reason and sometimes just by accident. [5] However, the extent of the brutality in *The Story of the Two Knights* is greater than usual. It seems that the more difficulty they face in continuing their lives, the more brutal they become. Their long hard years of being a knight-errant must have blunted their sensitivities.

SQUIRE 1 is killed accidentally when he tries to catch THE DAUGHTER on the orders of KNIGHT 2. THE DAUGHTER tries to protect herself with a razor. SQUIRE 2 loses his life in a fight against an imaginary Giant, Briareus, the son of heaven and the Earth, who has fifty heads and a hundred arms - what we see is a silhouette of a big windmill: the episode borrowed from Cervantes' *Don Quixote*.

When the two Knights finally reach the point when they are alone, and thinking of going to bed with their 'young bride,' THE INNKEEPER's DAUGHTER, they find that she has committed suicide.

> KNIGHT 1: Our bride is preparing to welcome us to her bed. [*He slowly goes to the table and sits on the chair.*]
> KNIGHT 2: That's fine. I'm tired of being prudent. [*Sitting down on the chair*] Our adventure is coming to an end. This time when I'm called, I'll go to her bed to be caught in her trap... and then have her cut my throat...
> KNIGHT 1: That sounds alright. But do you think she will think of what to do about me after that?
> KNIGHT 2: I'm sure she will...

> *The light behind the curtain goes off.*

> KNIGHT 1: The light has gone... It seems she's ready. Go and act the role of a stupid groom...
> KNIGHT 2 [*standing up slowly*]: It's been a long journey... And so has yours.
> KNIGHT 1: Yes...

> *KNIGHT 2 goes to the curtain and throw it open.*

> KNIGHT 2: ...
> KNIGHT 1: What's wrong?

KNIGHT 2: She's dead… cut her own throat.

KNIGHT 1: …

(KNIGHTS p.282, l.3-21)

They are tired of their adventure and want to put an end to their life. When the two Knights know that THE DAUGHTER has refused them by her death, they hope that somebody stronger would come to finish everything for them (KNIGHTS p.284, l.3-7).

As the play proceeds, we feel more and more that there are connections with *Waiting for Godot*, although at the same time it is still only the resemblances between the stage settings of the two plays which give us any immediate clues to those connections. But, if we look at the subject matter, our confusion is soon dispelled. DIDI and GOGO are waiting, waiting, and waiting and receive a message which says that their long-awaited Mr. Godot is going to visit them soon. But Mr. Godot does not yet turn up. So, they again wait, wait and wait. All their lives they just expect something that will perhaps take them out of the situation they are in. Meanwhile the two Knights have travelled, travelled, travelled, and finally come back to the place where perhaps they once passed by when they were much younger and being filled with the aspiration. They expect to be given something that they have been looking for through their journeys of adventure but it is still not given. And perhaps Mr. Godot will never turn up and the two Knights will never be able to stop travelling. Similarly, life is a sort of endless and seemingly futile repetition, and that repetition itself is the only meaning of the life.

The dialogues at the end of the play become shortened and more sophisticated, and sound rhythmic and poetic - Betsuyaku's dramatic language seems here to have reached the summit of true simplicity. It is ironical to note the similarities with Beckett's dramatic language which is also dry and lyrical, when we remember how Betsuyaku endeavoured in the early nineteen-seventies to overcome the influence of Beckettian theatre. After twenty years' travelling to find his own theatre, Betsuyaku has come back to where he started. So perhaps this play must be for the author the beginning of a new journey in search of his true theatre.

Notes: ———————————————————————————

(1) *The New Theatre (Shingeki)* (Tokyo: Hakusui Sha, 1987) No. 416, pp.130-167.

(2) The Parco Space Part 3, on the 8th floor of Shibuya Parco Building, Tokyo.

(3) It means 'the latest' of 1988, when this sentence was originally written.

(4) Japanese Title: *Hanyu no Yado.*

(5) e.g. ***The Kangaroo***

THE STORY OF THE TWO KNIGHTS TRAVELLING AROUND THE COUNTRY
– AFTER DON QUIXOTE –

By
Minoru Betsuyaku

Translated by Masako Yuasa

[IV] The Story of the Two Knights Travelling around the Country

The original text for the translation is from *Collected Plays of Minoru Betsuyaku (Vol. 16): The Story of the Two Knights Travelling Around the Country (Shokoku wo Henrekisuru Futari no Kishi no Monogatari: Betsuyaku Minoru Gikyoku Shū, pp.87-146)*, Tokyo: Sanichi Shobo, 1988.

CHARACTERS

KNIGHT 1
KNIGHT 2
SQUIRE 1
SQUIRE 2
THE DOCTOR
THE NURSE
THE PRIEST
THE INNKEEPER
THE DAUGHTER

Performance Poster (Leeds in November 1990)
Illustration by Kitty Burrows

The staging of *The Story of the Two Knights Travelling Around the Country* of this translation was from 27th November to 1st December in 1990 at the Workshop Theatre at Leeds.

The cast and the technical staff for the first English production of *Two Knights Travelling Around the Country* in the Workshop Theatre in 1990:

CAST

Knight 1	Greg Preston
Knight 2	Robert Burke
Squire 1	Emily McLaughlin
Squire 2	Alexandra Burton
The Doctor	Paul Lavin
The Nurse	Tanya Lees
The Priest	Jason Collidi
The Innkeeper	Adam Gamble
The Daughter	Lara Gisborne

TECHNICAL STAFF

Director	Masako Yuasa
Designer	Chris Jowett
Costume Designer	Kitty Burrows
Costume Assistants	Clare Huntley, Nikki Woodeson
Production Manager	Chris Jowett
Stage Management	Amanda Price, Alice O'Grady, Lisa Scorfield
Stage Crew	Donna Heppenstall, Lucy Carney
Lighting Design	Trevor Faulkner
Lighting Operator	Berkley Adams
Sound Designer	Peter Still
Sound Operator	Kim Greengrass
Properties	Tanya Lees

SCENE 1

Somewhere in the wasteland. A dead tree stands. A washed-out dirty wooden sign "THE MOBILE INN" hangs down from the tree. There are two crude beds by the tree. Some sail-cloth which is old and somewhat torn is suspended above the beds as a roof. There is an office desk and a chair beside them. Simple writing equipment, a hotel register book and a sign "INFORMATION" standing upright are placed on the desk. Down stage from the infromation desk there are a table and a few chairs, and a few glasses and a water jug have been left on the table. An enormous black silhouette of a windmill is seen behind these objects.

THE DOCTOR in a white coat, with a reflector on his head and a stethoscope hung round his neck, enters, followed by THE NURSE who carries a big black bag.

DOCTOR: Hey, look! What do you think it says here? [*Trying to read the sign*] Errr...

NURSE: It says the mobile inn.

DOCTOR: That's right. The mobile inn. [*Looking around*] So... do you know what that means?

NURSE: Are we staying at this sort of place tonight?

DOCTOR: I didn't say that. How many years have you been working for me? I am a doctor. So, I could give consultations to the guests at this inn. The people who come and stay at a place like this are mostly ill... well more than that... seriously ill.

NURSE: But there's nobody here.

DOCTOR: At the moment, no... however they'll be coming along soon. Anyhow this place is the mobile... [*He has forgotten what the sign says and tries to read it again.*] the mobile...

NURSE: It says the mobile inn.

DOCTOR: Yes, this place is the mobile inn... In other words, the innkeeper thought that somebody'd be bound to want to stay around here, so he built this here... But where is he?

NURSE: He might have moved on already.

DOCTOR: Nonsense... the mobile... [*He has forgotten the rest of it and tries to read it again.*] The mobile...

NURSE: It says inn.

DOCTOR: That's right inn... that means this can move as it is. So, it'd be stupid if only the inn-keeper had gone and the inn had been left behind... that's what I think... but can't you see him around somehwere close by?

NURSE [*Looking around perfunctorily*]: He doesn't seem to be here...

DOCTOR: I've got it.

NURSE: Has he passed on?

DOCTOR: Don't talk nonsense. Even if he had passed on, someone like his family and so on would be around, wouldn't they? It's not that. I say it must be a disease.

NURSE: A disease?

DOCTOR: Yes, and what's more, it was a sudden illness... [*Examining the place*] I can tell from a quick reasoning. Don't you think it looks as if they moved in a great hurry leaving everything behind? The attack must have come on suddenly... Do you think he was clasping his abdomen like this?

NURSE: Who are you talking about?

DOCTOR: The innkeeper.

NURSE: Well, I don't know.

DOCTOR: If he was, then it must have been his appendix. Appendicitis is the medical term. It might already have burst and peritonitis have set in. Dear, dear! If that is so, it'll mean a big operation. Have we parepared the sulphur medicine?

NURSE: Yes, I think we have... [*She puts down the bag and is about to take things out of it.*]

DOCTOR [*Stopping her*]: Not yet. Anyway, That's why all the family left him so suddenly. Really, if it were peritonitis, it would be terribly painful. We could use this table and [*pointing to the office desk*] that one as a sort of operating table. What do you think?

NURSE: Do you want me to move this over to that one?

DOCTOR: I've said, not yet. It could simply be appendix... Anyway, that is the reason why he is wandering around now, looking for a doctor...

NURSE: But I guess there aren't any doctors in this neighbourhood.

DOCTOR: What do you call this person under your very nose?

NURSE: Surely, except you, doctor, that's what I meant.

DOCTOR: That's... that's why... I say, in the end, he will have to come to me for help.

NURSE: Don't we have to let them know that you're here.

DOCTOR [*Sitting on the chair*]: How many times do I have to tell you? Doctors are sort of people whose value is enhanced when patients need to come and find them... so when they come back, don't look as if we've been walking around looking for patients. We must look as if we weren't a doctor and a nurse, and just happened to be here... In other words, when they come back from over there... Which way are they coming back from?

NURSE: Well, I don't know.

DOCTOR: Humm, it doesn't matter which way... We'll be facing in the opposite direction. Then, when they arrive and find us facing the other way, they'll ask whether I'm a doctor. I'll say, "Yes, I am," and they'll say, "Wonderful, we've been spared," somehow like that, it'll go... Do you see? It's at times like that, that I'm glad to be a doctor. [*Holding the water jug on the table*] Do you think it's water?

NURSE: Yes, I think so.

DOCTOR: Would it be all right to drink some?

NURSE: It belongs to the inn, doesn't it?

DOCTOR: I know that. But... don't you think they could be providing this free for passers-by?

NURSE: No, I don't...

DOCTOR: No, me neither...

NURSE: They put it here for the people who're staying.

DOCTOR: I guess so too. But, listen! If this is for them, if we put a bit of something in it, they would start getting diarrhoea in the night... See? We could do that...

NURSE: But doctor, you said, most people who come and stay at a place like this are mostly ill.

DOCTOR: Yes, I did, they are. But althought they are ill, many of them haven't noticed it ... just leave it to me... [*pointing at the bag*] there must be something in it ... something, like a laxative. [*He stands up.*]

NURSE [*Holding the bag under her arm*]: No, you can't.

DOCTOR: Why not?

NURSE: Because whenever you do that, you'll find you won't be able to cure it later.

DOCTOR: This time, I can cure it. Because it'll be simple diarrhoea. I'm not suggesting spreading dysentery or cholera. And even if I couldn't cure it, they'd only have taken a laxative. They'll recover by themselves with time... So, give it to me...

NURSE: No, I won't. [*She runs off.*]

THE PRIEST, carrying an open black umbrella and with a dirty sack over his soulder, enters reading the Bible.

PRIEST: Is anything wrong?

DOCTOR: No, no, nothing. [*To THE NURSE*] Come here, will you?

NURSE: Yes, sir. [*She sits on the chair.*]

PRIEST [*Looking around*]: Where's the patient?

DOCTOR: There aren't any patients here.

PRIEST: Surely not! You don't mean he's already passed on, do you?

DOCTOR: Why should someone die when they're in good health? And who are you?

PRIEST: I'm a touring Priest. I travel about in this area and pray for the dying. It's my job.

DOCTOR: Then why do you always follow us?

PRIEST: I don't. I simply follow God's will and walk around the places where I'm likely to find someone dying. Then, I don't know why, I always find that you have been there before me.

DOCTOR: Will yo please go somewhere else? Whatever you may think, we haven't found any patients here yet.

PRIEST: But this place... [*He tries to read the sign.*] Errr....

NURSE: It says the mobile inn.

PRIEST: That's right. The mobile type. In short this is an inn. And do you know what that means? It means the people who come to stay in a place like this often die, suddenly in the middle of the night... The doctor's efforts were of no avail, that's what people say... [*He sits on a chair and points at the water jug.*] Have you already put something in this water?

DOCTOR: No, we haven't.

PRIEST: Then I think I'll have a glass... [*He fills the glass.*] Anyway... I'm terribly thirsty...

NURSE: But don't you think they've provided it for the people staying at this inn?

PRIEST: I see. [*Pouring the water from the glass back into the water jug*] Ater all, you've already added something.

DOCTOR: Don't be silly. We haven't put anything in it. [*To THE NURSE*]

Why the hell did you say that?

NURSE: I only said that this water had been prepared by the people of this inn.

PRIEST: It must be a laxative, or something like that, that you've put in.

DOCTOR: Well, we were considering putting in a laxative, but we didn't. Nothing has been put in. [*To THE NURSE*] Isn't that so?

NURSE: Yes, it is.

PRIEST: Yes, you have.

DOCTOR: No, we haven't.

PRIEST: It doesn't matter. I'm not blaming you at all.

DOCTOR: Blaming us? Why should you? We haven't put anything in it.

PRIEST: So, I'm saying that I'm not blaming you, either. Putting effort into your business is a good thing… I wouldn't even be surprised if you'd added cyanide in this.

DOCTOR: Neither cyanide nor a laxative, we added nothing. [*To THE NURSE*] Hey, we didn't, did we?

NURSE: Did we? Sir, you must have heard that I said I wouldn't do that.

DOCTOR: Yes, you said no. That's why I gave up the idea because I thought you were right. [*To THE PRIEST*] It's true that… that we didn't put anything in it.

PRIEST: I said it's alright. It doesn't matter if it isn't cyanide.

DOCTOR: It is not cyanide. What's more we didn't put in a laxative, either. Isn't it you who wants to put some cyanide in rather than a laxative? [*To THE NURSE*] If he does that, he'll get his customers direct without our help.

PRIEST: It comes to the same thing. For, even if it were a mere laxative, you wouldn't be able to cure a patient with simple diarrhoea. Eventually they'll become my costomers.

DOCTOR: I'm sorry to say this but even if we couldn't cure them, we would charge the doctor's fee in our job.

PRIEST: That's the shoddy part of your profession. This might sound conceited, but in our case, we receive a fee only when we succeed. If our customers don't die, they'll take back their fees, even though we prayed a lot for them.

DOCTOR [*To THE NURSE*]: Listen, I'll cure the patients of diarrhoea tonight whatever happens, with all my power.

NURSE: But doctor, we haven't even put a laxative in it.

DOCTOR: That's true.

PRIEST: Yes, you have.
DOCTOR: No, we haven't.

THE INNKEEPER carrying a big basket of food has entered without being noticed.

INNKEEPER: What did you say you put in it? [*He picks up the water jug and looks in it.*]

THE DOCTOR, THE PRIEST and THE NURSE, each one is surprised and stands up.

DOCTOR: No, no, we were just explaining to him that we hadn't put anything in it.
INNKEEPER [*Looking at the glass*]: Someone must have drunk some.
PRIEST: You're mistaken... Well, yes, I poured water in it to drink some, but [*pointing at THE NURSE*] she said the water belonged to the inn, so I stopped doing it.
INNKEEPER [*To THE PRIEST*]: Is it you who drank this?
PRIEST: Listen, I'm telling you that I didn't drink it.
INNKEEPER: I see... Then, it's alright... [*He looks over the three again.*] Are you staying tonight?
DOCTOR: No, we aren't. Of course, we wouldn't mind staying tonight. We rather thought your guests would feel safer when they became ill and found us here.
INNKEEPER: I thought so. [*Putting away the basket and starting his work*] Whenever I open the inn, before the customers' arrival, the people who do business with them all turn up... the people just like you... But I'm pretty sure that there won't be anything doing tonight...
PRIEST: Nothing doing? Why not?
INNKEEPER: Wrong wind... [*Licking his forefinger and holding it up in the air.*] See? The wind is blowing from here to here.

The Three lick their fingers and hold them up in the air. The wind blows across the wasteland. From about this time the atmosphere on stage gradually gets shadowy and dense.

INNKEEPER: In other words, it means that I should have built this further west…for tonight… certainly at this moment there are four people wandering about… But all of them will turn away in that direction pushed by the wind. [*Returning to his work*] So, all of you, you'd better give up… We won't have any patients or dead people tonight.

DOCTOR: Well, then, how about us helping you to move this inn to the west where those four are going now?

PRIEST: I don't mind helping you.

INNKEEPER [*Continuing his work*]: I don't know how many years you've been doing this sort of thing, but you don't know much about business. At least with the inn, it puts up the value more when we let the customers find us for themselves. We aren't supposed to run after customers.

PRIEST: Then, what can we do?

INNKEEPER: Well, all we can do is to pray that the wind changes direction.

The singing of a song, 'There's No Place Like Home,' is heard with the sounds of the wind in the distance.

NURSE: I wonder what that is?

DOCTOR: It's a girl. It sounds like she's in a terrible pain.

PRIEST: She might be crying for help.

NURSE: It sounds like she's singing a song to me.

Before long the singing gradually gets closer and THE INNKEEPER'S DAUGHTER, putting up a parasol, enters slowly. She ignores the three who are stunned, walks around the table and finishes her singing at the centre stage.

DAUGHTER [*Facing the centre of the auditorium*]: Father, at last our long-awaited guests are arriving.

DOCTOR: Father? Is that me?

INNKEEPER: It's me! What are you saying? Doctor, do you have a daughter?

DOCTOR: No, I don't. So, I thought that was funny, too.

INNKEEPER: She is my daughter. Don't ever touch her… with your dirty hands! [*To THE DAUGHTER*] From which direction?

DAUGHTER [*Pointing*]: That direction.

INNKEEPER: I see. It seems the wind has changed direction.

DAUGHTER: No, it hasn't, but they turned when they heard my singing.

INNKEEPER: That does happen. There are customers of that sort. What did they look like?

DAUGHTER: They were a knight and his squire.

INNKEEPER: Knights? What are they?

DOCTOR: Knights are the people who…

INNKEEPER: I'm not asking you.

DOCTOR: I beg your pardon…

DAUGHTER: Knights are the people who ride horses, carry spears, wear helmets and travel about the country with their squires with the aim of punishing scoundrels.

INNKEEPER: I've got a bad premonition.

PRIEST: Is he riding a horse?

DAUGHTER: No, he isn't.

DOCTOR: Is he holding a spear?

DAUGHTER: No, he isn't.

NURSE: Then why do you call him a knight?

DAUGHTER: He's wearing a helmet.

NURSE: Is that all?

DAUGHTER: And he was with his squire.

INNKEEPER: Did he look strong?

DAUGHTER: You mean the squire?

INNKEEPER: No, the knight.

DAUGHTER: He was only just moving.

DOCTOR: In that case, he'll do fine.

INNKEEPER: How about the squire?

DAUGHTER: He was only just alive.

PRIEST: I see some hope here.

INNKEEPER: It sounds like we can manage this.

DAUGHTER: I'm worrying whether they can get here safely.

INNKEEPER: Are they so bad?

DAUGHTER: Yes, they are. When I first saw them, I thought that there were two dead trees standing. But when I looked closer, I found they were moving.

The wind blows.

NURSE: One trouble after another.

DOCTOR [*To THE INNKEEPER*]: I just want to make one thing clear. If they die before they get here, are they still your customers or not?

INNKEEPER: It's obvious. All the people walking towards here are my customers.

DOCTOR: In that case, I shall take their last pulse.

PRIEST: And I shall pray for them after you.

DAUGHTER: Shall I go and look for them? To check if they're still moving.

DOCTOR: Will you?

INNKEEPER: No, let's wait.

PRIEST: What if they never get here?

INNKEEPER: If they don't get here, we can go and pick them up. Anyway, all of you, will you please go somewhere for the time being? We must prepare for welcoming the guests.

DOCTOR: Why? How about all of us welcoming them together?

PRIEST: That's right...

INNKEEPER: They're my customers... [*To THE DAUGHTER*] You look after this table... [*He goes to the information desk.*]

DAUGHTER: Yes, Father. [*She folds the parasol, puts on the apron and is about to clean the table with a dishcloth.*]

PRIEST: But they're ours too...

INNKEEPER [*Doing some work*]: They turned this way because my daughter sang a song... Otherwise they would have been blown in that direction by the wind.

NURSE: Here they come!

INNKEEPER: Do they?

DOCTOR: Already?

NURSE: But is that them?

A voice: "Get out of the way! Get out of the way!" is heard and something approaches from the distance.

INNKEEPER: It's true, they're coming. Watch out! This is terrible. Hey, move the table. Put away the water jug. The chairs as well! Quickly! Careful! Hey!

KNIGHT 1, who wears a helmet made of a squashed washbasin and holds a long cane with some dirty cloth tied on the top end, sits on a chair in a hand-cart.

SQUIRE 1, who also wears a helmet made of a squashed saucepan, runs bustling onto the stage pulling the hand-cart in which KNIGHT 1 is sitting.

SQUIRE 1: Get out of the way, get out of the way, get out of the way, get out of the way, get out of the way…
KNIGHT 1 [*Shouting as if he were threatening somebody ahead*]: Wooow!

Following THE INNKEEPER's instruction, THE DAUGHTER moves the water jug and glasses, THE PRIEST and THE INNKEEPER himself move the table, and THE DOCTOR and THE NURSE move the chairs just in time to make way for the hand-cart. The hand-cart runs straight through.

DOCTOR: What was that?
INNKEEPER [*To THE DAUGHTER*]: Was that them?
DAUGHTER: No, that wasn't them? I think those I saw were much thinner and slower than that.
PRIEST: I'm glad it wasn't them. I don't think they are as strong as they look, but at any rate they looked terribly reckless.

While each of them moves the chairs, the table and so on back where they were…

DAUGHTER: The man I saw looked much thinner and slower, and quieter and more intelligent.
NURSE [*Turning back and looking*]: In that case, is that the one?
DAUGHTER [*Peering in the direction in which THE NURSE is looking and affirming*]: Yes, that's the one.
DOCTOR: Which one?
DAUGHTER [*Pointing*]: The one, over there.
DOCTOR: Eh? [*Changing the angle*] That one? You mean that?
INNKEEPER: Which one is that one?
NURSE: Can't you see the one over there? No, no, not that far, just there.
INNKEEPER: Well…
PRIEST: He doesn't seem to be moving, does he?
DAUGHTER: Yes, he does. If you look hard, you'll see he's moving.

All the people look hard at him.

DOCTOR [*Overbalancing*]: Oops… it's true… he moved.

DAUGHTER: You see…

INNKEEPER: Faster than I thought.

PRIEST: Although he isn't as fast as the last one.

NURSE: But the other one isn't moving.

DAUGHTER: He'll move soon.

DOCTOR: I wonder if he is feeling unwell?

INNKEEPER: Now, all of you, will you please go somewhere?

PRIEST: Please don't say that.

DOCTOR: They might be ill.

DAUGHTER: Our guests would be embarrassed… if they saw so many people welcoming them.

INNKEEPER: Yes, they would. I don't want to embarrass my guests.

As the three are about to retreat pushed by THE INNKEEPER, KNIGHT 2, who wears a ragged frock coat and a helmet of a squashed wash-basin, slowly walks in with a cane which has a dirty cloth tied on the top.

KNIGHT 2: Hello, all of you… Are you surprised? Well, you shouldn't. There isn't an army division launching an attack behind me… [*Walking slowly*] However, if you don't want the things around here to be broken, you'd better put them away quickly. Because I'm running through here like a GALE from now. [*Once more checking the way he said it*] Like a GALE… [*To THE DAUGHTER who approaches him*] Would you please try saying that?

DAUGHTER: Like a gale? [*She supports KNIGHT 2 who is unsteady on his feet.*]

KNIGHT 2: That's right… It means like a strong wind. What's more it's a gale. This means even your eyes can't catch me… But what are you doing here, all of you?

Daughter: We've been waiting for you, sir.

KNIGHT 2: It's no good you're waiting for me…Because I'll run through … like a gale… by flapping my frock coat… Do you see my frock coat flopping?

DAUGHTER: Yes … but, since you're here… how about stopping for a short rest? That person over there seems terribly exhausted, too.

KNIGHT 2: That person over there? (*Pointing to Stage Right*) You mean him?

DAUGHTER: Yes.

KNIGHT 2: No more hope for him.

KNIGHT 2 has already approached the table. THE INNKEEPER stands near the table. The other three have been pushed away by THE INNKEEPER under the tree Stage Left.

INNKEEPER: No more hope? [*He offers KNIGHT 2 a chair to sit on.*]

KNIGHT 2 [*Sitting on it naturally*]: He has departed this life over there, as we say, 'Alas! At last.'

PRIEST [*Involuntarily coming closer*]: Is he dead? [*He is driven back by THE INNKEEPER.*]

KNIGHT 2: If you feel like doing so, I appreciate it if you would pour him a handful of sand later.

DAUGHTER: But hasn't he been travelling with you up to now?

KNIGHT 2 [*Becoming a little sorrowful*]: Yes, he has. I'm not saying this because he's gone but he was hopeless… really, he was.

INNKEEPER: But, what will you do about his belongings?

NURSE: Just a moment. He moved just now.

DOCTOR: Moved?

DAUGHTER: It's true… he's moving.

KNIGHT 2: Don't worry. It's his so-called 'hour of death'… In other words, we all come to want to move a bit just before we pass on. It doesn't mean he's alive… He's simply moving.

NURSE: But he is walking.

PRIEST: It looks as if he's trying to come towards us.

INNKEEPER [*To KNIGHT 2*]: What shall we do?

KNIGHT 2: Well… can't you find something like a stick around?

INNKEEPER: A stick? [*He looks around.*]

DAUGHTER: What are you going to do with a stick?

KNIGHT 2 [*Noticing his own cane*]: Oh, this will do. With this… [*handing the cane to THE INNKEEPER*] his … [*pointing to the back of his head*] here… go and strike him here hard.

DOCTOR: Are you going to kill him?

KNIGHT 2: No, I'm not. He's already dead. Only, I'm letting him know about it because he hasn't noticed it yet.

DAUGHTER: I think he's smiling at you.

KNIGHT 2: Smiling?

DAUGHTER: Yes.

KNIGHT 2: Why is he smiling?

INNKEEPER: Well, I don't know.

NURSE: I suppose he must be pleased to know that he's able to move.

KNIGHT 2: He's awful really. I'm not pleased at all to know he's able to move. But he believes it makes me happy too. Well, listen, let's pretend we're not here when he comes over here.

PRIEST: If we do that, what'll happen?

KNIGHT 2: If we do that, he will think there's nobody around here and go away.

SQUIRE 2: Hello, good evening.

SQUIRE 2, who wears a helmet made of a squashed saucepan, carries a big dirty sack and holds a short cane, comes in almost crawling.

KNIGHT 2: Please remember that we aren't here.

SQUIRE 2 [*Ignoring what KNIGHT 2 said and approaching the table*]: I'm terribly sorry that I'm late, sir. Normally I get to the place first and tell people that my master is arriving soon, so please give him a warm welcome. But unfortunately my shoelace was broken…

KNIGHT 2 [*To all the others*]: That's a lie.

SQUIRE 2 [*Ignoring him*]: It had been threatening to happen since this morning and finally it did. So, I reluctantly asked my master to go first. Oh, dear! [*To THE DAUGHTER*] What a beautiful lady! Are you the daughter of this inn by any chance?

DAUGHTER: Yes, I am. [*She runs off.*]

SQUIRE 2: Needless to say, I was well prepared to get my revenge if something happened to my master because I asked him to go first on his own. [*To THE INNKEEPER*] Are you the owner of this inn?

INNKEEPER: Yes, I am. [*He runs off.*]

SQUIRE 2: That's the responsibility of a squire who travels with a knight. If my master died when he drank water served by the inn… [*Pointing to the water jug on the table*] I'm not talking about this… Before his body was buried… of course I wouldn't forget the courtesy of pouring a handful of sand for him, but who put poison in this water…?

DOCTOR: Nothing has been put in it.

SQUIRE 2 [*Looking into the water jug*]: Is this empty, then?

PRIEST: No, of course there's some water in it.

SQUIRE 2: So, the question is who added poison to the water, and who made my master drink it and killed him.

KNIGHT 2: Someone, make him shut up!

SQUIRE 2: I'd like to pursue this point here, now. All of you, please listen. The reason why I have to pursue it is…

KNIGHT 2: Shut him up.

INNKEEPER: But aren't we supposed not to be here?

KNIGHT 2: But, we are here in fact.

SQUIRE 2 [*To THE NURSE*]: Was it you who put poison in it?

NURSE: No, it wasn't me.

KNIGHT 2: Oi…

DOCTOR [*To SQUIRE 2*]: Your master is saying that you should shut up, mister.

SQUIRE 2: I'm going to, sure… [*He puts down the bag.*]

INNKEEPER [*Taking the bag and while carrying it into the inner part of the inn*]: He's shut up, sir.

SQUIRE 2: I'm not talking just because I want to talk. But when I stop talking just for a few seconds, my master thinks I might be dead. So I must talk, all the time, before my master thinks I'm dead, even if I don't want to, in order not to be thought to be dead by my master.

KNIGHT 2: He hasn't shut up at all.

INNKEEPER [*Coming out of the inner part of the inn*]: Shut up!

SQUIRE 2: Yes, sir. [*He sits on the chair and lays his face on the table.*]

KNIGHT 2: You see? When I look at this sod, I sometimes come to think there are some people who might be better off dead.

DAUGHTER: But isn't he your squire?

KNIGHT 2: That's why… [*Trying to take off the helmet*] Let… let me take off my helmet… it doesn't look there's anyone who's likely to do us any harm around here. [*Finally taking off the helmet helped by THE DAUGHTER*] When I'm with him, simply standing somewhere near him, he makes me feel as if I were being put through an ordeal of life.

PRIEST [*Approaching SQUIRE 2*]: He seems truly exhausted.

KNIGHT 2 [*To THE INNKEEPER who is about to put away the helmet*]: Put it somewhere close by, will you? I might need it in an emergency. [*To THE PRIEST*] No, he isn't. He doesn't know what it means to be exhausted.

DOCTOR: Would you mind if I examine him briefly?

KNIGHT 2: No, I wouldn't. It's up to you whether you examine him or not. I've always offered him freely for people's research, without charge, of course.

DOCTOR: Without charge? I didn't mean that it would be free this case.

KNIGHT 2: Are you going to pay me some money then?

DOCTOR: No, no, I didn't mean that…

NURSE [*Having been taking SQUIRE 2's pulse during the conversation between KNIGHT 2 and THE DOCTOR*]: Oh, dear!

DOCTOR: What is it?

NURSE: I don't feel any pulse.

DOCTOR: No pulse?

NURSE: No. [*She stands up, frightened.*]

INNKEEPER: Is he dead?

NURSE: Well, his pulse isn't beating …

PRIEST: He looked so well until only a few minutes ago though…

SQUIRE 2: That's why… [*looking up reluctantly*] that's why, didn't I tell you? When I stop talking for a second, soon my master thinks that I might be dead.

KNIGHT 2: It wasn't me who said you were dead.

SQUIRE 2: Whoever it was, I ought to keep talking.

KNIGHT 2: You ought not. [*Pointing to THE NURSE*] This woman didn't think you were dead because you were quiet, but because you didn't have any pulse… [*To THE NURSE*] Look, you must understand he's never had a pulse.

NURSE: He hasn't got a pulse?

KNIGHT 2: No, he hasn't. So don't ever think that he's dead even if you don't feel any pulse. If you want to know whether he is dead or alive, check whether he's talking or not.

SQUIRE 2: That's why I ought to keep talking.

KNIGHT 2: Shut up! [*To THE NURSE*] And there are occasions when he's alive even if he's quiet… [*To SQUIRE 2*] So you may keep silence now.

SQUIRE 2: Yes, master. [*He sits down and lays his face down on the table again.*]

KNIGHT 2: I wish you'd stop poking your noses into his affairs now… People who would be better off dead often want to stay alive really.

DOCTOR: Excuse me, sir… but if he hasn't got a pulse, how does he manage to be alive?

KNIGHT 2: How does he manage? That's exactly what I want to know. Could it be true that he talks instead of having a pulse?

SQUIRE 2 [*Looking up*]: Am I supposed to talk?

KNIGHT 2: No, you aren't.

SQUIRE 2: I see… [*He faces down.*]

KNIGHT 2: Anyway, let's not only stop poking our noses into his affairs, but also stop talking about him. We must stop thinking of him as well.

DAUGHTER [*Coming out of the inner part of the inn and to KNIGHT 2*]: Do you mind if we get your dinner ready?

KNIGHT 2: Dinner? What is that?

DAUGHTER: What we mean by dinner is … well… Eh? Excuse me sir, but did you just ask me what dinner was?

KNIGHT 2: Yes, I did.

DAUGHTER: Well, so… what we mean by dinner is … like this [*making an incomprehensible gesture*] for example, imagine that the thing in this hand is a fork and the thing in the other hand is a knife and…

Some clattering metal noises: 'Gachan! Gachan!' approach the stage. SQUIRE 1, who wears a helmet made of a saucepan, metal breast-plate and leggings, from which knives and forks hang, with a chain around his waist, and holds a rusty spear, enters like a robot. SQUIRE 1 who passed by once comes back formally dressed. There are two small holes in the saucepan so that he can see forward through them, but in fact he seems not to be able to see very well and tries to sense the atmosphere.

SQUIRE 1 [*Stopping and not to anybody in particular*]: Good evening. Is anybody here? I suppose there must be somebody around here. It's funny. [*Making some clattering noises: 'Gachan!', 'Gachan!' and turning around awkwardly*] Is anybody here?

KNIGHT 2: Yes.

SQUIRE 1: Oh, there is… [*Moving noisily*] Where are you?

KNIGHT 2: I'm here.

SQUIRE 1: Oh, you're there. I thought that you were here. [*Moving noisily*] Well, I can't find you.

KNIGHT 2: Not there, here!

SQUIRE 1 [*Moving*]: Where?

INNKEEPER: Here, we're here. [*He bangs the table with a glass.*]

SQUIRE 1: Will you please stop saying here or there and just tell me north or south, or east or west... oh, I've found you.

KNIGHT 2: What are you?

SQUIRE 1: I've come along.

KNIGHT 2: We know that. Because the way you've come along wasn't so very quiet. What I'm asking you is why you've come along? I don't think you came along to sell flowers.

SQUIRE 1: I didn't come to sell flowers. I came here to fight a duel.

KNIGHT 2: A duel?

SQUIRE 1: Yes.

KNIGHT 2: Who with?

SQUIRE 1: With you.

KNIGHT 2: What'll happen after that?

SQUIRE 1: After that? You mean after someone's won the duel?

KNIGHT 2: Well, yes...

SQUIRE 1: The one who's won the duel sets the person free.

Needless to say, SQUIRE 1 meant THE DAUGHTER, but KNIGHT 2 mistook the person for THE INNKEEPER.

KNIGHT 2 [*Pointing to THE INNKEEPER*]: You mean this person?

SQUIRE 1: Yes...

KNIGHT 2: I'd rather lose a duel than set him free.

SQUIRE 2 [*To SQUIRE 1*]: Aren't you talking about his daughter?

SQUIRE 1: Yes, of course.

KNIGHT 2: Oh, you mean her?

SQUIRE 1: Is there anyone else here apart from her?

KNIGHT 2: I see, you mean her... [*To THE DAUGHTER*] Well, maiden, are you unfree?

DAUGHTER: No, sir, not that much.

KNIGHT 2 [*To SQUIRE 1*]: She says she isn't that much unfree.

SQUIRE 1: But at least she thinks she's a bit unfree.

KNIGHT 2: All right, then.

SQUIRE 2: Are you going to do it?

KNIGHT 2: It can't be helped... anyway, this business of standing up is a nuisance. [*To SQUIRE 1*] Oi, Squire, are you going to do it with that spear?

SQUIRE 1: Me? It's not me who's going to do, I mean, if you are talking about the duel.

KNIGHT 2: Then who's going to do it?

SQUIRE 1: Who? [*Looking around and calling out to KNIGHT 1 as if he were just near them*] Master… master… [*A little louder*] Master… [*To all*] Excuse me, but can you see my master somewhere about there?

SQUIRE 2 [*Standing up and going to SQUIRE 1*]: Your master? What does he look like?

Except KNIGHT 2 who is sitting on the chair, and THE INNKEEPER and THE DAUGHTER who are preparing the meal, everyone else goes to SQUIRE 1.

SQUIRE 1: So, he looks like… [*making a gesture with his hands*] this and…

DOCTOR: Is he round?

SQUIRE 1: No, he isn't… He isn't round, just very ordinary like…

All the people act as if they were looking for something on the ground in some way.

NURSE: But aren't you talking about a person?

SQUIRE 1: Yes, it is a person since he is my master.

NURSE: Then isn't he bigger than that?

SQUIRE 1: Yes, he is big. Because he's bigger than me.

PRIEST: Bigger than you?

SQUIRE 1: Yes.

PRIEST: Then he's up somewhere? [*He looks upwards.*]

DOCTOR: Do you mean he's floating in the air?

SQUIRE 1: Certainly not. He stands properly like this…

DOCTOR [*To THE PRIEST*]: Since he isn't floating in the air…if we look around in the normal way like this…

KNIGHT 1, who wears a helmet made of a squashed wash-basin and a dirty long coat, and holds a long cane, slowly walks in.

KNIGHT 1: The one you are looking for is of this type?

SQUIRE 2: This is the one… [*To SQUIRE 1*] Isn't it?

SQUIRE 1: Which one?

NURSE [*Turning SQUIRE 1's face to KNIGHT 1*]: Over there.

SQUIRE 1: Yes, this one…Master, where have you been? I just guessed that you'd be in this area so… [*He is about to go close to KNIGHT 1.*]

DOCTOR: He isn't round.

PRIEST: No, he isn't.

KNIGHT 1 [*Walking towards the table*]: I am elusive, so when you expect me to be here, I appear from over there. [*Saying to SQUIRE 2, while pointing at SQUIRE 1*] Please don't let him come any nearer.

SQUIRE 2: But isn't he your squire?

KNIGHT 1: It seems he believes so, but I don't. [*He sits on the chair.*]

SQUIRE 1 [*Still getting closer to KNIGHT 1*]: But I've asked for a duel properly.

KNIGHT 1: And did you win?

SQUIRE 1: Did I win? Well, is it me who's going to do it? I mean, fight a duel?

KNIGHT 1: No, it isn't really, but… I only thought if you had fought it before my arrival, I wouldn't mind… [*To KNIGHT 2*] Are you pretending not to be here?

KNIGHT 2: No, I'm not. I've never been here at all from the start.

KNIGHT 1: I see. I thought you mightn't have been… Mind you I'm not here, either.

KNIGHT 2: Well, I thought so.

KNIGHT 1 [*Pointing to the water jug on the table*]: Is that water?

DAUGHTER: Yes, it is. Would you like some? [*She pours some water in the glass.*]

KNIGHT 1: No, I didn't mean that. The reason why I asked you if it was water was, because I wondered if it might have been poisoned. Have you poured it already?

DAUGHTER: Yes, I have, I'm sorry.

SQUIRE 1: That's all right. Then, let me drink it in place of him.

The glass is about to be passed from THE DAUGHTER to SQUIRE 2, then from SQUIRE 2 to SQUIRE 1. THE DOCTOR, THE NURSE and THE PRIEST avoid the glass as if not so intendedly and go behind SQUIRE 1.

KNIGHT 1: No, don't let him drink it.

SQUIRE 2 [*Holding the glass*]: Why not? This fellow says he wants to drink it.

KNIGHT 1: He drinks water all day, all the time. If he drinks any more, he'll get rusty and won't be able to move. Give it to me…

The glass is handed from SQUIRE 2 to THE DAUGHTER and from THE DAUGHTER to KNIGHT 1.

SQUIRE 1 [*Chasing it*]: Please let me drink it. I'm terribly thirsty.

KNIGHT 1 [*Looking into the glass*]: No, you mustn't. There's so much in the glass.

SQUIRE 1: Please, master.

KNIGHT 1: Well, then, you can drink half of it…

SQUIRE 1: Half is fine.

KNIGHT 1 [*To THE NURSE beside him*]: Will you drink half first?

NURSE: Yes, sir. [*She takes it involuntarily and gulps it down.*]

A short silence. THE NURSE groans, stares her eyes out, tears her throat and falls. All the people keep still. Coming to himself, THE DOCTOR runs to THE NURSE and examines her.

DOCTOR: She's dead. [*Standing up absent-mindedly.*]

SQUIRE 2: It had been poisoned after all. Look, it had been poisoned as I said. That's why I warned you a while ago that there might have been some poison added, in other words, someone might've put poison in it and…

KNIGHT 2: Shut up!

SQUIRE 2: Yes, master…

PRIEST [*To THE DOCTOR*]: Wasn't it you who added the poison?…

DOCTOR: No, it wasn't me. Well, my nurse knows that I didn't do that… this [*realising the situation and pointing at THE NURSE*] this nurse, she was the only one who knew.

The wind blows… There are two portions of dinner on the table.

KNIGHT 1 [*Wiping the fingertips with a napkin*]: How about taking it away? On second thoughts, it's not so bad to dine looking at a corpse…

Excluding two knights at the table and THE DAUGHTER, the people on stage pick up the corpse together and go off stage. THE DAUGHTER serves wine in the glasses for the knights.

DAUGHTER: Please enjoy your dinner. [*She goes off to the inner part of the inn.*]

When the knights are left alone on the stage, they begin to look like mere old men than knights.

KNIGHT 2 [*Holding a glass and having a sip*]: Was it you?...

KNIGHT 1 [*Having a sip, too*]: What?

KNIGHT 2 [*Suggesting the direction in which the corpse was carried*]: The one that did that.

KNIGHT 1: It was only my way of greeting ... [*He gives sounds of supressed laughter: ku-ku-ku.*] Have you seen that? It's what people call 'sleight of hand.'

KNIGHT 2: Well, I must say you were quite skilful but if I were you, I'd have gone for her ears.

The basket of bread is placed in the centre of the table and while tearing and eating bread...

KNIGHT 1: Her ears? What do you mean by that?

KNIGHT 2: Pouring poison into the ears produces a slow effect... The slower the poison works, the greater the pain it causes... She might have writhed in agony from about there to over there at least... I think she only went from there to there.

KNIGHT 1: No, no, I think it was more to there.

KNIGHT 2: Still if we had put it in her ear, she'd have moved to over there. What's more, with an awful lot of agony...

KNIGHT 1: But, listen, then how could one have told her to drink the water in the glass with her ears?

KNIGHT 2: So, I must admit there's a problem there...

A church-bell rings in the distance.

KNIGHT 1: A church-bell is ringing... Oh, isn't it nice?

KNIGHT 2: What?

KNIGHT 1: I mean... a person died, a church bell rings and the night has fallen...

KNIGHT 2: Yes... and what makes me feel indescribably good is that it isn't me who died.

KNIGHT 1: That's the thing. Yes, that's the thing my friend.

Blackout.

SCENE II

The same setting as SCENE I. The corner where the beds have been placed is screened by a dirty curtain. Meanwhile KNIGHT 1 and KNIGHT 2 are still at the table taking their time having dinner. In the dark behind them stand THE DOCTOR, THE PRIEST, SQUIRE 1 and SQUIRE 2. They seem to be waiting impatiently for the two knights to finish their meal. Now and then they come out to check the knights and go back disappointed. THE INNKEEPER also pokes his head out from behind the curtain from time to time. The sounds of wind.

KNIGHT 1 [*Stopping his hands abruptly and facing up*]: Oh!

KNIGHT 2: What is it?

KNIGHT 1: Do you think autumn has come?

KNIGHT 2: Autumn?

KNIGHT 1: Yes, when I looked up just now, I felt something like that in my nose.

KNIGHT 2: In your nose? It's not autumn.

KNIGHT 1: No, not autumn?

KNIGHT 2: No, it isn't autumn… You don't feel autumn in your nose.

KNIGHT 1: I see… Then, what was it that I felt in my nose just now?

KNIGHT 2: It was love.

KNIGHT 1: Love, was it?

KNIGHT 2: Yes, it was. When one gets old, one feels love in the nose.

KNIGHT 1: In the nose. [*Going back to his plate*] I thought it might be.

KNIGHT 2 [*Pointing at KNIGHT 1's dish*]: Is that nice?

KNIGHT 1: Awful.

KNIGHT 2: I thought so. When I tried it a little while ago it tasted awful.

KNIGHT 1 [*Keeping on eating nonchalantly*]: Why didn't you say so before?

KNIGHT 2: I wanted to hear what you'd say about it.

KNIGHT 1 [*Tasting*]: Awful…

KNIGHT 2: Then I was right. I thought it was truly awful.

KNIGHT 1 [*Pointing at the other thing on his plate*]: How about this one?

KNIGHT 2 [*Staring at the same thing on his plate*]: I'm positive, it'll taste worse.

KNIGHT 1: Shall we try?

KNIGHT 2: Yes, let's.

KNIGHT 1: But wait.

KNIGHT 2: What?

KNIGHT 1: I felt love a moment ago.

KNIGHT 2: Yes, in your nose.

KNIGHT 1 [*Blowing his nose with the napkin*]: Anyhow, in other words, I shall be loved by someone.

KNIGHT 2: Or I shall be.

KNIGHT 1: But it's me who felt the love. This, my nose felt it.

KNIGHT 2: The wind's been blowing in this direction, hasn't it? So the love came from there and made a turn like this...

KNIGHT 1: Does love make turns?

KNIGHT 2: Yes, depending on the wind direction. [*He goes back to his plate.*]

KNIGHT 1 [*Also going back to his plate*]: Do you think it's the innkeeper?

KNIGHT 2: What?

KNIGHT 1: The one who's sending you love.

KNIGHT 2: It might be that maiden.

KNIGHT 1: You mean the one who's died?

KNIGHT 2: No, the one who hasn't died yet.

KNIGHT 1 [*Tasting the food in his mouth*]: How is it?

KNIGHT 2 [*Also tasting the food in his mouth*]: This?

KNIGHT 1: Yes.

KNIGHT 2: Once I ate horse dung with salt. This falls a little short of that.

KNIGHT 1: Once I ate it without salt. This falls more or less the same level.

KNIGHT 2: You mean it tastes awful?

KNIGHT 1: Did you think that I meant it was tasty?

KNIGHT 2: No, no, I guessed you meant awful, but... By the way what did you do with your horse?

KNIGHT 1: Don't ask me about my horse... I don't want to remember it.

KNIGHT 2: Alright. I won't... It's all the same to me. You've eaten it, haven't you?

KNIGHT 1: Yes, I have. I ate it crying all the while.

KNIGHT 2: I cried too when I was eating mine. The only thing that consoled me was that it was quite tasty.

KNIGHT 1: Tasty?

KNIGHT 2: Fairly...

KNIGHT 1: Then why did you cry?

KNIGHT 2: Why? It's because it was the horse which I had been riding... Although it was awfully uncomfortable to ride.

KNIGHT 1: The reason I cried was that it tasted terrible.

KNIGHT 2: Tasted terrible?

KNIGHT 1: Yes, it did. It tasted awful. It would have been much better riding it than eating it since it was that bad.

KNIGHT 2: Perhaps you might've forgotten to put salt on it.

KNIGHT 1: Salt?

KNIGHT 2: It's the same with horse dung… it's crucial with horse meat if it is to taste good, that you put some salt on it, and some pepper.

KNIGHT 1: Salt and pepper… [*Looking over the table*] Hey, isn't there anything left to eat?

KNIGHT 2: It seems we've finished mostly.

KNIGHT 1: But that horse would have been no good even with salt and pepper. But I must admit it walked well…

KNIGHT 2: Things are like that. When a horse can walk well, it tastes bad.

KNIGHT 1: That's right. What's more, the point is, after you've eaten it, it's too late to say that it would have been a better idea to keep it alive.

KNIGHT 2: Exactly, and it makes you cry.

KNIGHT 1: Yes, it does.

KNIGHT 2: Hey, how about ordering one or two dishes just as a mere morsel?

KNIGHT 1: That would be a good idea. However tasteless they might be, they couldn't be as bad as that horse.

KNIGHT 2 taps the glass with the end of his fork, 'chin-chin.' THE DAUGHTER comes out.

DAUGHTER: What can I do for you?

KNIGHT 2: Um, well, we'd like to try one or two more dishes. Anything would do… Well, they won't be very good in any case… we know that, but…

DAUGHTER [*A little bewildered*]: Are you going to eat them?

KNIGHT 2: That's right. We are not intending to stamp on them.

DAUGHTER: Excuse me sirs, but will you please wait for a moment? [*She runs off to the inn.*]

KNIGHT 2: That maiden isn't so bad.

KNIGHT 1: You think so?

KNIGHT 2: You saw her too.

KNIGHT 1: Yes, but I didn't smell.

KNIGHT 2: Shall I call her again? [*Holding the fork*] When I tap the glass, she comes out.

Just as KNIGHT 2 is about to tap the glass, 'chin-chin,' THE INNKEEPER gives a cry "Woooow!" from inside and at the same time an empty food-basket is thrown out. THE INNKEEPER come out.

KNIGHT 1: What's the matter?

INNKEEPER: What's the matter? Did you say that you were going to eat more?

KNIGHT 2 [*Flinching a little*]: Well, one or two dishes.

INNKEEPER: One or two dishes? Look at this. [*Pointing at the empty food basket*] Nothing's left any more… It's you who've eaten up all the food.

KNIGHT 1: We said we wouldn't mind how bad it tasted.

INNKEEPER: Whether it tastes good or bad, whatever you may say, there's nothing left here… [*Holding the basket in the hand upside down*] Look, not even a few breadcrumbs.

THE PRIEST, THE DOCTOR, SQUIRE 1 and SQUIRE 2, being aware of the situation, come out of the dark area nervously.

INNKEEPER: Until last night this basket was [*making a mountain with his hands*] heaped up with food like this. But you came and ate it up all!

DOCTOR: All of it?

INNKEEPER: Yes, all of it.

THE DAUGHTER appears.

INNKEEPER: All the food, including what we are going to eat tonight. What's more, I had kept the food for tomorrow's breakfast and lunch as well. You old buggers, you ate it all up!

KNIGHT 2 [*To KNIGHT 1*]: Friend, are you singing a song?

KNIGHT 1: No, no, I'm not singing a song.

PRIEST [*To THE INNKEEPER*]: Why didn't you tell them beforehand?

INNKEEPER: Why didn't I… [*To THE DAUGHTER*] Why didn't you tell them that they had eaten up their share?

DAUGHTER: Well, I was going to, but they kept ordering, little by little, one more dish and one more dish…

SQUIRE 2: Even so, apparently the food in the basket was getting less and less, when you saw that, you should have noticed... that our share would be taken up... We were waiting... waiting for our table. Because somebody [*pointing at THE INNKEEPER*] yes, it was you... you said that we could eat dinner when the table became free.

INNKEEPER: I know. But there's nothing we can do, is there? These buggers ate it all up.

SQUIRE 1 [*All of a sudden loudly*]: Eeeeh?

SQUIRE 2: What's the matter?

SQUIRE 1: No dinner tonight?

SQUIRE 2: Not only no dinner tonight. No breakfast tomorrow, either.

SQUIRE 1: Eeeeh?

SQUIRE 2: No lunch, either.

SQUIRE 1: Eeeeh?

DOCTOIR: Alright. Let's calm down. What's done is done. [*To THE INN-KEEPER*] Listen, what I would say for now is...

KNIGHT 2 [*To KNIGHT 1*]: Friend, are you still eating something?

KNIGHT 1: No, I'm not. I just found a grapeseed here and it had got a little fresh, so I was chewing it. [*He spits a grapeseed out of his mouth.*]

DOCTOR: So what I suggest is... [*To THE INNKEEPER*] we must just wait you go to town to get some food in that basket and come back here with it.

KNIGHT 2: Nonetheless, under the circumstances, when you found something like that, you should have shared it with everyone.

KNIGHT 1: Yes, I should have ... Can't you find it somewhere over there? You might be able to taste it if you chew it.

DOCTOR [*Stopping THE PRIEST who moves forward involuntarily*]: Stop it! It's disgusting... [*To THE INNKEEPER*] Now you know what to do, so grab the basket quickly and...

INNKEEPER: Even if I go to town now, they won't open the market before dawn. If I do the shopping after that, I won't be back here until tomorrow evening.

PRIEST: Then we won't be able to eat anything until tomorrow evening?

SQUIRE 1: Eeeeh?

SQUIRE 2: Oh, no, that can't be right. There must be something. [*To THE INNKEEPER*] I think, you are keeping your food separately, aren't you?

INNKEEPER: No, we aren't.

SQUIRE 1: Eeeeh?

INNKEEPER: If you like, you can search us. There's nothing left. Those old fools ate it up completely. [*He goes off.*]

KNIGHT 2 [*To THE DAUGHTER*]: Maiden, give me a toothpick.

DAUGHTER: Yes, sir.

KNIGHT 1: Give me two as well.

DAUGHTER: Yes, sir. [*She goes off.*]

KNIGHT 2: Why do you want two?

KNIGHT 1: Because I use one for upper teeth and one for the lower teeth… to avoid mixing up the flavours.

KNIGHT 2 [*To the inner part of the inn*]: Hey, give me two as well.

DAUGHTER [*Off stage*]: Yes, sir.

SQUIRE 2 [*Approaching*]: Would you please listen to me, master… if you've finished your dinner, you'd better…

DOCTOR [*Stopping SQUIRE 2*]: Don't!

SQUIRE 2: What?

DOCTOR: Better leave them alone. It's too late to say anything, don't you think? Let's leave them there and we'd better find the solution to this problem on our own.

PRIEST: Find the solution? What solution do you hope to find?

DOCTOR: Listen… if we leave things to the Innkeeper, he won't go out until tomorrow morning… so, in that case…

THE DAUGHTER appears with the toothpicks.

DAUGHTER: I'm sorry it took me long. Here are your toothpicks. [*She wipes the toothpicks and holds them out.*]

KNIGHT 1: Thank you. [*He takes the toothpicks.*]

KNIGHT 2 [*Also taking them*]: Isn't there any dessert?

DAUGHTER: No, there isn't.

KNIGHT 2 [*To everybody*]: Hey, when the dessert comes it's yours.

SQUIRE 1: What?

KNIGHT 1: Dessert!

DAUGHTER: I said there's no dessert. [*She cleans the table.*]

SQUIRE 2 [*To SQUIRE 1*]: Leave them. [*He pulls back SQUIRE 1.*]

KNIGHT 2: But unfortunately, they say there isn't any dessert.

PRIEST: Let's move away a bit. [*He tries to make the people move away from the table.*]

KNIGHT 1: Oi, are you running away from us?

PRIEST [*Offended*]: What are you saying? You two, it was you who caused all of this…

DOCTOR: Don't… [*Pulling THT PRIEST back and going farther away from the table*] One of us is going to town now and when the market opens tomorrow…

KNIGHT 2: If you don't mind eating cheese, there are two pieces left. What do you say?

SQUIRE 2: Let's go.

The four people go off leaving KNIHGT 1, KNIGHT 2 and THE DAUGHTER on stage.

KNIGHT 1: Hey, I've got some cheese…

KNIGHT 2: They've gone. [*To THE DAUGHTER*] Are they very shy?

DAUGHTER: Well, I don't know.

KNIGHT 1 [*To KNIGHT 2*]: Where's the cheese?

KNIGHT 2: In the pocket of the apron.

KNIGHT 1: Which apron?

KNIGHT 2: That one.

THE DAUGHTER stands transfixed.

KNIGHT 1 [*To THE DAUGHTER*]: Give it to me.

DAUGHTER: But…

KNIGHT 2: You've been told to do so, to hide it, by your father, haven't you?

DAUGHTER: ……

KNIGHT 1: If you don't give it to me, I shall call everyone and ask them to search you.

THE DAUGHTER takes two small pieces of cheese wrapped in paper out of the pocket of her apron and puts them on the table.

KNIGHT 1 [*Putting them in his breast pocket*]: I'll keep them.

THE DAUGHTER is about to go off with the tableware.

KNIGHT 2: Don't move. [*He taps the fork on the glass, sounding 'chin-chin.'*]

THE INNKEEPER comes out of the inn slowly.

INNKEEPER: What do you want?

KNIGHT 2: Lend me your ears.

INNKEEPER: My ears. [*He goes closer anxiously.*]

KNIGHT 2: Which is your hearing ear?

INNKEEPER: Hearing ear?

KNIGHT 1: Which ear do you listen to other people's words with?

INNKEEPER: I listen with both ears usually.

KNIGHT 2: Then, give me whichever is cleaner.

INNKEEPER: What on earth are you up to? [*He offers an ear to KNIGHT 2.*]

KNIGHT 2: Is this the cleaner one? It's revolting, although one could say that's a mere detail.

INNKEEPER: Ouch! [*He draws back hurriedly.*]

KNIGHT 2: Don't. Don't make a mountain out of a molehill. I haven't finished my talk yet.

INNKEEPER: What's the talk about? [*Going close*] Anyway, please get on with it quickly and just leave out what is unnecessary… [*He puts his ear closer to KNIGHT 2.*]

KNIGHT 2: So…

INNKEEPER: Ouch! Ouch! Hey, what have you done? [*He presses his ear, moves away and writhes about.*] Help, Daughter…!

DAUGHTER: Father!

INNKEEPER [*Groaning*]: Hey, quickly, some medicine… Hey… [*He goes off to the inner part of the inn.*]

DAUGHTER: Father! What's the matter? [*She goes off to the inner part of the inn.*]

From the inner part of the inn there is the groaning of THE INNKEEPER and the sounds of falling and breaking. THE DAUGHTER's cry: "Someone! Come and help! My father's…" The voices of the people rushing to THE INNKEEPER: "What's the matter?" "What's wrong?"

KNIGHT 1: What did you use?

KNIGHT 2: This... [*Holding the toothpick in his hand*] I've put that on the end of this... [*He places it in a small paper sac and carefully puts it away in his breast-pocket.*]

KNIGHT 1: Well, that's one way of doing it...

KNIGHT 2: He was thrashing about from over to about here, wasn't he?

KNIGHT 1: But... [*Standing up slowly*] I know a better way.

KNIGHT 2: Where are you going?

KNIGHT 1: To the duel. Don't you remember?

KNIGHT 2: Well, yes, I do... [*Also standing up slowly*] Which way are you going?

KNIGHT 1 [*Pointing to Stage Right*]: This way.

KNIGHT 2: Then [*pointing to Stage Left*] I'm going this way.

KNIGHT 1: That's fine. When we've walked all the way around here and met up again, please attack me without hesitation. [*He walks to Stage Right.*]

KNIGHT 2: Alright, I will... [*He passes by KNIGHT 1, walks to Stage Left and stops abruptly.*] If you lose the duel, what am I going to tell them?

KNIGHT 1 [*Also stopping*]: If you lose the duel, I'll tell them that you fought bravely and were killed.

KNIGHT 2: Alright, then I'll say the same.

The two knights part slowly to the right and to the left and go off. The wind blows. THE PRIEST comes out and sits at the table. THE DOCTOR comes out and sits at the table.

DOCTOR: He's dead.

PRIEST: I know.

DOCTOR: He was bleeding from the ear.

PRIEST: Do you know what this means?

DOCTOR: What?

PRIEST: This means we can't ask him to go to town and get some food for us.

DOCTOR: Someone else can easily go.

PRIEST: But who knows where the town with the market is?

SQUIRE 1 and SQUIRE 2 appear absent-mindedly.

SQUIRE 2: Do you know where my master's gone?

PRIEST: He's gone off somewhere. Might be enjoying a short stroll after din-

ner.
SQUIRE 1: It's the duel. They've gone to have the duel.
DOCTOR: The duel? The duel for what?
PRIEST: It's for…

THE DAUGHTER appears.

DAUGHTER: Your Reverence, will you please pray for my father?
PRIEST: Certainly.
DOCTOR: What happened while we weren't here?
DAUGHTER: We really don't know. Only there were two pieces of cheese in the pocket of my apron and …
SQUIRE 1: What was in your apron, did you say?
DAUGHTER: Two pieces of cheese…
SQUIRE 2: Where?
DAUGHTER: Here… [*She is not wearing the apron any more*] Well… in the pocket of the apron I was wearing until a little while ago.
PRIEST: And? What happened to the cheese?
DAUGHTER: It was found and I was told to take it out…
DOCTOR: By whom?
DAUGHTER: By those two…
SQUIRE 1: By my master?
DAUGHTER: Yes.
SQUIRE 2: Did he eat it up?
DAUGHTER: No, I think he put it away in his pocket…
PRIEST: And carried away?
DAUGHTER: Yes.
DOCTOR: Damn!
SQUIRE 2: Do you think he's still got it?
SQUIRE 1: I'm sure he has…
PRIEST [*To THE DOCTOR*]: Shall we chase him?
DOCTOR: What will you do after that?
PRIEST: Well…
DAUGHTER: Emm…will you please pray for my father?
PRIEST: Oh, that.
DOCTOR: No, it's not that. Now we understand about the cheese, but what happened to your father.

DAUGHTER: They called my father because they thought that he had told me to hide the cheese.

SQUIRE 1: And?

DAUGHTER [*To SQUIRE 2*]: And your master was whispering something into my father's ear, very close… and soon my father started thrashing about holding his ear…

The wind blows.

PRIEST [*To THE DAUGHTER*]: Was it your father who told you to hide some cheese?

DAUGHTER: No…

SQUIRE 2: Then, he didn't know anything?

DAUGHTER: I happened to keep some cheese which was left this morning in my pocket.

DOCTOR [*To SQUIRE 1 and SQUIRE 2*]: What are your masters?

SQUIRE 1: They are knights, sir.

DOCTOR: We know they are knights.

SQUIRE 1: What's more, they're knights who travel around the country. The difference between an ordinary knight and a travelling knight is if an ordinary knight just sits quiet, the world stays as it is, but if a travelling knight sits and does nothing, it inflicts damage on the world. That's why a travelling knight must go around the country all the time, correcting injustices or removing evils.

PRIEST: If he does nothing, the world suffers. Is that so?

SQUIRE 1: That's right.

PRIEST: It's not if he does something, the world suffers, is it?

SQUIRE 1: No, it's not.

In the distance mixed with the sound of the wind, KNIGHT 1's voice: "Yaaaah!" and KNIGHT 2's voice: "Ooooohh!" are faintly heard.

SQUIRE 2: Did you hear that? The duel has started.

SQUIRE 1: The one who wins the duel will win this maiden's love.

DAUGHTER: Excuse me, your Reverence, but will you please start praying for my father soon?

PRIEST: Oh, yes. [*He stands up.*]

DOCTOR [*Also standing up*]: Maiden, did you know that?
DAUGHTER: Did I know what?
DOCTOR: So, whichever of them the one who wins the duel will win your love.
DAUGHTER: No, I didn't…

THE DAUGHTER and THE PRIEST go off to the interior of the inn.

DOCTOR: What does it mean to win her love?
SQUIRE 1: After the duel, they correct injustice or remove evils for her sake.
DOCTOR [*Without understanding*]: Umm, I see.

THE DOCTOR goes off to the interior. The sound of the wind… The two knights' voices: "Eeei!" and "Yaaaah!" are heard once again in the distance.

SQUIRE 2 [*Sitting on a chair*]: They're still fighting.
SQUIRE 1 [*Also sitting on a chair*]: It'll last all night.
SQUIRE 2: Are you hungry?
SQUIRE 1: Yes, I am.
SQUIRE 2: But let's not think about it. The more I think about it, the hungrier we become. That's how the stomach is. Can't you think of anything else to think about?
SQUIRE 1: No, I can't think of anything to think about. [*He fidgets restlessly.*]
SQUIRE 2: You can't think of anything to think about? You can't be like that. Because we human beings tend to meditate on things all the time… For example, in my case [*noticing that SQUIRE 1 is restless*] what are you doing?
SQUIRE 1: Yes, well, I feel a bit itchy… [*He stirs some more.*]
SQUIRE 2: Itchy? There! You're thinking about it at this moment, that you're feeling itchy… In other words, people are always… Hey, what's the matter?
SQUIRE 1: What's the matter? I've told you that I've got an itch.
SQUIRE 2: So, you are thinking about feeling itchy now and…
SQUIRE 1: I'm not thinking about it, I feel itchy… Hey, help… help me!
SQUIRE 2: You ask me to help you, but it can't be helped … Because it's you who's got an itch.
SQUIRE 1: But… Oi…

SQUIRE 2: Where do you feel itchy?

SQUIRE 1: Here… on my back…

SQUIRE 2: On your back? [*Noticing the armour*] Can' t you take this off?

SQUIRE 1: No, I can't.

SQUIRE 2: Why not?

SQUIRE 1: Because it's locked. [*Gesturing key with his hands*] One like this is kept by my master.

SQUIRE 2: Then, we can't do anything.

SQUIRE 1: Yes, but listen…

SQUIRE 2: I'm listening. I don't think you'd feel any better if I scratched outside the armour, would you? [*He scratches SQUIRE 1 outside the armour.*]

SQUIRE 1: No, that doesn't work.

SQUIRE 2: Just give up.

SQUIRE 1: Give up? How can I give up? I can't…

SQUIRE 2: Be patient.

SQUIRE 1: No, I can't… Oi…

SQUIRE 2: Think about something else.

SQUIRE 1: I've told you that I haven't got anything to think about.

SQUIRE 2: How about thinking about being hungry? You are very hungry at this moment.

SQUIRE 1: I'm not hungry.

SQUIRE 2: Yes, you are. You haven't eaten since last night… Hey, really, think about it seriously. We won't have anything to eat even when tomorrow morning comes. Are you thinking?

SQUIRE 1: I'm trying but I can't because it's too itchy…

SQUIRE 2: Just think! You're in danger of dying of hunger. We don't die when we feel itchy but we do die when we get hungry.

SQUIRE 1: Oi, help! I'd rather… die of hunger… Can't you find a stick or something?

SQUIRE 2: A stick? What for?

SQUIRE 1: Listen, you are going to stick it down my back…

SQUIRE 2 [*Having found the cane*]: But I don't think it'll go in.

SQUIRE 1: Then please hit me with it! Here… hit me here…

SQUIRE 2: Hit you?

SQUIRE 1: Yes, I don't mind., so please hit here hard.

SQUIRE 2: You mean like this? [*He gives a heavy blow on SQUIRE 1's back.*]

SQUIRE 1: Harder!

SQUIRE 2: Harder? Do you think that'll be alright? [*He gives a heavier blow.*]
SQUIRE 1: More, more, more, more…

SQUIRE 2 begins hitting SQUIRE 1's back with the cane continuously very hard. THE DOCTOR, THE PRIEST and THE DAUGHTER are astonished and come out.

DOCTOR: What are you doing?
SQUIRE 2 [*Pointing at SQUIRE 1*]: He's got an itch. [*He goes on hitting.*]
PRIEST: He's got an itch?
SQUIRE 2: Yes.
DOCTOR: If he's got an itch, why don't you scratch him?
SQUIRE 2: We can't scratch him because it's as if he were in a tin can.
PRIEST: But don't you feel sorry for him?
SQUIRE 2: He asked me to do this.
DAUGHTER: How about scratching the part there out of the armour?
SQUIRE 2: I see, scratch the part out of the armour.
SQUIRE 1: It's my back that itches… My back.
SQUIRE 2 [*To THE DAUGHTER*]: It's his back that itches…
SQUIRE 1: Harder… more…more…

KNIGHT 1 slowly walks in from Stage Right leaning on his cane. He is exhausted and injured by the fight. SQUIRE 2 notices him and that makes SQUIRE 1 notice it too, as SQUIRE 2 stops hitting him.

SQUIRE 1: Oh, master.
KNIGHT 1: I'm alright, so don't move from there, I'll walk to you. Hey, do you
    see I'm walking?
SQUIRE 1: Yes, I do, master.
KNIGHT 1: Aren't I walking?
SQUIRE 1: Yes, you are, master. Did you win the duel then?
KNIGHT 1: Yes, I did. As soon as we met, we knew who would be the winner.
    Oi, am I walking?
SQUIRE 1: Yes, you are, master.
KNIGHT 1: Then, it was true that I won… Where's the chair?
SQUIRE 2: It's here, sir. And what happened to my master?
KNIGHT 1: Move the chair in this way a bit more, will you? I'm not sure if I

can move round to that spot.

SQUIRE 2: Is this alright?

KNIGHT 1: That'll be fine… [*He sits on the chair.*]

DOCTOR: You're bleeding. I'll treat you.

KNIGHT 1: It's only a scratch.

DOCTOR: At least it needs disinfecting, so as not to get germs in.

SQUIRE 2: Well, so… what happened to my master?

KNIGHT 2 walks in slowly from Stage Left, leaning on his cane. He is exhausted and injured by the fight.

SQUIRE 2 [*Noticing*]: Master!

KNIGHT 2: Calm down. Don't make a big fuss. I'm alive… Whatever might have happened, I'm alive and talking at this very moment. Eh? Am I talking now?

SQUIRE 2: Yes, you are, master.

KNIGHT 2: Then, I'm alive no matter what. But don't be so pleased about it… think about my opponent. He's bleeding from the mouth and writhing in agony in the dark. No, don't come to me. I'm coming to you, what's more, just look at me, I… I will make a detour…

SQUIRE 1 [*To KNIGHT 1*]: Master, who did you fight with?

KNIGHT 1: Who?

SQUIRE 1: The other master has just come back.

SQUIRE 2 [*Changing the position of the chair*]: Is the chair alright here?

KNIGHT 2: Yes, that's fine. Don't miss this. The way I sit down on that from this side, it'll be marvellous… [*He sits on the chair.*]

DOCTOR [*To KNIGHT 2*]: Please sit still. I'm going to treat the wound.

KNIGHT 2: It doesn't need it.

DOCTOR: But at least let me disinfect the wound.

KNIGHT 1 [*To KNIGHT 2*]: Friend, what's the matter?

KNIGHT 2: What's the matter? What? [*Noticing*] Oh, is that you? Have you been there?

KNIGHT 1: Have I been here? Friend, have you been to the duel?

KNIGHT 2: Yes, I have. You must know that. We went out together a little while ago.

KNIGHT 1: And did you win?

KNIGHT 2: Yes, I did.

KNIGHT 1: So did I. In that case who did I defeat?

KNIGHT 2: Think it over carefully. Don't you think you might've lost the duel?

KNIGHT 1: But if I had been defeated and snuffed it, why am I here at this moment? I walked back here on my own… [*To SQUIRE 1*] Wasn't that so?

SQUIRE 1: Yes, you walked back here.

KNIGHT 2: That's true. What's more, I'm here, too… On top of that I'm talking. [*To SQUIRE 2*] Haven't I been talking for some time?

SQUIRE 2: Yes, master, you've been talking for some time.

DOCTOR [*To KNIGHT 2*]: I've disinfected the part for the time being, but if it gets hurt later, tell me. [*To KNIGHT 1*] You, too. I also have pain-killers although they cost rather a lot.

KNIGHT 1: Thank you… Doctor, would you like some cheese? [*He takes a small lump wrapped in paper out of his breast-pocket.*]

DOCTOR: Cheese? [*He receives it.*]

PRIEST: But isn't that what this maiden was keeping?

KNIGHT 1 [*To THE DOCTOR*]: Put it in your mouth quickly, it's the only piece left…

DOCTOR: Yes… [*He puts it into his mouth and swallows it.*] Ugh… [*He presses his hand to his throat and keeps still for a moment.*]

PRIEST: What's going on?

THE DOCTOR opens his mouth wide and spits out a mouthful blood. It dyes his white coat red. He covers his mouth with his hand and runs off to the inner part of the inn, shouting out "Waaaa!" THE PRIEST, THE DAUGHTER, SQUIRE 1 and SQUIRE 2 run off by following THE DOCTOR. They say, "What's the matter?" "What happened?" "What's wrong?" and so on. A louder cry "Waaaaa!" and a sound of falling over are heard.

KNIGHT 1: He's dead.

KNIGHT 2: Was it the cheese?

KNIGHT 1: No, it was the butter. I had hidden a razor blade in the butter.

KNIGHT 2: Did it cut his throat?

KNIGHT 1: Yes, it cut his throat.

KNIGHT 2: It must've sort of slid down his throat…

KNIGHT 1: Yes, too smoothly to feel pain…

KNIGHT 2: But what do you think? Did he notice that it was a razor blade before he died.

KNIGHT 1: Didn't you see his eyes? When he stood bolt upright there pressing his throat, he knew it.

KNIGHT 2: It could be right... His eyes showed it.

THE PRIEST comes out absent-mindedly.

PRIEST: Errr...

KNIGHT 1: What do you want?

PRIEST: Please don't kill me...

KNIGHT 2: Why not?

PRIEST: Why not? Because I don't want to die yet.

KNIGHT 1: Why don't you want to die yet?

PRIEST: Why don't I? I... I just want to live a little longer.

KNIGHT 2: What will you do?

PRIEST: Well, I will live and...

KNIGHT 1: It's meaningless just to keep on living.

PRIEST: But it wouldn't cause much harm if I lived. I'll be fine when I'm given a little food and a little drink.

KNIGHT 1: Would you fancy eating some cheese? [*He takes cheese out of his breast-pocket.*] There's one more piece left.

PRIEST: No thanks you.

KNIGHT 2: How about some water? [*He shakes the water jug.*] There's some left.

PRIEST: No, I don't want any water, either.

KNIGHT 2: Then how will you survive? There's nothing to keep you alive here, is there?

PRIEST: But I want to live.

KNIGHT 1: So how?

PRIEST: How? At least you don't need to kill me, do you? Since I'm living like this...

KNIGHT 2: We aren't killing simply because we want to...

PRIEST: Then, why do you kill people?

KNIGHT 2: It's because if we don't kill, we will be killed.

PRIEST: Who, who's ever tried to kill you? None of us has done you any harm.

KNIGHT 1: No, you haven't... I think it's better for you to know, so I'm telling you this...it's because it's too late to do anything after we've been attached.

KNIGHT 2: In other words, we've always taken the initiative... as it's called 'winning a game in which one has made the first move.'

PRIEST: I'm sure you'll always win, because we've neither tried to harm you nor thought about it... At least I haven't got any thought of causing you any harm at all.

KNIGHT 1: In that case you cannot complain when you're attacked.

PRIEST: Why? I'm not going to do you any harm.

KNIGHT 2: Listen, if you don't want to be killed by us, you must kill us ... It's the only way left to you.

PRIEST: I can't do such a thing. I can't kill you.

KNIGHT 1: Otherwise, it'll be you who'll be killed by us.

PRIEST: No, I can't.

KNIGHT 2: Yes, you can. I'll show you how to kill us. [*He takes a thin cord out of his breast-pocket.*] Use this to strangle me.

PRIEST: No, I won't.

KNIGHT 1 [*To KNIGHT 2*]: Are you willing to die for him?

KNIGHT 2: I'm only teaching him how.

KNIGHT 1: It's no good spoiling him. We'd better kill him since he says that he doesn't want to kill us.

KNIGHT 2: Hey… listen, I'm telling you to teach you how. Go and tie the end of this cord to that tree.

PRIEST: What are you going to do with it?

KNIGHT 2: Just do it.

THE PRIEST takes the end of the cord and ties it to the tree.

PRIEST: Is this alright?

KNIGHT 2: Yes, and pull the cord in this direction... that's right... and wind it around my neck.

PRIEST: How?

KNIGHT 2: How? Don't you even know how to wind the cord? Do it like this… [*He winds the cord around THE PRIEST's neck.*] And, you go a little farther away while turning yourself around. [*He makes THE PRIEST go a little farther with the winding cord.*] Then you must pull this… [*He pulls the cord.*]

PRIEST: Pull?

KNIGHT 2: Otherwise, you wouldn't die. [*He pulls the cord.*]
PRIEST: Please stop! [*He is choking.*]
KNIGHT 2: If I stopped, [*pulling the cord*] you would survive.

THE PRIEST makes a groan, kneels and slumps over.

KNIGHT 2: If I give another pull, I'm sure he will die. Do you think he's learning that he's killed if he doesn't kill?
KNIGHT 1: Yes, I do. He's learned it with his own flesh and bones.
KNIGHT 2: Then it's worthwhile being killed. [*He pulls the cord with a jerk.*]

THE PRIEST gives a low groan, "Ugh!" and falls. KNIGHT 2 loosens the cord... The sound of the wind.

KNIGHT 1 [*Looking over KNIGHT 2's contrivance*]: Is this the way you do it?
KNIGHT 2: That's right. Do you see? If you tie the other end there, you need only half the strength. In other words, the tree pulls as much as I do. That's physics... And the most wonderful thing about this method is that the person to be killed helps me to prepare and all I have to do is just to sit and wait here.
KNIGHT 1: It's a lazy way of killing...
KNIGHT 2: We can't manage a large number if we don't take up this sort of idea. [*He claps his hand: "pon-pon."*]

SQUIRE 1, SQUIRE 2 and THE DAUGHTER appear absent-mindedly.

KNIGHT 1: Clear him away.
SQUIRE 2: Another one?
SQUIRE 1: This is the fourth victim already...
KNIGHT 1: But it's getting better... At least this one learned that he'd be killed if he didn't kill. But, of course, it was too late when he learned it.

SQUIRE 2 unties the cord around the tree and carries the corpse away helped by SQUIRE 1.

DAUGHTER [*A littler vaguely*]: It must be my turn next. Aren't I right? [*Walking slowly*] You are going to kill me this time... It's alright. I don't mind being killed… I'll fall down covered with blood. But be careful, I won't be killed so easily. If you approach me carelessly, it could be you who'll get injured.

KNIGHT 2: Have you got a sharp instrument?

DAUGHTER: Yes… [*She hides her hand which holds something behind her back.*]

KNIGHT 1: Show it to me.

DAUGHTER: No, I won't.

KNIGHT 2: Why not?

KNIGHT 1: Why can't you just show it to us?

DAUGHTER: … [*She moves her hand to the front and shows something wrapped in a white handkerchief. When she opens the handkerchief, she has a razor.*] Here it is.

KNIGHT 2: Does it cut well?

DAUGHTER: Yes, it does. My father sharpened it every morning…

KNIGHT 1: Come to me.

DAUGHTER [*Drawing back*]: No, I won't.

KNIGHT 2: Come and cut [*pointing his throat*] here with it. Or [*pointing at KNIGHT 1*] cut his if you like… [*To KNIGHT 1*] She might find it easier to cut your throat.

KNIGHT 1: Really? [*Feeling his own throat*] But if she's going to cut here, she's got to be very good.

KNIGHT 2 [*To THE DAUGHTER*]: Maiden, have you never done this before?

DAUGHTER: No, never.

KNIGHT 1: In that case [*pointing at his wrist*] here would be better. [*To THE DAUGHTER*] Cutting here can't kill us quickly, but [*pointing at the throat*] it's much easier than here. Just cut out straight.

KNIGHT 2 [*To KNIGHT 1*]: Behind the ears, that's another place to cut. It sounds a bit hard to do, but it's not really… [*To THE DAUGHTER*] I mean, after cutting here deeply … in this way, you must turn your wrist over… it's very important… well, only if you can do this…

KNIGHT1: If she can turn her wrist over, she should scoop out the eye-balls. After all that's more glamorous.

KNIGHT 2: If you want a glamorous way, it's the nose.

KNIGHT 1: What do you do to the nose?

KNIGHT 2: Cut it off.

KNIGHT 1: But we should use a more practical method this time… [*He glances at THE DAUGHTER and shuts his mouth.*]

THE DAUGHTER cannot bear to hear their conversation and stays squatting down, covering her mouth with the handkerchief. SQUIRE 1 and SQUIRE 2 come in absent-mindedly.

SQUIRE 1 [*Looking at THE DAUGHTER*]: What's going on?
SQUIRE 2: Are you going to kill her, too?
KNIGHT 2: On the contrary, she's going to kill us, so we are teaching her how.
KNIGHT 1 [*To SQUIRE 1*]: You, go and help her… to kill us.

THE DAUGHTER runs off to the interior of the inn without speaking.

KNIGHT 2: Catch the girl.
SQUIRE 2: Yes, master. [*He runs after her to the interior.*]
SQUIRE 1: Why?
KNIGHT 1: Wait and see. He'll be killed by her. She's got a razor in her hand… and it's been well sharpened.
SQUIRE 1 [*Upset and to the interior*]: Hey! You! Hey! [*He is about to go off to the interior.*]

THE DAUGHTER's screaming voice: "No! Don't do that!" is heard. At the same time there are SQUIRE 2's groans: "Ugghh," followed by the sound of him falling over.

KNIGHT 2 [*To SQUIRE 1*]: Go and look, will you?

SQUIRE 1 goes off to the interior.

KNIGHT 1 [*Standing up*]: I don't like to criticize but your methods are always lazy.
KNIGHT 2: You may be right… I'm bored with killing… In other words, bored with being alive. Haven't you ever thought like this? Someone whose hands move quicker than ours appears in front of us soon and kills us before we think about killing him, that's what I wish…
KNIGHT 1: Look, the windmill's begun to go round.
KNIGHT 2 [*Also standing up*]: The windmill? Is the wind blowing?

SQUIRE 1 comes out.

KNIGHT 1: How was it?

SQUIRE 1: He's dead… Got his throat cut.

KNIGHT 2: How about the girl?

SQUIRE 1: I couldn't find her anywhere.

KNIGHT 1: Run away!

SQUIRE 1: Me?

KNIGHT 1: Yes.

SQUIRE 1: No, I won't.

KNIGHT 2: Will you kill us then?

SQUIRE 1: No, I won't do that, either.

KNIGHT 1: Do you want me to kill you?

SQUIRE 1: No, I don't.

KNIGHT 2: Then, what are you going to do?

SQUIRE 1: I will fight with the Giant Briareus.

KNIGHT 1: Who's the Giant Briareus?

SQUIRE 1: He's over there. He began to move just now.

KNIGHT 1: That's a windmill.

SQUIRE 1: No, that's the Giant Briareus. That famous wise man Felson changed him into a windmill so that he could deprive me of the honour of fighting the Giant Briareus. Master, please tell me to go. Tell me to go and fight the Giant Briareus. [*He takes the spear.*]

A short silence… The sound of the wind.

KNIGHT [*Rather quietly*]: Go… Go and fight the Giant Briareus. And be killed…

SQUIRE 1 couches the spear, suddenly shriek out, "Yaaah," and then runs off crying out loudly, "Haaaaah!" At the same time the sound of hooves is heard loud and clear, and then with the scream of "Waaau," it becomes lower and further away. Before long we hear SQUIRE 1 and his horse bumping into the windmill. SQUIRE 1 cries out, "Gyaaah!" and then it becomes quiet. The wind blows.

KNIGHT 1: What a fool…

KNIGHT 2: However, it's good that a young fool kills himself by his foolishness, while it's also good that a sensible old man survives through his prudence...

A dim light is on behind the curtain which screens two beds and the silhouette of THE DAUGHTER changing her clothes shows on the curtain.

KNIGHT 1: Our bride is preparing to welcome us to her bed. [*He slowly goes to the table and sits on the chair.*]

KNIGHT 2: That's fine. I'm tired of being prudent. [*Sitting down on the chair*] Our adventure is coming to an end. This time when I'm called, I'll go to her bed to be caught in her trap... and then have her cut my throat...

KNIGHT 1: That sounds alright. But do you think she will think of what to do about me after that?

KNIGHT 2: I'm sure she will... Anyway, she's desperate... and at least she's found one of the ways to bewitch us by turning on her charm.

The light behind the curtain goes off.

KNIGHT 1: The light has gone... It seems she's ready. Go and act the role of a stupid groom...

KNIGHT 2 [*standing up slowly*]: It's been a long journey... And so has yours.

KNIGHT 1: Yes...

KNIGHT 2 goes to the curtain and throw it open.

KNIGHT 2: ...

KNIGHT 1: What's wrong?

KNIGHT 2: She's dead... cut her own throat.

KNIGHT 1: ...

KNIGHT 2 closes the curtain slowly, comes back to the table and sits on the chair. The sound of the wind.

KNIGHT 2 [*Noticing the cheese left on the table*]: Is that the cheese over there?

KNIGHT 1: Yes, it is the piece that we left before, do you want it?

KNIGHT 2: Yes...

KNIGHT 1: Hang on... [*Taking another piece out of his breast-pocket*] There's another piece. [*Putting it on the table*] I took two from the girl and the one I gave the Doctor was butter. Which one do you take? [*He puts two pieces.*]

KNIGHT 2: I'll take this one. [*He takes a piece.*]

KNIGHT 1: Then, I'll take this one.

The two strip off the paper and slip the cheese into their mouth casually. They read each other's condition.

KNIGHT 2: No change.

KNIGHT 1: No.

KNIGHT 2: Haven't you put anything in it?

KNIGHT 1: No, I haven't.

KNIGHT 2: Then why did you make me choose?

KNIGHT 1: I thought she might have put something in it.

KNIGHT 2: She wouldn't do such a thing.

KNIGHT 1: You know, the Nurse died when she drank the water from the water jug. I hadn't put anything in the glass at that time... In other words, the poison had already been put in by then.

KNIGHT 2 pours water out of the water jug into the glass and drinks it slowly. KNIGHT 1 looks at him. No change is seen in KNIGHT 2.

KNIGHT 2: Why did you lie?

KNIGHT 1: Why do you rush to death?

KNIGHT 2: You aren't willing to kill me, are you?

KNIGHT 1: No, I'm not.

KNIGHT 2: Why not?

KNIGHT 1: Because I'm tired of...

KNIGHT 2: Killing?

KNIGHT 1: No, tired of living. What's more, when I became tired of living, I lost my enthusiasm for killing.

The church bell is heard from afar with the sound of the wind.

KNIGHT 2: The bell's ringing.

KNIGHT 1: Because someone died...

KNIGHT 2: But we are alive...

KNIGHT 1: We can't help it.
KNIGHT 2: Until when?
KNIGHT 1: Until coming here from over there…
KNIGHT 2: What's coming?
KNIGHT 1: The one who will kill us.
KNIGHT 2: Is he coming?
KNIGHT 1: We must wait…

The sound of the church bell… The two sit still as if they were praying…

KNIGHT 2: Can you feel the earth moving?
KNIGHT 1: The earth?
KNIGHT 2: Yes. If you keep still like this… you can feel this earth moving slowly.
KNIGHT 1: Hum… [*examining*] yes, I can.
KNIGHT 2: Is it autumn now?
KNIGHT 1: Yes, it's autumn.
KNIGHT 2: Then, we're slowly moving towards winter now.
KNIGHT 1: Yes, towards winter.
KNIGHT 2: You see?
KNIGHT 1: Yes, I do.

The two face each other over the table and keep still as if they were frozen.

Blackout.

END

Bibliography of Betsuyaku's Plays (1969-1990)

Collected Plays of Minoru Betsuyaku: The Match Girl/The Elephant (Matchi Uri no Shojo/Zo Betsuyaku Minoru Gikyoku Shū) (Tokyo: Sanichi Shobo, 1969).

includes:

(1) The Match Girl (*Matchi Uri no Shojo*)

(2) A Scene with a Red Bird (*Akai Tori no Iru Fukei*)

(3) The Kangaroo (*Kangarū*)

(4) The Fallen Angel (*Da-Tenshi*)

(5) Another Story (*Aru Betsuna Hanashi*)

(6) The Elephant (*Zō*)

Collected Plays of Minoru Betsuyaku (Vol. 2): Alice in Wonderland (Fushigi no Kuni no Arisu Betsuyaku Minoru Dai ni Gikyoku Shū), ed. Kisaji Kikuchi (Tokyo: Sanichi Shobo, 1970).

includes:

(1) I am Alice (*Ai Amu Arisu*)

(2) The Spy Story (*Supai Monogatari*)

(3) The Gate (*Mon*)

(4) A, B and a Woman (*A to B to Hitori no Onna*)

(5) Alice in Wonderland (*Fushigi no Kuni no Arisu*)

Collected Plays of Minoru Betsuyaku (Vol. 3): The Rebellion of the Soyosoyo Tribe (Soyosoyo Zoku no Hanran Betsuyaku Minoru Dai san Gikyoku Shū), ed. Keigo Tagawa (Tokyo: Sanichi Shobo, 1971).

includes:

(1) The Rebellion of the Soyosoyo Tribe (*Soyosoyo Zoku no Hanran*)

(2) The Tapir (*Baku*)

(3) A Yellow Parasol and a Black Umbrella (*Kiiroi Parasoru to Kuroi Komorigara*)

(4) Dr Maximilian's Smile (*Makushimirian Hakase no Bisho*)

(5) A Yellow Sunday (*Kiiroi Nichiyobi*)

(6) The Town and The Zeppelin (*Machi to Hikosen*)

The Move (*Idō*) (Tokyo: Shincho Sha, 1971).

Collected Plays of Minoru Betsuyaku (Vol. 4): The Story Written with Numbers (Sūji de Kakareta Monogatari Betsuyaku Minoru Dai yon Gikyoku Shū), ed. Kisaji Kikuchi (Tokyo: Sanichi Shobo, 1974).

includes:

(1) A Blue Horse (*Aoi Uma*)

(2) The Sea and a Rabbit (*Umi to Usagi*)

(3) A Scene with a Corpse (*Shitai no Aru Fukei*)

(4) An Old Banger and Five Gentlemen (*Ponkotsu Sha to Gonin no Shinshi*)

(5) The Legend of Noon (*Shogo no Densetsu*)

(6) The Story Written with Numbers (*Suji de Kakareta Monogatari*)

Chairs and the Legend (Isu to Densetsu) (Tokyo: Shincho Sha, 1974).

Collected Plays of Minoru Betsuyaku (Vol. 5): Bubbling Boiling (Abuku Tatta Ni Tatta Betsuyaku Minoru Gikyoku Shū), ed. Kisaji Kikuchi (Tokyo: Sanichi Shobo, 1976).

includes:

(1) A Demolished Scene (*Kowareta Fūkei*)

(2) A Scene with a Bus-stop (*Basutei no Aru Fūkei*)

(3) Bubbling Boiling (*Abuku Tatta Ni Tatta*)

Collected Plays of Minoru Betsuyaku (Vol. 6): The Short Months (Nishi Muku Samurai Betsuyaku Minoru Gikyoku Shū), ed. Kisaji Kikuchi (Tokyo: Sanichi Shobo, 1978).

includes:

(1) The Short Months (*Nishi Muku Samurai*)

(2) A House, a Tree and a Son (*Ikken no Ie. Ippon no Ki. Hitori no Musuki*)

(3) A Place and Memories (*Basho to Omoide*)

Collected Plays of Minoru Betsuyaku (Vol. 7): I am the Father of the Genius Idiot Bakabon (Tensai Bakabon no Papa Nanoda Betsuyaku Minoru Gikyoku Shū), ed. Hajime Takemura (Tokyo: Sanichi Shobo, 1979).

includes:

(1) I am the Father of the Genius Idiot Bakabon (*Tensai Bakabon no Papa Naroda*)

(2) Dance Dance Snails (*Mae Mae Katatsumuri*)

(3) Water-Bloated Corpse (*Umi Yukaba Mizu Tsuku Kabane*)

(4) Days for Insects (*Mushi-tachi no Hi*)

Collected Plays of Minoru Betsuyaku (Vol. 8): Mother, Mother, Mother (Mazā, Mazā, Mazā Betsuyaku Minoru Gikyoku Shū), ed. Kisaji Kikuchi (Tokyo: Sanichi Shobo, 1980).

includes:

(1) The Information Desk (*Uketsuke*)

(2) A Little House and Five Gentlemen (*Chisana Ie to Gonin no Shinshi*)

(3) A Small Path to the Tenjin God Shrine (*Tenjin-sama no Hosomichi*)

(4) Mother, Mother, Mother (*Mazā, Mazā, Mazā*)

Collected Plays of Minoru Betsuyaku (Vol. 9): The Blooming Tree (Ki ni Hana Saku Betsuyaku

Minoru Gikyoku Shū), ed. Kisaji Kikuchi (Tokyo: Sanichi Shobo, 1981).
includes:
(1) A Corpse Which Creates an Atmosphere (*Funiki no Aru Shitai*)
(2) The Red Elegy (*Seki-shoku Eregi*)
(3) The Blooming Tree (*Ki ni Hana Saku*)

Collected Plays of Minoru Betsuyaku (Vol.10): A Corpse with Feet/ The Meeting (Ashi no Aru Shitai/Kaigi Betsuyaku Minoru Gikyoku Shū), ed. Kisaji Kikuchi (Tokyo: Sanichi Shobo, 1982).
includes:
(1) A Corpse with Feet (*Ashi no Aru Shitai*)
(2) I am not Her (*Sono Hito dewa Animaseni*)
(3) The Disease (*Byoki*)
(4) The Meeting (*Kaigi*)

Collected Plays of Minoru Betsuyaku (Vol. 11): The Snow Lies on Taro's Roof (Taro no Yane ni Yuki Furitsumu Betsuyaku Minoru Gikyoku Shū), ed. Kisaji Kikuchi (Tokyo: Sanichi Shobo, 1983).
includes:
(1) Ten Little Indians (*Sohite Dare mo Inaku Natta*)
(2) Who's Right Behind Me (*Ushiro no Shōmen Dare*)
(3) The Snow Lies on Taro's Roof (*Taro no Yane ni Yuki Furitsumu*)

Collected Plays of Minoru Betsuyaku (Vol.12): Mary's Lamb (Meri-san no Hitsuji Betsuyaku Minoru Gikyoku Shū), ed. Kisaji Kikuchi (Tokyo: Sanichi Shobo, 1984).
includes:
(1) A Lullaby Preventing Sleep (*Nemutcha Ikenai Komori Uta*)
(2) Star Time (*Hoshi no Jikan*)
(3) Mary's Lamb (*Meri-san no Hitsuji*)
(4) A Crime at the Street Corner (*Machi Kado no Jiken*)

Collected Plays of Minoru Betsuyaku (Vol. 13): Hiking (Haikingu Betsuyaku Minoru Gikyoku Shū), ed. Kazuo Arakawa (Tokyo: Sanichi Shobo, 1985).
includes:
(1) When We Open the Window, We See the Port (*Mado o Akere ba Minato ga Mieru*)
(2) The Room (*Heya*)
(3) Tadpoles are Frogs' Children (*Otamajakushi wa Kaeru no Ko*)
(4) Hiking (*Haikingu*)

Collected Plays of Minoru Betsuyaku (Vol. 14): Lieutenant Shirase's Expedition to the South Pole (Shirase Chui no Nankyoku Tanken Betsuyaku Minoru Gikyoku Shū), ed. Kazuo Araki (Tokyo: Sanichi Shobo, 1986).

includes:

(1) An Escaped Convict Who Carries a Hot-water Bottle (*Yutanpo o Motta Datsugokus-hū*)

(2) The Cleared Evening Sky (*Yūzora Harete*)

(3) Lieutenant Shirase's Expedition to the South Pole (*Shirase Chūi no Nankyoku Tanken*)

Collected Plays of Minoru Betsuyaku (Vol. 15): Giovanni's Journey to His Father (Jobanni no Chichi e no Tabi Betsuyaku Minoru Gikyoku Shū), ed. Kazuo Araki (Tokyo: Sanichi Shobo, 1988).

includes:

(1) The Salad Murder (*Sarada Satsujin Jiken*)

(2) Toilet This Way Please (*Toire wa Kochira*)

(3) A Voyage Round Giovanni's Father (*Jobanni no Chichi e no Tabi*)

Collected Plays of Minoru Betsuyaku (Vol. 16): The Story of the Two Knights Travelling Around the Country (Shokoku o Henrekisuru Futari no Kishi no Monogatari Betsuyaku Minoru Gikyoku Shū), ed. Shigeru Hatakeyama (Tokyo: Sanichi Shobo, 1988).

includes:

(1) An Inari Shrine Around the Corner (*Muko Yokocho no O-irari-san*)

(2) Hide and Seek (*Mo ii Kai, Mada da Yo*)

(3) The Story of the Two Knights Travelling Around the Country (*Shokoku o Henrekisuru Futari no Kishi no Monogatari*)

Collected Plays of Minoru Betsuyaku (Vol. 17): Count Dracula's Autumn (Dorakyura Hakushaku no Aki Betsuyaku Minoru Gikyoku Shū), ed. Shigeru Hatakeyama (Tokyo: Sanichi Shobo, 1990).

includes:

(1) A Squid Eraser (*Ika Keshigomu*)

(2) Momotaro Born in a Peach (*Momo Kara Umareta Momotaro*)

(3) The Red Moon (*Akai Tsuki*)

(4) Count Dracula's Autumn (*Dorakyura Hakushaku no Aki*)

APPENDIX [II]
Table of Betsuyaku's plays (1960-1988)

Headings
- (1) Title
- (2) Month and year of staging
- (3) Staging group and director
- (4) Length of play (in hours), number of acts or scenes (if more than one)
- (5) Number of characters
- (6) Genre
- (7) Subject matter
- (8) Relationships between characters
- (9) Costumes and properties
- (10) Location and design
- (11) Lighting, sound and special effects
- (12) Miscellaneous notes

1
- (1) The Room to Let
- (2) April, 1960
- (3) Freedom Stage (*Jiyu Butai*) of Waseda University; Suzuki
- (12) unpublished

2
- (1) A, B and A Woman
- (2) November, 1961
- (3) Freedom Stage of Waseda University; Suzuki
- (4) 1/2 hour; 2 scenes
- (5) 2
- (6) naturalistic, sadistic
- (7) the strong and the weak, class conflict
- (8) 2 childhood friends
- (9) a book, a fruit knife, a pen
- (10) indoors, a red carpet, chairs, anywhere in the world
- (11) 'a tune like a beautiful memory'

3
- (1) The Elephant
- (2) April, 1962
- (3) New Freedom Stage (*Shin Jiyu Butai*); Suzuki
- (4) 2 hours; 3 acts

(5) 10
(6) surrealistic, absurd
(7) victims of the A-bomb in Hiroshima
(8) a man, his wife and their nephew
(9) a bicycle-cart, a rag-doll, an umbrella, rice-balls
(10) indoors, in the ward of a hospital, Japan
(11) night, daytime, morning

4 (1) Another Story
(2) 1962 (staged 1968)
(3) Waseda Small Theatre (*Waseda Sho Gekijo*); Suzuki
(4) 1/2 hour
(5) 4
(6) ritual, absurd
(7) old parents to be sent to an old people's home
(8) the parents and a daughter, a man from the home
(9) table and chairs, furniture, tableware
(10) indoors, in a room in a flat, anywhere in the world

5 (1) The Gate
(2) May, 1966
(3) Waseda Small Theatre; Suzuki
(4) 1 hour
(5) 3
(6) socialistic, naturalistic
(7) people wishing to run away from reality, having to face it
(8) a civil servant and a shoe-shine boy
(9) 2 big trunks and a knife
(10) outdoors, in a city, the wall
(11) evening; an evening bell

6 (1) The Fallen Angel
(2) September, 1966
(3) Drama Project 66 (*Engeki Kikaku 66*); Kobayashi
(4) 1 hour
(5) 9
(6) absurd
(7) returning to the same place, not able to go anywhere
(8) 2 men and six travelling blind people
(9) a rag doll as a corpse, a blue balloon, an astronomical telescope, a record player
(10) outdoors, anywhere in the world
(11) evening - night; the sounds of the wind and the river, a shriek

7   (1)   The Match Girl
    (2)   November, 1966
    (3)   Waseda Small Theatre; Suzuki
    (4)   1 & 1/2 hours
    (5)   4 (plus 2 off-stage)
    (6)   fantasy, absurd
    (7)   child prostitution in the aftermath of World War II
    (8)   A sister and her younger brother, a middle-aged couple
    (9)   an English style tea-set, biscuits, a pram
    (10) indoors, in a living room, old fashioned table and chairs, anywhere in the world
    (11) evening; an old popular song
    (12) received the 13th Kishida Playwright Award

8   (1)   A Scene with a Red Bird
    (2)   1967
    (3)   Drama Project 66; Hideo Kanze
    (4)   2 hours; 6 scenes
    (5)   17
    (6)   fantasy, absurd
    (7)   courage to tell the truth to the world
    (8)   a sister and brother, the people in the town (a Catholic priest, a postman, a may-
          or etc.)
    (9)   an incense-burner, a pram, a bicycle
    (10) outdoors, a city square with a clock tower,anywhere in the world, two coffins
    (11) day-time; music for a carnival

9   (1)   Dr. Maximilian's Smile
    (2)   June 1967
    (3)   Waseda Small Theatre; Suzuki
    (4)   1 hour; 2 scenes
    (5)   5
    (6)   surrealistic, naturalistic
    (7)   the definition of sympathy and hypocrisy
    (8)   a nurse, a doctor and child A-bomb victims
    (9)   a big fish bowl, a rag-doll with torn legs
    (10) indoors, in a research hospital, Japan
    (11) night

10 (1)   The Kangaroo
    (2)   July, 1967
    (3)   The Atelier Group of The Literature Theatre Company (Bungaku-za Atorie no

Kai); Fujiwara

(4) 2 hours; 6 scenes
(5) 11
(6) fantasy, absurd
(7) a misfit in society
(8) a man and people at a quay
(9) a rag doll, a postage stamp, a Japanese dagger
(10) outdoors, anywhere in the world, at a quay, a bench, a street light, a coffin
(11) evening - night; a masked singer with a guitar

11 (1) An Old Banger and Five Gentlemen
(2) 1969
(3) The Group Company (*Gunzo Za*); Iijima
(4) 1 hour
(5) 5
(6) absurd
(7) 5 people who cannot tell the time, date or direction, except relatively
(8) 5 men wearing worn out formal suits
(9) Chaplinesque costume, a letter, a newspaper, shoes, cigarettes
(10) outdoors on a road, an old banger, anywhere in the world
(11) autumn; the sound of the wind
(12) the influence of Beckett's Godot is clearly seen.

12 (1) The Spy Story
(2) 1970
(3) Drama Project 66
(4) 2 & 1/2 hours; 6 scenes
(5) 12
(6) musical, surrealistic
(7) finding one's own identity
(8) a spy and the people in the town
(9) a big envelope, a telephone, a wash-basin for fishing in
(10) outdoors, anywhere in the world, chairs for the chorus, an electricity pole, a bench, a red pillarbox
(11) daytime - evening
(12) a musical; contains a class-room scene

13 (1) I am Alice
(2) 1970
(3) The Actors' Small Theatre (*Haiyu Sho Gekijo*); Hayano
(4) 3 hours; 5 scenes
(5) 33

(6) fantasy, absurd

(7) criticism of authoritarian power

(8) Alice, a gentleman, members of the royal family

(9) period costume, a cage, a violin, a bird in a cage, a goldfish, a parasol, signs for the scenes

(10) a mixture of parts of Japan and a foreign country; stagehands move the scenery

(11) daytime - night; noisy music, the howling of animals, classical music

14 (1) Alice in Wonderland

(2) 1970

(3) The Actors' Small Theatre; Hayano

(4) 2 hours; 5 scenes

(5) 31

(6) fantasy, surrealistic, absurd

(7) finding one's own identity

(8) Alice and her family (circus), doubling as the royal family

(9) properties for the circus

(10) outdoors, anywhere in the world, a big-top in the desert, an execution tower, a trapeze, tables and chairs

(11) night - daytime - dawn

(12) contains a class-room scene

15 (1) The Town and the Zeppelin

(2) 1970

(3) The Youth Actors' Theatre (Seihai), Sueki

(4) 2 hours; 5 scenes

(5) about 40

(6) fantasy, symbolism (cubism)

(7) the meaning of family life

(8) a man, a woman and her brother and mother, the people in the town

(9) a suitcase, toothbrushes, catalogues

(10) outdoors, anywhere in the world, public places, a huge zeppelin

(11) a steam engine

16 (1) A Yellow Parasol and a Black Umbrella

(2) 1970

(3) Drama Project 66; Kobayashi

(4) 1/2 hour

(5) 6

(6) fantasy, symbolic/ surrealistic

(7) the man-woman relationship

(8) two couples

(9)   a telephone, a tea-set, an umbrella, a big rag doll (baby), a tape recorder
(10) outdoors and indoors, anywhere in the world, a bus-stop, a table and chairs
(11) daytime; a bell, muttering, a children's song

17 (1)   A Yellow Sunday
    (2)   1970
    (3)   unknown
    (4)   1/2 hour
    (5)   6
    (6)   surrealistic
    (7)   the past and the present
    (8)   two men, a married couple in the cave, a couple walking
    (9)   a toothbrush, stomach medicine
    (10) outdoors, Japan, in a cave, on a street
    (11) afternoon - evening, autumn; sports day at school

18 (1)   The Rebellion of the Soyosoyo Tribe
    (2)   1971
    (3)   The Actors' Theatre
    (4)   2 hours; 6 scenes
    (5)   18
    (6)   symbolic/ surrealistic, cruel
    (7)   death by starvation
    (8)   a mother and daughter, Mr. X, a cripple
    (9)   a wooden coffin
    (10) outdoors and indoors, an electricity pole, a bus-stop, a bench, a whale museum
    (11) dazzlingly bright; a noon siren, sounds of chewing
    (12) The Soyosoyo Tribe died out a long time ago. They lost their language and so could not tell anyone that they were starving. Each scene is named after an angel.

19 (1)   The Tapir
    (2)   1971
    (3)   May Company (*Gogatsu Sha*); Sueki
    (4)   2 hours; 5 scenes
    (5)   18 +
    (6)   naturalistic
    (7)   death by starvation
    (8)   an artisan, a delivery man and his wife, a brass-band
    (9)   a suitcase, an old cage, an umbrella, a pram
    (10) outdoors, a town, a wasteland, an electricity pole, flags of all nations
    (11) night; music - A Lullaby Preventing Sleep
    (12) A carnival gives a European atmosphere. Long absurd speeches. Based on Kafka's

The Hungry Artist

20 (1) A Blue Horse
(2) 1972
(3) Studio Nova; Watanabe
(4) 1 hour; 10 scenes
(5) 11
(6) puppet theatre, fantasy
(7) real kindness and hypocrisy
(8) a blind woman and her younger brother who has a crutch, a travelling couple, the people in the town
(9) an apple, a pram
(10) outdoors and indoors, a small house, an electricity pole, an execution tower, a pillarbox
(11) a baby's cries, harmonica
(12) 'A blue horse' is a symbol of famine, because the horse keeps eating forever.

21 (1) The Move
(2) September, 1973
(3) The Hand; Hayano
(4) 2 hours; 7 scenes
(5) 9
(6) absurd
(7) a continuous move to new places in everyday life
(8) a married couple, their baby and parents, a man, another couple
(9) household goods in a bicycle-cart, a parasol <nenneko>: a short coat worn by a nursemaid, flags of all nations, tea and biscuits
(10) outdoors in Japan, on the street, an electricity pole
(11) daytime; the sounds of the wind
(12) set in the postwar period, Japanese names

22 (1) The Sea and a Rabbit
(2) 1973
(3) Studio Nova
(4) 1 hour; 8 scenes
(5) 15
(6) puppet theatre, surrealistic/cubist
(7) the rights and responsibilities of settling in one place
(8) a man, a pimp and his woman, a watcher, animals (a rabbit and a dog)
(9) a telephone hanging from the ceiling, a head (an informer)
(10) indoors and outdoors, anywhere in the world, a cellar, a sea coast, a town square
(11) evening; the sound of waves, a telephone, the barking of a dog.

(12) 'I have never dwelled and I never will'

23 (1) The Legend of Noon
   (2) 1973
   (3) Group Nack; Sueki
   (4) 1 hour; 3 scenes
   (5) 4
   (6) naturalistic, absurd
   (7) one cannot forget the war experiences, or the crimes of that time
   (8) a man, a woman, two invalids
   (9) invalids' costumes, sunglasses, <Taisho-goto> (a Japanese musical instrument), a parasol, a wooden box for satsumas, the sun flag <hinomaru>
   (10) outdoors, Japan, on the street, a white wall
   (11) noon; Japanese national anthem (*Kimigayo*)
   (12) Why do we eat? Betsuyaku's logic: Please kill me in order to help me prove my innocence of having stolen anything.

24 (1) Chairs and the Legend
   (2) August, 1974; Sueki
   (3) The Hand
   (4) 1 & 1/2 hours
   (5) 7
   (6) naturalistic, cruel
   (7) human relationships in a group
   (8) a woman at an information desk, 4 men, 2 women
   (9) chairs, a parasol
   10) outdoors, anywhere in the world, an open space, a bus-stop, an information desk and chair, 5 chairs
   (11) daytime
   (12) a game of musical chairs

25 (1) The Story Written with Numbers
   (2) October, 1974
   (3) The Atelier Group of the LTC; Fujiwara
   (4) 1 & 1/2 hours; 6 scenes
   (5) 7
   (6) naturalistic, absurd
   (7) the group suicide of a religious sect
   (8) 4 men, 2 women, a narrator, the believers
   (9) a kettle, a balloon, bandage, a screen of black and white stripes, traditional Japanese food, a wooden box for satsumas
   (10) indoors, Japan, the Nichiren Centre

(12) Based on a historical incident in the early Showa era.

26 (1) A Scene with a Corpse
   (2) 1974
   (3) performed at a concert of the singer, Lily; Kobayashi
   (4) 1/2 hour
   (5) 2
   (6) boulevard comedy
   (7) the meaning of life and death
   (8) a man and woman who pass by
   (9) photographs of people who were helped to commit suicide
   (10) outdoor, on the street
   (11) children's songs

27 (1) A Demolished Scene
   (2) March, 1976
   (3) The Circle (En); Takahashi
   (4) 1& 1/2 hours; 4 scenes
   (5) 7
   (6) naturalistic, absurd
   (7) the psychology of human beings and food
   (8) a mother, a daughter and her husband, a salesman, a marathon runner, a couple
   (9) picnic food, a beach parasol, strawmats, a bicycle, an old record player
   (10) outdoors, anywhere in the world
   (11) a record which gets stuck
   (12) Human pettiness towards food is described as passers-by eat the picnic food left after the family have committed suicide.

28 (1) Bubbling Boiling
   (2) April, 1976
   (3) The Atelier Group of the LTC; Fujiwara
   (4) 2 hours; 10 scenes
   (5) 6
   (6) ritual, symbolic, absurd, omnibus style
   (7) family matters
   (8) a husband and wife, their parents, a beggar, an invalid
   (9) food on trays, a telephone hanging from an electricity pole, strawmats, a golden screen, flags of all nations
   (10) outdoors, Japan, a pillar box, an electricity pole
   (11) evening, daytime, snow
   (12) a very Japanese atmosphere is created visually and symbolically, Japanese names

29 (1)   A Scene with a Bus-stop
   (2)   1976
   (3)   Group Nack; Sueki
   (4)   1/2 hour
   (5)   2
   (6)   naturalistic
   (7)   a lonely woman tells a lie to a man in order to keep up communication
   (8)   a woman and a man, passers-by
   (10) outdoor, Japan, on the street, a bus-stop, a bench
   (11) daytime; voices from the radio

30 (1)   The Short Months
   (2)   May, 1977
   (3)   The Atelier Group of the LTC; Fujiwara
   (4)   1 hour
   (5)   5
   (6)   naturalistic, cruel
   (7)   the courage to face reality
   (8)   two married couples and a beggar
   (9)   a bicycle-cart, futon, a baby's toy, an umbrella, a short coat worn by a nursemaid
         <nenneko>
   (10) outdoors, on the street, an electricity pole, a bench
   (11) evening; the sounds of the wind, howling dogs
   (12) a trap to catch a beggar

31 (1)   A Place and Memories
   (2)   July, 1977
   (3)   The Hand; Sueki
   (4)   1 hour
   (5)   6
   (6)   naturalistic, cruel
   (7)   marriage
   (8)   a salesman, a woman, a blind woman and her younger brother
   (9)   a black umbrella, a salesman's suitcase, a postcard of the Ganges
   (10) outdoors, Japan, on the street, a bench, a bus-stop, a red pillarbox
   (11) evening
   (12) a bus-stop to which buses never come

32 (1)   Water-Bloated Corpse
   (2)   February, 1978
   (3)   The Atelier Group of the LTC; Fujiwara
   (4)   1 hour; 6 scenes

(5) 4
(6) naturalistic, absurd
(7) war experiences
(8) 2 invalids, their supposed parents
(9) invalids costume; sunglasses, <*Taisho-goto*> (Japanese musical instrument), a black umbrella, a wheelchair, sheets, tools, a sun flag <*hinomaru*>, strawmats
(10) outdoors, Japan, on the street
(11) evening, no moon; a war song <*Taisho goto*>
(12) an invalid dies from refusing to relieve himself - influenced by Betsuyaku's war experiences

33 (1) A House. a Tree. a Son
    (2) March, 1978
    (3) The Circle; Takahashi
    (4) 1 hour
    (5) about 10
    (6) naturalistic, absurd
    (7) problems of being unmarried, buying a house, etc.
    (8) an unmarried woman, a couple deceived by an estate agent, their parents
    (9) rice balls, rice crackers, a bird cage, household goods, a charm from Narita Shrine
    (10) outdoors, Japan, in the park, a bench, a pillarbox, an electricity pole
    (11) evening
    (12) social pressures: to have a house, grow a tree, have a son

34 (1) Dance Dance Snails
    (2) October, 1978
    (3) The Snail; Murai
    (4) 1/2 hour; 3 scenes
    (5) 2
    (6) surrealistic, cruel
    (7) hatred born out of married life
    (8) a woman school teacher and a detective sergeant
    (9) dolls for the Doll Festival, sweet saki, <*bon bori*> a paper covered lamp stand, a rope
    (10) indoors, Japan, a red carpet for the dolls, a pillar
    (11) lights from the <bon bori>; sounds of the man sawing, a song for the festival, Bach
    (12) based on the Arakawa Murder
         "the way of weighing an elephant: cut into pieces", the boundary between the real and unreal, Japanese names

35 (1) I am the Father of the Genius Idiot Bakabon

(2) October, 1978
(3) The Atelier Group of the LTC; Fujiwara
(4) 1 hour
(5) 9
(6) comic fantasy, absurd
(7) confusion of judgement
(8) Bakabon (a cartoon character) and his family, 2 policemen, people in the neighbourhood
(9) policemen's uniforms, the cartoon characters' costumes; a desk and chairs, a telephone, poison, rice paper, cigarettes, an umbrella
(10) outdoors, Japan, on the street, an electricity pole, a public toilet
(11) daytime; the theme song of the TV Cartoon programme
(12) based on Fujio Akatsuka's comic strips of the same name

36 (1) Days for Insects
   (2) June, 1979
   (3) The Jan Jan Theatre; Kishida
   (4) 1/2 hour
   (5) 2
   (6) naturalistic, absurd
   (7) the rituals of eating together
   (8) an old married couple
   (9) food on the table, a newspaper, a telephone
   (10) indoors, Japan, the living room, a low table, a worn-out lamp shade
   (11) evening; door bell, telephone bell
   (12) one of Betsuyaku's dramatic devices in the meal scenes, the fine description of the food. Japanese names.

37 (1) A Little House and the Five Gentlemen
   (2) July, 1979
   (3) Group Nack; Sueki
   (4) 1 &1/2 hours
   (5) 7
   (6) absurd
   (7) 5 men, a mother and daughter
   (8) the value of things is set by how others think of them
   (9) a crutch, a bottle, a worm at the end of a fishing-rod, a chain, a knife
   (10) outdoors, anywhere in the world, on the street, cardboard boxes
   (11) daytime; Dvorak
   (12) resemblance to An Old Banger and Five Gentlemen
        Man 3: Why don't we build a house?
        Man 4: We can't! Because if we do, we have to think of somebody to be our

mother or to be our daughter, like the people who've just been here.

38 (1) Mother. Mother. Mother
   (2) September, 1979
   (3) The Hand; Sueki
   (4) 1 & 1/2 hours; 6 scenes
   (5) 9
   (6) naturalistic, cruel
   (7) religion
   (8) a father and the people of the town, a businessman and his wife
   (9) a first-aid box, a pram and a rag doll (child), a chair, a sheet of newspaper, chiropodists' medicine
   (10) outdoors, anywhere in the world, an electricity pole, a bench
   (11) a red sun the colour of blood; a god's voice from a speaker, echoing cries of 'Mother'
   (12) a very positive attitude towards everyday life

39 (1) A Small Path to the Tenjin Shrine God
   (2) October, 1979
   (3) The Atelier Group of the LTC; Fujiwara
   (4) 1 hour; 2 scenes
   (5) 10
   (6) naturalistic, hysterical
   (7) a sister's love and and feeling of responsibility for her younger brother
   (8) a sister and her younger brother, people who pass by
   (9) black suits, a crutch, a bicycle-cart, a bicycle, a balloon
   (10) outdoors, an electricity pole, lamps without shades hanging from the electric wire
   (11) afternoon - evening; children's song
   (12) the opening of the play is very interesting:

Man 1: Excuse me.
Woman 1:(Turning back and stopping) Yes?
Man 1: Did a tiger pass in front of your house?
Woman 1:A tiger? No...
Man 1: When you say "No" do you mean that the tiger passed by by saying "No"?
Woman 1:No, it didn't, no tigers!
Man 1: When you say "No, it didn't, no tigers!" do you mean that the tiger
       passed by "No, it didn't, no tigers"?

This sort of conversation continues for two pages - playing with words and logic in a very Betsuyakuesque way.

40 (1) The Blooming Tree
   (2) June, 1980
   (3) The Youth Theatre Company (Seinen Za); Ishizawa
   (4) 1 hour; 6 scenes
   (5) 7
   (6) surrealistic, symbolic
   (7) two generations share a house, juvenile violence
   (8) a grandmother, her son and his wife, her grandson
   (9) a banquet
   (10) outdoors, a cherry tree in full bloom, in a garden, a big wardrobe, a straw mat
   (11) chattering voices in the wardrobe, voices on the phone
   (12) bears a resemblance to Kafka's The Trial, Japanese names

41 (1) The Information Desk
   (2) June, 1980
   (3) The Snail; Murai
   (4) 1/2 hour
   (5) 2
   (7) a receptionist waits for someone to register
   (8) a single woman, a married man who wants to see a doctor
   (9) a telephone
   (10) indoors, a large office building, an office desk, two chairs, an information desk with a sign on it
   (11) daytime; a large noise
   (12) names of Japanese international charities

42 (1) The Red Elegy
   (2) September, 1980
   (3) The Atelier Group of the LTC; Fujiwara
   (4) 1 hour; 6 scenes
   (5) 16
   (6) realism
   (7) infighting between leftist groups, the sense of failure in the political movements of the 60s and 70s
   (8) a former student group
   (9) abandoned household goods, a miniature train, a bandage
   (10) indoors and outdoors, Japan, on the street, in a room, in a park, a swing, an electricity pole, in a hospital
   (11) popular songs of the time, the Internationale
   (12) the title is borrowed from a graphic novel <Gekiga> by Seiichi Hayashi

43 (1) A Corpse Which Creates an Atmosphere

(2)   October, 1980
(3)   The Circle, Takahashi
(4)   1 hour
(5)   12
(6)   naturalistic, absurd
(7)   problems in a hospital, medical ethics
(8)   a father, his son and his wife, doctors and nurses
(9)   a trolley with a corpse on it, hospital beds and side tables, chairs
(10) indoors, Japan, the basement floor of a hospital
(11) the smell of incense; the sutra chant
(12) the play is built up in a way very similar to I am the Father of the Genius Idiot Bakabon

44 (1)   I am not Her
   (2)   June, 1981
   (3)   The Snail; Murai
   (4)   1/2 hour
   (5)   2
   (6)   marriage
   (7)   a single woman and a widower
   (8)   2 people introduced through a marriage bureau
   (9)   an attache case, a C.V., a handkerchief
   (10) outdoors, Japan, a bench
   (11) evening; the wind blows
   (12) a remote resemblance to Albee's The Zoo Story

45 (1)   The Disease
   (2)   October, 1981
   (3)   The Atelier Group of the LTC; Fujiwara
   (4)   3/4 hour
   (5)   9
   (6)   naturalistic, absurd
   (7)   consciousness of one's disease
   (8)   a passer-by, his wife, a nurse and a doctor, a tramp
   (9)   an office desk, chairs, a water jug, medical equipment
   (10) an outdoor casualty centre, anywhere in the world, hospital beds
   (11) daytime
   (12) the presence of God

46 (1)   The Meeting
   (2)   February, 1982
   (3)   The Hand; Sueki

(4) 1 hour
(5) 12
(6) naturalistic
(7) a discussion
(8) stage hands, people attending the meeting
(9) a map, a desk and chairs, a Dunhill lighter
(10) outdoors, Japan, on the street, an electricity pole with a telephone hanging from it
(11) daytime
(12) Japanese names

47 (1) A Corpse with Feet
(2) June, 1981
(3) The Snail; Murai
(4) 1/2 hour
(5) 2
(6) naturalistic, absurd
(7) man-woman relationships
(8) a man and woman passing by
(9) a corpse in a futon bag, a gift from a wedding
(10) outdoors, Japan, on the street at a level-crossing barrier, a bench
(11) evening; the warning bell of the level-crossing, passing trains
(12) Japanese names

48 (1) The Snow Lies on Taro's Roof
(2) October, 1982
(3) The Atelier Group of the LTC; Fujiwara
(4) 2 hours; 7 scenes
(5) 15
(6) symbolic, surrealistic
(7) monarchism and the individual
(8) invalids, a couple, an assassin, a page, a man from the Department of the Imperial Household
(9) things for playing house, a strawmat, a crutch, sunglasses, a white sheet, a big map hanging on a wall
(10) outdoors, Japan, on the street, an electricity pole
(11) evening, snow; children's songs, a war song
(12) based on the 2.26 incident Japanese names

49 (1) Ten Little Indians - the ten little Indians who are waiting for Godot
(2) December, 1982
(3) Honda Theatre Production; Fujiwara
(4) 2 hours; 6 scenes

(5) 10
(6) naturalistic, absurd
(7) a parody of Ten Little Indians by Agatha Christie, and Waiting for Godot by Samuel Beckett
(8) the characters of Christie's novel
(9) a rocking horse, a motor-cycle, a record-player, a table set for tea, a pistol, a syringe
(10) outdoors, a Western country, wasteland, a big chest
(11) evening - night - morning
(12) dead people revive and dance, this is also found in The Kangaroo and I am the Father of the Genius Idiot Bakabon

50 (1) Who's Right Behind Me
   (2) March, 1981
   (3) The Circle; Takahashi
   (4) 2 hours; 4 scenes
   (5) 4
   (6) naturalistic, hysterical
   (7) the problem of finding a spouse, the father-daughter relationship
   (8) 2 unmarried sisters, their father, a man
   (9) a hose, an English style tea-set, biscuits, cheese, a toilet kit, a suitcase
   (10) indoors, a western style drawing room, a mound of furniture
   (11) evening (tea-time); laughter

51 (1) Star Time
   (2) June, 1983
   (3) The Snail/Hitaka Project; Murai
   (4) 1/2 hour
   (5) 2
   (6) fantasy
   (7) the eternity of heavenly time, a woman tricks a man into eating his own cat
   (8) a woman opening a restaurant, a man looking for his cat
   (9) food on a plate, a table cloth
   (10) outdoors, Japan, trees in the wood, a table, 2 chairs, lightbulbs hung on trees
   (11) evening; footsteps
   (12) Japanese names

52 (1) A Lullaby Preventing Sleep
   (2) June, 1984
   (3) The Snail/Hitaka Project; Murai
   (4) 1/2 hour
   (5) 2

(6) fantasy

(7) communication

(8) a man who does not feel that he is alive, and a woman sent by a 'conversation service'

(9) an old table, chairs, a telephone, three miniature houses, an electricity pole

(10) indoors, a Western style room in a flat

(11) the sound of the wind

(12) memories of childhood, Japanese names

53 (1) Mary's Lamb

(2) 1984

(4) 1/2 hour

(5) 3

(6) fantasy, surrealistic

(7) was a train crash an accident?

(8) a former station master, the son of his former girlfriend, his wife

(9) miniature train set on a table, puppets (dolls)

(10) indoors, in a room

(11) the sounds of steam engines

(12) real actors and miniature objects, Western names

54 (1) A Crime at the Street Corner

(2) October, 1984

(3) The Hand; Sueki

(4) 1 hour; 2 scenes

(5) 8

(6) naturalistic, absurd

(7) the real job under the superficial job

(8) people working for the secret service

(9) semaphore flags, mourning dress

(10) outdoors, on the street, an electricity pole, a bus-stop, a bench, a signalling stand

(11) daytime, night

55 (1) Hat Sellers' Tea Party

(2) December, 1984

(3) The Circle, Kobayashi

(4) unpublished

56 (1) When We Open The Windows, We See the Port

(2) January, 1985

(3) The Actors' Theatre Production; Sueki

(4) 1— hours; 2 scenes

(5) 6
(6) surrealistic, absurd
(7) the parent-child relationship
(8) parents, their son and daughter, their spouses
(9) a butterfly net, an insect cage, a suitcase, letter, a tea-set on a trolley, pine seeds, walnuts, a diary
(10) indoors, in a room, old furniture, a triangular tent, a miner's lamp
(11) the Wedding March

57 (1) The Room
    (2) June, 1985
    (3) The Snail; Murai
    (4) 1/2 hour
    (5) 2
    (6) surrealistic
    (7) the lonely life of a single woman
    (8) a woman, a man
    (9) a candlestick, a letter, an apple, bread, an old table, a chair, a telephone
    (10) indoors, Japan, a room
    (11) telephone bell, footsteps, shrieking voices, calling voices
    (12) Japanese names

58 (1) The Insects
    (2) July, 1985
    (3) Sapporo City Culture and Education Centre Production; Murai
    (12) unpublished

59 (1) The Hiking
    (2) November 1984
    (3) The Atelier Group of the LTC; Fujiwara
    (4) 1 hour
    (5) 6
    (6) naturalistic, cruel
    (7) the challenge of anti-conventional manners
    (8) parents and daughter, an invalid, a man who has been to the public bath
    (9) a wheelchair, sunglasses, picnic food, a plastic dustbin, an accordion, a beggar's collecting box for the invalid
    (10) outdoors, on the street, an electricity pole
    (11) night
    (12) Man 1: This is an electricity pole, just an ordinary one. In other words, an electricity pole stands, like this, here or there and when you are tired you can lean on it, or sometimes dogs piss on it...

60 (1) Tadpoles are Frogs' Children
   (2) November, 1985
   (3) The Circle, Takahashi
   (4) 1 hour; 2 scenes
   (5) 10
   (6) naturalistic, cruel
   (7) understanding life and death
   (8) a woman who has lost her child in an accident, an army officer, a nurse, a grave digger, passers-by
   (9) a shop mannequin, a coffin, a bicycle, an army sword
   (10) outdoors, Japan, in the park, a swing, a climbing frame
   (11) evening; wind, a children's song, the Dead March from Saul
   (12) Japanese names

61 (1) The Cleared Evening Sky
   (2) November, 1985
   (3) The Atelier Group of the LTC; Fujiwara
   (4) 1 &1/2 hours; 2 scenes
   (5) 6
   (6) naturalistic, cruel
   (7) people's words create reality
   (8) a salesman, people who say that they have seen an animal in a cage, a mother and daughter, a zoo-keeper
   (9) mourning dress; a stretcher, a rope, a bandage, a crutch, a white sack
   (10) outdoors, anywhere in the world, open space, an electricity pole, an old cage, some chains
   (11) evening; wind, a harmonica, the sound of an old-fashioned gramophone
   (12) playing with words: the names of the animals 'lions', 'bears', 'tigers', 'people'

62 (1) An Escaped Convict who Carries a Hot-water Bottle
   (2) June, 1986
   (3) The Snail; Murai
   (4) 3/4 hour
   (5) 2
   (6) naturalistic, absurd
   (7) the justification of murder
   (8) a man from an investigation agency, a woman who lived with the man he is looking for
   (9) a big suitcase containing a pillow, a hot-water bottle, a blanket, an ash tray, flowers in a vase etc.
   (10) outdoors, Japan, on the street, a street light, a plastic dustbin, a bus-stop, a bus

timetable, a bench
(11) night; passing buses

63 (1) Lieutenant Shirase's Expedition to the South Pole
   (2) September, 1986
   (3) The Hand; Sueki
   (4) 1 &1/2 hours; 2 scenes
   (5) 9
   (6) absurd
   (7) consciousness and will to reach 'the new world'
   (8) the Lieutenant Shirases, their groups of 4 men and 2 women, a brass band
   (9) a table and chairs, an English tea-set, arctic exploration equipment (e.g.goggles, rope etc.)
   (10) outdoors, Japan, an electricity pole, a side of a ship, the flags of all nations
   (11) daytime - evening - morning; wind; the band plays children's songs
   (12) based on an historical incident, uses old newsreel photographs and narration

64 (1) Giovanni's Journey to His Father
   (2) May, 1987
   (3) The Atelier Group of the LTC; Fujiwara
   (4) 1 & 1/2 hours; 8 scenes
   (5) 11
   (6) fantasy
   (7) returning home
   (8) Giovanni, his dead father, his mother, the people in the village
   (9) a crutch, a black umbrella
   (10) outdoors, anywhere in the world, a station, a screen, a cloth hanging from a lighting bar
   (11) a red sun, red snow, smoke; wind
   (12) based on Miyazawa's story resembles A Blue Horse and The Sea and a Rabbit

65 (1) The Salad Murder
   (2) November, 1986
   (3) The Atelier Group of the LTC; Fujiwara
   (4) 1 hour; 4 scenes
   (5) 4
   (6) realism, psycho-drama
   (7) parents who killed their son and daughter to gain money from an insurance company
   (8) the couple, a salesman selling a token of acknowledgement for the receipt of a funeral present
   (9) a tray of cat litter, used tea leaves, tea cups, a vase, shoes

(10) indoors, Japan, a Japanese style tea table, a household Buddhist altar, a cupboard

(11) a voice on the radio

(12) Masae (the wife) hears on the radio news that a wife asked her husband to buy two pre-packed salads, but when the husband bought only one, killed him. Masae claims that there was at least a misdeed to be punished by murder in that case, whereas her children had committed none.

66 (1) Toilet This Way Please

(2) June, 1987

(3) The Snail; Murai

(4) 3/4 hour

(5) 2

(6) naturalistic, absurd

(7) the value of life, what is important and what is not

(8) a woman trying to commit suicide, and a man whose job is to show the way to a public toilet

(9) a wooden box for satsumas, a rope, a big rag doll, a chipped bowl, a bag

(10) outdoors, Japan, on the street, a street lamp, a bench

(11) the Japanese national anthem

67 (1) A Story about the Star Town

(2) July, 1987

(3) Drama Project 66; Kobayashi

(12) unpublished

68 (1) Funaya

(2) October, 1987

(3) Drama Project 66; Kobayashi

(12) unpublished

69 (1) Another Place

(2) October, 1987

(3) Drama Project 66; Kobayashi

(12) unpublished

70 (1) An Inari Shrine Around the Corner

(2) June, 1988

(3) The Snail; Murai

(4) 1 hour; 4 scenes

(5) 7

(6) naturalistic, absurd

(7) a daughter who left home returns bringing misfortune with her, and accidentally

burns the village and her mother
- (8) a woman, her mother, a man wounded in a political attack, a nurse, passers-by, an invalid
- (9) a bandage, a crutch, a bag, a musical instrument <Taisho-goto>, a bicycle-cart, a strawmat
- (10) outdoors, Japan, the precincts of a shrine, a red sacred arch <torii>, gravemarkers <sotoba>, a reed screen, a white flag, a bench, a bus-stop
- (11) daytime, flames; a song at the shrine
- (12) inspired by an old children's song

71 (1) Hide and Seek
- (2) 1988
- (3) The Circle
- (4) 1 hour; 2 scenes
- (5) 8
- (6) naturalistic, absurd
- (7) a father returns home thirty years after he abandoned his family
- (8) the father, 3 children, 2 grandchildren born as a result of their incest, a maid, a male passer-by
- (9) mourning dress; candles, a bandage, sheets, a table, a sofa, a sideboard, a rope
- (10) outdoors and indoors, a kennel, a streetlight
- (11) night

72 (1) The Story of the Two Knights Travelling Around the Country
- (2) October, 1987
- (3) The Parco Space Part 3; Kishida
- (4) 1 & 1/2 hour; 2 scenes
- (5) 9
- (6) fantasy, absurd
- (7) the meaning of life
- (8) 2 Knights and their Squires, a doctor, a nurse, a priest, an innkeeper and his daughter
- (9) armour made from old pans; a water-jug, cheese, a razor, a doctor's bag with equipment, chairs and a table, food on plates, a cart
- (10) outdoors, in the wasteland, a mobile inn, a dead tree, beds, a big windmill
- (11) daytime - night
- (12) based on Cervantes' Don Quixote

BIBLIOGRAPHY

Other Works of Minoru Betsuyaku

Collected Criticisms of Minoru Betsuyaku: the Strategy towards Words (Kotoba e no Senjutsu). Tokyo: Karasu Shobô, 1972.

Collected Fairy Tales of Minoru Betsuyaku: The Lonely Fish (Betsuyaku Minoru Dôwa Shû). Tokyo: Sanichi Shobô, 1973.

The Space with an Electricity Pole (Denshinbashira no Aru Uchû). Tokyo: Hakusuisha, 1980.

The Enumeration of Animals (Kemono Zukushi). Tokyo: Heibonsha, 1982.

The Enumeration of Tools (Dôgu Zukushi). Tokyo: Yamato Shobô, 1984.

Lines in Scenes (Serifu no Fûkei). Tokyo: Hakusuisha, 1984.

The Enumeration of Birds (Tori Zukushi). Tokyo: Heibonsha, 1985.

The Masterpieces (Meiga Gekijô). Tokyo: Okokusha, 1985.

Tangesazen on his Horse (Uma ni Notta Tangesazen). Tokyo: Riburopôto, 1986.

Beckett and Bullying (Beketto to Ijime). Tokyo: Iwanami Shoten, 1987.

Nowadays Business Come-and-Go (Tôsei Shôbai Orai). Tokyo, Iwanami Shoten, 1988.

Collected Fairy Tales of Minoru Betsuyaku: A Study of Winds (Betsuyaku Minoru Dôwa Shû). Tokyo, Sanichi Shobô, 1988.

The Way of Spending Everyday (Hibi no Kurashi Kata). Tokyo: Hakusui Sha, 1990.

Japanese Language Publications

Yamazaki Masakazu, *Collected Essays of Masakazu Yamazaki: The Theatrical Spirits (Yamazaki Masakazu Dai-ichi Essei Shû: Gekitekinaru Seishin)*. Tokyo: Kawade Shuppan, 1966.

Collected Plays of Beckett, Vol. 1 (Beketto Gikyoku Shû 1) trans. by Andô Shinya & Takahashi Yasunari. Tokyo: Hakusui Sha, 1967.

Collected Plays of Beckett, Vol. 2 (Beketto Gikyoku Shû 2) trans. by Andô Shinya & Takahashi Yasunari. Tokyo: Hakusui Sha, 1967.

Abe Kôbô, *Collected Plays of Kôbô Abe, Vol. 11 (Abe Kôbô Zen Sakuhin Shû 11)*. Tokyo: Shinchô Sha, 1973.

Ibaragi Ken, *Thespis Series: A Short History of Japanese New Theatre (Tesupisu Sôsho Nippon Shingeki Shô-shi)*. Tokyo: Mirai Sha, 1961.

The Outline of Contemporary Japanese Plays Vol. 7 (Gendai Nihon Gikyoku Taikei 7), ed. Kikuchi Kisaji. Tokyo; Sanichi Shobô, 1972.

Suzuki Tadashi, *The Sum of Interior Angles (Naikaku no Wa)*. Tokyo: Jiritsu Shobô, 1973.

Kan Takayuki, *Asahi Selection 178: The Postwar theatre (Asahi Sensho 178: Sengo Engeki)*. Tokyo: Asahi Shinbun Sha, 1981.

Kazama Ken, *From the Theatre-Wasteland (Engeki no Kôya Kara)*. Tokyo: Seikyû Sha, 1984.

Mori Hideo, *The Complete Smatterings of Contemporary Japanese Theatre (Gendai Engeki Marukajiri)*. Tokyo: Shôbunsha, 1983.

The Collected Interviews of Tadashi Suzuki (Suzuki Tadashi Taidan Shû), ed. Ogawa Michia-ki. Tokyo: Riburopôto, 1984.

Senda Akihiko, *The Dramatic Renaissance (Gekiteki Runessansu)*. Tokyo: Roburopôto, 1983.

Senda Akihiko, *The Voyage of Contemporary Japanese Theatre (Gendai Engeki no Kôkai)*. To-kyo: Riburopôto, 1988.

The Complete Listings of Shingeki 1989 (Shingeki Benran 1989) ed. Toshimizu Tetsuo (Tokyo; Teatoro Sha, 1989.

Migel de Cervantes, *Don Quixote (Don Kihôte Vol. 1, 2, 3, & 4)*, trans. by Aida Yû. Tokyo: Chikuma Shobô, 1987.

The Collection of Contemporary Literature Vol. 24: Takamura Kôtarô, Hagiwara Sakutarô and Miyazawa Kenji (Gendai Nihon Bungaku Zenshû 24: Takamura Kôtarô/Hagiwara Sa-kutarô/Miyazawa Kenji). Tokyo: Chikuma Shobô, 1954.

The Collection of Contemporary Literature Vol. 27: Kikuchi Kan and Muroo Saisei (Gendai Nihon Bungaku Zenshû 27: Kikuchi Kan/Muroo Saisei) Tokyo: Chikuma Shobô, 1955.

The Collection of Contemporary Literature Vol. 64: Natsume Sôseki II (Gendai Nihon Bungaku Zenshû 64: Natsume Sôseki II) Tokyo: Chikuma Shobô, 1956.

Japanese Language Periodicals

The New Theatre (Shingeki), no. 395, 416, 417, 419, 431, 436 & 446. Tokyo: Hakusui Sha.

Teatro (Teatoro), no. 522, 543, 548, 554 & 555. Tokyo: Teatoro Sha.

English Language Publications

Esslin, Martin, *The Theatre of the Absurd*. Harmondsworth: Penguin, 1961.

Absurd Drama, with introduction by Esslin, Martin, . Harmondsworth: Penguin, 1965.

Comic Drama, ed. W.D. Howarth. London: Methuen, 1978.

Merchant, Moelwyn, *The Critical Idiom 21: Comedy*, ed. Jump, John D.

Styan, J.L., *Modern Drama in Theory and Practice Vol. 1*. Cambridge: Cambridge Universi-ty Press, 1981.

Styan, J.L., *Modern Drama in Theory and Practice Vol. 2*. Cambridge: Cambridge Universi-ty Press, 1981.

Styan, J.L., *Modern Drama in Theory and Practice Vol. 3*. Cambridge: Cambridge Universi-ty Press, 1981.

Beckett, Samuel, *Waiting for Godot*. London: Faber and Faber, 1956.

Beckett, Samuel, *Endgame*. London: Faber and Faber, 1958.

Beckett, Samuel, *Collected Shorter Plays of Samuel Beckett*. London: Faber and Faber, 1984.

Samuel Beckett: *Collection of Critical Essays*, ed. Esslin, Martin. London: Faber and Faber, 1965.

Fletcher, John, *Beckett; the Playwright*. London: Methuen, 1972.

Ionesco, Eugene, *The Bold Prima Donna*, trans. and adapted by Watson, Donald. London:

Samuel French, 1958.

Ionesco, Eugene, *Rhinoceros/ The Chair/ The Lesson*, trans. by Prowse, Derek and Watson, Donald. Harmondsworth: Penguin, 1962.

Pinter, Harold, *Pinter Play: One*. London: Methuen, 1976.

Pinter, Harold, *Pinter Play: Two*. London: Methuen, 1977.

Pinter, Harold, *Pinter Play: Four*. London: Methuen, 1981.

Pinter, Harold, *The collection and the Lover*. London: Methuen, 1963.

Pinter, Harold, *Other Places*. London: Methuen, 1982.

Pinter, Harold, *One for the Road*. London: Methuen, 1984.

Almansi, Guido, and Henderson, Simon, *Contemporary Writers: Harold Pinter*, ed. Bradbury, Malcolm and Brigsby, Christopher. London: Methuen, 1983.

Camus, Albert, *Caligula/ Cross Purpose/ the Just/ The Possessed*, trans. by Gilbert, Stuart, Jones, Henry and O'Brien Justin. Harmondsworth: Penguin, 1984.

Kennedy, Andrew, *Six Dramatists in Search of a Language*. Cambridge: Cambridge University Press, 1975.

Dewhurst, Keith, *Don Quixote*. Ambergate: Amber Lane Press, 1982.

Hoggett, Chris, *Stage Craft*. London: Adam and Charles Black, 1975.

Abe Kôbô, *The Man Who Turned into a Stick (Bô ni Natta Otoko)*, trans. by Keene, Donald. Tokyo: University of Tokyo Press, 1975.

After Apocalypse, trans. by Goodman, G. David. New York: Columbia University Press, 1986.

Goodman, G. David, *Japanese Drama and Culture in the 1960s*. New York/London: Sharpe, 1988.

Modern Japanese Drama, trans. by Takaya, T. Ted. New York: Columbia University Press, 1979.

Schodt, L. Frederic, *Manga! Manga! The World of Japanese Comics*. Tokyo: Kodansha International Ltd, 1983.

SCOT: Suziki's Company of Toga, trans. Hoff, Frank, Matsuoka Kazuko and Takahashi Yasunari. Tokyo: SCOT, undated.

Yuasa, Masako

Masako was born in Osaka and currently lives and works in Osaka's Sakai City. She is a member of the Japanese Society for Theatre Research. She gained her Master's degree in Theatre Studies in 1986 at the University of Leeds in the United Kingdom, for which she wrote a dissertation on *Kunio Shimizu and his work*, and her Doctorate in 1990, also from Leeds University, for which she wrote her thesis, *The Plays by Minoru Betsuyaku*.

Masako taught Japanese language and theatre at Leeds from 1990 to 2000 and story-telling at Osaka Kyoiku University (Osaka University of Education) from 2002 to 2011. She was an honorary research fellow in drama translation at the University of Hull in the United Kingdom from 2005-2008. In 2017, she received a Citizen Award from Osaka City for her work on the Chikamatsu Project.

Masako has translated and staged several contemporary Japanese plays at the Workshop Theatre at Leeds, including ***He Died at His Peak*** *(Hana no Sakari ni Shinda ano Hito)* by Kunio Shimizu, ***The Kangaroo*** *(Kangarū)*, ***I am the Father of the Genius Idiot Bakabon*** *(Tensai Bakabon no Papa Nanoda)*, ***A Corpse With Feet*** *(Ashi no Aru Shitai)* and ***The Story of the Two Knights Travelling around the Country*** *(Shokoku wo Henrekisuru Futari no Kishi no Monogatari)* by Minoru Betsuyaku, ***Futon and Daruma*** *(Futon to Daruma)* and ***The Man Next Door*** *(Tonari no Otoko)* by Ryō Iwamatsu, ***Paper Balloon*** *(Kami Fūsen)*, ***New Cherry Leaves*** *(Ha-Zakura)* and ***Love Phobia*** *(Renai Kyōfu-byo)* by Kunio Kishida. ***A Corpse with Feet*** was broadcast on BBC Radio 3 in October 1991 and staged by the Royal Shakespeare Company in January 1993.

Bi-lingual work: *Bilingual edition of Three Sewa-mono Plays by Chikamatsu Monzaemon* (Shakai Hyôronsha).

Translated works with annotations: *The Story of the Two Knights Travelling around the Country* (Alumnus), *Futon and Daruma* (Alumnus), *Kunio Kishida -three plays* (Alumnus). *"A Corpse with Feet by Betsuyaku Minoru and the Snail Theatre Company," Asian Theatre Journal*.

Joint works: *20 Seiki no Gikyoku I and III (The Criticisms on Japanese Playwrights' Works in the 20th Century Vol. 1 and 3)*, Shakai Hyôronsha, *Half a Century of Japanese Theatre: 1990 Part 1 and Part 2*, by Kinokuniya Company Ltd, *Kishida Kunio no Sekai (The World of Kishida Kunio)*, by Kanrinshobō, *Toshi no Fikushon (Fiction of a City)* by Seibun-do. *Miyamoto Ken no Gekisekai (The Theatrical World of Miyamoto Ken)* by Shakai Hyôronsha. Contributions to *The Cambridge Guide to Theatre*, Cambridge University Press, *Who is Who in Contemporary World Theatre*, Routledge.

Articles: *"Gendai Nihon-Engeki ni okeru Junsui-Engeki kara Fujōri-Engeki eno Nagare no Kōsatsu (Aspects of Contemporary Japanese theatre from the Pure Theatre to the Theatre of the Absurd)", The Journal of the Japanese Society for Theatre Research*, No. 34 (an English full version, *Leeds East Asian Paper* No. 53).

Four Plays of Minoru Betsuyaku

2023 年 12 月 25 日　初版第 1 刷発行

著　者　　湯浅雅子

発行人　　松田健二

発行所　　株式会社 社会評論社
　　　　　東京都文京区本郷 2-3-10　〒 113-0033
　　　　　tel. 03-3814-3861 ／ fax. 03-3818-2808
　　　　　http://www.shahyo.com/

装幀・組版デザイン　　中野多恵子
印刷・製本　　　　　　倉敷印刷株式会社

printed in Japan